THE HUSBANDS

THE HUSBANDS

A Novel

Holly Gramazio

Doubleday   *New York*

Copyright © 2024 by Holly Gramazio

All rights reserved. Published in the United States by Doubleday, a division of Penguin Random House LLC, New York. Simultaneously published in hardcover in Great Britain by Chatto & Windus Limited, London, in 2024.

doubleday.com

DOUBLEDAY and the portrayal of an anchor with a dolphin are registered trademarks of Penguin Random House LLC.

Front-of-cover art based on an illustration by Laralova/Shutterstock
Jacket design by Emily Mahon

Library of Congress Cataloging-in-Publication Data
Names: Gramazio, Holly, author.
Title: The husbands : a novel / Holly Gramazio.
Description: First edition. | New York : Doubleday, 2024.
Identifiers: LCCN 2023030831 | ISBN 9780385550611 (hardcover) |
ISBN 9780385550628 (ebook)
Subjects: LCGFT: Novels.
Classification: LCC PR9619.4.G736 H86 2024 |
DDC 823.92—dc23/eng/20231017
LC record available at https://lccn.loc.gov/2023030831

MANUFACTURED IN THE UNITED STATES OF AMERICA
1 3 5 7 9 10 8 6 4 2
First American Edition

For Terry, my favourite husband

THE HUSBANDS

CHAPTER 1

The man is tall and has dark tousled hair, and when she gets back quite late from Elena's hen do, she finds him waiting on the landing at the top of the stairs.

She yelps and steps backwards. "What—" she starts, then tries again. "Who are you?"

He sighs. "Fun night?"

Carpeted steps lead up to the man and the dim landing. This is definitely the right flat, isn't it? It must be: her key worked. She's drunk, but she's not drunk enough to commit breaking and entering by accident. She steps back again, and feels for the light switch, keeping her eyes on the stranger.

She finds it. In the sudden glare, everything is as it should be: the angle of the steps, the cream of the walls, even the switch under her fingers, a moment's resistance then *click*. Everything except him.

"Lauren," he says. "Come on. Come up and I'll make you some tea."

He knows her name. Is he—no, it's been months since she had that guy round, and he was blond, he had a beard, this isn't him. A burglar? How would a burglar know her name?

"If you leave," she says, "I won't report this." She will absolutely report this. She reaches behind to the door handle, and tries to turn it, which takes a lot of fiddling but she isn't going to look away, especially not now that—oh god—he's coming down the stairs. She backs out of her flat and into the hall, takes careful steps until she's grappling with the front door until that pushes open too, warm summer air thick behind her. Out through the spatter of irregular raindrops—but not so far that she can't still see him.

He's crossing the hall, then he's outlined in the doorway, bright light behind him.

"Lauren," the man says, "what are you doing?"

"I'm calling the police," she says, digging in her bag for her phone, hoping it has battery left. The pocket where it should be is occupied instead by a tiny cactus in a painted pot, from today's workshop. The phone itself is further down. It lights up and she rummages, grabs it, pulls it out.

But as she does, she sees the lock screen.

And: it's a picture of herself, standing on a beach with her arm around the man in the doorway.

Two per cent battery, flicking to one. And his face. Unmistakable. And hers.

She grabs with her other hand for the little cactus, holding it ready to throw. "Stay where you are."

"Okay," he says. "Okay. I'm staying here." He's taken a few steps outdoors, feet bare. She looks again: his face glowing from the phone, his face in the night in front of her. He's wearing a grey T-shirt and soft tartan trousers. Not trousers, she realises. Pajamas.

"Right," she says, "come out further," and he does, sighing, another half-dozen barefoot steps on to the pavement, and now she has enough space to edge around him towards the front door, past the closed blinds of the downstairs flat. "Stay there," she says, facing him as she circles. He turns, watching. She steps up through the door, on to the tiles of the hall, and risks a glance to confirm: yes, the closed door to Toby and Maryam's to one side, the open door to her own flat directly behind her, familiar stairs, the right house.

"Lauren," she hears the man say. She spins and shrieks and he stops, but she told him to stay where he was, and he's moved! She slams the front door in his face, then steps quickly into her flat and slams and locks her own door. "Lauren," he's still saying from outside. She thumbs her phone again to ring the police after all, but it lights up—his face—and then darkens. Out of battery.

Shit.

"Lauren," and sounds of the outer door rattling. "Come on."

She runs up the stairs and across the landing and grapples in the kitchen for her charger. She'll phone someone, she'll call Toby downstairs even. But then she hears footsteps, and the man's coming up, and somehow he's in the flat. He's *in the flat.*

She spins and strides to the kitchen door. "Get the fuck out," she says into the landing, holding the cactus firmly. She's ready. If he comes any closer, she'll throw.

"Calm down," the man says, reaching the top of the stairs. "I'll get you some water." He takes a step towards her, and she does it, she throws, but the cactus goes wide, past him, and it hits the wall and bounces off and rolls towards the stairs, *thud, thud, thud-thud-thud,* accelerating down the steps in an otherwise silent night, coming to a stop with a final thud against the door at the bottom.

"What's wrong with you?" the man says, keys clutched in his hand. That's how he got in: he stole her spare keys. Of course. Maybe he logged into her computer and changed her phone remotely, and that's why his picture's on her lock screen. Is that possible? "Fuck's sake," he says. "Go and sit down. Please."

He turns off the light on the stairs, and switches on the landing light instead, the big square landing with all the rooms leading off it, the big grey landing she passes through a dozen times a day.

Which is, somehow, blue.

And it has a rug. It never had a rug before. Why is there a rug?

She can't stop to look: the man's walking towards her. She backs across the rug, which feels thick and soft even through her shoes, towards the door to the living room. It's right above Toby and Maryam's bedroom. If she screams, she thinks, they'll hear. But even in the dark, the room doesn't seem right.

She feels for the switch.

Click.

Light falls on more strange objects. The sofa is dark brown, and surely when she left this morning it was green. The clock on the wall has Roman numerals instead of normal numbers, and it turns out Roman numerals are difficult to read, VII, XIIIII, VVI. She has to squint to stop them from blurring. Her old vase on the shelf has tulips in it, her wonky lino print of an owl is gone. The books are wrong or in the wrong place, the curtains have been replaced with shutters. Most of the pictures are wrong and one of them—one of them is *very* wrong. One of them is of a wedding featuring—and she steps up to it, nose almost to the glass—*her.* And the man.

The man who has entered the living room behind her.

The husband.

She turns around and he holds out a pint glass filled with water. After a moment she takes it and notices, for the first time, a ring on her finger.

She transfers the glass to her right hand and spreads her left in front of her, turns it over palm up, ring still there as she folds her fingers in and touches it with the tip of her thumb. Huh.

"Come on," the husband says. "Sit down. Drink up."

She sits. The sofa is the same shape it used to be, despite the colour. And it has the same uneven give.

The husband sits too, over in the armchair, and at first she can't see whether he's wearing a wedding ring as well, but he leans forward and there it is: bright on his finger. He's watching her. She watches him in return.

She is, she thinks, very drunk, so it might be that she's missing something obvious. But she's been given a drink by a man she's never met before and, if anything, the fact that she may be unexpectedly married to him should make her more rather than less wary.

"I'll . . . drink this in a moment," she says, carefully, clearly, enunciating each syllable (although there do seem to be more of them than usual).

"Okay."

If he's meant to be here, why isn't he in bed? "Why aren't you in bed?"

He sighs. "I was," he says. "You didn't exactly make a stealth entrance."

"I didn't know you were here!"

"What?" he says. "Look, drink the water and take your dress off and we'll get you ready for bed. Do you need help with the zip?"

"No!" she says, and grabs a throw pillow, pulls it in front of her. Shit. She's never seen him before. She's not taking her dress off in front of him.

"Okay, okay, don't—shh, it's fine, drink your water." His tired face. Round cheeks with a flush of red. "Okay?" he says.

"Okay," she says, and then, after a moment: "I'll sleep here. So as—so as not to disturb you. You can go."

"Do you want the spare room? I'll clear the bed—"

"No," she says. "No. This is good."

"Okay," he says again. "I'll get your pajamas. And the quilt."

She stays upright, still careful, as he leaves and comes back in. The pajamas are her own old set that she bought from the big Sainsbury's, the ones with Moomins on them, but the quilt is another new thing: dark-blue and light-blue squares, alternating, arranged like patchwork but it's just a print. She doesn't like it.

"I know, but look at it this way," he says, "if you chuck up on it you'll finally have an excuse to throw it out."

This doesn't make sense, "finally," but everything is intense and confusing and she doesn't want to argue. The room is buzzing gently.

"Okay," she says. They seem to be taking it in turns to say "okay" and sighing or waiting, which perhaps is what marriage is like; this is the first time she's tried it.

The husband turns on a lamp and then turns off the overhead light. "You good?" he says. "Do you want some toast?"

"I had chips." She still has the taste in her mouth. "And chicken." She is a vegetarian but not when she's drunk.

"Okay," he says once more. "Drink your water," he adds again, just before he closes the door. She hears him in the kitchen, then the bedroom, and then nothing.

Well.

She goes to the door and listens for a moment. Silence on the landing, and through the flat. She puts on her pajamas, step by step like she's in a school changing room: first the shorts over her underpants, then the dress over her head, then the pajama top on over her bra, then the bra off, unhooked and her arms wriggled out one by one until she can pull it triumphantly from an armhole, at which point she overbalances and tumbles back on to the sofa with a thump and a clatter as her dead phone falls off the cushions and on to the ground.

She freezes, waiting to see if the husband comes back. Nothing.

A creak, maybe. A truck or a bus outside, up on the main road.

At least now she's sitting down.

Another rumble of a car outside. Maybe a train, further back, although it's late for that. Perhaps she's imagined it, and the husband.

If she hasn't imagined him, there's a strange man in her house. She pushes herself back up to stand unsteadily one more time.

Quiet steps to the table in the corner, and she takes a chair and carries it—slowly, slowly—over to the door. She hasn't ever done this before but she's seen it in so many movies: you wedge the chair and it keeps the door shut, right? She sets it down and balances it, the back hooked up under the handle. It takes her a couple of tries, but finally it's there, jammed in place, and she looks at it and goes to sit on the sofa and figure out what to do next, and then she's asleep.

CHAPTER 2

She wakes to find that she's feeling less drunk and much, much more terrible.

The room is bright, the slats of the shutters tilted to let in warm light, turning everything yellow.

She stands up. It goes mostly okay. Looks around. The chair she used to barricade herself in last night is on its side lying next to, but in no way blocking, the door, which is half-open, letting in noises from the rest of the flat: footsteps, a clatter.

The husband.

She is not feeling her best, but she picks up her dead phone and rights the fallen chair and peers out. The sound is coming from the kitchen.

She rushes across the landing into the bathroom, on tiptoe, and locks the door. She's torn between emptying her bladder and throwing up; opts to prioritise the second, leaning over the bowl as she gives in to the rising thrust of a good drunken chuck.

Her headache dissipates right away, and her nausea subsides, leaving behind a glorious clarity that she knows will last for twenty minutes at most before her body realises it has outstanding issues to address. At the basin, she swirls water around her mouth, spits it out, then drinks again and swallows this time. She wants very much to brush her teeth, but on the corner of the sink sit two unfamiliar toothbrushes, one yellow, one green. Toothpaste on her finger, then.

It's been a while since she last drank this much.

"Lauren?" the husband calls from outside the door, so close.

". . . Yes," she says. "Give me a minute."

"I'll put on some breakfast."

She stares at the door, waiting to hear him move away, then washes her face, cleaning away the last remnants of the night's glitter and mascara. Takes her pajama top off, wipes herself with a washcloth: face, shoulders, under the breasts, under the arms. She can shower when she's figured out what's going on with the husband.

Her clothes from last night are in the laundry basket. He must have come into the living room while she was sleeping and picked them up. The dress is dry-clean only and the laundry basket is absolutely the wrong place for it, but underneath it she finds last night's bra and a man's shirt, boxers, a grey jumper she recognises as hers and a pair of leggings she doesn't. Bra, jumper, then she swaps the pajama pants for the leggings and looks in the mirror.

Concealer? Mascara? No. She's not going on a date: she's trying to find out why this man is in her house. She's clean, or clean-ish, and that's enough.

She unlocks the door.

○ ○

The husband (cardigan, trousers) is in the kitchen, where the walls are not the yellow she remembers but rather the same blue as the landing. Her toaster (unchanged), a coffee machine (new), a tiny table with two stools squeezed in against the wall (new). Something is frying on the stove.

"It's alive," the husband says as she walks in. "Here," he adds, and hands her a coffee, turns back to the machine to make another. "Bacon's nearly ready."

"I'm a vegetarian," she says without conviction.

"There are no atheists in foxholes," the husband says.

There's a charger plugged into the wall, its cord lying in a loop across the little table. She sits at the stool on the far side and connects her phone. He constructs a sandwich and puts it in front of her on the table.

If he was a murderer, he could have just murdered her last night—waiting till the morning and poisoning her with a bacon sandwich would be a roundabout way of doing it. And when she takes a bite, the sandwich is good, really good: crispy-edged, salty, buttery, the chew of fresh bread, the tang of brown sauce. She had started to avoid pork even before she went vegetarian; pigs are as clever as a human three-year-old, she heard once, the same day she went to her nephew Caleb's third birthday party, and that was it. But throwing out a sandwich now wouldn't save any pigs. And by the fourth or fifth slow bite, she is feeling a little bit better.

"So," the husband says, sitting opposite her with a sandwich for himself. "Good night?"

It had been such a good night. She remembers painting the cactus pots in that little shop, then drinks while the pots dried, then a big dinner, and karaoke, and a cocktail bar, and then dancing, and more drinks, and shoving late-night chips into her face, salty and greasy, while Elena took photos of the two of them posing in the mirrored tiles of the chicken shop, its lights glowing warm in the cooling night. She remembers Elena promising not to abandon her for a married-person life of married-person things, *you know I would never.* She remembers climbing to the top floor of the night bus to Norwood and sitting down and seeing the moon impossibly huge in the sky. She remembers looking out at London through the spatter of summer rain on the window, traffic lights and strangers and kebabs and the wide bridge and the long journey towards streets where the city relaxes and spreads into suburbs.

And then: arriving home, and finding the husband.

"Yeah," she says. How does a conversation with a husband work? "What about you? What did you get up to?"

"Went for a swim," he says. "Tidied up a bit. Helped Toby fix that window so they won't get in trouble with their landlord." Okay, she thinks, the husband knows Toby. He continues: "Finally put those boxes up in the attic. Might turn over the veg patch today."

He sounds very industrious. She doesn't have a vegetable patch, but perhaps he's brought it with him. The whole flat has become a spot-the-difference puzzle: more cookbooks, the dent in the wall from when she swung the door too hard that time has disappeared, a light is still sitting askew in its socket. The cactus pot she painted yesterday is on the windowsill, and the cactus lopsided inside it. The husband must have collected it from the bottom of the steps for her. He does seem nice.

Which doesn't stop it from being disturbing that he's here.

He appeared while she was out. If she leaves and comes back, might everything be normal again? "I'm . . . going to go for a walk. Clear my head," she tries.

"Want some company?"

"No, I'm okay." Maybe she's misunderstanding something and as soon as she gets a little air, it'll all make sense.

She finds socks, shoes, keys. Back in the kitchen for her phone, which has charged to thirty per cent. The husband is chewing cheerfully on the last of his sandwich. She opens the fridge for a hangover Coke but there's only a can of grapefruit-flavoured water. She takes that instead.

Down the steps and outside, and she looks back at the house, those new shutters.

The rest of the street. Houses, an empty dumpster halfway up towards the main road, trees and their green leaves. She walks away from the house, counting twenty steps, then looks behind her: the shutters are still there.

When she reaches the corner, she can see the bus stop from last night. As far as she can tell, it's the same as it always was. Behind it, the petrol station, and kids talking over each other, their bikes leaning against a wall. She crosses the road, sits down on the bus stop's tilted bench, and pulls her phone out.

The lock screen is still her and the man, standing together, the sea behind them.

She touches the screen, and it demands a passcode. Maybe this, too, will have changed; but, no, it unlocks to the code she's used for years.

She opens her photos first, and scrolls backwards through last night. The bus ride, the chicken shop, the bar, the other bar, the pottery workshop with everyone's plant pots lined up together, Elena's with the diamond patterns, Noemi's with its elegant looping dicks. Fine. Then she filters to show selfies only, skims the past year: some with just her but more with her and the husband, squinting into the sunlight. Further into the past: he's still there, in and out of the pictures. He has a beard. It's gone again. They're on a hill. They're by a tree. They're in front of a swan; the swan is approaching them; she's trying to feed the swan; the swan isn't happy.

She looks up from the impossibility of it, the man's face on her phone against the sunny day. One of the kids at the petrol station is kicking a plastic bottle along the pavement while the other keeps goal. A taxi pulls in across the road and lets someone out.

She checks her sent messages: lots of hearts to Elena, *I LOVE YOU I KNOW YOU'RE GOING TO BE SO HAPPY*, and a photo back from her of their chicken-shop reflections captioned *It must be difficult for everyone else that we're so beautiful*. In another thread Lauren finds she has sent a *HOME SOON I WILL SEE YOU HOM SOON YESS HELLO SOON* to—ah, here we go—a Michael.

The husband is called Michael. She scrolls up through the messages.

Another one to him, from two days ago: *Lemons, dishwashing liquid, thx!*

Another: a picture of a pear with big googly eyes stuck on it.

One from him, a few days earlier: *Almost there see you in five.*

When she searches her own messages for "Michael," she finds she's mentioning him constantly to everyone: Michael's away for work, Michael's training for a half-marathon so he can't come out to the pub, Michael's bringing panzanella to the barbecue. Michael this, Michael that. Nobody has responded with *What the hell, who's Michael?*

Well. If her friends know about him, maybe one of them can explain.

She finds Toby in her phone; the husband mentioned him, and he lives downstairs, he should know what's going on. *Hey,* she messages, *am I married.*

An almost immediate reply: *Last I heard,* he responds. *Tall kid, nice face. Lives with you. You know the one*

Okay when did we get married

The response: *14 April. Is this a quiz? Do I win?*

14 April. This year? A couple of months ago, if so. There weren't any pictures of a wedding in her photoroll, but she looks in her messages instead, and eventually finds, sent to her mum: *These are the first few—we'll get the rest from the photographer in a month or two.*

And then, four photos.

A group shot first, the one she saw in the living room. Her in a cream dress, long sleeves, flared skirt to mid-calf, pink heels, a bunch of pink flowers (not roses, something else). No veil. The husband, Michael, in a dark-brown suit. Her mum. Her sister and Elena and a woman she doesn't know are bridesmaids in different shades of green. Strangers: his friends, his family.

The next photo: just her and the husband, dancing. Looking at each other. He's smiling, she's serious.

The next: signing papers.

And the last: her and Michael again, kissing. She touches her lips. They're dry.

So, she had a wedding.

She's married. She has a husband, who is back at the flat.

A message from him pops up on the screen, as if to confirm: *Hey if you pass a shop could you get a light bulb? Screw-in, not bayonet.*

She almost drops the phone—it's as if he's caught her spying on him—but she calms herself and messages back, *Sure.* That's the kind of thing you say, right?

Okay, what else? First, she searches *Michael* in her email and finds a surname: Michael Callebaut.

She has also, apparently, become a Callebaut. Well. It's a step up from Strickland.

She googles the husband but there are a bunch of Michael Callebauts, so she adds *london,* scrolls through the image results. God, does she even remember what he looks like? Yes: there he is, gazing at her, a headshot in front of stone.

It's from an architectural firm that lists him halfway down their "About Us" page. The company's website has pictures of churches, a library, a hall in the financial district, a fairground. She can't always tell whether their designs are real photographs of things they've built or computer mock-ups of things they've imagined.

An architect, though! What a perfect job for a husband. Ambitious yet concrete, artistic yet practical, glamorous yet without an industry-wide drug problem. No wonder he's filled in the dent in the kitchen wall and planted a vegetable garden. Wait, might her job be different in this new world? She checks, and no: she's still a business advisor at the council, persuading companies to move to Croydon and helping local residents set up new projects. Her calendar is highlighted blue instead of green, but it has most of the same meetings, maybe in a different order.

Still. Plenty of other changes to be getting on with. "Lauren

Callebaut," she says out loud, trying it out. She opens the can of water and takes a sip. It's metallic and unpleasant, somehow tasteless and sour at the same time, but she takes another. Perhaps this is her new life: she drinks grapefruit water now.

○ ○

She walks back slowly, carefully, picking up a light bulb at the petrol station and dawdling, stopping a moment at the corner to her road, trying to give normality a chance to re-establish itself; but as she nears the house she can still see, in the living-room windows, shutters instead of the curtains that were there yesterday.

The front door: no. Not yet. She circles around the side instead, sidles past the bins, takes in the house from the back, looks up towards the bedroom and the kitchen where she can see that a ceramic jar she has never owned is sitting just inside the window, stuffed with utensils.

The garden has changed a little. Toby and Maryam's side, visible across the low fence, is the same as always, enthusiastically started but erratically maintained. Her half—hers and Michael's, she supposes—is looking a little better than it used to, with the vegetable patch at the back (it's very minimal, some peas and lettuce). A row of pinkish flowers along the fence. A half-filled bowl with dry pellets by the outdoor tap. She has a cat. Or Michael has a cat? They have a cat together?

What is my cat called, she messages Toby.

She texts her sister, Nat, too, *Quick question, what do you think about my relationship situation*, and Elena, *Was anything weird for you when you got home last night?*

She gets a call right away from Nat, and answers, but it turns out it's Caleb with Nat's phone.

"Auntie Lauren!" he says. "Do you want to listen while I do some karate?" Then there's rustling noises, and a yell, and a thud.

"Caleb," she calls. "Caleb. Is Mummy there?"

"No! She's giving Magda a bath! I'll do the kick again."

At this point she'd take any adult. "What about Mamma?"

"No! They say getting Magda in the bath is a job for two! Did you hear it?"

God, she loves him but this is not the time. "Caleb. I'm going to have to go. Give Mummy her phone back, okay? And tell her to call me. You can send me a video of the karate, all right?"

"I'll give it to her if you get Uncle Michael!" Caleb says. "Uncle Michael always listens to me."

Huh. Maybe Caleb has more to contribute to this than she thought. "Yes. Caleb. What can you tell me about Uncle Michael?"

"He loves it when I show him my good kicks," Caleb says decisively. "And his favourite dinosaur is the triceratops and his favourite bird is the swan."

"And you've seen him a lot?"

"I'm his favourite nephew!"

"Caleb. Do you remember the wedding? When Uncle Michael and I got married?"

"It was boring," he says. "Tell Uncle Michael to call me about some kicking," and he hangs up.

She looks at the phone.

"Are you okay?" Toby says from the other side of the fence. He's on the steps outside his back door, holding his phone. Steady voice, big dimple, unflattering baggy T-shirt. It's good to see not everything has changed.

"Yeah," she says, "just—I didn't have a husband yesterday. And now I've had a husband for months? Who likes to practise kicks with my nephew? I mean, as far as I can tell he's perfectly pleasant."

"I like him." Toby has always been good at taking things in stride. During lockdowns the two of them had hung out in their respective gardens while Maryam was at the hospital, drinking cups of tea and chatting quietly, and he had been dependable and unruffled and a comfort in the strangeness. It feels good to say, out loud, what's happened now.

"It's very surprising," she says. "And apparently we've got a cat?"

"Yeah?"

"What's it called?"

"Gladstone," he says.

"Like the prime minister?"

"Yeah, because of the sideburns, you said."

Lauren is sure she doesn't know what Gladstone's sideburns looked like. What did Gladstone do? How racist was he? Does she have a problematic cat? This is perhaps not her most pressing issue.

"How long have I been seeing Michael?"

"Wait, do you really not remember? Are you—did you hurt yourself? Do you want me to get Maryam?"

"No, I'm fine," she says. "I don't need a doctor. I'm just joking, ignore me, I'm good."

○ ○

Around the front, she hesitates again. The main door, the tiled hallway, her own front door, the stairs.

"Hello," she calls out, tentative, and the husband pokes his head out to look down from the landing. "Welcome back," he says. "Good walk?"

"Yeah," she says. "Sure." Up the stairs, one at a time.

"Did you get the light bulb?" the husband asks.

"Oh," she says, and fishes in the bag, holding it out as she reaches the top. "Yeah, here."

She's going to have to tell someone what's happened, she thinks. Maybe she's even going to have to tell this man, this husband. But first, she needs a little sit. "Do you want a cup of tea?"

"That'd be great," he says. "Just gimme a sec. The attic light was out when I was up there yesterday, let me change it while I remember."

"Yeah," she says, "okay." She heads into the kitchen while he stays on the landing and pulls the ladder down—hears him jerk it to one side at the place where it always catches, like he's lived here for years. In the fridge, she is confronted by three different milks in a row: oat, cashew, dairy. God, and what if he drinks it black? He's an architect, after all. She'll just have to ask, and if he thinks it's weird, then so be it. Maybe it'll be a way into a conversation that she still doesn't know how to start. "Do you want milk?" she calls out, stepping back on to the landing with the blue mug in her hands.

"What?" says an entirely different man, climbing down the ladder from the attic.

CHAPTER 3

The second man is even taller than the first, and more strongly built. He has the short cut and wavering hairline of someone who is balding young and not at peace with the fact, but he is startlingly good-looking, his cheekbones sharp, his olive skin flawless, a dark-green T-shirt fitting him closely.

"Uh," she says, looking at his face and then his forearms (his forearms!). He, too, is wearing a wedding ring.

"Is that for me?" he says, nodding at the mug. A slight accent: Turkish, perhaps? The mug in her hands is yellow with thin black lines.

". . . Yes?"

"Great," he says. His eyelashes are dark.

She doesn't move.

"Are you okay?" the maybe-Turkish gratuitously handsome husband says after a moment. His immaculate eyebrows furrow in concern. She looks up at the attic, searching for Michael, then back at the landing. Its walls—usually grey, more recently blue—are white. She steps backwards and peers into the living room. The wedding picture is gone.

"You're not still hungover, are you?" the man asks.

"No," she lies, and switches her focus back to him. "Were you just in the attic?"

"What? Yes. You saw me."

"Was anyone else there?"

"Where?"

She looks at the dark square. "Up there. Is Mich— Was there anyone in the attic?"

"Like a squirrel? Mice? I don't think so. Do you want me to check?" He stands, one hand on the ladder, teetering between irritation and concern. The mug is still warm in her hands.

"Yes," she says.

"Are you sure you're okay?"

"Yes. Yes, if you could check, please."

The husband tightens his shapely lips and climbs partway back up the ladder, and then continues, up, up, all the way in, his bare feet (uncalloused, perfectly formed) disappearing before her eyes. There's a moment of movement and brightness above her, like a flash of sunlight through train windows, and a sharp crackle.

A moment later a blue furry slipper emerges from the trapdoor. And another.

Huh.

The third husband is less attractive than the first two, with a rectangular head and a sunburn across his pale nose. His red-brown hair sticks out at all angles. She is still holding the mug (it's now pink). Her hands are hot; she shifts her grip. His slippers have purple spots and black claws and she thinks they may be *Monsters, Inc.* themed.

"We really should clean it out up there." From his voice he is, perhaps, Welsh, she's not sure. He dumps a bag on the ground and, without waiting for a reply, he goes back up, climbs halfway in, brings down another bag he must have left by the hatch, and heads up again, all the way this time. Another moment of light, bright and then dark, and a sound, a fuzz. And moments later—and it's almost not a surprise, this time—another new man calls out, "Lauren, Lauren, look what I found," loud and plummy, like an agitated professor. "It's the most remarkable thing. It's extraordinary."

This time the feet that emerge are bare again, and so are the legs, and so too is the shockingly round white bottom that follows them. She takes two quick steps backwards as the bottom's owner finishes his descent and turns to face her, then spreads his arms. This husband is shorter than the others and extremely thin, other than those remarkable buttocks, with sharp-edged shins, visible ribs, and a narrow but very long penis which he points to with both hands. "It's a penis!" he says.

She stares. As he points she sees that he, too, is wearing a wedding ring. He is wearing nothing else.

"Not funny? Come on, I don't have any clothes on!" When she doesn't react he waits a moment, then again he says, in the same excited and informative tone: "Penis!" This time he sparkles his fingers to either side of it, *ta-da*, and twists around to flop it from side to side.

Lauren shifts her grip on the mug, ready to throw hot tea over him if he gets any closer.

"We can take it on *Antiques Roadshow*," the husband says, jiggling. "Nice specimen, beautifully crafted, excellent condition, very unusual to see one of this size." To be fair to him, the penis really is extraordinarily long.

Lauren is torn between wanting to look into the attic, and not wanting to get any closer to either it or the naked man. She compromises by doing nothing.

"An exceptional piece," the man adds, undaunted. "No? Still not funny? Never mind, hold on a minute, I found something else too," and he climbs back up into the attic and thankfully she never finds out what the next stage of his joke was going to be. Instead: the buzz, the flicker of light, and the man who climbs down thirty seconds later is fully clothed in jeans and a T-shirt, and even an apron that, when its wearer turns, says THIS IS WHAT A FEMINIST COOKS LIKE. Pink tips to his hair, which she's not at all sure about, but she can deal with the hairstyle once she's dealt with the man.

"Nah," he says. "No sign of it."

She still has the mug in her hands. He steps towards her and she holds it out automatically. "Cheers," he says, and takes it. "Are we out of milk?"

"I forgot," she says. She feels slow, she's still working it out, but the flat is different again, different carpet beneath her feet when she looks down; everything is changing every time, but always behind her back; her gaze holds everything in place until she looks away, and when she turns around it's like someone has flipped a card or pulled a lever and exposed a new world.

The apron husband takes the tea to the kitchen, and she hears him open the fridge. She looks into the living room, at the new walls and the sofa and the books.

"Are you okay?" the husband says, stepping back on to the landing, whose walls, now that she has glanced away and back, have settled into pale orange. "What's up?"

She looks at the open attic.

"I thought I heard something," she says, then adds, "maybe a squirrel," shamelessly copying from the husband with the eyelashes and the forearms. "Could you check?"

"Shit, really? God, I hope it's not rats again." The husband balances his now-milky tea on the radiator and heads straight up the ladder, pauses halfway. "What did it sound like?" he says.

"Chittering," she says firmly. "It's very plausible," she adds, because it is.

"I'm not sure rats chitter," he says, doubtful.

He climbs. The sound, the thick white noise. She stares straight ahead, eyes trained on the pale-orange wall opposite, a vintage advertisement for trains: THE MATLOCKS FOR A RESTFUL HOLIDAY, EXPRESS SERVICES & CHEAP FARES. If the change happens again, she will catch it.

Music is playing from behind her in the living room, something old, a man singing. She doesn't let it distract her. She stays focused, even as footsteps above her head move towards the trapdoor, and anything, she can see: no asking him to check for sounds above, no *just pop this box up*, no promise of a nice surprise.

They are, she supposes, fighting. He goes into the bathroom, and she looks around for a name, something to orient herself; but he's only gone for a moment, not even closing the door, then across to the kitchen to grab a bottle of water from the fridge and back to the landing. He stops.

"What time are they getting here?" he says.

"Uh. I don't know."

"Well, find out, then," he says. His feet are heavy on the stairs; the door at the bottom slams closed, then the outer door a moment later. She heads into the living room, new objects wherever she looks, and watches from the window: he walks then lengthens his stride, accelerating up the road, past the dumpster, away from the house, out for a run.

Her flat is empty again. But everything is wrong. In the living room her original sofa has reappeared, but the junk-shop coffee table she was so proud of finding for £10 has gone, the dent in the kitchen wall is back, the television is smaller, strange throw pillows. The hundreds of tiny signs of a new husband. And she has not taken to this one at all.

She checks her messages. He must be Kieran.

Then her photo library, and the video she tried to take of his absence from the attic isn't there. And it's worse than that, because in her photo reel she finds Elena's pottery party, and the first, but not the second, and no late-night chicken shop. As far as her phone is concerned, she came home early.

She scrolls, checks, and it's not just that there are no late-night messages from Elena: there's nothing from her for weeks, nothing on Instagram except a note about a misdelivered parcel, nothing to recall. A few to Zarah at work. Regular enough messages from Mum, no advice, no instructions, no links to articles she ought to read, just *Thinking of you, let's chat soon* or pictures of the kids.

at the corner of her eye patterned trousers descend, but she is still looking ahead at the wall, trying to catch the world in the act; then the man pushes the ladder up and she can't help herself, she flicks her eyes to look at him. Black, slender, wearing glasses, the pattern on his trousers a green check. When she looks back at the poster, it has become a framed print of a fluorescent ice-cream cone. The walls are off-white.

"Could you leave the ladder?" she says to the new husband. Shirtsleeves rolled up, no wedding ring but perhaps he's taken it off to do chores.

"Okay," and he pulls it back down. "Only for a few minutes, right? It's hot up there, don't want the whole flat to warm up."

"Sure," she says. Her phone: the lock screen this time is a picture of her niece and nephew. A small table on the landing: no letters, but a wallet which she flicks open. She finds a name, Anthony Baptiste, on an organ donor card.

"Anthony," she calls.

"Yeah?" he says from the living room.

She walks back over to the ladder, touches it.

"Yeah?" he repeats. "You said something?"

She'll film, she thinks, record him going up, someone else coming down. Get some evidence.

"Have another look in the attic," she says, steadily.

"What?" he says. "Why? Is a bucket of water going to fall on my head?"

"No. Nothing's going to happen. I just need you to have a look."

"Why?"

"It's okay," she says. "It's a—it's a surprise. A gift. This will all make sense in a moment." She is massively overpromising on the explanatory power of the attic, but she manages a smile.

"It's not a big rubber spider, is it? You know I can't do jump scares."

Weirdly nervous is one of her types, actually. She likes men at the extremes of self-assurance, men who know what they want and are either confident they can have it or terrified they can't; she can imagine being into this guy.

"No," she says. "You'll love it. No rubber spiders." She's talking herself into a corner she has no way of getting out of, but the evidence so far suggests that she simply won't have to. "You'll be so happy," she adds, bold with promises. "I've been planning this for months."

Anthony lets the frown lapse into a puzzled smile, and glances upwards, then hands her his mug and climbs, his head to the trapdoor. A little further.

"What am I looking for?" he says, halfway in. His body stretches away from her, framed by the attic; she touches the button on her phone, starts filming.

"Keep going. I can't wait for you to see it. This is the best thing I've ever done for you."

He climbs again. Again, one foot in, and then finally, finally, his lagging foot disappears from sight. The attic brightens, and this time she can see that the light is coming from the bare hanging bulb. It flares, illuminating the wooden struts on the underside of the roof, then fades.

"Hello?" she calls out towards, she can only imagine, another man, another husband. She steps back, the flurry of novelty revealed as she turns, a new world flicking into place behind her back. The walls have changed again, even though she was pointing the camera at them the whole time. She feels clearheaded—maybe in this version of the world she drank less last night, or maybe things are starting to make sense. A sound from above.

"What's it like up there?" she calls out, wondering who's going to answer.

CHAPTER 4

It's the fucking attic, what do you think it's back. A pile of towels drops straight thro thumps against the bottom of the ladder, the floor.

She watches the husband (the sixth? sev wards, sneakers, joggers, a T-shirt, one of t holds a phone while you run.

He is tall and pale and angry about som ing up the towels and refolding them, an spare room, then he turns to leave but she' and juts his chin, waiting for her to let hi

"There should be two more towels," sh way. She'll send him up and replace him mood.

"They're my fucking towels," he say are."

"I was sure there were six."

"Well, you were wrong."

Okay, then. "Maybe you could gr

"What, so now you want to use t

As far as she's aware she has no sounds like they are, somehow, a sounds like a lot of things might might be mostly sore points. Th

When she catches herself in a mirror, she is surely paler than she ought to be this far into summer, paler than she was yesterday, and her hair, pulled up into a bun, is wrong. She loosens the elastic. Yes: usually her hair is cut to shoulder length, but now it falls three or four inches further, and somehow this is the thing that makes the world intolerable, that sends her dizzy even though she is not, in this version of the world, hungover. She is aghast in her own body, she shrinks back from it, feels her fingers trembling, goose-bumps, a hollow in her stomach edging up towards her chest.

She wants the long, wrong hair gone so absolutely that she thinks about taking the kitchen scissors and chopping it off. But instead she ties it back up. The husband will go, and the hair with him.

○ ○

Everyone has bad days, of course. Everyone yells at their partner sometimes, or so Elena claims; Lauren herself has usually kept it to snippy asides, and her relationship with Amos, her longest, ended quietly on a day four years ago when he was supposed to move in but instead phoned her from a roller-coaster queue at Alton Towers to say that he thought perhaps they were moving too fast.

But nothing about this marriage looks good.

And if she wants to get rid of this guy, she has no time to wonder what's going on, no time to refuse to believe it, to pinch herself, to call one of her reduced number of friends.

The situation, however new to her, is clear. She has been provided with a husband, and each time that husband goes into the attic, he is replaced with a different husband. Where the husbands come from, how many there are, even in some cases their names: mysteries she can address in due course. But the basic mechanics are undeniable, and so is the fact that the current husband is— well, perhaps safest just to say *a dud*.

○ ○

Back on the landing, the attic hangs above her like a threat. But she has a plan.

She finds a speaker in the kitchen, a grey cylinder, and connects to it with her phone. Disable Bluetooth, re-enable Bluetooth, press a button, Forget About This Device, start the whole process again. She begins to worry, listening for the door, but the connection eventually works. It's taken her, what, four minutes? Five? It's fine. Plenty of time.

Okay, stage two. She steps up the ladder, one foot and then two, then another rung, then one more. She's holding the speaker in one hand. This is safe, she tells herself, trying to tamp down her fear. The husbands have only changed when they've gone all the way in. But her other hand is clutching tight on to the topmost rung, then she takes a deep breath and sticks her head up into the darkness.

And: it's her attic.

In the murk there is only furniture, and boxes, and a dark shape that she flinches from before realizing it's a half-disassembled Christmas tree. There is no Michael, no naked man with a hemispherical bum, no Anthony, no handsome man looking puzzled. There are no frozen husbands propped against the walls, no golden door through which they exit and enter, no wisps of bright-green smoke, no ghosts sitting around a table playing poker for the chance to exit the attic. No figures hanging upside down from the rafters like bats and breathing, in-out, in-out, in unison. No bodies stacked like carpets to unroll into life.

Only the attic, and the light bulb, which is, admittedly, starting to glow just a little.

Okay. Priorities. It's been . . . ten minutes since Kieran left? Twelve? How long does she have?

She reaches as far into the attic as she can without stepping any further. The light brightens above. The speaker crackles as she rests it on the floor, then pushes. Back down the ladder for an umbrella, then back up and she uses it to poke the speaker in further, out of arm's reach, another crackle as she pushes it through the dust. Far enough that nobody could reach it without climbing in.

Then she ducks her head back out and gasps for air on the bright landing. The light above her dims.

Down the ladder, and she tries streaming through the speaker from her phone. From above: a quick burst from yesterday's playlist, songs that Elena's friends added during the pottery workshop.

She opens YouTube to search for the right sort of noise.

She finds it.

Back in the living room, she looks for Kieran on the road outside. She doesn't search through her phone for wedding pictures, proof of their life together. Whatever the situation is, she's fixing it. She doesn't need to know.

It's been fifteen minutes, then twenty. Twenty-five. She hates running, the visibility of it, the traffic, the people who run by faster; she doesn't know how long a run is meant to take, but shouldn't he be back soon? He'll be coming from the top of the road, unless he's circled round to the lane.

Which he has: she sees him at last, halfway between the lane and the house. It takes her a moment to recognise him. She has, after all, spent only a few minutes in his company. She was looking for a pale-faced runner but he's walking instead, then leaning over with his hands on his knees, then standing back up, flushed bright red. She has one minute, maybe two.

She's calm. This will work. This will work, won't it? What if the attic refuses the exchange? What if she was only meant to have seven husbands and Kieran is the culmination? Seven is a fairy-tale number, seven feels like the sort of thing that might be true.

No. She can cross that bridge if she comes to it: for now she has no choice but to trust the attic. She starts the video playing, and there's an ad, *Is HelloFresh worth the money? Absolutely!* But then she can skip and there's the sound of water or, as the video title calls it, *Two Hours of Broken Pipes Murmuring Water Rainfall Soothing ASMR* playing through the open trapdoor and, yes, when she turns the volume up as far as it goes she can hear it through the flat: drips, a gush, a rattle.

She rushes to the bedroom, heads in and closes the door. She was going to get under the bed but it's a different bed, solid to the ground. The wardrobe, then; Kieran's clothes are in there too, and the smell of an unfamiliar laundry detergent, all wrong, but this is no time to be fussy.

She nestles down, pulls the hanging swag of coats around her, angles herself so the doors sit flat, one leg extended in front, hoping away any cramps. Softness and dark, with a crack of light. Trickling water, muffled but still audible from the attic above. And the door at the bottom of the stairs—she feels the reverberations as it closes, and hears the husband's footsteps coming up, and then, as he steps on to the landing, his breath, loud and fast.

CHAPTER 5

"Could you not even close up the fucking attic," she hears him call. Then he goes into the kitchen; the splashing of a tap, multiplying the water sounds.

"Lauren," he says. The door to the bedroom opens, but he doesn't come in. *Listen to the noise*, she thinks. *Listen to the attic*. It's louder now, with the bedroom door open. She hears a creak that could be from the ladder, and another; perhaps he's climbing, though probably not far enough to change, maybe not even far enough to see in. She thinks about the Bluetooth speaker's light, and whether it'll give everything away.

"Lauren," she hears him call again. Come on, she thinks, it's water noises in your attic, are you not going to investigate, but then her phone lights up with a call from him, illuminating the clothes and her own hands and the inside of the wardrobe door; and up above, in the attic, the ring sounds, relayed through the speaker, loud, *biddle-de-beeep, biddle-de-beeep*. Fuck, *fuck*.

She turns the phone face-down on to her knee to hide the light but the noise continues; she flips it back and tries to silence it, fumbles.

"What the fuck, Lauren," she hears the husband say, his voice coming from outside the door and then again, crackling from above, relayed through the speaker in the attic, a half-moment later, and she hangs up successfully this time and tries to restart the water sounds, but she must have done it wrong because the hen-night playlist starts again, the Veronicas loud above her.

She hits stop and stays motionless as she hears him swear again and climb up the ladder, and—yes—stop a few steps up and then start again.

And another step. Another.

And the static, that sharp crackle, louder than usual. And she hears someone climbing down.

It's worked. It must have.

"Hey" is all the voice says, but she is almost sure it's not him. And again, from the landing: "Lauren? Where have you got to?"

This time it's clear: the vowels, the rhythm of the voice. A new man. She falls out of the wardrobe, flopping an old coat on to the ground and dislodging shirts and dresses, trailing one of them behind her, through the changed-again bedroom and on to the landing where she hugs, hard, the new husband, who is maybe her height or maybe a little shorter, and he has his shirt off which reveals a tattoo of ivy curling over one shoulder and which makes him, as she squeezes, the first husband whose chest she has touched. Her hair on her shoulders, the right length again, and smooth floorboards under her feet.

"Hello there," the husband says, and laughs. She leans back to look at him. His eyes crinkle at the corners; his hair is short and sits in loose curls, like a mass of flowers. He is wearing jeans and canvas shoes. He is solid, tanned, smells of dirt and sunlight. She cannot tell how old he is, though the eyes suggest older than her. The change of husband can't have affected the weather, but the landing is glowing. Maybe it's the floorboards, or the new yellow walls.

"Hello," she says, and feels herself grinning.

"Want a coffee?" he asks, smiling back.

"I would love a coffee." She never did drink any of the tea that she and the other husbands kept handing around.

The husband laughs again, like he's enjoying her delight, which she tries to tamp down but she can't because it *worked*, she got rid of Kieran and the attic has gifted her this joyful coffee-bringer. She stands back from his naked chest, a little embarrassed.

"Wanna drink it in the garden? I'll bring them out."

"Perfect," she says. The garden! She's always meant to use the garden more.

She steps back again to take it all in. The flat, though it feels brighter than before, is a mess: papers on the kitchen counter, towels on a chair in the corner, cables, a box of empty cans waiting to go down to the recycling bin.

"Hey," she says, "you're not going back up, are you?" and she nods her head towards the attic.

"Ah, no, I'm done," the husband says. "Sorry, should've closed it up."

"Good." She pushes the ladder away. "Don't. Promise you won't go back in."

He looks at her. "What's up?"

"Nothing," she says. "Just, no more attic today, okay? Or tomorrow. I had a—like a premonition of you falling. So steer clear."

He laughs. "I promise. No attic."

The carpet has gone from their stairs, but there's a runner down the middle, green. And when she heads around the side to the back, she finds an arch of maybe-roses, and she steps through and finds herself in a real garden.

Flowers and grass and a wooden table. A dozen little brown birds that take off as she approaches. In the back corner, a big netted box with mazy branches inside and a blackbird outside gripping on and pecking through the holes. The fence dividing their side of the garden from Toby and Maryam's is a wooden lattice, taller and growing all over with vines, some of them green and some with clusters of tiny white flowers and some pouring with long purple strands; but there's a gate in the middle of it, connecting the two halves.

Lauren checks her phone, and her texts to her friends are back, her adventures last night. Even an Uber home instead of the bus. Wait, is she rich now? She owns half her flat, of course; she and Nat inherited it together from their grandmother. So certainly she is rich enough that she knows better than to complain about money in front of her friends. But is she casual £45-car-ride-to-Zone-4 rich? Maybe!

She takes a picture of the newly lush garden, the chairs, the trees, the vines.

Maryam comes out of the kitchen next door with a laundry basket, and heads over to unpeg tea towels from the washing line.

"Hi there," Lauren calls out. "What a gorgeous day!"

"Oh, hi," Maryam says. "Yeah, it's nice, isn't it?" She looks up at the sky like it's a surprise. This is part of why she and Toby work so well together, Lauren has always thought: Toby notices and Maryam acts.

"Hey," Lauren says. "Have I ever had a cat?"

"I guess," Maryam says. "You seem the type."

"No, I mean while I've lived here."

Maryam unpegs another towel and looks over. She is always distracted, Lauren thinks, until she's not, and then for a moment you're the most important person in the world. She feels it: the switch as Maryam moves her from background to foreground, puzzled. "What?" she says. "No. I don't think so. Right?"

It is, Lauren supposes, a weird question for her to have asked. "You're right," she says. "No cats."

Maryam frowns, but lets it go, heads inside with the towels. Inconclusive! But on the side of Gladstone never existing?

Lauren takes a seat behind the table and kicks her legs out, face in the shade but her body stretching into afternoon sunlight.

The sun is picking out the hairs on her legs, sparse but clustered just below the knee; she has, she supposes, grown lax about shaving, a married woman. A *wife*. She doesn't like that her body keeps changing like this, without her say-so, not just the world but herself in it. She pulls her chair forward to put the legs under the table, free herself of the sight until she can shave them later, then she looks up towards the kitchen. The husband is barely visible inside, a dark shape moving.

There's a pot of daisies on the table. She picks one, and pulls off a petal, two, three. She's halfway around when the husband appears under the arch of maybe-roses. He's carrying a tray, with two small cups and a packet of chocolate digestives, half-empty, twisted at the end. He's put a T-shirt on, and she gets a good view as he approaches: lopsided nose; big wide eyes, eyebrows that reach towards each other along hard ridges but stop just shy of meeting in the middle. Flip-flops for the garden. Still hard to tell how old he is but, from a distance, the crinkles around the eyes are less of a distraction: about her age after all, perhaps. And he's smiling.

He seems like a husband she can live with for a while.

CHAPTER 6

The birds, the insects, the distant thrum of traffic, the husband chewing his chocolate digestives. She takes it in, relaxes into having solved the Kieran problem; she deserves a break before she deals with the more challenging question of the husbands at large. She sneaks glances at this one, his broad fingers.

"Garden's looking good," she says.

"Yeah," he says. "The hydrangea's really come round."

"I . . . agree."

"It's over there," he says, and points.

"I knew that."

"Sure you did."

He doesn't seem annoyed, though; maybe this is a *thing* they have, a running joke. If you live with someone for years you must make your fun where you can. "Love that humbrudger," she says, testing, and he smiles, and they lapse into silence again.

She watches him out of the corner of her eye.

He slaps at a mosquito.

She takes another sip of the coffee.

"This coffee is good," she tries.

"Yeah," he says, "it's the end of the packet we got from that cafe."

It's difficult to make conversation with a husband whose name she doesn't even know. But, fortunately, it doesn't seem necessary. The husband is happy to sit and sip his coffee.

"Oh, I paid the plumber," he says once.

"That's great," she says, which seems to be the right response. "Thanks for sorting that out," she adds, experimentally.

She can't keep from smiling at him as he sits there, though, so pleased and thoughtful, and he smiles back.

○ ○

She lingers in the garden when he goes back in; pulls out her phone, tries Nat again. "What? What's happened? Are you okay?" Nat says on answering, which is fair; they aren't usually spur-of-the-moment-phone-call sisters.

The sun has clouded over, but the day is still warm. "Yeah," Lauren says. "I'm fine. I just wanted to catch up."

"Uh. Maybe tomorrow? I'm on my way to get Caleb from karate and I'm trying to get Magda in the car and she"—she whispers the next word—"she *bit* me this morning. Obviously I love her."

"Yeah," Lauren says. "Sure. Just quickly," deep breath, "you know my husband?"

There's a moment's silence.

"What, Jason?"

Jason! Yeah, he looks like a Jason.

"Jason," she says. "Do you like him?"

"What? Yes, of course. Why?"

"Oh, I'm just—testing something out." Perhaps a convincing tone matters more than what she's actually saying. "Is there anything bad I should know about him?"

"I mean, the chewing, I guess? But we've talked about that. Magda, *no*," the sound of rustling, "she thinks she can eat keys. Did I tell you she got fired from nursery?"

The chewing? What chewing? "You didn't."

"At one and a half years old! I've had to take next week *off* and we're trying to find somewhere else for her but they have *waiting lists*. Waiting lists, to sit in a room and lick Duplo. Look, I have to go—"

"Okay," Lauren squeezes in. "One more thing, did you ever notice anything weird about the attic here?"

"What? No. Is there a problem? Is it the water tank? I've told you, you have to call someone immediately when it makes those noises, you can't wait till it breaks. Come on, you should know all this. I'm not your landlady."

"Does that mean I can stop paying you rent?" Wait, she thinks: in the old world she paid Nat monthly for her half of the flat, but what if it's different here?

But no, it seems like she's got away with it. "Yeah," Nat's saying. "Very funny. Look, I have to go and pick up my *non-biting* child, but I'll drop you a line tomorrow."

She tries Elena next, but doesn't get an answer, which makes sense; Elena's always been a sleep-through-the-hangover girl. And Toby: *Hey, have I ever had a cat?* The husbands don't know they're appearing and disappearing, Maryam knows nothing about Gladstone, but will Toby remember their talk from the morning?

o o

Inside she discovers, looking through papers piled on the kitchen counter, that the husband is called Jason Paraskevopoulos, and that she's kept her own surname, perhaps for political reasons or perhaps for ease of spelling.

"I've still got a bit of a headache," she says, rinsing out the mugs, looking into the darkening garden below. It's loud with birds, louder than she's used to, louder than she'd like even at this late stage of a hangover.

"What, a headache like a bad case of having been extremely drunk last night?" Jason says.

"Yeah, I dunno, feels different." She is preparing the ground for separate beds, trying to make it natural. She likes Jason, but she isn't ready to share a bed with him as husband and—she swerves away again from the thought *wife*—as husband and her. "I hope I'm not coming down with anything."

Jason is sceptical, but allows the possibility. "Maybe it's your turn with that cold I had," he says, generously. "It should only last a couple of days."

"I suppose I was bound to get it."

This is so plausible that he brings her Panadol and orders a curry ("The usual?" he asks). While they wait, they watch *Mindhunter*, which they are four episodes into. She doesn't think much of it but perhaps there's backstory she's missing. The curry arrives halfway through, and her "usual" turns out to be chickpeas. She was hoping for paneer, but at least it's vegetarian.

She needs time to think. What's the earliest she can get away with going to bed? Once they've cleared up the takeaway containers the sun has set, at least. "I'll sleep in the spare room," she says. "Feels like I'm going to be pretty restless."

"Nah, you're the sick one," Jason says. "I'll take it. Plus I have some emails I need to sort out before the week kicks off. Monday tomorrow, early start for me."

Ten almost unbearable minutes—thanking the husband for the peppermint tea he makes her, then for the splayed-open book on the history of mushrooms she's supposedly reading—before he finally runs out of questions to ask or things to offer. Is that it? She thinks that might be it.

"Good night," she says.

He leans in through the door to kiss her and she looks at his curls and his smile and decides, fast, that she's okay with it, and tilts her face towards his; but then at the last minute he swerves: "Oh wait, if you're sick we'd better not."

"Yeah, good point." She is, she realises, a little disappointed.

He steps away and closes the door.

○ ○

He's still there, she knows he's still there (and she can hear him, flushing the toilet, fetching something from the kitchen). But in the bedroom, it's just her, lamplit and secret.

Clothes are still spilling across the floor from when she climbed out of the wardrobe and sent them awry. She shakes out the brides-maid dress for Elena's wedding, crumpled inside its garment bag; almost two weeks to go until the day, though, plenty of time to iron it later. Everything else she just shovels in and closes the door on; she can sort it out in the morning.

One of the mismatched tables by the bed has a hair tie and the right sort of charging cable, so she supposes that side is hers. She sits delicately, and switches off the lamp.

In the darkness everything is familiar again. The moonlight from outside falls as it ought to across an almost correct room.

She does not sleep.

First, she scrolls through the photos on her phone, back and further back.

Plenty of them look familiar. Maybe not the exact photos she took, but close enough. A particularly good sunset, glimpsed between two blocks of flats. Nat's wife, Adele, on a picnic blan-ket, smiling and looking down at tiny Magda, whose baby face is contorted into an enormous scowl. Nat and Caleb standing ankle-deep in the fountain at the V&A, red-brick walls all around. A fish-and-chip shop called Fishcotheque. A cheese board she maybe remembers, or maybe that was a different, similar cheese board.

Some photos are new. A restaurant she's never been to; graffiti on the floor of a tube carriage reading *two dozen eggs please*. The biggest difference is that she keeps finding hills, big jagged hills, a picnic laid out in fog on a hill, a large bird in a thorny bush on a hill, her on a hill, her and the husband, her and strangers, all on a hill. It's looking suspiciously like she's taken up hiking.

She scrolls back through three or four years of photos before the world starts to look more like she remembers. Caleb as a toddler; her and Amos in a park; her and Elena and their friend Parris, back before Parris moved out of London. She switches the lamp back on and writes a list of husbands in the back of the mushroom book:

MICHAEL
(HANDSOME)
(SLIPPERS)
(NAKED)
ANTHONY
KIERAN
JASON

She stares at it, then remembers *(Feminist Apron)*, who was either before or after *(Naked)*.

She's not sure what to do with that information. She'll come back to it.

She writes: *when they go into the attic, they change*

And: *the light comes on, there's a sound*

And: *something is different in the past, maybe*

That's not getting her anywhere either.

She goes to her phone again and checks her emails, to see if anything important has changed in her day-to-day life. And: shit. She no longer works at the council. Instead, she is an office manager for the big hardware store and garden centre down the road. A hardware store! She doesn't even know whether a Phillips-head screwdriver is the one with a cross or the one with a line. She does at least know that a Phillips-head screwdriver is a thing that exists, but that probably doesn't count as extraordinary specialist expertise.

Monday morning tomorrow. She searches her sent mail until

she finds one from six months earlier, calling off sick; she sends the same message again, to the same address. Food poisoning, apologies. She can worry about work on Tuesday.

Back to her investigations. She searches for *Jason Paraskevopoulos* and finds his website: Garden Design and Maintenance.

She reads through WhatsApp, messages to friends, a Discord filled with strangers making jokes about flapjacks and tagging her. She has an Instagram account but the last time she posted was eighteen months ago, a picture of a foggy graveyard, and two months before that a cinnamon swirl. When she flicks through the people she follows it's mostly names she doesn't recognise and it feels like freedom: *she doesn't need to look*.

o o

She had not expected, heading out on Saturday afternoon, that Elena's party would be the least eventful part of her weekend. It's three o'clock in the morning, not quite twenty-four hours since she got on that night bus. She stands and walks out on to the landing towards the just-ajar door of the spare room. Pushes it a crack further, until she can see a dark mound on the bed. Another push, a half-step forward. The husband is breathing, in and out, and clutching one of his pillows to his chest.

CHAPTER 7

Lauren wakes before seven to the sound of the husband getting ready. She climbs out of bed quietly, sneaking on tiptoes, twisting the door handle like she's trying not to startle it. She can hear that he's in the kitchen. Is it still him?

"Hey," Jason says. "You're up! How you feeling? Get a good long sleep?" Still the crinkles at the corner of the eyes, a smile when he sees her.

"Not bad," she says.

"Big week for me. You off work?"

"Yeah," she says, "I need a day to rest up."

When he leaves she watches from the living-room window. He gets into a van parked halfway up the road, big logo on the side, a tree in the centre. And when he pulls out at the top of the road and turns right, the tightness in her shoulders dissipates, the tension of holding herself together releases.

The flat is hers again.

She sits on the sofa, lies back, closes her eyes. It's okay. It's all okay.

She wakes again at ten thirty and showers until she feels clean and new; blow-dries her hair, shaves her legs. Her legs themselves may be a little wider than they were, more clearly muscled. She raises and lowers one thigh on the toilet where it spreads against the plastic.

There are hiking boots in the wardrobe, and one of those jackets that's all zips and toggles. But there are some trousers she's owned for years and a green T-shirt she's had since uni, and a shirt she thinks she almost bought once and decided was too expensive. She puts it on.

She starts to pull down the ladder to the attic.

Stops. Feels sick.

Pushes it back up.

She should eat. She toasts some bread and spreads it with peanut butter, but it's a different brand than the normal, thick and too sweet. It sticks to the roof of her mouth. She is calm but beneath the calm something is fluttering. She has to get out of the house. She leaves the toast where it is, one bite taken; grabs her phone.

She looks up at the staircase as she leaves, the green runner, then closes the door.

○ ○

It's better outside; she breathes deeper the further away she gets. Look: the bus stop again, still where it used to be! The arts centre where she keeps thinking she should see a show at some time. The sky, the road, the cars, the trees, the petrol station. The gentle slope of the hill under her feet as she speeds up.

There's an argument to be made that she should go to hospital. The evidence really does seem to indicate that she's married. She has nothing to support her conviction that on Saturday afternoon she wasn't; the most likely explanation is not that her attic is creating and transforming men but rather that she is in some way ill, that there is—this is one thing the internet has suggested—a gas leak, or that she took something at Elena's party and it's still wearing off.

But she doesn't want to go to hospital. She wants to sit outside and maybe have a coffee.

Or even, she thinks as the hill levels out and the pub at the corner comes into sight, its tables arrayed in the sunlight: a beer. She wouldn't normally drink on a Monday or at eleven thirty in the morning, let alone both, but these are exceptional circumstances. In fact, go big or go home, and she's definitely not going home.

At the bar in the empty pub, she asks about a cocktail menu.

The woman at the bar says, "Yes?," then ducks and rummages, and brings up a laminated sheet. Bright liquids glow from complicated glasses that the pub does not, Lauren is certain, own.

"I will have," she says after a moment of examining the sheet, "a Merry Berry Fascination. And a flat white."

The woman squats below the bar again, and this time brings up a ring binder, flips through printouts of cocktail recipes. "This might—you know what, I'll bring it over."

"Lovely, thank you." Lauren smiles. "I'll be just outside."

○ ○

She finds a bench that lets her face away from the sun, and waits until the door opens, and the woman brings out a coffee and a bright-pink cocktail in a wine glass. "We're out of the little umbrellas," she says, apologetically.

"Thank you so much," Lauren says. The Merry Berry Fascination is sweet and bubbly. It has a slice of apple in it.

From her bench, Lauren looks towards the crossroads. A man with a shopping bag, standing there like the world hasn't changed. She checks the time in Spain and tries a message to her mum: *Hi! Hope everything's okay! Weird question, but what do you think about Jason?*

A few minutes later, a reply: *Hello darling, lovely to hear from you. I've always liked Jason. He's obviously very fond of you. I'm running short on proper tea bags and marmite, could you send some over.*

She thinks about calling Nat again, Toby, even spilling it out to Jason, although that's a bad idea. Probably he wouldn't believe her and he'd go up into the attic to prove her wrong—or worse, he *would* believe her, and then he'd refuse to go up there ever again. She likes him, but she's not sure she's ready for that level of commitment.

Besides, Elena is the one she tells everything.

Going to Elena's tonight, she sends to Jason, *she's really stressed about the wedding.*

Next: Elena. *Hey I need to talk, can I come over,* she sends; it occurs to her belatedly that perhaps Elena will have other plans. Still, it's a Monday night, two weeks out from her wedding. *I can help you blow up balloons*

She checks the phone's step tracker, numbers occasionally huge from hiking: 28,300; 35,600. A lightning monitor, which she opens, and a flurry of red and yellow dots pop up to the west.

Then she hears back: *7 p.m. You will arrange almonds,* Elena messages, *and you will like it*

∘ ∘

It's two o'clock when she finally runs out of terms to search on her phone: *men appearing in attic* (news stories about secret living spaces), *attic transformation* (expensive renovations), *husbands disappearing* (more news stories, plus quite a lot of bigamy, which is almost but not exactly the opposite of her own problem). She tries *husband magically came out of attic and when he goes back in he turns into someone else.* A real mix: a woman who hid a secret lover in her attic; an abusive man; someone writing to an advice column because her husband has realised he's gay; the plot summary for *Flowers in the Attic.*

She's going to have to pull down the ladder again and look.

But when she gets home, the husband's van is parked back in its spot. The irregular hours of a gardener; and that, she thinks, means no attic investigations. She can't quite hide the rush of relief, the gratitude and fondness she feels about this permission to keep ignoring the overwhelming question. Jason has rescued her a second time.

When she gets inside, he emerges from the bathroom in his underwear, again revealing the tattooed ivy that winds over his shoulder. He is wet-haired, presumably recently showered, and he looks—he always looks—so pleased to see her.

"I was wondering where you were!" he says.

"Yeah," she says, "just out for a walk. I'm so glad you're here! I'm feeling a lot better."

"Oh, are you?" he says, and comes over towards her. "Exactly how much better are we talking?"

"A fair bit," she says, then gets his meaning.

Well. She likes him. She is still flushed with relief that his presence has allowed her to delay investigating the attic. And it's been a few months. Why not?

"A whole lot better," she adds, stepping towards him.

He pushes his underpants downwards.

This is normal, she tells herself as they move to the bedroom. He is naked in front of her and this is normal to him. She unbuttons her shirt and this, too, is normal; as far as the husband knows, she has been naked in front of him hundreds, thousands of times. Only she knows that this has never happened before.

She strips her trousers off and sits on the edge of the bed, her anticipation switching to uncertainty, looking up at him and his grin, this man to whom she is married, and she's slept with people she's just met before, that's not the issue: it's the *husband* bit. She has never slept with a husband before.

But she lies back as he jumps enthusiastically on to the bed, and then before she can say anything he has rolled over and is diving straight in, his head at her groin.

She lets her legs widen, surprised. She would have preferred a gentler on-ramp, she thinks, looking along her body at his industrious head, but he knows what he's doing. Tongue firm, enthusiastic, efficient, her body is increasingly into it as her mind catches up—yes, there he is, working away; she touches his loose curls with one hand. And after surely less than three minutes, maybe four, she finds herself stretching out in satisfaction, her legs straightening to either side of his shoulders, while in her head she is still thinking about the logistics, about how often he believes he has done this, about the lampshade above her that she has noticed for the first time is the wrong colour.

And then, still grinning, he kneels up on the bed and tilts his head, gesturing towards the penis, a sort of "Hmm?" like he's offering her another chocolate digestive. She nods, and he wriggles into place for his turn at an orgasm.

His takes a little longer, but the whole thing is done in not much more than ten minutes.

Gosh. Married life, she thinks.

o o

She takes her clothes with her to the bathroom and washes, gets dressed. The husband is in the kitchen, still naked, eating the leftover toast she abandoned in the morning.

"That's been there since breakfast," she says. It's mid-afternoon—it can't taste good.

"Waste not, want not," he says.

He's a loud eater, and he isn't quite closing his mouth. This must be what Nat meant about the chewing. She feels her postcoital fondness recede a little.

"When are you going over to Elena's?" he asks.

She'd almost forgotten. The clock says half past three. Is she ready for another couple of hours with the husband?

"We could fit in another *Mindhunter*?" he says, and wet nodules of toast are still visible on his teeth as he talks.

No. "I need to pick up a couple of things on the way," she says. "I'll eat at Elena's, don't wait up if you've got an early start."

"Hey, am I back in the bedroom tonight?" he calls out as she's leaving.

At this point, why not? "Yeah, I'm probably over whatever it was."

"Great," he says. "I missed you last night."

He really is enthusiastic.

○ ○

Lauren gets to Walthamstow at half past four, with two and a half hours to kill before she's meant to meet Elena. She sits down at a cafe to search through her phone again but she can't stand it, so she walks instead, fast and directionless. Past coloured doors, a pawn shop, a cat warming himself on the lid of a black bin, the big murals of a neighbourhood newly determined to be fashionable. Delivery bikes gathered outside the Nando's. A mattress leans against a wall; someone has scrawled LITTERING IS A CRIME MATTHEW on it in permanent marker.

She stops at a dessert bar and gets two scoops of ice cream, rosewater and mint choc chip, and the woman gives her three free wafers. "Have more if you want, love, they're past their best-before so I can't sell them." She eats, then sets off again. She'll say this about the hiking: she walks for two hours and barely notices it, no burgeoning blisters, no tired legs.

And when it's finally almost seven, and she heads to Elena's flat, she is so happy to find it unchanged. Messier, with the wedding so close—the kitchen table is covered with index cards, guest names arranged around notional tables—but the walls, the furniture, the plates are the same as they always were.

"Oh my god," Elena says, flops down on to the sofa and kicks her legs up. "Weddings are terrible. You should have told me how much work this would be. I mean, you did, but you should have made me believe you."

"I guess I should have," Lauren says. She has been listening to Elena's plans and looking at dresses and talking about flowers for months, and it's been fun but also a weird thing to do, single: to help someone plan a party that's all about how they're definitely not like you. How different would it have felt with a husband of her own?

"I haven't cooked," Elena says, "I mean, obviously, you saw the kitchen. I'll order noodles in a minute."

"Yeah, great."

"And we can arrange the almonds after that," Elena adds. "But tell me what your thing is first, sorry. I don't know why I'm like this, the wedding's all I can think about. Why do I care about where the gift table goes? Why do I care about whether the fairy lights are warm white or cool white? Warm's better, right?"

"Yes," Lauren says firmly. "Definitely warm."

"God, I'm doing it again. Tell me your thing." And Elena sits herself up straight, leans forward, pushes her phone away from her on the coffee table. Attentive. Listening.

Now that Lauren's presented with the moment, it's not quite straightforward. You can't just say *My weird attic is magic*.

"Okay," she says. "My weird attic is magic. It's been creating a whole bunch of husbands, and I don't know what to do."

CHAPTER 8

Oh yeah," Elena says. "Like, a hundred husbands? A thousand?"

God, imagine. "Eight or nine. One at a time, though."

"Probably for the best," Elena says. "You've got that spare room, but even so."

This isn't the *Oh wow that's so strange but I definitely believe you, tell me more* response that she'd ideally have liked, but it's also not the *Ah you need to see a doctor immediately* that she'd feared.

"So," she says, "obviously I don't really know what's going on."

"No," Elena says, "I can see that. I know we studied different subjects at uni but I don't think either of us covered magic attics."

Their friendship has always been built on Elena's convictions and Lauren's cooperation. Way back in her first weeks at university, Lauren had been so relieved to find a friend who seemed to know what she was doing, and who was willing to make it up if she didn't, to order a particular beer despite not really knowing what a *sour* was or whether she'd like it (she didn't), to declare that of course sneakers were fine for a night out (they were), to collude in hanging out at a particular table where a particular boy might just happen to walk past, "No, it's a better place to study, it's nothing to do with Nick" (it was). After uni, when Nat moved out of the flat and Elena took over her room, they'd invented the rules of adulthood together, a friendship sustained by never saying "Oh no, that can't be right, that's not how it works."

She doesn't believe Lauren, of course. But she's joining in anyway. And what's more important? To be believed or to have the conversation?

"I thought you might be able to help," Lauren says. "Like—do you know where I met Jason?"

"At Noemi's party, right? Just after you and Amos broke up."

Four years ago. That fits with what she saw, scrolling back through photos.

"Why did I like him?"

"Oh, huh. Hair? That cheesecake his mum makes? The way he's, you know, constantly adorned with birds and flowers like a Disney princess? That ladybird he rescued from a Pizza Express, which by the way I still think he planted there to impress you. Not that that's a bad thing. Shows dedication."

Lauren tries a different approach. "Did anything weird happen when you got back from your hen party?" she asks.

"Like what?"

"Or while we were out. Did I seem okay?"

"Yeah? What's up?"

"Did I mention Jason?"

"Yeah, there was a full ten minutes where you wouldn't stop talking about how being married was so great and I was going to love it. Why?"

She's going to need to be more direct. "Okay," she says. "I know how this sounds, but I really do have a magic attic and it really is producing husbands for me."

"Yeah, you mentioned," Elena says, still entirely unfussed.

"This is a genuinely true thing and I don't know what to do," Lauren says. She's not sure how much clearer she can be.

Elena looks at her like it's obvious. "You go through them till you find the best one," she says. "Hot, rich, funny, good cook, gets on with his family, you get on with his family too, works as a fight choreographer for mid-budget movies."

"Yeah," Lauren says. "I guess."

"You know the wedding is really, really soon, right?" Elena says. "If this is a complicated way of telling me that actually marriage sucks and I shouldn't do it, you're going to need to be a lot less oblique."

"It's not," Lauren says. "It's not that. It's . . ." and then she stops.

She could insist. She could cry, say *No, this isn't a joke, this is real*, say *I know it doesn't make any sense*. She could really try, and of course Elena wouldn't believe it was happening, but maybe she'd at least accept that it wasn't a joke.

But then that would be it: Elena worried, phoning people, googling things that Lauren has already googled, and of course, of *course* she'd just assume that her own wedding had prompted some sort of breakdown. And for ever after, this conversation would be a thing Lauren did, just before the wedding. A story she made up, a delusion she suffered.

"No," she says. "You should absolutely get married."

"That's what I thought. But the farm," Elena says, "called today and said they only have a hundred red chair covers. So we need to either pick another colour, or I guess have half red and half white? Does that seem okay? God, I hate that I genuinely care about this. Sorry. Let's order food. And if you're still up for the almonds we could do that while we wait." She gestures at the floor, which is crowded with tulle and ribbons and big plastic bags of sugar-coated almonds in bright colours.

o o

It doesn't take Lauren long to get the hang of it. Five almonds: red, orange, pink, white, gold. Gather the tulle. Tie a bow. While they work, she lets herself drift through wedding chat, paying half-attention: final thoughts on poems for the reading; whether to ask the farm to keep the hens in their coop because it's practical or let them roam free because it's picturesque; brainstorming new entries for the list of songs that the DJ is forbidden to play.

When the noodles arrive, they eat on the only corner of the kitchen table that isn't occupied by the seating plan. Lauren spots herself and Jason at a table to the left.

In the real world it had been a tiny, tiny disappointment to her that she was just a bridesmaid and not the maid of honour. It's a tiny, tiny disappointment that it hasn't changed here, though at least she won't have to give a speech, or have Jason at the head table chewing with his mouth open.

She looks at her neighbours.

"You're okay with Amos and Lily, right?" Elena says, pointing. "Neither of them knows the other guests, and we were at their wedding so we had to invite them. But I've got a special table for people who had kids and regret it—if you want, I could put them there and give them a miserable time."

"No," Lauren says. "It's fine. Whatever's easiest. It'll be good to catch up."

It will not be good to catch up. The thing about having a really judgemental partner, she thinks, is that it's actually kind of great, as long as they like *you*. If someone hates the world, and you're the only exception, then surely that proves something. When she and Amos had been together, judging people had been a shared hobby and a shortcut to calibrating who she wanted to be. People who boast about never using recipes: *judged*. People who don't take their empties back to the bar even if they're walking past it: *judged*. People who take their empties back even if it's out of their way and who make sure the bar staff see them doing it: *judged doubly*. Amos had particularly deplored people who sighed loudly at train delays, because *We're all on this train, you're not special, there's nothing uniquely bad about the delay to your specific journey.* But also: people who wore turquoise tights, or velvet anything, or perfume to the cinema. Houses with names. Doorbells with cameras. Sparkling

she looks through windows, listens at a closed door while delivery drivers criss-cross on motorbikes and pigeons gather at a loaf of bread that's spilling out of its bag across the pavement.

Nothing.

And on the bus back home, she thinks: she can't call in sick for ever.

So on Thursday she gets up early and goes in to the combination hardware store/garden centre where she supposedly works. It's terrifying to just turn up; she has scoured the company website and her emails but she still doesn't know what she does or how.

She arrives half an hour before opening and stands across the road. Staff members walk through a side gate, roll out trolleys of plants on to the pavement. At least she's admin and not public-facing; she won't have to try to figure out how to work a card machine while a queue of customers stares.

She has tied her hair back, which feels efficient. And a few minutes before she's due to begin, someone opens the main shop door, so she doesn't have to try to sneak in through the side gate and hope there isn't a code. Inside: a counter, where a staff member nods hello as she walks past. A row of saws and hammers and snippers and screwdrivers. A small display of ornamental water features. A door with a sign reading STAFF ONLY, and she summons all her determination to push it open, but it reveals only a small yard with mismatched garden furniture, and a guy with a long beard, smoking. "Morning," he says.

Eventually she finds an unmarked door behind the lengths of wood that leads into a narrow office with small louver windows. Hot, no air-conditioning. She has only been there a couple of minutes, and is still figuring out which empty desk is hers, when a different man comes in with a plastic folder and says, "Oh, you're back, good, could you run this order for me?" then immediately leaves. A phone on maybe-her-desk rings; it's someone called Bev, who wants to know if C040338-14 has come in yet.

"I'll get back to you," she learns to say, "just catching up on the last couple of days!" but she will not get back to anyone. In the next hour, the man with the plastic folder returns twice to hand her more pieces of paper, she can't figure out who her boss is, the beard guy carries in a sawhorse and leaves it half blocking the door and asks her to "sticker it up," and in the end she takes the eleven different forms that she's received over the course of the morning and runs them through the shredder before pushing past the saw-horse to take an early lunch at eleven thirty and then not go back.

That night she's preoccupied, and Jason tries to cheer her up. "Come on, let's go round the corner for a pizza."

And it's nice of him, but the conversation drags and he is again chewing with his mouth open and she's sorry, but she's going to have to send him back.

○ ○

You can't stay married to someone for ever just because they climb out of your attic one afternoon. He rescued her from Kieran and she's grateful for that, but she's known him for four days, not even very interesting days. All they've done is watch *Mindhunter* and launder their hiking trousers and drink coffee. She doesn't owe him the rest of her life.

She doesn't want to take him to the wedding, Elena and Rob declaring their eternal love, Amos and whoever the hell Lily is judging his messy eating. And thanks to the attic, she doesn't have to: she can send him away without even having an awkward conversation about it.

So the next morning she ignores the work emails piling up and the replies to her previous off-sick emails, and the four calls that come up on her phone as *Christine (work)*, and she eats ice cream and lies on the sofa and reads. And now that she knows she's changing everything, that there are no consequences to her actions, she calls

Elena just before Jason gets home and has another go at telling her what's going on, *The thing I told you about the attic, I know how it sounds,* and of course Elena doesn't believe it but she does, eventually, believe that Lauren believes it. And it all happens like she thought it would, the worry, *Look, I'm coming over, don't go anywhere, keep the windows open, is there something wrong with the gas? Is Toby working from home, can you go down there?*

And then Jason gets back, and the time has come.

"Welcome home," she says.

"You're back early," he says.

"Yeah, I finished early." She is experimenting further with her new *this explains everything* tone.

"That's great," he says.

"Anyway, I thought I heard something in the attic, I don't suppose you could have a look?" An incantation, a little question.

"Yeah, sure."

"I'll get dinner started while you're up there."

"What are we having?" he says.

"Your favourite." Probably he has one.

She watches from the kitchen doorway as he pulls the ladder down.

"Hey," she says as he's about to go up. "Thank you." And she kisses him on the cheek, avoiding the too-wet mouth.

"No worries," he says, and smiles, and then he's climbing.

CHAPTER 9

The moment his foot disappears, doubt washes through her. Perhaps she will receive only worse and worse husbands, maybe he was the best available, this was her chance and she's fucked it up.

It's only a few seconds before a new man starts coming down the ladder. And keeps coming. He is bewilderingly tall, his entrance revealing more and more of his long body. No, she thinks. It's Friday. Elena and Rob's wedding is Saturday next week, eight days away. What she wants right now is to find someone to take with her, and when they go they will have to camp in a field together, and there is simply too much of this man for a tent. "Sorry, just a sec," she says before he even unfurls his whole self to her. "I heard something, could you look again?"

The next husband puts a foot down the ladder. He is wearing shoes with individual toes. Again: no.

Before the husband after that even appears, she hears a sound from the living room and turns to look: *Mindhunter* on the television, the same episode she saw with Jason. No.

But it's working, the process is working.

The next husband is wearing sneakers, and jeans, and a blue shirt with a small geometric pattern on it. He looks South Asian, solidly built but not ostentatiously muscular. His tongue juts out of the corner of his mouth as he climbs down the ladder, concentrating, and she likes that, it's cute. He is carrying an irregular blue vase in one hand, which he takes into the kitchen, and she follows him.

"Hey," he says, and smiles. She leans forward to kiss him, and he smells like the sea.

So far, so good.

And, even better: she hears a noise in the living room, and when she investigates it's her sister, Natalie, lying on the sofa, scrolling on her phone.

Perfect! She will have to find out whether or not the husband owns a suit. She'll have to look up her own job. But so far: she likes him. She can imagine taking him to the wedding, sitting at a table with Amos, admiring some horses, sharing a tent. And, bonus: she gets to talk to her sister! Without the kids! It's been weeks since she last went round to Nat's, and maybe years since she saw her without children. If the husband is a disappointment she can always exchange him later.

She turns back to the kitchen. It'll be easier if they go out: she doesn't want to chat to Nat and figure out the husband all at once. "Hey," she says to him, too quietly for Nat to hear, "Natalie's stressed about Magda stuff, I might take her out to the pub and calm her down a bit?"

"Okay," he says. "Magda stuff?"

"You know. Nursery. I'll tell you later."

"Sure," he says. He's not just cute: he's also obliging!

Then she goes through to Natalie, and: "Hey, he's"—with a head gesture when she realises she doesn't know the husband's name—"got a bit of a headache, maybe we could go to the pub and let him have a nap?"

"God, really? I just lay down. I've taken my shoes off. This is half my flat, remember, you can't just kick me out."

"Come on," Lauren says cheerfully, consequence-free, "up up up."

o o

This time the pub's outdoor tables are busy, despite the sky threatening drizzle, but the dark interior is almost empty. Lauren considers ordering a bottle of their most expensive white wine but she might want to stay in this world for a while and she hasn't checked her bank balance yet. She goes for the third-cheapest instead. Not the second cheapest! Fancy!

While she waits for the bartender to check the fridge downstairs ("We don't sell a lot of this one"), she finds the husband in her phone: Ben Persaud. She skims through photos. The two of them at a city farm, Ben beaming, patting a donkey. The two of them in a cafe sharing an elaborate ice-cream sundae. The two of them triumphant outside an escape room with unfamiliar friends, their hands joined and thrust aloft. Amos, of course, thought escape rooms were ridiculous, a hobby for people who *missed doing home-work*, but she's never going to find a husband that's immune to every possible way that Amos could disapprove of a person.

Anyway, she knows where to turn for the real dirt. "Okay," she says to Nat as they sit, "tell me the top thing I'm doing wrong in my life." Where else is she going to get such immediate access to detailed knowledge about herself, her husband, her marriage, and whatever's not quite right about any of them?

"What? No. Let's just have a nice drink."

Of course the one time she wants to be told what she's doing wrong is the time Nat won't cooperate. Maybe she can ask again after a glass or two of wine.

"Besides," Nat says, "the deadline for that promotion was last week, right? So you've missed it anyway."

Work! God, if it's just *work* that she's doing wrong then that's fine. "I guess I have," she says, and leans back in her chair. What a magical thing to discover, that *not applying for a promotion* is her life's worst mistake.

"What a lovely day," she says, which is not at all true.

"Sure," Nat says.

"How's everything with you?"

"Yeah, pretty good."

Hmm. Lauren's been so preoccupied with the husbands (not unjustly, she thinks!) that she's struggling with a normal conversation. "How's Magda? Did you find a new playgroup?"

Nat frowns. "What?"

Maybe Magda is better behaved in this version of the world, and hasn't yet been kicked out for taking after her mother.

"Okay," she says instead. "How's Adele?"

"I don't know, I haven't seen her in years."

Wait. Shit.

"Sorry," Lauren says, "give me a moment. I know this seems weird. You used to date Adele?"

"Yes?"

She nods. "But . . . you broke up?"

". . . Yes." Nat is watching her, waiting for something, waiting for this to make sense.

"Look. Indulge me. I'm sorry, but can you tell me exactly what happened?"

"I've apologised for this a hundred times, Lauren, if you can't let it go, then—"

"No," she says. "It's not that. I promise I'll explain in a minute. Please, Nat, just tell me what happened."

Nat leans back. "Okay," she says after a moment. "Fine. Adele and I broke up at your wedding because you were my little sister and you seemed so sure of things, you'd known this guy *four months* and you were getting married at this huge fucking party and I don't even know how you had time to plan it, and Adele and I had been together for years and I still wasn't sure. Twenty of your guests heard us break up. I'm crying in the background of half your wedding photos. The food was delicious."

It's hard to take this in. If Nat and Adele broke up years ago, how long has Lauren been married, how far back do the changes go this time? Why would she get married to someone *four months* after meeting him? If she rushed into it like that, can it possibly be as good a marriage as it seems? But most importantly, she thinks, piecing it together: "Ah. Fuck. And you don't have any children."

"What? No. Of course I don't have children. Is this because of what I said about your work? You literally asked me, what was I supposed to do, lie?"

"No," Lauren says, "shit, sorry, I'll fix this." She gets up from the table and starts to head outside but Nat follows her, so she pivots and goes into the toilets instead and locks herself in the big accessible stall, and calls—Ben, right? Yes, he's in her messages. She calls Ben. She ignores Nat, who is outside the door saying, "*Look, are you okay?*"

"Ben," she says, "are you still at home? I have a super-urgent question and I know this is going to be annoying but I need you to go into the attic and find a green box on a shelf. I need you to check it's there and send me a picture. I want to prove to Nat I still have it, she's really worried. I'll do the washing-up and laundry and I'll clean the bathroom, all of it, if you check right now, you're the best, thank you so much, I love you." She hangs up. This is, she thinks, the first time she's said "I love you" to a husband.

And she listens to Nat knocking, thinks about the step-by-step process Ben will be going through: pulling the ladder down, getting shoes on maybe. It shouldn't take more than a minute or two but Nat is still out there in the corridor, which means Caleb and Magda still don't exist, and she tries to breathe steadily but can't quite pull it off, and how long can it possibly take to climb into an attic?

The gap between knocks extends. Three seconds. Five, ten. Twenty.

She feels her chest unknot.

She splashes water on her face.

And she unlocks the door, and nobody is out there in the corridor, and she phones Nat, and gets a voicemail message, and phones again, and again, and again, until eventually Nat picks up, *What's wrong, is it Mum*, and how can Lauren explain? "No," she says, "I just wanted to say hello." And she can hear, in the background, a furious baby shouting, a little roar over and over. "Is that Magda? That noise?"

"What? Yes, of course. Lauren, you don't call eight times in a row to say hello! I thought someone was in hospital."

"I know," she says, "I'm sorry. Can I talk to Caleb?"

"What?"

"I've got a dinosaur fact for him. It's a really cool one."

"Are you drunk?"

"No, I just have a dinosaur fact."

She waits. "Okay," Nat says eventually. "But he's meant to be doing his spelling. So only for a minute." And she hears Nat calling, and feet running, and then it's Caleb on the other end, and god, the relief.

"I don't like dinosaurs any more," Caleb says immediately. "I like space now. Uncle Rohan told me a meteorite killed all the dinosaurs and space is more powerful."

Uncle Rohan: the new husband, probably.

"Yeah," Lauren says, "I think that's true. Okay. I won't tell you a dinosaur fact." She didn't have one so this is for the best. "You can get back to your spelling now if you want."

She sits down in the pub where she was before, and takes deep breaths. It's all okay.

But she is going to have to be more careful.

She stands up and heads outside, where she leans against the wall. Michael. Nude guy. Feminist cook. *Monsters, Inc.* Kieran. Jason. Tall guy. Another half-dozen and she can't even remember why she dismissed them. Ben. And whoever's there now, whoever climbed down when Ben climbed up, Uncle Rohan.

o o

She will, she decides, keep him for the night unless she thinks he's a genuine danger: she will send nobody back for a bad T-shirt or a haphazard approach to home deodorizing, for cutting his own hair, for rewatching *The Wire*, for filling the living room with Funko Pops. She does not have the fortitude, tonight, to explore the parameters of the attic or mount a campaign to find the perfect escort for the wedding.

And besides, the rules of this situation are becoming clearer to her. All of her husbands are men that some version of herself might have chosen to marry, and who might have chosen to marry her. None of them are going to be radically dissimilar from the husbands who have already visited.

She will go home and she will meet another man. A man who—she can see as she rounds the corner—has changed nothing fundamental about the flat. And he will be a plausible husband for her. He will not be an astronaut or the king of Ruritania or a man whose great dignity forbids him the use of ladders.

He'll just be some guy.

o o

She unlocks the flat door. The carpet on the stairs is back.

"Heya, I'm home," she calls out.

"Prithee, fair maiden," says a husband in a red embroidered doublet and diamond-patterned tights, his brown skin glowing with health, his dark hair tied back with an enormous bow.

"Whence comest thou?" he says. "What outlandish garb thou wearest!"

Ah.

CHAPTER 10

The husband is, it turns out, performing in the local amateur dramatic society's rendition of *Rosencrantz and Guildenstern Are Dead*, taking the role of the Player, and he has brought the doublet home to get used to moving around in it but also because he finds it extremely funny. The uncanny radiance of his complexion is stage makeup, which he wipes off carefully in the bathroom, but he leaves the doublet on.

"I promised I wouldn't eat in it," he says, emerging to fetch a beer from the fridge, "but I never said anything about drinking. Or, y'know—" and he wriggles, the huge flounce around his hips amplifying the movement. His calves in bright tights are extraordinarily shapely.

Lauren is about to smile and offer to make tea, but she sees the ridiculous flounce-wiggle, and the calves, and the confidence, and the sense of *fun*, and thinks: actually, why not?

A dozen husbands in and she has barely touched most of them, has had extremely efficient sex only with Jason. This is more novel. She's pretty sure she's never before had sex with a man within five minutes of meeting him. She has certainly never had sex with a man in a bright-red Elizabethan doublet.

The ponytail is a clip-on, extending from the bow; without it the husband looks less at home in the doublet and hose. His calves, however, remain shapely with the tights in disarray around them.

She pushes him back on to the bed while he's still got the ruff and the doublet on. Their fabric folds puff up as she crawls on top, *pfuff.* It's adorable.

He doesn't undress completely until they finish; then he pulls off the tights and unclips the ruff, and hangs the costume carefully in the spare room.

She walks naked to the bathroom with her phone, and looks him up. Yep, Rohan. He works at the council, where he's Temporary Assistant Director of Electoral Services. She's back at the council too; they must have met at work.

She sleeps well next to him, on the other side of the bed than the one she occupied with Jason. And the next morning, Saturday, she sleeps in, and when she gets up Rohan is making her a cup of tea, which she suggests they take into the garden. When she gets there it's back to its straggly self, weatherworn deck chairs and a few technically alive plants, but she now, thanks to Jason, knows that the two in bloom are nasturtiums and geraniums, though she's not sure which is which.

○ ○

Maryam is outside, and she leans over the fence to chat.

"We just got back from the market," Maryam says. "I got some of those little pastries you were talking about," to Rohan, "with the plum? Haven't tried one yet, we can have them after dinner."

"They're so good," Rohan says.

"I hope so. If I'm going to break my sugar fast it had better be worth it."

"Yeah, how long since you last had cake?"

"Cake? Literally your wedding. But I had a crêpe in May when we were in Paris for Toby's birthday. And I licked a macaron."

"I don't get the point of macarons," Rohan says. "I like a pastry with heft to it. Something between your teeth." He's got charm. A charming husband! Who wouldn't want one of those!

"I'll chuck out the ones I bought and pop a bit of leather in the oven for pudding, shall I?" Maryam says.

"Let's not get carried away. Seven, right?"

"Seven." Maryam smiles.

"What should we bring?" Lauren says.

"The usual," Maryam says. "Just yourselves. And some wine. Definitely bring wine."

○ ○

Rohan heads out after lunch: he has a rehearsal at the arts centre across the road. If she keeps him long enough, Lauren thinks, she'll go to see him perform, and she'll be able to cross "go to that arts centre some time" off her to-do list.

She should spend her spare afternoon researching the husband situation, but it's been a big week. She deserves a break. Instead she lies on the sofa and does precisely nothing.

○ ○

Rohan gets back and pulls a bottle of white wine from the cupboard and puts it in the freezer to chill. "Don't let me forget and leave it there till it explodes."

Lauren nods. She even sets an alarm on her phone.

He changes into a smart button-up shirt at half past six, which seems like overkill for dinner downstairs, but he looks good, and a little fussiness in dress bodes well for the wedding.

Her alarm goes off at ten to seven: *DON'T EXPLODE WINE.*

"Do we know what we'll be eating?" she asks.

"I think her new hobby's spending money on cheese," Rohan says.

And, indeed, they enter the flat downstairs—almost the same as her own flat in layout, the living room and bedroom swapped,

but painted throughout in rental off-white—and they find a huge
cheese board: grapes, dates, dried apricots, an orange cheese and a
yellow one and one that's covered in grey ash, four different sorts
of cracker.

"Hello," Toby says.

"Welcome," Maryam says, beaming her attention on them both,
but especially Rohan, standing behind the cheese board with her
hands on the table and leaning forward.

It's odd. Something's wrong. Maryam never stays focused like
this on anyone. She doesn't *lean*. Lauren looks between them and
thinks: Maryam and Rohan are having an affair, or they're considering it, dancing around the edges of flirtation and frisson.

What the *hell*.

She has been cheated on before, but not for years, at least as far
as she knows. Not since university. And this is not acceptable. Toby
and Maryam are her perfect match, her proof that two imperfect
people can make something work, something straightforward
and good. Not Elena and Rob's fights and reunifications, the two
months during lockdown when Elena moved back into her spare
room for a break. Not Nat and Adele's exhausted parenthood. Just
two people who are happy with each other, two people who are
careful and fond, Maryam's distraction against Toby's calm and
low-key attentiveness.

How *dare* they disrupt that?

Rohan is bound to be interested in return. She barely knows
him, and he may just be warm and flirtatious by nature; certainly
he seems as affectionate with Toby as he is with Maryam. But
Maryam is so pretty and has such huge eyes. Some people speak
as if their every word is conjured anew, never repeated from past
conversations; they create their thought and hand it to you like a
cross-stitched bookmark. Rohan is, perhaps, a little like this. But
Maryam listens either barely at all or, when she's focused, like it
is *your* every thought that has been made afresh. How can Lauren

expect an actor, someone whose hobby is literally having people pay attention to him, to resist that lure?

She doesn't care unduly about Rohan. It's a blow to her pride, but she didn't expect to keep him long anyway; certainly, she now realises, she would have exchanged him before the opening of his am-dram production of *Rosencrantz and Guildenstern Are Dead*, which she can only imagine will be interminable.

She cares a little more about Maryam, about this betrayal by a friend.

But the main affront is to her model of ideal happiness.

Does the possibility of this affair imply that Maryam and Toby's relationship is less perfect than she thought? Maybe. But maybe it just implies that circumstances can ruin anything. If she cycles through another ten husbands and finds that Maryam is seducing them all then, sure, she'll have wider concerns. But if this is a one-off then she can simply ensure that things go no further.

Maryam is continuing to lean towards Rohan, her hand casually on Toby's arm. Rohan is, to be fair, still showing their two hosts equal attention, and even including her, his boring wife of a number of years, the specifics of that number still in question. They are discussing the cheeses; Maryam is pouring wine; Maryam is laughing becomingly; Maryam is, and this is the real surprise, leaning forward towards Lauren and kissing her lightly on the mouth.

Oh, she thinks.

They're not cheating. They're *swingers*.

Though aren't swingers all white and in their forties? She's sure she read that in an article somewhere; their group doesn't quite fit the demographic. Maybe they could be polyamorous instead? She's vague on the difference, but they are in London's outermost suburbs and none of them, as far as she is aware, work in tech, so this does still fit more closely with what she knows of swinging than with what she knows of polyamory.

It's also entirely in line with what little she knows of amateur theatrics.

She is not, however, into it. She can see how in another world she might have been won over, determined to maintain the happiness of her husband, flattered by Maryam's attentions, curious about what it would have been like if she and Toby had ever got together. But standing in her neighbours' living room, having given up Jason's fruit trees and immaculate garden, and Ben's happy friends and ice-cream sundaes, having lost all that just so she and her new husband can make out with their slightly more attractive neighbours: no. She isn't subject to the sexual constraints of most marriages, she has the option of not serial but perhaps parallel monogamy, she doesn't *need* to do this for the novelty of two strange mouths and the perky attentions of a new penis; so she leans back from Maryam's soft kiss, smiles, and says, "I've just remembered I left another bottle of wine in the freezer. Don't want it to explode!"

Out the front door, into her own, up the stairs, and once again she opens the attic, its dark square above her, and pulls down the ladder.

She sets up the dripping noise, though she can't find a speaker in this world so she slides her phone in, maximum volume, facedown, as far as she can, groping above her in the dark, a tiny crackle when her hand goes in but not enough to stop the video from playing.

And she waits.

Finally—seven minutes later, eight? What sort of care is this to show your beloved wife?—she hears him come up the stairs.

"Lauren?" he says as he nears the top, then rounds the corner. Except it's not him. He hasn't even come to check on her himself: he's sent Toby.

CHAPTER 11

Y ou okay?" Toby says, hands in his pockets, a little awkward.

"Yeah," she says. "There wasn't any wine in the freezer after all."

"Okay," he says, but it sounds like a question, and he glances up towards the attic and the noise.

"It's my phone. Playing drain noises—it's complicated. Look," all of a sudden, before she's even realised she's going to say it, "I want to talk to you about something."

"Okay."

When she tried to tell him before, it didn't go well, but she launches in, one last attempt. "I have a . . . magical attic."

He looks at the open trapdoor. "Like, *Magic Faraway Tree?* Strange worlds?"

"A bit. Like, it creates husbands for me."

". . . Huh?"

She decides to start from the beginning. "You know Elena?"

"Elena who did a speech at your wedding that was just reading out all the drunk texts you'd ever sent her? Elena who made me throw my jacket on the bonfire at that party last year because she thought it didn't suit me? Yes, I know Elena."

This sounds plausible, within the range of things Elena might do. "A week ago," she says, "I went to Elena's hen do and when I came back there was a husband here. I was wearing a wedding ring, and so was he, and there were photos of us on the wall. His name was Michael."

"He'd replaced Rohan?"

"No. Before he turned up I was single. I'd never been married. Then this husband appeared. Then he went into the attic and when he came down he was a different guy. Then another different guy. And another one, and eventually Rohan. And maybe I should have kept one of the others because I am not up for"—and she gestures widely—"this? Like, what's going on? Why did you follow me up instead of Rohan? Why is your girlfriend all over my husband? Are we meant to . . ." and she circles her hand in the air, too embarrassed to even say it.

"Not if you don't want to!" Toby says.

"But we . . . have? In the past?"

". . . usually only on Wednesdays, we rescheduled because Maryam had to swap shifts. Look, Lore, have you really forgotten all this? Do you want some tea? Do you want me to get Maryam?"

Yeah, yeah, Maryam's so wonderful, she's got stethoscopes and those lights for looking at your pupils and she's a great kisser. "I haven't *forgotten*," Lauren says. "It just hasn't happened to me. This is new. I met Rohan yesterday. I've never experienced one of your Wednesdays."

She knows how it sounds. People are very often wrong. Attics are very rarely magical. But she is more certain than ever. She's pissed off that her husband—her husband who she doesn't even like that much, but it's the principle—is canoodling with Maryam. She's concerned for Toby, her friend, who she is meant to be canoodling with in turn but who she does not believe is particularly into her or the shared household situation. She feels within her the unlikeliness, the long and slow steps that must have been required to bring her here. The misgivings she must have pushed down, the advice columns she must have read, the conversations with Elena.

This isn't something she might have *forgotten*. If this had happened for real, she would know it.

"Have you looked in the attic?" Toby says.

"A bit."

"Do you want me to check it out?"

"No! What if it changes everyone? What if I get a new neighbour?"

He frowns. "I'll just look."

She thinks. The husbands have only changed when they're entirely inside the attic; she's looked in herself and been fine.

"Yeah," she says. "Okay. But be careful, if it starts doing anything weird then come straight down. Other than the light glowing a bit, that's actually normal."

"Okay." And they look up, and he climbs, towards the hatch and the dripping noise. His head enters. She waits for the light. But: nothing. No flicker, no in-rush of white noise like the sudden tide.

Well. That's new information.

Toby takes his phone out of his pocket and, as far as she can tell, turns the flashlight on. She should get an umbrella and ask him to scrape her dripping-sounds phone back along the floor so she can switch it off.

But when she turns back, umbrella in hand, Toby's climbing again. "No!" she says but it's too late, his foot is disappearing, and he's in there, he's gone, and she shouldn't have let him look, this is her fault. She stares up, panicked.

"What?" Toby says and looks down at her, framed by the darkness.

"Are you okay? What are you doing up there? I said to just look!"

"I am," he says.

"I meant, from the ladder. God. Anything could have happened!" Has he changed?

"Oh," he says. "Sorry. Should I come down?"

It's a bit late for that. "No," she says. "I guess it's fine."

"I'll have a look, then?" His face disappears.

No buzz. Only footsteps. The drain noise playing from her phone stops. A click, and the yellow attic light comes on above her, solid, steady. Normal. And Toby returns to view.

"It looks fine to me," he says.

"That's enough," she says, "turn the light off and come down," and he does: the same shoes he'd had going up, familiar legs, his old face.

"Maybe it's just the husbands that change," she says.

"Yeah?" He holds her phone out. He's wondering, she thinks, whether this is a joke that she's inviting him to go along with, or if he should worry.

"I'm not imagining it," she says. "I'll show you." And she steps up the ladder, two rungs, and holds her arm above her head, into the space of the attic. She's *not* imagining it, is she? It's real? And as her hand enters: the glow above, fainter than usual but undeniable. The crackle.

"Shit," Toby says.

"See?" It's a relief, suddenly, that he's seen it. She comes down the ladder and heads into the kitchen and rummages, finds the flashlight, unbroken in this world. When she comes back out, Toby has his head up through the trapdoor again.

"What was that?" he says. "Have you had an electrician out?"

"It's," and she doesn't know how many more times she's going to have to say this, "my weird fucking magic attic. I told you. Get down," and he does. She steps up again, raises her arm, flashlight on: its glare grows brighter as soon as it enters the attic, brighter still, then *crack*, the flare, the noise. She steps down again and holds the flashlight out to Toby.

"God," he says, "you need to get someone to look at that. It seemed fine when I was up there. It can't be safe. When did it start? Has Rohan had a look?"

Has Rohan had a look. She has explained the attic situation as clearly as she can, she has shown him the crackle and the light, and he cannot take it in.

She is, she's surprised to realise, crying, and he steps forward and puts an arm around her in a way he never would normally, too intimate, and his face is too close to hers, and that's wrong too, and how is it this, *this*, after the week she's had, that has her in tears?

She's annoyed to be so scared. She's annoyed to be crying. She's annoyed that the husband, the not-even-all-that-much-to-her-taste husband, is downstairs with Maryam and cannot be returned immediately to the attic.

She's annoyed that the nice freezer-chilled open bottle of wine is downstairs too. She pulls free of Toby's arm and strides into the kitchen and there's no cold white wine but there's an open bottle of red, for cooking she supposes, but it'll do, and when she can't find a wine glass she pours it into an espresso cup, then downs it and refills.

She's also annoyed, she realises, that Toby has slept with her but she hasn't slept with him, an unjust imbalance of knowledge. This, at least, she can remedy, and she kisses him, which feels like a practice kiss on her own arm, his lips firm but barely responsive, and he hesitates and asks if she's okay, and she says yes, yes, she was worried about the attic but she'll get an electrician in, and fuelled she supposes by her distaste for the whole situation, she takes him to the bedroom where they have deeply, *deeply* unremarkable sex.

○ ○

In the bathroom afterwards she thinks about the cliché of people's sexual tastes, that everyone wants what they don't have in life, the CEOs tied up in expensive boudoirs and mocked by women in difficult boots, the shy bookworm who pounces with eager delight in bed, and she thinks: not always. She and Toby are both easily led in real life, amenable, happy for others to make the decisions, perhaps a little too anxious about getting it wrong. And they are noncommittal but helpful in bed as well. Polite, certainly, engaged with their partner's intentions; but helpfulness cannot exist in a vacuum, it cannot take the form of a series of expectations mutually imagined and joylessly fulfilled.

Sooner or later, somebody has to want something, and then admit to it.

o o

She is unclear on the etiquette of whether they should go back to Maryam and Rohan now, whether they have breached standard procedures already.

She'll rewrite this whole thing soon, dodge repercussions, summon a new husband and with him a new world. She will ensure that Maryam remains devoted to Toby, and the pair of them will continue to provide their neat model of two people who can be happy.

She's been too vague in her search, too unclear about what she wants from a husband. It's time to focus. No swingers. No amdram enthusiasts. No open-mouth chewers. Just a nice man to keep for a week and take to a wedding. Not a perfect husband; just a perfect plus-one. She can worry about everything else later.

o o

In the end she allows Rohan to stay until morning; it's easier than launching into a late-night husband loop. She lies next to him in bed, tamping down her fury with the knowledge that he's about to vanish from the world.

In the morning she sends him up; no thank-yous, no goodbye kisses, just flare, flash, buzz.

In return she receives Iain, who is an aspiring painter with large glasses, his canvases ramming the spare room. She likes his bright smears of colour, which make her think of reflections in windows. She considers keeping him, as he is also funny and owns a grey suit. But every half an hour he has a new small complaint: that the ripe-and-ready avocado he bought is neither ripe nor ready, that a sculptor acquaintance won a residency that he missed out on, that his hay-fever medicine isn't in its usual place. No, she thinks.

His replacement is a guy named Normo (stubble, boxer shorts, somehow even larger glasses). He's an expert witness consultant; he finds people who know about printers or gunfire or the origins of different types of wallpaper, and arranges for them to appear in court. She likes him too, but then she goes to the bathroom and finds that (a) her period has just started, not ideal, and (b) the only product she has in the cupboard is a menstrual cup. She looks up a series of instructional diagrams on her phone, fold it like *this* or like *this* or like *that*, and she gives it a go, but the cup keeps springing open when it's halfway inserted, blood spattering across the tiles, and it gets slippier each time. She reads the FAQ, one last attempt, but all she learns is that there are two sizes of menstrual cups and that as a thirty-one-year-old she is recommended to take the larger, and she simply declines to remain in a world that comments immediately on the size of her vagina.

The next husband is a bit of a shock. It happens quickly, the four or five seconds of a climb down the ladder, but it's still slow enough that she goes through a whole multi-step process of realisation.

- The husband climbs down, carrying a box.
- He's tall, slender, his hair is like Amos's.
- He turns around.
- His hair is like Amos's hair because he is Amos.
- She is married to Amos.

That's one way to solve the issue of who to take to a wedding where she's going to have to share a table with Amos. But: no. "No thank you," she says aloud.

"What?" Amos replies.

"I think I heard a noise up there," she says, and sends him away.

After Amos she gets Tom, who is going through something, red-eyed and straggle-haired, and she feels cruel as she sends him back up, but what she needs is not a husband for better and worse but rather a husband for next Saturday. Tom is replaced by Matthias, one of those nervous Englishmen who are so pale that their noses glow red around the curve of the nostrils, all long thin fingers and knowing how to pronounce the names of obscure villages and reading Lytton Strachey. She does like nervous, but he's going to be terrible at making conversation with strangers. No.

Matthias gives way to Gabriel, who is situated at the hotter end of her husband range, but when she opens the door to the spare room she is shocked to find a child's bedroom. An occasional step-child? It doesn't look like a room where anyone lives full-time. Marker pens, Lego, a single poster of a dinosaur riding a rocket. She doesn't want children anyway, she's had an IUD in place for years, and she definitely doesn't want to take a divorced dad husband and his kid with her to this wedding.

So Gabriel turns into an even better-looking man named Gorcher Gomble, which is just too embarrassing to say out loud. *Meet my husband, Gorcher.* But she's struck a handsome vein: the next husband is, if anything, more attractive again, with glossy white teeth and a slow American accent. He is a bewildering presence in her home, which has changed only a little: like he's too relaxed, or the wrong aspect ratio or oversaturated compared to the grey weather. He is wearing a clearly recently ironed dark-blue shirt and, she can see at the neck, an actual real-life undershirt.

She doesn't know anything about him, but she knows he'd look great in a suit. Sure, she thinks. Let's give him a try.

CHAPTER 12

The husband is named Carter.

She calls in sick on Monday. If she keeps changing husbands every couple of days, she thinks, she will never have to work again: she could coast forever on the diligence of her past selves, constantly dodging to new worlds where she hasn't used her sick leave yet.

Her messages with Carter go back almost two years. She can't pinpoint the exact moment they met, but she thinks it might have been at a house party she remembers going to and leaving early; he's in her phone as *Carter (From Party) (Husband)*.

"Remember when we met?" she tries.

He grins. "Thank god for small bladders." So, perhaps the toilet queue.

They have separate finances, plus a joint account for bills and rent. They have blinds instead of curtains or shutters. They have a big American coffee machine, the sort where coffee drips through into a jug.

The spare room is set up with a single bed and Carter's clothes in the wardrobe, which surprises her since they shared the bedroom after he arrived (no sex; she went to bed before him so she could look through old photos and google him in secret). Perhaps he just has more clothes than previous husbands. Their past texts are affectionate and frequent, the occasional *Thanks, love you* among them.

She looks up their wedding, which is informative.

It's not that it's an immigration marriage exactly. They were definitely seeing each other. But they got married about seven months after they started dating, in the town hall with a party at the pub afterwards, her in a dark-red beaded dress with a big flouncy skirt and gold roses in her hair, him in a jacket and a shirt and no tie; and when she looks through her emails they sure do have a lot of paperwork around Carter's right to stay in the UK.

The party at the pub looks like a great time, though: fifty or sixty people, her friends, some strangers, kisses, confetti. And now it's a year and a half later, and here they are, still together.

The second night he's out late because he is, somehow, playing baseball (in *London;* she didn't know that was even possible). He gets back before she goes to bed, wet from a flurry of rain, the wave in his hair flattened against his head. "Don't hug me, I'm soaking, it started right when I got off the train," he says, and pulls his shirt up over his head. When his face reveals itself again, the shirt has set his damp hair awry.

o o

His pajamas are shorts and a V-necked T-shirt, and he offers to make her a hot chocolate.

They sit on the sofa with the window open while she drinks, listening to the slow drops of rain against the glass. "Hold on," he says, "it'll go for it again in a minute," but it never does; they open the bedroom window a crack too, and she falls asleep with him, waiting for a storm that doesn't come.

o o

On Tuesday she goes into work at the council. She's growing to like this husband, and if she might want to keep him around after the wedding instead of sending him on his way, she probably shouldn't just burn through all her sick leave.

This is the first time she's been to work since the husbands appeared, other than that visit to the hardware store, and she's nervous. But nobody even looks up when she walks in. First task for the day: she calls into a Teams meeting with a borough resident who's putting together a business plan for a new bakery that even has the same terrible name it did originally, Loaf Is What You Bake It. She talks through the forms then tries again to persuade him to consider different names, and again fails.

"It's not that all pun names are bad," she says to Zarah as they make coffee, and remembers the photo of Fishcotheque that she's had on her phone in at least two different versions of the world.

"There's a barber near Farringdon called Barber Streisand," Zarah says, "which my mum likes, she says it's a joke about a singer from the olden days."

Zarah is the youngest person in the office by almost a decade and enjoys horrifying the rest of the department with the fact. Lauren refuses to rise to the bait. "I know you've heard of Barbra Streisand," she says.

The whole day is shockingly normal. She takes her turn replying to the perpetual backlog of email enquiries about business rates and VAT and finding office space. She updates some slides for a webinar for her boss. The whole office is so much the same as it used to be that she has to keep touching her wedding ring. She messages the husband once, nervous, *How's the day?*, and he replies a few minutes later: a photo of a horse by a bus stop. *Not too bad*, he says. What possible job has him hanging out with a horse, in London, at ten past eleven? Riding instructor? Bookie? Literal cowboy? She googles Carter's name; he works on the video production side of a marketing agency. That makes more sense.

o o

She and Zarah pick up lunch from the falafel place around the corner. It's the usual guy, and he remembers Lauren's order like he always does. Doubt and panic creep in again, the impossibility of the husband system. By quarter past two she can't take it any more, and she runs out before the weekly catch-up to stand in the stairwell and phone Carter.

He doesn't answer. She calls again five minutes later.

"Hey," he says, "is everything okay?"

Even now, worried, his voice is slow and gentle. "Yeah, sorry, I just—I was thinking maybe we could get dinner in town tonight. I could come and meet you." That's the sort of thing a married person might say, right?

"Oh," he says. "Yeah, I won't be done till almost eight, though, could you come over this way?"

"Sure. Let me know where to meet you. Message me." It will be more proof that he exists, she thinks. At four p.m. a message comes: an Italian restaurant in Pimlico.

○ ○

She arrives before him. He comes five minutes later; she stands up and he kisses her fleetingly on the lips, and again he seems out of place in this world. He eats spaghetti perfectly, fork in, a twirl, a whole compact little package in his mouth, a loose strand that he sucks in sharply with his lips parted in just the right way to conceal the food without allowing the sauce to slide off and gather in stains around his mouth. The perfect wedding dinner companion. He offers her a forkful and she thinks no, *no spaghetti on dates*, but: they're married. It's okay. She can eat a forkful of spaghetti.

"How was the horse?" she says.

"Enormous. Bit of a prima donna. What's the latest with your bakery guy, was that today?"

What a marriage they must have, that she tells him about her incredibly mundane video calls. Is it a good sign, that they share so much? Or a bad sign, that they have so little of real interest to talk about?

The waiter brings the dessert menu, and Carter leans over the table towards her. "What's maritozzi?"

"Dunno," she says. "Try ordering it." But he orders the tiramisu instead, and she goes for the maritozzi in response. It turns out to be a plate of tiny buns.

"Can I try?" he says.

"Nope." She pops one whole into her mouth, then relents.

"They're not great, are they?" he says after he's eaten one. "But I love you for trying." And she feels something unexpected, a little moment like stepping on a paving stone and feeling it shift, at the word "love."

Afterwards, they walk to the river, and lean over the wall near a triangular patch of grass. The Thames is at low ebb, exposing the wet green sides of the embankment. Old white buildings behind them, bulbous new flats to one side, wide patches of dirt in the threadbare grass. Empty glass towers, and cranes building more. A seagull is standing on the wall and staring at them, and she's not sure she's ever seen a seagull awake this late at night. She waves her arms at it, shooing; it remains in place, impassive.

"Oh no," Carter says. "I thought it'd be romantic to gaze out over the river, but it definitely isn't. I'm so sorry, I've brought you to the worst place in London."

"Nah," she says, "worst place in London is over on Cable Street. Where they said they were building a museum of women's history, but they put up a Jack the Ripper museum instead."

"Oh, I thought I heard that closed?"

"Did it?" She looks around. "In that case, yeah, this is the worst place in London."

He laughs and leans forward, a little husbandly kiss, and of course it can hold no particular charge for him because they have done this so many times. But for her it's new, and she's aware of her forearms, her shoulders, his breathing close to hers, and he's looking at her, noticing her response.

"Hello," he says, and laughs.

"Hello," she says back.

And then a man strides up to the wall right next to them, *right* there, perhaps two feet away on an almost empty street, yelling into his phone, and the night seagull squawks and takes off. "Yes," the man says, "I left it in the bin, but that was for *safekeeping*, so it wouldn't get lost! I put a piece of paper on top of the bin, which is a clear indication that I didn't want it to be emptied, it's like a beer mat on a pint glass, right? Exactly! And I'm sorry, but if you don't understand universal British symbols of communication, then I don't think you can blame me if the paperwork goes missing."

They pull apart. *Worst place in London,* Carter mouths, then, aloud, "Let's go home?" She's aware of his body next to hers on the train, but when they get back to the flat he's missed a call about the horse and he has to respond—"Sorry, I'll just be ten minutes"—and it turns into half an hour. And when he's finished, he has to pack for his work trip, and then it's late, and she lets the moment go. She does not, she finds, want to rush things with him.

○ ○

He's due back noon on Friday, and she swaps around her work-from-home days so that she's there when he gets in. And when he steps into the house, it feels right again. They go to bed at ten, because it's the day before the wedding and they have an early start, and she is feeling suddenly shy but she curls up to him, head on his shoulder, conscious of his arm around her and his breath in and out, the thud of his heart; then after ten minutes of that he says, "Okay, my turn," and tips her out of his embrace and leans against her shoulder instead, curling into the space between her arm and her body.

○ ○

Saturday: Elena's wedding day. Lauren wakes well before her alarm, creeps out of bed beside Carter, and goes to splash water on her face.

When she opens the kitchen windows, the air has the smell of a day that's getting ready to be hot.

She will have a convoluted journey before she even gets on the train, made more complicated by having to haul her dress and shoes in a bag, and a detour to pick up Elena's favourite cream-cheese bagel. "The tent and the present are on the landing," she says to Carter, who is half-awake in bed. "You're okay to bring them?"

"Yeah, no problem," he says sleepily, and smacks at her bottom as she walks away. "Wait, come back, I forgot something," he adds, and she does, and he sits up and reaches around and smacks the other buttock. "There," he says, so pleased with himself.

"Okay," she says, and laughs. "I'll see you later."

○ ○

Out at Aldgate, the dress in its zipped-up bag catching the leaflets that blow down the stairs as she walks up. Along the road to the two not-quite-identical bagel shops (thankfully, the one Elena believes to be morally superior in some indeterminate way is the one with the shorter queue). A walk through crowds into the weekend calm of the financial district, and on to a train at Fenchurch Street, where the slow, rattling carriage is almost empty.

She calls her mum, who doesn't answer, but calls back ten minutes later.

"Hey," Lauren says, "I didn't have a chance to send Marmite yet, sorry."

"What? No, don't, darling, I have a dozen jars in the pantry. Send me a Twix."

The Marmite must have been with a different husband. "Don't they have Twixes in Spain?"

"There's something wrong with them. Natalie thinks there's a special ingredient in the chocolate to stop it melting in the heat, which is clever but it doesn't taste right."

"Oh, okay," Lauren says.

"And of course you can't be good at everything," her mother says. "The Spanish do so well at the sea and wine bars, and that festival with the tomatoes. Olive oil. *Don Quixote.* So you can't expect them necessarily to make a good Twix."

"No, I suppose not."

"Picasso. Ham. I know you don't eat it but if you ever change your mind, the Spanish make such lovely ham. Anyway, darling, what were you after? Was it just about the Twixes?"

"No," she says. "It's about Carter."

"Carter! What a nice young man he is," her mother says. "You know, there's an American bar that's opened quite near the beach here. It seems very authentic, they show basketball on the television and you have to tip the bartenders. Next time you come you must bring him."

"Okay, I'll do that."

"Was that what you wanted to talk about? Are you coming out to visit? It would be lovely to see you both, except of course it shouldn't be during August because everything is so expensive then, and anyway I don't think you're set up for the heat, you get so flushed to the face and your hair gets terribly lank."

"No," she says. "I mean, maybe. I just wanted to know if you like him."

A moment's silence. "Well, yes, of course," her mother says. "I won't try to say I wasn't worried about the wedding at the time, but it's turned out nicely for everyone."

"Okay," Lauren says. "Thank you. That's good to know."

o o

She gets out at the country station and phones the number for a taxi. Its route winds past hedges and cows towards the farm, which is hung about with sun-faded bunting. A rabbit hops past as she gets out, a bird circles overhead, a woman in an apron ushers her into the big farmhouse. It's all extremely bucolic, though the day is beginning to heat up.

Inside, Elena's maid of honour, Noemi—who is in a white cotton robe over only her knickers, effortlessly glamorous, or maybe, Lauren thinks, effortfully glamorous, but either way it works for her—anyway, Noemi is sipping a coffee, and Elena is lying on a sofa, her head off one end, her legs up against the wall. She has her eyes closed, and her hair is hanging towards the floor.

"Hey," Lauren says.

"Ugh," Elena says as she hauls herself upwards and opens her eyes. "Going to be thirty-three degrees, did you see? It's too hot. Can you check if we're allowed in the pond? Can you get married underwater?"

"Stop panicking. Eat this," and Lauren hands over the greasy bag.

Elena pulls the bagel out and shoves it into her mouth, tears away a chunk of it with her teeth. "Gub-spub," she says, then chews and swallows the first mouthful, and repeats: "Godsend."

"How's it going?"

Elena swallows another mouthful. "Terrible. Why am I getting married? And if I have to get married, why would I get married to an *accountant* who can't even make an *omelette*? Catastrophe. Where is my helicopter pilot, my chef, my leader of a revolutionary street dance troupe?"

"As I recall," Lauren says, "the helicopter pilot you went on that date with was a liar who turned out to be an accountancy student, so I think you must just have a thing for accountants."

"You absolutely do," Noemi says. "Remember when you used to masturbate to the Count from *Sesame Street*?"

"I didn't *masturbate*," Elena says. "I was *four*. I didn't even know what masturbating *was*."

"Pigeons don't know what shitting is but that doesn't stop them," Noemi says.

"I just wriggled around a bit."

"That is one hundred per cent not how my speech is going to tell it." Noemi pours three more coffees.

"And you don't want someone who can make an omelette. You hate it when other people cook," Lauren says. "Remember when I had you round for dinner and you brought a whole pan of soup, on the bus, just in case?"

"It's not my fault I don't trust English cooking," Elena continues, "which is another issue. Why am I marrying someone *English*?"

"You are also," Lauren points out, "English." Elena's mother is from Turin, but Elena herself was born in Croydon and hasn't even got around to applying for an Italian passport.

"It's not the same."

Lauren is pretty sure that Elena is just trying out thoughts, indulging herself, saying the worst things she can think of now so that she doesn't say them later.

"Yeah," she says. "Maybe you're right, maybe it's a mistake. Send him back, get a new one."

Noemi takes her robe off and starts unzipping her dress bags.

"Don't get married at all. Spend the money on flying lessons. You be the helicopter pilot." She glances up at Lauren, and mouths, *She'll be okay*, and Lauren nods.

Elena groans. "It's too late," she says.

"It's never too late," Lauren says. "Wanna run?"

"We'll go with you if you do," Noemi says. "But I've got a big work thing on Tuesday so I don't think I could do, you know, Peru. Leamington Spa, maybe?"

Elena rotates, sits up straight. "You two are terrible at pep talks."

"Yeah," Lauren says. She's been through a lot of husbands lately and they weren't all good. She tries again. "I don't know, Rob's not perfect, obviously. But it's not like there's some magical version of the world where you wouldn't be a bit nervous right now, you know? You're getting married. It's a big deal. Being nervous doesn't mean he's the wrong guy. Being nervous is just part of the process. The question is whether you want to do it anyway. And if you don't, that's fine, we go out and tell everyone it's off. I mean, Noemi does, I'm not really into public speaking."

"Yeah," Noemi says, "I would be amazing at cancelling a wedding. I would knock that shit out of the park."

"God," Elena says, "fine, yes, congratulations, you've called my bluff, I guess I like Rob and I want to marry him."

"Good," Noemi says. "In that case, let's get you into this big fucking dress."

CHAPTER 13

Lauren never, she thinks, particularly wanted a wedding, never planned or imagined it, never saved pictures of wedding dresses to a secret folder. For a while when she was with Amos she wanted to be *married*, but not for the wedding, just for the certainty. Just for the feeling of a mind made up. She wanted to know that if something went wrong her first thought would be *How can I fix this?* and not *Should I leave?*

When Elena got engaged, it hadn't made her yearn desperately for her own big day; it had just made her think, *God, must be nice to have that one ticked off the list.*

She has seen so many of her own wedding photos, and she has looked happy in all of them, but the weddings themselves have been so different. She has seen herself in a dress, in a white jumpsuit, in a sari, in a sundress, in a church, in a bandstand, in a community centre. She has seen formal cutlery on tables in a hotel, a huge buffet with stacked serve-yourself plates, a burrito van. As far as she can tell, there's nothing that has been there through every wedding, nothing that every version of her past self has wanted.

Elena and Rob's wedding is good, though. The ceremony takes place under a veranda that juts out from the main farm building; for legal purposes it counts as indoors, with rows of chairs circled around it on the lawn. Picturesque chickens roam. Wind blows through leaves. Lauren cries a little during the ceremony, and some of it might be for the confusion of her own lost weddings, but mostly it's the usual: Elena and Rob seem certain and happy and they're making a decision even though nobody can ever really be sure about anything, and everything in the world is always falling apart.

Carter is the perfect escort. She looks round for him during the ceremony: he's near the back, on the far left. After everything's vowed and signed, she walks over. He's talking to an older man, an uncle maybe; nodding, turning as she approaches.

"Hey," he says, "I was just learning about woodpeckers," and he goes back to the maybe-uncle, carrying Lauren with him into the conversation.

She takes his hand and squeezes it and he feels like comfort.

o o

She only gets ten minutes with Carter before it's time for the photos, which take almost an hour, family members and friends configured in different charming pastoral poses, under that tree, in front of these roses, beside this goat (the goat tries, but fails, to eat the bridal bouquet). Just the groom's side. Just the bride's side.

She gets a minute to talk to Elena while Rob and his brothers pose for their pictures.

"Congratulations," she says.

"Yeah," Elena says. "Glad I went through with it in the end."

For a moment, Lauren feels an echo of her old feelings: just a little envy at the certainty, just a little worry about being left behind. It must be nice to be that sure of anything, to risk the mistake, to have the big party.

But of course, she remembers: in this version of the world, she's done it as well.

o o

The waiters circle guests on the lawn, dodging the picturesque chickens, carrying their bottles of champagne. Every time they orbit, people clamour for a top-up in case this is their last chance, and it never is. God, the cost of it, the glare of the sun.

"Does my hair look lank?" she asks Carter, remembering her mum on the train.

"What?"

"In the heat. Does my hair look lank? And is my face flushed?"

"No," he says. "What? You look beautiful. The little twiddly . . . bridesmaid bits in your hair, I don't know what they're called. Wait," he says, "do I look okay?" He looks down at himself, pulls his jacket straight.

She almost laughs at him before she realises it's a real question. "Yes," she says. "You obviously look perfect."

o o

By the time they gather in the tent to eat, half the crowd is edging towards drunk.

The seating arrangement is almost the same as the plan Lauren saw at Elena's the other night, despite the change of husband. Her main concern at the time had been Amos, but sharing a table with Toby and Maryam is also, she thinks, going to be a little weird, post-Rohan.

She's been avoiding them—they have a parcel for her that she has yet to pick up, she hasn't replied to a couple of messages. But they don't know about the swinging. She makes tense eye contact first with Maryam (that kiss) and, bracing herself, Toby (she's slept with him now; she resented it when the mismatch of experience went the other way around, but this is no better). She tells herself this is okay. She is okay.

At her seat, she picks up the bag of almonds and begins untying the ribbon. You are not, she knows, supposed to eat the almonds;

you're supposed to keep them as a souvenir then throw them out a decade later to lie immaculate in the dump for centuries, the last whole thing on this earth. But she has to do something with her hands. "It's lovely to see you both," she says to Toby and Maryam, weirdly, she thinks, and to Amos, who is joining the table, "Hi! It's so nice to see you."

"Yeah," Amos says. "You too. You've met Taj, right?"

Last she'd heard Amos was married to a Lily, but she supposes that makes sense, a change to her past could change his too. "Taj," she says. "Hi." Taj is short and fat and pretty with a wide triangle of hair, and she's wearing a grey jumpsuit that is *perhaps* not-black enough to be appropriate for a summer wedding, but only just. She looks like she absolutely doesn't want to be at a reception where she knows the married couple, her husband, her husband's ex, and nobody else. Amos murmurs something into her ear, and she half laughs.

The last two seats on the table are taken by ex-housemate Parris, who Lauren hasn't seen for at least a year, and her new girlfriend, Tabitha, who it turns out dated Rob at university and is so pleased that he's happy with Elena, *so* pleased, you couldn't *imagine* how pleased.

Dinner is strange, but mostly good.

Tabitha goes into more and more detail about how much she likes Elena and how she thinks that she's just great for Rob, how perfect, what a wonderful match. Maryam is delighted by her, and doesn't lean towards Carter, doesn't look at him from under her eyelashes, interacts with him no more than politeness requires; there's no accounting for tastes. Carter is wonderful, though, putting in the work to keep table-wide conversations going.

"They've been lucky with the weather," Taj says, and Lauren glances towards the sky where a bird still hovers on the immaculate breeze.

"We're the lucky ones," Amos says. "Imagine if we'd had to pitch our tents in the mud. They'd be okay, they're sleeping in the farm-house either way."

Carter did remember to bring the tent, right? She looks at him. "It's already up," he says. "Easy-peasy."

So competent! And during the main course, while Maryam pours from another bottle of wine, he leans over and whispers, "This is good, but our wedding was better."

God. It really is a shame she missed it.

"Do you think they'll have kids?" Maryam says, looking over at Rob and Elena on the top table.

"Dunno," Lauren says, although she knows Elena would like to.

"Rob always wanted kids," Tabitha says. "Even when we were still studying. He'll make a great dad, he's got the hands for it."

Someone is shuffling a microphone; there's a premature tap on a champagne flute. Speeches are imminent. Maryam grabs her glass and a half-empty bottle of wine from the table. "This is going to be interminable. Anyone want out?" She jerks her head towards the trees and the barn.

"I'm a bridesmaid," Lauren says. "Probably better not."

"Oh yeah. Anyone? Tabitha? Tabitha, c'mon, let's go."

Maryam and Tabitha sneak out, and Lauren thinks: that's a great call, actually. No loud whispers from Tabitha during the speeches. Good work, Maryam. And she takes a glass for the toasts (champagne, she remembers, was the only drink with bubbles that Amos didn't consider "for children") and sits back to listen.

The speeches are long and Rob's list of people to thank is vast, each parent individually, each specific brother and what he brought to the occasion, *Noemi for everything but especially talking Elena out of fleeing the altar, that must have been hard work this morning! Lauren for being such a good friend to us both over so many years and for your sterling work with the almonds.* But there are lovely moments too. And it's good to have Carter there to glance across at; the relax-ation of having home turf, someone to be with by default.

And even Amos, even Amos is mostly okay. He's easier to take when she has Carter by her side. And when the cake comes, and she is served a corner piece with frosting on three sides, way too sweet for her tastes, Amos looks at it and holds up his own plate with a centre piece and frosting on the top only, and he tilts it towards her with raised eyebrows, an offer. She nods, and they exchange plates, quietly, and neither of them says anything, but it feels good to be remembered like that, to have her tastes known and acknowledged. It feels a little like *being on good terms*, the thing that they have never quite managed.

o o

The sky's still light when they are ushered to the barn for the first dance. She and Carter are among the last to come through the big doors. She looks for the people she knows. Maryam and Toby and Tabitha and Parris on the hay bales at the back; Amos and Taj leaning against a wall, presumably listing the things wrong with everyone else in the room. Noemi talking to her preferred grooms-man. Elena's parents. Elena and Rob in the middle of the circle.

Outside, a bird is still looping in the sky, the sunlight golden and heavy. How beautiful. And then as the music starts, the bird dives, like a blessing for the dance, she thinks for a moment, embarrassed at her own cheesiness until the bird gets closer and closer still and even closer than that, and it's swooping down, down, down towards the picturesque chickens.

The chickens squawk and run.

They run towards the barn, where Rob and Elena are swaying together.

She grabs Carter's arm and he spins around. "Hawk," she says, and it only takes him a moment; he steps out and pulls her with him, and says, "Your skirt," and she holds it out as wide as she can with both arms and flaps it, shooing them away from the dance floor. The chickens turn for a moment, then they swerve back towards the barn again; but Carter is behind her, waving his jacket. The mass of the flock turns once more and runs, still squawking, but away from Rob and Elena's gentle waltz.

In the sky, the hawk is circling again.

The chickens cluster under a tree, anxious, loud. Lauren glances behind at the dance floor; a few people near the door are looking out.

"Do we just . . . leave them to it and hope it doesn't come back?" Lauren says.

"No," Carter says, "gimme a moment, I'm out of practice but we can do this."

We can do what? She watches as he lays his jacket over a nearby chair, then walks up to one of the chickens and bends down as he gets closer. Surely not? Surely that's not possible? But he scoops it from the ground, his hands over its wings, and it bocks once but doesn't even try to flap, relinquishes itself utterly to his hold.

He walks with it towards Lauren, so triumphant, his face delighted. "Still got it!" he says. "You try and keep them out of the barn if the hawk comes down again? I'll ferry them over to the coop?" And that's what he does: over the course of the first dance and the next song, he collects hens, first one at a time and then, as his confidence grows and she is more and more visibly impressed, two at a time, one in each arm. It's *magnificent*.

"Wanna get the last one?" he says.

". . . How?" she asks.

"Like it's a ball. Or a loaf of bread. Steady pace. Scoop it up. No doubts, just do it."

The hen is pecking in the grass where a kid spilled a packet of crisps earlier. "Okay."

"I believe in you," he says.

She takes firm steps and bends and puts her hands down, either side of the wings, soft feathers; she feels a flutter but she grasps and she lifts, and she's done it, the chicken lets out a loud protest but it's not struggling, and she's got it, she's holding a whole chicken.

"Oh my god," she says. "Now what?"

"Now we run, right? Make a break for it with our free chicken." And he leads her to the coop and cracks the door open and she pushes the chicken through, releases it, and it flaps out its wings and flicks its tail and runs away from her with one last indignant bock.

"That was the best thing I've ever done," she says.

"You're a chicken natural." And he takes one hand and twirls her to the music spilling from the barn. "You're so good at just trying stuff, you know," he says. "Maritozzi, catching chickens, jumping in a lake, that purple tofu milkshake at that restaurant. Marrying me. Why not, have a little adventure."

She has always thought of her willingness to go along with things, her outsourcing of decisions to friends and circumstance, as passivity, not courage. But observed and described by this man she likes so much, she can almost believe in herself as someone with an audacious spirit.

"What was your favourite thing about our wedding?" she asks him.

"The cake was good," he says. "I liked not getting kicked out of the country too. But maybe just the bit near the end where it had calmed down and we could relax and go *Yeah, we're married.*"

"Good pick." And she pulls him closer and holds her phone at arm's length, and takes a photo. It's not great: half of both their faces, dark with the bright barn door behind taking focus. "We're a very blurry couple," he says.

Back in the barn, they join in the dancing and, eventually, a haphazard conga line. Later on, in the dark, warm fairy lights blink by the bar in the tent. The murmur of people talking under trees, the rival sound of crickets.

Carter is blurry in the tent that night as well, as they lie on the air mattress and listen to singing, bickering, someone pissing too close, an irritated sheep. They're warm together on a warm night, and she sleeps better than she has since the husbands came.

○ ○

She barely drank during the wedding, in case bridesmaid duties called, but in the morning there's breakfast sandwiches and mimosas in the tent, and she takes two of each, then a third mimosa. The day is overcast and cool, and the guests are bedraggled in a mix of practical camping clothes and now-crumpled wedding outfits. Lauren is wearing her bridesmaid dress without the petticoat, plus sneakers for practicality and a big grey cardigan for warmth. Carter brought a spare shirt but it's orange; he wasn't, he explains, expecting the day to be cold enough that he'd want to wear his bright blue suit jacket over it. They look ridiculous. She doesn't care.

On the train back to London, Carter reveals a bottle of prosecco and another of orange juice, smuggled from the farm. They mix their own mimosa in a water bottle and share it, swig and swig about.

In a taxi from Fenchurch Street, they're both a little drunk; not too much, the right amount. "Hey," Carter says to her, seriously, "I like you so much."

She laughs. "I like you too. You're very pretty."

"I know," he says, so solemn. "It's the symmetry. I'm very symmetrical in the—in the face."

When they get home they kiss on the stairs. She touches the tip of one of his cheekbones, and his earlobe, and the arch of an eyebrow. Then she leans in again, her hands back by his waist to gather a handful of his crumpled shirt in each fist, and she pulls him towards her, but the steps are narrow and her bags are still over her arm and the tent over Carter's, swinging in the way, thumping into the wall, so they walk up laughing, there's no rush, and she goes to make some coffee while he rummages in the living room. "Hey," he says, "do you know where our wedding photos are?"

"Nah," she says. "Try the bookshelves," which seems like a passable guess.

She has wedding photos on her phone too. She goes to find them but instead she's distracted by the pictures she took last night, and especially by her and Carter, her arm extended, in front of the barn in the dark. It's not a good photo but it's something she *remembers*, even if it only happened yesterday. It would be good to remember their own wedding but she's happy to remember Elena's instead. Flowers on the table; chickens, disgruntled in their coop; the goat; Noemi giving her speech. The coffee has started bubbling through the machine but Carter is still rummaging. She hopes he can find them; she'd like to see something physical, to touch an artefact of their wedding day. Then they'll kiss again, and go to bed, and she feels a flutter of nerves and anticipation in her chest and between her legs as she wonders what that will be like but: it'll be good. Whatever it's like, it'll be good. Because she likes him so much. Maybe this is love? Maybe this is the early stages of love.

The coffee machine hisses and drips. Buzz, splatter.

While she waits she scrolls through more photos, further back: her and Carter on a picnic, on the pier in Brighton, out in the back yard. In a lot of them Carter's looking straight at the camera, photogenic smile in place, but sometimes she'll find one where he's laughing and off-guard, or where they're squeezed into the frame together and he's looking at her.

The coffee starts to burble through the paper.

"Hey," she says, heading back out from the kitchen.

And she sees the ladder pulled down on the landing.

The warmth inside her empties out, and she closes her eyes, and feels instantly sober; no furtive mimosas on the train, no laughing up the stairs, their morning together is gone and Carter is too.

Oh, but she liked his accent and his undershirts and his face, his serious enthusiasm, his *smell*.

She liked being married to him.

And she'll never know how long it might have lasted, and she'll never see him ride a horse which she's sure he could do although it never came up, and she'll never lie in bed with him and listen for a rainstorm that doesn't come. All because he wanted to find their wedding photos. Because he liked her too.

She looks at her camera roll: no blurry faces in the dark. The flowers, a picture of Elena, one of Toby and Maryam, and one of her with some guy, just some guy, just some husband.

"Here we go," the man says, climbing down from the attic with a pillow.

Go back in, she thinks. Turn back. Please turn back.

CHAPTER 14

The new husband smiles at her, but she hates him straight away, hates his face, his beard, pushes past him and up the steps to the attic in case she can somehow call Carter back. The light bulb shines and buzzes, a food processor on a chair in the corner sparks, and he's not there, he's gone, and she pulls her head back down and sends the new husband away and the next one comes, the reset wiping away her tears, her face clean again. But she hates this one too. New tears start to swell and new chemicals surge through her body. If she swaps fast enough, maybe the attic will create another Carter.

Another husband, and once again for a moment her throat functions like normal, her refreshed new-world body is behind the news; but she can't change what happened, and again it's only a couple of seconds before the physiology of anguish re-establishes itself, and she's feeling it all again. Then there's another new husband, and another, and she can't get a good set of tears going, every new husband clears everything away, ten of them, fifteen, it's like smashing plates, like throwing bricks. Send him back, send him back, until finally she peters out.

On a man who, it turns out, is called Pete. He seems . . . fine. "You okay?" he says as she showers and puts on pajamas and tells him she's going to have a nap, and he touches her gently on the shoulder.

She's not going to keep him: it's no start to a relationship, having the husband you really like swapped for some guy with an insufficiently maintained moustache. She lies in bed, trying to think and then trying not to think. She gets up in the late afternoon feeling nauseous. The storm has still not broken.

She wants Carter back.

She sends Pete away and gets a husband with weird-shaped elbows. The one after that has an accent that reminds her of Carter's and that seems like a bad idea. Then a man who is red-eyed and hung-over and attempting to resolve the issue by having two different beers at once. Then a man who is maybe ten years older than her and the house is too clean, honestly, and the shelves are empty, where are her books? Where's the little cactus pot she made with Elena?

She is aware that she is being unfair.

Okay. She tells too-clean husband that she's going out for a walk, and heads away from the railway station and up the hill to the park, where she dodges happy families and dog-walkers, heads to the lake, looks at ducks. She's vague on the details of duck mating but she knows it's unpleasant and involves a corkscrew-shaped penis, so arguably things could be worse.

Under a tree, out of the drizzle, she tries to talk herself out of feeling bad: she barely knew Carter, this isn't a divorce, this is like a third date with someone who never replies to your message. But even if she didn't know him well they were still *married*, the third date became a thirtieth and a three hundredth became a life.

Maybe she should take off for a week, go to Milan or New York, get into debt on a nice hotel and room-service pancakes. Come back and hope the husband is still around to let her reset everything.

The drizzle is getting worse, turning into the storm she waited for with Carter that never came.

Her phone rings, and it's Felix, who she supposes is the husband.

"Hey," he says, "it's bucketing down, where are you? Do you want me to drive round and pick you up?"

Drive. They live in London, what do they have a car for? It's ridiculous. Maybe that's why there weren't any books in the flat, they had to sell them to pay for petrol.

Still. It's very much raining.

"Yeah," she says as she retreats further under the tree, watches the ducks splash. "Yeah, that would be good. I'm in the park, I can get to the big gate?"

"I'll come now. We should be heading off soon anyway."

Heading off. The last thing she needs on a day like this, wet and stroppy, is an excursion. Why would they have planned anything for the day after a wedding? What is it? A mother-in-law? A bottomless brunch? A trip to IKEA? She'll fake illness and send this Felix off on the excursion on his own and get a few hours to herself, she thinks. Exchange him when he gets back.

o o

The car that pulls up is . . . nice. It's dark green, and she doesn't know cars but it looks new. Is this right? She didn't pay that much attention to the husband earlier but she leans forward to check his face before getting in and it's him, right? She's not getting into a strange man's car?

She is, but it's a strange man she's married to. "That came on suddenly," the husband says.

"Yeah," she says. "I guess it was holding off till after the wedding."

"Very thoughtful." The husband is white, with grey eyes and a slight accent that she can't quite place. Perhaps he is Swedish, or Norwegian. He's older than she thought at first—she'd imagined maybe ten years on her but it's probably at least fifteen. But he has thick hair and a calm demeanour.

In addition to the calm demeanour he also has, she discovers, a house in the country.

o o

It happens like this. "Oh, could you have a look in the attic later?" she says as the car waits at a pedestrian crossing. "I'm trying to find that big red blanket. I want to send it over to Elena when she gets back from the honeymoon, she always loved it when she lived here. I couldn't see it, but maybe I was missing something?"

"I'll have a look," Felix says. "But maybe it's at home? I thought we moved those boxes over?"

"Oh," she says. "Maybe. Never mind."

"I'll check, though."

"No," she says, "you're right." She doesn't want him disappearing until she's figured out what he means by *at home*.

Back at the flat she has to let the husband go ahead of her through the doors, because instead of keys they have a number pad and an entry code. Her suspicions grow stronger as she makes coffees, with a pod machine this time, trying milk-no-sugar for Felix and finding that the fridge is almost empty: the milk, some butter, a cluster of pickle and jam jars towards the back.

They don't live here.

On her phone, she summons up a map of photos arranged by location. They cluster in South London but also near a village to the south-west, the opposite direction to the farm where Elena got married just yesterday. It's not far from where she and Nat grew up, actually, but that can't possibly be why she's spent so much time there. She checks the pictures. Some fields; a sheep; a glass-walled conservatory with wicker furniture; flowers, and more flowers, and trees, and even more flowers.

She checks her work email and finds that she doesn't in fact have work email, or at least not on her phone. It isn't clear to her whether this means that she doesn't have *work*, but her calendar gives no indication of meetings: there is only a dinner, a coffee, "the girls." Is she a *lady of leisure*?

o o

After the coffees Felix says he has a couple of things to deal with, and opens his laptop on the table. She takes the chance to look in her wardrobe, and it's almost empty. A man's suit, a few shirts, a dress and a jumpsuit, which like the car are . . . nice. The jumpsuit is from TOAST, a shop she is tangentially aware of but has never thought about because—and she confirms with a search—everything costs an absolute comedy amount, in the case of this jumpsuit: £465. The dress is asymmetrical with a collar she doesn't understand, and comes from a shop she hasn't even heard of, but it seems from what she can tell like a recent purchase that came in at £1,125.

This isn't taxi-to-Zone-4 rich. This is *rich* rich.

"Hey," Felix calls out, "this is taking longer than I thought, could you make sure everything's ready for the guests? If we get going in the next hour or so we could stop at the Shepherd on the way back?"

She's putting it together: they live somewhere else but she still owns this flat; this is an Airbnb. This is *her* Airbnb, which is to say she runs it, which she confirms by opening the app and seeing landlord-side messages. They didn't camp over at the farm last night because they *have a car*, so they just drove back here, a convenient stop halfway between the wedding and their real home.

She never thought she'd marry for money, but Felix is handsome enough in his lightly professorial way, and he drove out to pick her up; she's had worse husbands. She is still, she thinks, in no mood to give him a fair chance. But she could absolutely be in the mood for a holiday.

Out in the country, far from London, it'll be logistically awkward to exchange him down the line—but you know what, she thinks, let's go. She's been directing everything towards the wedding and the perfect husband, and the wedding's over, the perfect husband has vanished from everyone's memories except her own. So why not fuck off to a life of luxury for a week?

CHAPTER 15

She isn't sure what readying things for the guests involves. It looks like they've sorted out the bed already, and the old sheets are in a pile near the door. She pours the milk down the drain and takes the carton to the recycling bin outside (she's found the codes to get back inside in her outgoing Airbnb messages). Back upstairs, there's a cabinet in the kitchen with a padlock, hanging open; inside she finds toilet paper, cartons of UHT milk (she puts one in the fridge), little containers of shampoo and conditioner and shower gel, eight identical bottles of wine and a pile of paper bags with a card stapled to each one reading WELCOME in a curly handwriting font. She puts some wine and a bag on the table on the landing and steps back. Seems plausible? She closes the cupboard and clicks the padlock shut. Is this right? From the kitchen window she can see the back garden: some new garden furniture and a few plants in big pots looking sullen. Maybe she should water them; or maybe they've already been watered too heavily by the storm. She heads downstairs and around the back to take a look.

Maryam opens the door from her kitchen. "You off again?" she asks.

"Yeah, I think so."

"Next time you have guests like that last lot I'm putting in noise complaints to our landlord and the council," Maryam says.

Oh. "Okay," Lauren says. She's not sure what to add. "Sorry about that. It won't happen again."

"It probably will," Maryam says, looking at her with absolutely the wrong sort of attention. "I'm just telling you what's going to happen when it does." Then she closes the door again.

Well, at least if Maryam's pissed off at her and the husband, she won't be trying to fuck them. Lauren checks her messages to see if she's still on good terms with Toby at least, and—they're not *not* on good terms but they're not talking often, and she only has to scroll back a couple of screens to find *Just wanted to let you know that your guests this weekend had people over, the carpet hasn't been helping with the noise,* which for Toby is a seething screed of fury. Also, she realises, she didn't have a bridesmaid dress in the wardrobe, though it's not clear whether that's because she wasn't a bridesmaid yesterday or just that she's already sent it off for dry-cleaning.

Still, she finds the photo Elena sent of the two of them, just like on the night everything changed, so they're still close. And she's in touch with Nat, who has both her kids. There's a group chat with names she doesn't recognise, another message popping up as she checks; she turns off notifications.

Felix is closing down his laptop when she gets back upstairs. He checks a safe in the bedroom and says, "Ooh, nearly forgot these," holding up a couple of, she guesses, jewellery boxes? Fine. Their car is also clearly, very clearly, fancy, now that she sees it in less rain, though it's not, thank god, the kind of sports car she might have expected given Felix's age and younger wife (that said, she's thirty-one, and a sports car would perhaps go better with a twenty-two-year-old).

They drive south-west. Ten minutes in, Felix puts a podcast on. It's about what economists can learn from trait inheritance in snakes, and it is very, very boring, hosted by three men with almost identical voices, two of whom are called Matt, and it's calming to just sit there and look out the window. She is going along with it. She is on holiday. She is allowing herself to take some time. The Matts interview a woman named Maddie, who is an economist or possibly a snake breeder.

o o

The Shepherd turns out to be a pub that does Sunday roasts until eight p.m.; they're just in time. She goes for the mushroom Wellington. It costs twenty pounds and the pastry is soggy, but the gravy is excellent.

"Beautiful wedding yesterday," the husband says.

"Oh," she says. "Yeah." Then after a moment: "Could you explain that trait inheritance economics thing? I feel like I didn't really get it from the podcast." She doesn't want to talk about the version of the wedding that she must have lived with this man, to hear how it was different, to find out whether the chickens ran into the barn, to let Felix's version of the day blot out her memories of the day with Carter.

o o

It's dark when they leave the pub. She feels like a child being driven somewhere. A low wall. A turn down a road through a field. Past trees, and a house rises up, grey stone, three rows of windows above each other, pointed rooftops.

Lights flick on as they approach. They park, and Felix pulls both of their little suitcases out of the boot.

Even the door is huge.

Felix unlocks it with a code, and they step through to a wide alcove, and beyond that to a tiled entrance hall the size of her living room with a staircase looping the edges. She can't see any details, just the dim shapes of doorways in the walls. The house is silent, no traffic, no downstairs neighbours, too late for birds.

"Lights!" Felix calls into the quiet, and lights fade on. The dim shapes clarify. Closed doors all around them, and one double set standing open, giving on to a living room filled with dark wood, enormous sofas, a tightly patterned rug covering almost the whole floor, a room so big that the spill of the hall light illuminates it only a little, and at first glance Lauren almost misses the neon-yellow piano.

Felix opens a door to the left, and she follows him into another hall, which lights itself gently as they walk through. More closed doors. She stays close to the husband, a little intimidated by the scale of it, the strangeness. He leads them through the corner of a vast dark dining room, with what must be twenty chairs around the table, and into a kitchen, a big one, with a whole separate eight-person dining table in the middle.

Felix opens the fridge and pulls out a bottle of water, the ones like cylinders. She reaches out to turn on a light to see it all better, but there are half-a-dozen switches on the panel. She tries the top left. Blinds roll down the windows. She flicks it back; they stop. She tries a different switch, and they close further.

"You okay there?" Felix says.

She doesn't want to try saying "Lights!" in front of him, in case it doesn't work. She steps away from the panel. "Yeah."

He closes the fridge and goes out through another door. She starts to follow him, but then he closes it behind him, and she figures it out: a toilet. Okay.

She's alone, and the night air outside the windows seems closer and denser than in London; no cars, no lights, just the dark.

She'd assumed Felix was a lawyer or something, but do lawyers get *this* rich? She doesn't know his surname; when she checks, he's just Felix B. in her phone, and there are no bills or unopened letters by the door for her to rummage through. There's the slight accent, of course. She tries searching for "Felix lawyer London," "Felix banker London," "Felix Norway oil London," "Felix tech millionaire London," and when none of those seem to bring up the specific Felix in question, "Felix Scandinavian lord London" and "Felix London organised crime."

The door clicks, and he's back. "Hey," he says. "I wanted to get a bit more work in before the week kicks off, that sound good?"

"Sure," she says. "Perfect. Yes. Great."

"I'll be an hour or so."

"Okay," she says, and starts to ask a question—*is it okay if I look around* or *how do the lights work* or *where should I wait*—but he is her husband, of course, he is her husband and this is her house.

○ ○

He pulls out his laptop and sets up on the kitchen table. And that's it. His attention is on the computer, and she is on her own.

The door she assumed was a toilet actually leads to a big store-room, and a laundry off it, and a bathroom on the other side, and a big back door with a number-pad lock. She opens it, and looks into the dark, which is close and surprisingly cold, and if she goes out she won't know the code to get in again. Back through the kitchen, then, where Felix is engrossed in his work. Through the long murky dining room, where she gets a closer look at the uphol-stery: old-style wooden chairs, but covered in tie-dye fabric, rough to her fingertips when she touches it. And back to the entrance hall.

There's another set of double doors. She pushes them open. They reveal another living room, half-visible, dark shapes hanging from the ceiling. "Lights," she tries, quietly at first and nothing hap-pens, and then she pulls herself together and says it loudly, and the room complies. The dark shapes reveal themselves as taxidermied birds, hanging from the ceiling, their wings outspread. A peacock. Three magpies. Fifteen or twenty little brown sparrows. Dozens of birds, hanging at different heights but all facing towards her and the doorway, suspended in flight. What the fuck.

It's also right next to the first living room, the one with the yellow piano, like *right* next to it.

Her instinct is to take a photo immediately and send it to Elena, but presumably she already did that the first time she came here, or else somehow in this world she thinks a dead bird room is stylish and welcoming. She backs away and closes the doors again. No thank you. Then, tentative now, she opens the last set of doors from the entrance hall. A conservatory, rammed with plants. She should like it, but the walls are floor-to-ceiling glass and the invisible outdoors is pressing inwards. No.

The stairs circling the entrance hall are wooden, with the edge of each step painted a different colour. The design here is really something, half–old country house and half-hallucination. As she walks up she finds that one of the steps creaks, though. Money can't buy everything.

At the top of the stairs there's a wide dark room. She tries a sharp "Lights!" again, and they come on. She is in yet another living room, although this one has a billiards table and three pinball machines and an arcade machine controlled by a full-sized fake motorcycle, so she guesses it's technically a games room. She pulls the plunger on one of the pinball machines and releases it, but the machine's turned off, there are no balls in play, so nothing happens except the echoes of a loud *thwack*.

This is the largest room yet, with three separate sets of windows. The world outside might as well not exist, for all she can see of it through the glass, even when she walks right up and pushes her face against it, cups her hands to keep out the light.

A corridor. A bathroom. A bedroom: empty. Another bedroom: empty. Another. A study, Felix's she supposes, with rows of folders in a glass-fronted cupboard. In a few of the rooms the "Lights!" trick doesn't work so she tries a couple of switches and ends up unscrolling more blinds over the windows, or in one case causing the bed to whirr and screech and rise to a semi-recline.

There's only one bedroom with signs of an inhabitant: a kid's room, video-game posters on the wall, framed and hanging from the picture rail. A desk with a couple of exercise books and a big computer. A stepchild, then. That makes sense; she feels like a second wife, maybe even third. Out in the corridor, and another corner, and she is back in the games room.

Up the stairs again, one last floor. Only two doors at the top. One leads into another untouched bedroom, walls that shade from orange at the bottom to pink at the top. She loves and hates it at once. Someone in this house has terrible taste, and she's beginning to suspect it might be her.

Behind the other door lies a room which is, she supposes, *their* room. A huge bedroom, a huge bed, as wide as it is long. More doors (she's leaving most of them open behind her as she goes, she realises, but that's good; she'd get lost otherwise). A bathroom. A dressing room full of men's clothes and mirrors. Another: hers, more angled dresses, high collars, unexpected waists, two whole drawers of pajamas. And one last door which opens, of course it does, on to a final living room. An L-shaped sofa, two armchairs, a kitchenette in the corner, an irregularly shaped bookshelf filled with the objects you buy because you've got an irregularly shaped bookshelf and you need something to put on it: a porcelain fish, an hourglass, a slide rule, a jar filled with small ceramic pinecones.

It's the most normal room she's found, although it's still so dark outside that she pushes a window open and turns on the flashlight on her phone and shines it out, just to confirm that the world still exists. Trees, the edge of another building, the wall of the house extending below her. Half the weirdness of the house, she realises, is the quiet; presumably the windows are immaculately soundproofed, but with this one open she can hear the wind, and an occasional clatter, and the yowl of some distant animal.

She sits on the almost-normal sofa, which gives way like a bed beneath her, and searches. She finds the husband in her emails. He is called Felix Bakker, he is Dutch, and he is a chief financial officer. Technically this should make sense to her, since she does work in business support; perhaps that's how they met, perhaps his company is one of the big multinationals that they've been trying to woo to Croydon. But after another few minutes of searching it is still not clear to her what he actually does. It is, however, clear to her from her emails what she does, which is: almost nothing.

She winces in anticipation when she looks for their wedding, imagining castles, cathedrals, twelve-pronged candelabras. But instead she finds maybe forty people in a villa in Italy. Nat (heavily pregnant with, presumably, Magda), Adele, Caleb, her mum, Elena. There's a boy who looks ten or eleven who is, she guesses, the owner of the room with the video games.

It's all . . . surprisingly restrained, considering.

She's still going through photos when Felix joins her. "Sorry that took a while."

"That's fine." She is here to get over a man who no longer exists. She's in no rush. She can sit in any number of different living rooms, nap gently, bathe in one of the giant baths, shower under a contraption where water falls from the ceiling, sit in the outdoor hot tub that she has seen in a couple of pictures on her photoroll. She will dampen herself in every conceivable way.

Plus: there's no television in here! In fact, she can't remember seeing one in any of the four living rooms. Perhaps they have no television at all? Perhaps this is finally a husband where she doesn't have to watch—

"*Mindhunter?*" he asks, then "Projector on!" in his talking-to-the-house voice. A square lights up bright on the wall opposite the sofa.

CHAPTER 16

Felix's alarm goes off at seven. She gets up with him. It's a struggle to haul herself out of the bed, which is firm and yielding at the same time, but it seems polite. The windows, now that it's daylight, show distant hills, trees, patterned fields. On her way down to the ground floor, she realises she can see a smudge on the glass in the games room from where she tried to peer through last night.

"What are you up to today?" she asks Felix.

"Just meetings," he says. "Oh, I'm taking the Canadians to the range tonight, you're still okay to pick up Vardon and get him off to bed?"

Vardon: the son, she supposes. "Yeah, what time was that again?"

"The usual," he says, unhelpfully.

Once he's gone to work she tries to make coffee. There's a machine on the sideboard in the kitchen, the sort that connects to its own water line. She presses the biggest button she can find: a small puff of steam emerges from a hole.

"Coffee machine on," she tries in a firm voice. No.

"Make coffee." No.

She presses a smaller button. A light flashes red. "Coffee!" she says quickly, in case. The light goes green, then red again, then turns off with a clunk.

Okay. She can't go to the pub or the petrol station and get a cof-

"Yeah," she says. "Of course. Do you . . . need anything? Water? Juice?"

"Bit later, maybe? I should get this started first. You know, work up a sweat."

Is he flirting? He has his gardening gloves on, so she can't tell whether he's married. If he is, then this is inappropriate. Or maybe it's part of the job? She's briefly offended on behalf of his hypothetical wife, who is not her.

The gravel shifts beneath her. "It's looking good," she says. "Pulled out a few weeds earlier."

"Yeah, the rain and then the sun really got them going." She has heard him say this about weeds before.

"Okay," she says. "I'll leave the conservatory open in case you need the bathroom or anything. I've got a bit of work to do"—shit, she doesn't have work, does she? Does he know that?—"but I'll make some coffee and bring it out in an hour or so?" She remembers the machine. "Some tea."

"Perfect," he says.

Jason Paraskevopoulos. In her husband's garden.

CHAPTER 17

This new information will not fit in her head, it keeps spilling out; she needs paper, a whiteboard.

Okay.

Priorities: at some point today, she has to pick up what's-his-name, Victor, Vander. Judging from his room and the wedding photos he's maybe twelve, so presumably she's collecting him . . . after school? Around three o'clock? She'd been in no rush to figure it out before but now her thoughts are too busy; she needs to start answering questions and this is the simplest one.

The child's name is *Vardon*, her emails tell her, and she confirms that he's Felix's son, her stepson. Emails about him go between Felix and an Alicia, probably the mum; Lauren and a mysterious Delphine are copied in—the nanny, some searching confirms.

The emails mention Vardon's school, and she looks up its website, which doesn't say when the school day ends but does have an address: about twenty minutes' drive away.

She sets an alarm for half past two and clears out that corner of her mind.

○ ○

She is back in the conservatory, door open, and occasionally she hears distant gardening. Jason's footsteps on gravel. The van door opening, closing again.

She finds his website: gardens and landscaping, South London and Sussex. It has a photo of the garden beds outside the conservatory and the orchard behind them, labelled *Private garden, West Sussex*. The pictures are from spring, daffodils still out, pink and white blossoms crowded on trees that are now thick with leaves. More gardens: a courtyard with low hedges; a pathway lined with young trees and archways, and another shot of the same pathway labelled *five years later*. He's doing well.

Okay, then. What about the other husbands? If Jason is real, then they must be real too.

One question fills her head, but she doesn't dare approach it directly. She thinks at it sidelong, sorts through the other husbands first.

Michael—what was his surname? Husband Number One. Callebaut. Michael Callebaut. He has a child, a daughter; there are photos of the little girl on Michael's Instagram, where she is standing on benches or running through parks or wearing a tiny chef's hat and stirring a bowl. No sign of a mother until she scrolls back and finds an anniversary post: *Two years since Maeve left us*, a picture of bluebells in a wood, *always her favourite. Miss you forever.*

God. The poor guy. The poor woman.

Kieran, whose surname she doesn't think she knows. She does a few searches anyway, in the news as well in case he turned out to be a murderer instead of just an angry husband, but there's nothing.

After Kieran it was Jason, who's—yes, coming into view behind the trees, following a path she hasn't explored yet, with a wheelbarrow and some seedlings. She angles her screen away from the outdoors. After Jason and a few fly-by-nights it was Ben, who has moved to Dublin, and Rohan the swinger, who is, she finds, appearing that very night in an amateur production of *The Pirates of Penzance* in Richmond, safely away from Toby and Maryam's perfect happiness. Good riddance.

Outside, the sunlight dims, then shines bright again.

She's getting off-track. Rohan. Iain, the painter. Normo, the expert witness consultant. She tries to keep them in chronological order, to stay calm.

And then she reaches him.

Carter.

She has always been so good at not googling her exes, and yet.

He is back in America.

He's back in America, and that's so far away, but it means, it must mean that he wasn't just out to marry anyone, that he wouldn't take any desperate step to stay in the UK; it means he liked her, her-her not her-as-a-passport. It was real.

He's seeing someone. Of course he would find a partner, of course he wouldn't live an eternally thwarted life without her, he would just *be happy with someone else*, and she feels it in her stomach, her groin, the compression in her chest and at the back of her knees as she scrolls and scrolls: Carter with this laughing woman, her wide sunhat, her perfect eyebrows, a mug of coffee, they're on a boat with friends at a party, it's winter and they're wrapped in jackets (he looks so good in a coat). When she scrolls back far enough they're in Hallowe'en costumes, and they are *adorable*, not the half-arsed non-costume or skimpy sexy-something that would have let her feel superior; he is Mr. Tumnus, with furry trousers and cardboard hooves, and she is the White Witch in a charity-shop wedding dress that seems to have pushed a Bedazzler beyond all reasonable measures.

Fuck.

She could fly over. She has so much money. She could book a flight, probably *first class*, it would be like sitting in yet another living room while people bring her wine. She would land and find Carter and stand near him and, what, watch him order a coffee? Orchestrate a meeting? Hire him to do whatever it is he does with some more of her husband's money? Try to win him away from someone he obviously loves as much as he obviously loved her?

The clarity of his joy in being with this woman is so visible in the pictures; she recognises it from when they were together, when he looked with delight at her instead of this interloper.

Even if she could do all that, it would mean she'd be stuck in this world: returning Felix to the attic would reset everything, leave Carter oblivious again. So absolute best-case scenario: she flies over, wrecks someone's relationship, gets together with an ex who doesn't remember her, divorces Felix, and is for ever someone who used her husband's money to go and hunt down a guy who she had, in this world, never even met.

She should be thinking about the wider implications of the husbands, their continued existence, their life in the world without her, but it's too big, she can't tease out what it means. Will she run out of husbands, if they're being selected from a pool of men she might have married, rather than generated afresh? Is she going from most likely husband to least? The other way round?

She tries again, coming at it from another angle.

Start small. The current situation, this house, Felix. If she sends Felix up to the attic again this house won't vanish but will instead remain and she will be replaced by, at a guess, some other brunette fifteen years Felix's junior.

She looks at texts from him—minutes of scrolling, all their past messages. Recently: affection when one of them is away. Practical information, times, meeting places. Before that, fond teasing, photos, running-five-minutes-late, and jokes: *okay, I'm shunning capital letters like a young person; I told you I could be flexible. look: I won't even use a full stop* and she guesses she can see how the relationship developed. Before that, far enough back, *It was lovely to see you*, and *Thanks for a lovely night*, bandying the word "lovely" back and forth, lovely lovely lovely.

She searches her messages for Carter, just in case; nobody of that name in her phone.

Then she checks Jason.

She has his number in there, because he's her gardener; for a moment, panicked, she thinks she's tapped on it and rung him accidentally, but no, the messages unfold, photos of the garden, notes, questions. *What do you think of one of these for the courtyard* and a picture of a cactus hung about with Christmas baubles, but mostly serious: *maybe these* and a few pictures and flower names, twisting vines with pastel glossy spheres in half a dozen colours, a white starry flower that she thinks they had in their garden back in Norwood Junction.

The messages grow more formal as she winds backwards; then him, *Yeah, give me a call and let's discuss,* and her, *Hey, sorry to message out of the blue but do you still do gardens in Sussex? I might have some work . . .* and back years before that, from her, *No worries, I've got a lot on too—it was great to get to know you a bit better, stay in touch!* and him, *Hey, I had a great time but it made me realise I'm not in a place to date right now.*

She looks up again. Jason in the courtyard garden, nestling new flowers into place, white and yellow. So they went on a date, years ago, maybe after an earlier-than-usual break-up with Amos (if she even dated Amos in this version of the world). And he blew her off but kind of politely, and he did go to the effort of sending a message, which she knows she's supposed to appreciate, though in fact she's always preferred a quiet ghost.

And three years later she got in touch to get him to come and *do the gardens* and flirt with her at her new husband's ridiculous country house, where she is, as far as she can tell, a lady of leisure and an occasional Airbnb host.

The texts seem tonally perfect, just looking for someone to help deal with the gardens, but she must, *must* have meant to rub it in: look, you turned me down but another man didn't, see how rich I am. Look, I care so little about your rejection that I would be delighted to see you tend my enormous garden, which by the way I have. Because it's easy—she assumes, though obviously she's never tried it—to google *local gardener* and find someone. Presumably most people who need gardeners do not obtain them by going on two dates with someone then texting them years later.

This whole process is making it difficult to maintain a sense of herself as a nice person who means well.

She looks out into the garden again. Jason has moved closer, this side of the orchard.

Is she *meant to be* with Jason? Is that why he's been returned to her? She's caught in renewable husbands until she makes the right decision? It's hard to be sure when there's no direct line of communication with the attic process beyond sending husbands back and seeing what happens.

She gets up and leans out through the door. "Come on," she calls to him, "surely you can take that tea break?"

○ ○

After the tea, they walk through the garden to the wall in question.

"Okay, so," Jason says, "we were talking about green and white, and the obvious thing to do is shove in some jasmine and watch it go, right?"

"Yes," she says. She pulls a flower from a big bush, dozens of clustered petals, and starts pulling them off as they talk.

"But I think it'll feel better to make a long-term decision even if it won't pay off for a few years. So I was wondering about some old-fashioned climbing roses? We could go with the Blushing Pierre de Ronsard, which starts out this gentle pink, which gives a bit of texture, but then it opens white. Or there's the Lamarque, which is like a more sophisticated version of yer good old Iceberg." He holds out a tablet, scans through pictures.

"Yeah, makes sense." She is so intrigued by how much this version of her knows about plants. Even when she was married to

Jason he wouldn't have said anything like that to her: he looked after the garden, and she appreciated it. She lets the last petal drop.

"You know you should always start with the answer you want, right?"

"What?"

He nods at her hands, the empty stem. "No guarantees, but usually flowers have an odd number of petals. That's why you start with *He loves me*, right? Whatever you begin with, that's probably the answer you'll get in the end."

"I didn't know that," she says.

Would she marry this man? She supposes she did, once.

"I should get back to it, anyway," he says. "But I'll send over the slides and you can have a look, lemme know what you think."

"Of course," she says. She can have an opinion on roses. Even if she won't be around to see them bloom.

CHAPTER 18

She spends the rest of the morning in a corner of the conservatory, hunting for more details about Carter, as if the right search terms will open a database of all his possible lives. She tries *parallel worlds*, *alternate husbands*, getting nowhere. She takes a break to poke at the coffee machine, which remains uncooperative.

She does, in an alcove in the kitchen, find a screen that flicks through a dozen CCTV views of the house: front door, main hall, two of the living rooms, the driveway where she pauses to watch Jason dig out a weed and check his phone. The kitchen: she can see herself standing, looking at the screen, her stiffening back, movement as she turns to look up. Above the cabinets, a squat grey cylinder is nestled discreetly. She has to force herself to turn away from it and look through the rest of the screens: the conservatory, too, though not from an angle where anyone could tell what she'd been googling, thank god. A shed. A room with a bike and a treadmill and a weights machine which she hasn't seen in the house, perhaps another shed. Nothing in the bedrooms. But she doesn't like it.

She feels worse still when she finds a dropdown that allows her to select "other properties," and pulls up a cottage somewhere, and then the view down her own flat's stairway, and her living room, almost bare, with two strangers on the sofa. She has to stop; there's a hollowness in her stomach and a buzzing in her temples.

Jason knocks on the conservatory door to say goodbye. The clouds are thickening, and the air is warm when she opens the door, rushing in to mix with the cool inside. The rain comes back half an hour later. It thuds on the conservatory roof, first one drop then another and then hundreds, irregular and fast, and then it stops.

Her alarm goes off. Shit, yes, she needs to pick up Vardon, *Vardon*, what a name. She feels airy, loose, like all the emotions in her body have separated into constituent parts which are floating inside her, unconnected.

She parks a couple of minutes' walk from—well, from the place her phone tells her she often goes at 3:20. Women cluster nearby, and one man. No, another two over by the gates. Most of them are in expensive athleisure, or a Zoom-from-home work-top-with-leggings combo. If she has to do this again she should find her own fancy yoga pants. Maybe she should even do some actual exercise.

After a couple of minutes the boy from the photo comes up to her, sulky-faced. "Vardon," she says.

The boy glares. "I told you, it's Mikey." Makes sense; if she were a child named Vardon then she would absolutely want to be called Mikey instead.

"I'm sorry, Mikey," she says. He is unplacated. "How was your day?"

"Can we go? I don't want them to see me with you." He keeps glaring as they walk to the car, and then he climbs into the back seat. He is, she guesses, treating her like a chauffeur to make a sulky almost-teenager point. This might, she thinks, be hurtful if she were truly making an effort to connect with him.

"Do you . . . have any Pokémon?" she tries.

He rolls his eyes and lets out a disgusted *uggggghh*.

"I dunno, do you have any homework, then?"

"I'm *twelve*," he says. What's she supposed to conclude from that? Too old for Pokémon? Too young for homework? The other way round?

"You sure are," she says.

"I want a McDonald's," he says.

"Really?"

"Yes!"

She pulls over and looks it up; there's a drive-thru twenty minutes away. "It'll take half an hour to get there," she says. "Do you want to spend an hour in the car with me for a burger?"

He thumps his small body back against the seat, letting out another grunt of despair. "Just take me home."

At the front door, she realises she still doesn't know how to get through the keypad lock, but Mikey stomps ahead of her and punches in a number. A small light turns green.

Once he's through the door he runs upstairs. That's okay! They don't have to spend time together. He'll have a new stepmother in a week.

Instead, she pulls out drawers in her wardrobe until she finds fancy workout gear. Perhaps this will help her to feel less like she is on the brink of non-existence, of dissolving into the air.

She finds Mikey in his room. "I'm going to be in the gym," she tells him. He stares at her impassively then pulls his headphones back on and returns to his game. "What's the code to get in? I've forgotten."

"It's one thousand shitty fuck fuck," he says.

Okay. "If you don't want me to go to the gym," she says, "we can hang out here and bond."

He lets out a half-grunt, half-wail. "I don't *know* the gym code, I'm not *allowed* in case I *drown*. Look on your phone."

"Oh," she says, "okay." She starts by looking for a special app, which she does kind of find: an icon with a camera and a dial which opens up an interface to their CCTV system. She closes it quickly. The actual entry codes are in a notes file, unencrypted. Felix probably wouldn't approve. One nine-digit string for the house; an eight-digit for the outbuildings.

It's still hot outside. She looks round corners, tries doors; heads to a shed that turns out to be filled with rakes and soil, and another that wasn't on the CCTV and that she doesn't have a code for, before she finally finds the gym.

There's sports equipment, tennis rackets, balls. Machines, weights. A treadmill.

And there's something else: the smell of chlorine.

Mikey did say *drown*. And: yes. A door on the far side opens on to a pool room. The pool itself, ten or twelve metres long; wicker chairs; three medium-alive plants; glass walls facing away from the house and over browning fields.

An actual swimming pool.

There's half a dozen buttons on the panel by the door, and two of them turn the lights on and off, and one seems to start a gentle wave rocking through the pool, but the cover is still on so she turns the wave off right away. Then another button, and the cover retracts: a slowly growing blue rectangle.

She takes off her yoga pants, and steps in. The water over her ankles is cold for a moment and then perfect. The cover is still retreating before her, and she follows it, deeper and deeper, past her knees, and then she pulls her top off and throws that to the side too and, after a moment's thought and another glance to double-check for cameras, her sports bra. She's in to her knees, her waist, she falls back into the water; she's floating, her hair around her. The tension stretching over her skin relaxes. She stands again, then falls back again and the emotions disarranged inside her float, just a little, into place.

She can't research husbands in a pool. She can't make notes.

She can't search for evidence, she can't look up her old workplace or examine a wedding album. She can only be in her body.

○ ○

She stays for maybe an hour; her fingers are puckering and it's hard to leave, but she can come back with a bathing suit and goggles, and she probably shouldn't leave the kid too long (if anything happens to him, she can reload the world, but even so). Plus, she realises, she's hungry, an uncomplicated physical hunger like she hasn't felt since the husbands came.

○ ○

There are boxes and boxes of fancy delivered ready meals in the fridge. She calls the kid. "Take your pick," she says to him. He shuffles through and wrinkles his nose and asks for burgers, which they don't have, or ice cream, which they do. "Go for it," she tells him, giving him the carton and a spoon. Parenting is easy! At least if you never have to make any decisions whose ramifications will last for longer than a week! She goes for an apricot-and-chickpea tagine herself because it needs the least amount of time in the oven, and while she's waiting she breaks off a chunk of cheese and eats it straight.

After dinner she sits in the creepy death living room, which doesn't have a camera, presumably because the hanging birds would get in the way. She scrolls through pictures of Carter in Denver with someone else, and closes the page, and opens it again. She calls Natalie, who doesn't answer, and their mother, who does but who only has a few minutes because she has to rush out to the residents' meeting or else Sonia will get her way about the eucalyptus and that'll just be the thin edge of the wedge.

A message appears: a group chat about the kid. His mother is reminding her and Felix that he isn't to have nightshades. She thinks that's okay; she's pretty sure ice cream doesn't have any nightshades in it.

Just before eight o'clock the kid comes downstairs with a long, serious-looking toy gun, all black and green, and he tells her he's going to shoot squirrels.

"Uh," she says.

"It keeps me active," he says.

"I . . . don't think that's a good idea."

His groan is more disgusted than ever. "Fine. I'll do target practice in the barn."

"I don't . . . You're twelve," she says. "I don't think you're allowed to have a gun." He's not even allowed in the swimming pool alone.

"I've told you," he says, "it's an air rifle."

"I think—let me talk to your dad about it." This isn't normal, right?

"What am I meant to do instead?"

Isn't that what cartoons are for? She gets him back to his room by promising that as long as he doesn't leave she won't check up on what he's doing. He agrees reluctantly; refuses point-blank to brush his teeth. He also refuses to let her take his air rifle. "It's mine," he says, "it was a birthday present."

○ ○

She tries Nat again, who answers this time.

"Hey," Lauren says, "you know Vardon. Mikey."

"Yeah," Nat says. "Look, I know he's lonely but I don't think Caleb had a great time when they hung out. Plus four years is a big age gap when they're that old and Vardon does a lot of stuff Caleb's not allowed to."

"No, it's not that. I guess it's kind of that. He's got an air rifle. Is that normal for a twelve-year-old?"

"It doesn't surprise me," Nat says. "But it's not legal."

"I don't know," she says, "I guess his mum's okay with it? I should just let him do what he likes?"

"Honestly," Nat says, and sighs, "I don't know what to tell you."

○ ○

When Felix gets back, Mikey is asleep, angelic. Lauren makes raspberry tea, big pyramid-shaped bags, in their upstairs-living-room's kitchenette.

She mentions the air rifle, and Felix laughs. "It's a good break from video games," he says. "I know you don't like it, but Alicia and I both grew up hunting. It's normal in the country. And it's just an air rifle."

It sounds like they've had this discussion before.

"Oh, I bought you something," Felix says. A sports car? Tickets to Coachella? One of those antique machines where the planets circle each other on long rods, encrusted with jewels? But no: it's a packet of American pretzel M&M's, which she's never tasted but supposes she must like in this world. She eats one, and yep: there's something about them, the crunch or the contrast of textures.

"Thank you," she says.

"C'mon, give me a couple." He leans towards her.

"No more than three," she says. He takes two and looks up at her through his surprisingly thick eyelashes, the crag of his middle-aged eyebrows above them; he's smiling, affectionate, pleased that she's there. In bed, he lies on his back, one hand extended to rest on her side as they fall asleep on the impossibly comfortable sheets.

○ ○

The thing about being extremely rich, she thinks, after finding a drawer of bathing suits the next morning and returning to bob in the swimming pool again, is: it's *great*. After sharing her medium-sized flat with so many unexpected husbands, it's magical to have this much space, the hills before her, the trees, the summer haze. Air-conditioning—it's another hot day today, and if she was at home she'd be dropping ice cubes down her top to cool off. Here, she almost enjoys the heat of the short walk from the main house to the pool.

What does she usually do with her days? It seems she doesn't, for example, wash the sheets or mop the floors; she's in the pool now partly because there's a strange woman in the main house, cleaning, tidying, washing out the mugs from last night's raspberry tea.

Maybe the answer really is: not much?

○ ○

She can't stay, of course.

Well. She supposes she can't stay.

It's clear that at least one version of her decided that she *could* stay.

You shouldn't stay with a husband just because he's got a country mansion, it's true, but also, you shouldn't *dismiss* a potential husband because his house is too nice.

In fact, spurning a husband because of his wealth would be bad for the world, because through this particular husband she has access to money and power. She could donate, say, even half of her clearly enormous clothes budget, and think of how much good that could do. Or her travel budget! She's searched her calendar and email for flights, and found a mix of business- and first-class tickets that have, staggeringly, been forwarded to her by a travel agent, which it turns out is a job that still exists. If she travelled premium economy instead, which would still be much nicer than standard economy, she could donate the difference in cost to good causes, and that would absolutely do more for the world than she could dream of in her old life. So from one perspective, some people might hold that she had a moral obligation to stay.

She's not going to, she thinks, kicking off backwards from the side and putting her arms out and feeling the water surge around her. But she can see how it might have happened before. In theory.

CHAPTER 19

She decides that her holiday will last for one week exactly. She came in on a Sunday; she will leave on the following Sunday, or on Monday since Felix is, it turns out, going to Switzerland on Friday morning and won't be back till Sunday evening.

They have sex on Wednesday night, at his instigation. The experience is less weird than it was with Jason, and *way* less weird than it was with Toby. Felix's tastes run lazy: he invites her to do the work, twisting and licking and wiggling while he reclines fondly. This isn't her usual approach, but she appreciates the transparency of his desires, and he is older than her, after all, his chest hairs silvered, the oldest man she's slept with, probably; so she feels youthful by comparison, enjoys his laid-back aesthetic appreciation with none of the self-consciousness she might have felt perched atop a younger man. She moves and squirms and watches his reactions, his little shifts in expression, his minute changes in breathing. It's nice to give her smooth and expensively maintained skin a proper audience. She is surprised to find herself really getting into it, and suggesting a repeat on Thursday.

The rest of the time they circle in their own orbits, intersecting briefly. She makes up a mnemonic for the main entry code so that she can get in and out of the house with confidence: 635324847, count out the letters of *regard the dozen men in your upstairs room, octopus* (mnemonics have never been her strong point). Felix brings her small things for approval, like the M&M's or the no-capital-letters text message, a gin and tonic in which he has placed a small flower ("Those are the edible ones, right?"), a shawl when she's sitting out in the garden and it starts to get cool. Each time he does it he waits for her acknowledgement, and she thanks him and says how nice it is, and he smiles, satisfied, and goes about his evening. She brings him a biscuit in return once, while he works in his office, and he's not half as pleased as when he brings her something.

o o

She does feel a little lonely sometimes.

She messages Toby, who responds slowly, and she remembers the tension around the Airbnb.

She drafts an email to Carter, which of course she does not send, not even from the fake email address she makes just in case. God, if she'd only had more time with him, if she knew his secrets, his history, enough details to put in an email and say *I know this sounds unlikely but how else would I know about the bubblegum you stole when you were six*, but all she has is the time they spent together.

She calls her mum, who mostly wants to talk about all the houses near her in Spain that she thinks Lauren should buy: "It just makes sense for you to have a place here, and of course Natalie and her friend and the children could stay as well, because I know they'd like to visit more but there's just not space for them in my little cottage."

"Sure," she says, "send me some links." She can pretend that she's going to buy a Spanish villa, why not?

She's been trying not to bother Elena on her honeymoon, but after spending twenty minutes trying to figure out how to get the pinball machines working, she gives in and flops down on the games-room sofa and sends *Hey how's married life going?*

Amazing, Elena messages back a few minutes later. *God, to think I have to go back to work in a week. Disgusting.*

Just explain you've decided to stay away and hang out on islands for ever, she replies.

We can't all marry evil millionaires, Elena writes back.

It's a joke, of course, Lauren thinks. Felix probably isn't evil. She's looked up the company he's CFO for, Wardrell Stern, and they're a generic tech company that offers "solutions."

But just in case, she searches for the company name and "evil." Ah.

She finds . . . a lot. Some of it is full internet garbage: someone who thinks Wardrell Stern rigged the New Zealand elections and is causing chemtrails (as far as she can tell, Wardrell Stern have no presence in New Zealand or, indeed, the upper atmosphere), some elaborate anti-Semitism stemming from the fact that one of the company founders is named Elijah Wardrell (Elijah Wardrell does not actually seem to be Jewish).

But she also finds that:

The cameras in their house have records that are stored centrally and have been shared with police.

Wardrell Stern cameras and facial recognition software have been used at busy public events to identify people with outstanding warrants.

Wardrell Stern drones have been used in patrolling national borders.

Wardrell Stern microexpression analysis solutions have been used to provide employers with Wardrell Stern's opinions on whether employees are lying about being sick, stretching the truth during job interviews, or allowing their attention to drift during camera-monitored work-from-home sessions. Wardrell Stern is in a pilot programme to use these same microexpression analysis solutions to assess benefits claimants and insurance claimants, and to assist in border control interviews.

Wardrell Stern is . . . maybe not good.

She should have known something was off when she found the creepy cameras.

She looks up from her phone. Of course, of *course* it was too good to be true that she should have a countryside castle to live in for ever. She was going to stay, she realises, of course she was going to stay, a week at a time at first and then for ever, and now she can't, she has to send Felix back before she goes through whatever convoluted thought process got her to the point where she could ignore Wardrell Stern and the cameras in every room and joke with Elena about evil millionaires.

She's doing it already, she feels it at the edge of her thoughts: *if I decided to stay before it can't be that bad, there's probably more to it than some guy on the internet knows.* Enough. Felix is going in the attic. She's going to go back to her little flat, which she is appalled by, the size of it, the warmth, the constant proximity to the husbands; how has five days in a mansion taken her to the point where her *flat that she owns with her sister* feels like a trap? She needs to get back to thinking of this as the holiday it was always meant to be. Swimming. Good food. A nice, distant husband she doesn't have to spend too much time with. And then home.

She would rather have Carter than this mansion, she reminds herself, and it takes a moment but that still feels true. She finds the pictures of him with his beautiful girlfriend again. There's a new photo; they're by a lake. She's never been to America but it seems like everyone is very invested in lakes there.

o o

Felix is still away for work so there's nothing she can do; it's just her, alone, wandering from room to room, watched over by the cameras. She covers one of them with a tea towel and receives a pop-up notification on her phone ten seconds later, *camera obstruction.*

She spends Saturday evening sitting outside in the garden, avoiding the house and its allure and its menace. Felix messages her around midnight: *Hey lovely! You out having fun? Noticed you haven't been in the house tonight*

Fucksake. It's bad enough that there's cameras all through the house without knowing that he's actually looking at them. She walks into the conservatory and waves. *I'm here! Just been outside, enjoying the garden!*

o o

On Sunday she tries to enjoy the end of her holiday, but once she's opened the most expensive bottle of wine she can find and swigged from it while floating in the swimming pool one more time, she finds she doesn't want to drink the rest. Maybe she could read? Go for a walk? Call her mother again, talk more about the Spanish house she's not going to buy, get the credit for that, although what's the point when it's going to be wiped clean? She goes for a drive and ends up in a farm shop, where she watches chickens in their coop and wonders if they would let her scoop them up.

o o

Felix is due back around eight. She tells him she'll have dinner ready. A nice last night—a pleasant few hours to wipe away all the weirdness. She finds a dhal recipe that she thinks they have all the ingredients for, although it's clearly not a kitchen where anyone regularly cooks from scratch.

"Wow," Felix says when he returns, looking at her in her apron, and at the bubbling saucepan. "This looks good."

"Tastes good too." She's been testing it throughout, and when it wasn't good she microwaved a different dhal from the freezer and stirred it in, just out of sight of the cameras. She thinks she remembered to jam the container to the bottom of the bin.

"I missed you," he says, and they kiss lightly.

"Got to keep stirring," she says, brandishing the wooden spoon. It's almost time.

They eat at one end of the long dining-room table, since she did, after all, cook. Felix even lights a candelabra, which flickers and illuminates the tie-dye chairs stretching away to the distant dark end of the room.

"Oh," she says, idly, carefully, "I think I left some papers in the old London flat. Up in the attic. I know we brought most of my stuff over but I've had a real search and I'm pretty sure we missed at least one box. I know it's a pain but there aren't any guests staying at the moment. If you're going to be in town tomorrow could you pop in on your way home and grab it?"

CHAPTER 20

She gets up with Felix again in the morning. She can make coffees now: she presses the third button from the left, then says "flat white" and "macchiato."

Felix will be late home, he says; maybe nine or nine thirty. He will bring her box of papers.

She has, then, twelve hours or so to get ready for re-entry.

She decides to spend her last day of luxury doing research, by which she means hanging out in the pool room and watching time-loop movies on her laptop (she has realised, belatedly, that it doesn't actually matter if it gets wet).

Not that she's in a time loop exactly. In a time loop, the horror is that there's no progress, just a constant uncontrollable reset; there's no point doing anything because its effects will never play out long-term. But the corresponding advantage is an infinity of time: no ageing, no long-term penalties for messing up, no death, and the gift-or-curse of extra years, decades, centuries. Time to learn theoretical physics or flawless piano-playing or a dozen languages or how to come to terms with your childhood, time to become a better person.

She isn't getting any extra time, not objectively. She has received no miracle of agelessness. Each new husband does not reset the calendar; time moves forward like it always did, and she is, she supposes, moving forward with it.

It's only been three weeks since the first husband arrived,

but the details of her old life are distant and airy, long weeks of nothing changing, days sliding into other days. What did she do? What was it like? She'd put things into her calendar, and the things would come up and she'd do them. Drinks after work on Thursdays. Swimming before work on Tuesdays. Tea with Toby mid-morning if they were both working from home. The cinema maybe once a month. She'd been making a lot of frittatas before the change, she remembers; she'd got out of the habit of reading; sometimes she would walk through the further-away park to see the roller skaters. She and Elena had gone to Florence for a week-end in April. Sometimes she'd think about whether she ought to try to find someone to date, and then she'd consider the whole long process, and decide: no. She'd been happy enough, she thinks, carrying on with her life, habits and friendships and regular gro-cery orders to carry her from week to week with no real risk of anything going wrong.

○ ○

She should get a move on. It would be a bad idea to be standing inside Felix's multi-camera house at the moment he ceases to be her husband.

At four o'clock she walks to their room, pulls on an asymmetri-cal silk dress that she hasn't worn yet, and takes one last circle around the ridiculous house. Walks through the garden. Pinches an unfurling rosebud off the bush and tucks it behind her ear.

She daren't drive in case Felix goes into the attic mid-journey and the car disappears beneath her and she rolls through the air on to the road at eighty miles an hour, or it suddenly belongs to someone else who reports it missing. She walks to the station instead, about an hour. Her expensive shoes are, she is almost annoyed to discover, extremely comfortable even after a long walk on country paths.

The train is cool and gentle and, for five o'clock, not too busy. She's facing backwards, so the buildings rush away from her, then the gardens with trampolines, then the fields and the large sheep as they roll into the countryside.

She is relaxing into it, lulled by the movement of the train, when she gets a message from Felix. *Couldn't find the box, let's get Nia to have a look in storage tomorrow. On my way, see you soon.*

She stops, reads again.

And again.

He tried to find the box (and of course he couldn't—presumably there isn't one, she has no idea what's in the attic or isn't). And yet he's texting her, not his new alternate-universe wife.

He still knows her.

They're still married.

He didn't change.

She should have known not to rely on the attic for ever. Maybe it had a certain number of changes, and she's exhausted them. Maybe she's too far away, and it only works when she's within five miles. Maybe she needs to turn it off and on again.

Shit. *Shit.*

Okay. She checks her phone for big strange news, sunspots, the northern lights. In a way it's very normal for an attic not to transform your husband into a different husband, so it's a difficult problem to troubleshoot.

The train is rattling onwards, closer and closer to her old flat. And she thinks: what if she's stuck with Felix for good?

And if she is?

Other than the evil surveillance situation, he's a good husband. He's kind, he's thoughtful, he leaves her with plenty of time to herself. He maintains a level of detachment which she finds comforting: no farting and laughing about it, no pissing with the door open, no talking about feelings, nothing like the moment when Jason emerged from the bathroom with a cotton bud in one hand

and showed her a bright clump of earwax, jagged, a mountain, Jason wide-eyed in delight. She knows these habits are considered healthy by some but to be parachuted into them, to be invited to squeeze the spot on a stranger's bum or to look at some cool porn they found while you were out: it's too much. She cherishes the distant fondness she has with Felix. The space between them feels expansive, not forbidding.

The stepson isn't ideal; the squirrel shooting seems definitely bad. But Felix used to do it and he turned out okay, didn't he? Other than maybe being evil? And besides, the kid's only there a night or two a week.

If she stays, she thinks, she will know better than most rich people how to enjoy her miracle of wealth. She will be the sort of rich person that nobody hates, the sort of rich person who tips well and is polite and friendly and who people say is *actually surprisingly decent*. She won't take it for granted: the garden, the housekeeper, the pool, the clothes, ordering a meal based entirely off whim or nutritional value and not even a little based on cost. She hasn't chosen this life, but that doesn't mean she wouldn't make the best of it.

And if she has lost the option to leave, she has also lost the obligation.

Or, she thinks, if it doesn't feel like a good long-term plan she could even divorce Felix, and presumably do quite well out of it; there's nothing that says that once you're married to someone you have to stay that way for ever, other than she guesses technically the marriage vows. She searches for *easy UK divorces,* and finds that divorce is listed as one of the five most stressful things you can do, but she suspects the people who compiled the list hadn't tried infinite transforming husbands.

She should check the old flat. The surveillance app on her phone opens on views of the country house. But when she clicks to "other properties" there's a little red notification bubble, "today's activity," and it must be Felix getting the box that doesn't exist, except: it isn't.

It's a husband.

A *different* husband.

A video of the stairs, and a different man, neat hair, glasses, young. He's walking up, then he vanishes from view. She sees him in the living room too, with a glass of water.

A man in her house. Not Felix.

She's not supposed to have two husbands at once. It doesn't even make sense: how could a new husband be caught by cameras installed by the old one? But the rules are falling apart.

She calls Felix. It goes to voicemail. "Call me back," she says. Then she looks through her phone for pictures of the new husband, but there's nothing. No messages to anyone who might be him, either.

Her phone battery is running low, under twenty per cent. She didn't think it would need to last this long; she'd expected to be parachuted into another world. She didn't even bring a charging cable. Go faster, train, she thinks, as it rushes towards London, and she tries calling Felix again, and again, and again.

She is walking from Norwood Junction and is almost at her old flat, and down to six per cent on her phone, when he finally calls her back.

CHAPTER 21

"Hey," he says, "where are you? The app says you're in London?"

Of course the fucking app tells him where she is.

"The box," she says. "Sorry, this is important. Was anyone else at the house when you went to look for it?"

Two minutes, perhaps, from the corner of her street. Her fingers feel slippery where they touch the phone.

"What? Wait, let me check," and she hears a rustle, then Felix again, more clearly, switching from speakerphone maybe. "No, I mean I sent an intern, but he didn't mention seeing anyone, have you checked the cameras?"

It takes her a moment to absorb the sentence, to understand the situation.

She is turning the corner as she decodes it, and sees the house come into view with one all-encompassing realisation: *the attic is still working.*

"Hey," she says, "I'll call you back."

The man on the camera wasn't a husband. Of course Felix didn't get a train or a taxi or a company car and spend an hour coming to her old house. Of course he just sent an employee. Of course.

She has to stop in the street to bathe in her relief, to close her eyes, to feel it engulf her like the waters of the swimming pool.

She has had enough of this. She is done. She wants her new life.

And the thing is, as long as she's happy to *leave* this life, it doesn't matter how much of a fuss she makes on the way out.

So she picks up her stride and unlocks the front door—the codes in her Airbnb messages, one for the outer door and one for the flat—and she walks up her old familiar stairs.

The house is still the strange empty thing it was when she left a week ago. She looks in the cupboards in the kitchen for a phone charger, but finds only four half-empty jars of grey-green herbs and a row of untouched recipe books.

The cleaner, presumably, has set out a welcome package on the table in the hall, another of the folded-over bags. She opens it. There is tea, and some shortbread chocolate-chip biscuits. The bottle of red wine sitting next to it is worth (she looks it up) £5.49. It's a screw top, and much easier to open than most of the hundred-pound bottles she's been drinking during the week, so she takes a sip. It tastes fine, but she has to grudgingly admit that the very expensive wines were mostly nicer.

I am at home, she texts Felix. *My old home. I am not leaving.*

Her phone rings right away. She declines the call.

It rings again. She declines again, and texts *I am at the flat and I will not leave until you are here. I will explain later*, then she turns it to aeroplane mode to conserve battery and arguments.

Next: time to check the attic's still working. She pulls the ladder down, jerking to the left at the halfway point like always; in no world have she and the husband had it fixed. Two steps up, far enough that she can reach her hand in. There it is; the warm light. A crackle in the air. The attic, still doing its weird thing.

She doesn't want to go into the living room, under the gaze of the camera. Instead she takes a recipe book from the kitchen so that she has something to read while she waits, and heads into the bedroom, flops down on what she is pretty sure was her original bed. Brilliant Biscuits. Clever Cakes. Perfect Puddings.

She is looking through Scrumptious Scones when she hears the beep of someone unlocking the front door, and footsteps coming up. It can't be Felix, can it? Not already. No: it's a woman in a suit.

"Lauren?" the woman says in the hallway, switching the light on; it's been getting dark.

"Hello," Lauren says from the bedroom doorway. "I don't suppose you have a phone charger?"

The woman checks her bag. "No," she says. "Sorry."

"That's fine," Lauren says. "Are you here from Felix?"

"Yeah, I'm—I'm Siobhan, we met at the summer party."

"So we did," Lauren says with a grandiose gesture. "Welcome. I don't have much battery left so I can't call Felix directly, but I'd love it if you could tell him I'm okay, I'm just planning to stay here until he comes to see me."

"Is there anything—are you all right?"

"I'm well, thank you. How about you?"

"I'm good." Siobhan is young, surely not more than a couple of years into her position. It's unkind of Felix, Lauren thinks, to send her to chase down his wife.

Siobhan's still talking: "Would you like me to call someone? Do you definitely want Felix to come? Or is there something . . . I looked up a couple of organisations?"

It takes Lauren a moment. "Oh," she says, "god, no. I don't think so? No, I'm sure not." She looks at Siobhan. Imagine being, what, twenty-two? Sent by your boss to tend his wife's nervous breakdown, and having the moral fortitude to check if the wife is being abused. This isn't what Lauren wanted, some low-ranking employee forced to come to her flat long after work hours have ended. But: *no repercussions*, she reminds herself. Siobhan will be returned to her normal evening when Felix arrives.

"Would you like some wine?" she says. "Or some shortbread biscuits?"

"No," Siobhan says, "I'm good. Maybe some water?"

"Of course." Lauren goes into the kitchen and opens cupboards, looking for glasses. "Do take a seat," she adds, and Siobhan perches on a stool.

Then the doorbell rings.

Siobhan stands up.

"Don't be silly," Lauren says, "sit down, this isn't your job. I'm not impressed that Felix made you come here to sort out his problems. I hope you get paid overtime." She is momentarily inflamed with the desire for justice.

"I don't mind."

"Actually," Lauren says, "maybe if you could get it after all?" It's occurred to her that although this can't be Felix, who would use the code, it's not impossible that he's called some sort of rich-person emergency crew. Maybe a private ambulance that men can send to collect their recalcitrant wives, to take them to some sort of luxury treatment centre? She picks up the bottle of wine and the biscuits, heads back into the bedroom and closes the door. She has learned from that first night that a chair under the handle doesn't do anything so instead she drags the chest of drawers over to block the door completely. *Ooof.*

She hears someone on the landing with Siobhan: ah. Not luxury paramedics. Toby.

"Oh, hey," she says through the door.

"Uh, hi," he says. "Are you okay? I got a call from Felix."

Felix should learn to deal with his own problems. "I'm fine," she says. "I'm just not leaving till he comes. I've been very clear."

"Okay," he says after a moment; she hears Siobhan murmur something but can't make it out. "Can I come in?"

"I'd rather you didn't," she calls back. Last time she was in this bedroom with him it was extremely weird. "Tell you what, how about you make me a cup of tea?" She doesn't want one and isn't going to move the drawers to let him in, but it'll keep him busy.

She is trying so hard to do the right thing.

All she needs is for Felix to play his part.

A few minutes later, a knock on the door. "It's me," Toby

says, and the doorknob twists, and the door opens quietly out-
wards. Ah.

He looks at the drawers, puts a mug on them. "Uh, here's your
tea."

"I'm sorry about the noisy guests," she says. "Please tell Maryam
too. I'm going to put a stop to it."

"Okay," he says. "The important thing is that you're all right.
Are you sure I can't come in?"

"Yes," she says, standing behind the chest of drawers like it's a
shop counter.

He waits.

"Could you shut the door?" she says. And he hesitates a moment,
then closes it gently.

She looks up Carter. Three per cent battery and it's ridiculous to
use it on this, but there's a new photo of him and the woman. He
can't really be as happy as he looks, can he? He can't have put up
tents and chased chickens for her, and then stepped sideways into
another life he loves just as much.

Her battery ebbs lower; her phone turns itself off politely and
she is left alone on the bed. She hears the front door again: Toby
leaving, perhaps.

And then: more hubbub on the landing. And this time, at last,
it's Felix.

"Thanks," she hears him say to Siobhan; then he knocks at the
door and opens it a crack.

"Hey," he says.

"Hey," she replies. "I really thought the door opened inwards,"
she adds, gesturing at the drawers.

A moment of silence. "Siobhan," he says, "thanks, I can take it
from here."

Siobhan gathers her bag. "No problem," she says, almost convincing. "Happy to help."

Lauren watches Felix, who waits until he hears the door close.

"So, what's up?" She was expecting him to sound either worried or angry, but he's something else, carefully neutral, assessing.

"Well," she says. "If you go into the attic I'll explain. There's something up there I want you to see." The ladder is still pulled down behind him.

"I . . . don't think I feel comfortable with that," he says. "Unless you can explain a little bit more. You've got to see this is really odd, right?"

"I promise you won't regret it," she says, "it's nothing danger-ous, it's nothing disgusting. I can't explain it properly. But I'm ask-ing you to trust me. As your wife."

A moment, then: "I'm just going to need more than that," he says.

Okay.

"I don't like to have to do this," she says, "but you'll understand once you see it. I'm going to ask you one more time to climb into the attic. This simple thing, to oblige me, because you love me and you trust me."

Felix looks up at the ladder, and back at her.

"And if you don't," she says, "then I'm afraid I'm going to have to tell everyone your secret."

Like Jason with his favourite dinner, she thinks: presumably he has one.

His eyes widen, just a little. "My . . ."

"You know the one," she says. He is a multi-millionaire, he is chief financial officer for a definitely evil company, he has been divorced twice and married three times, he lets his son use an air rifle and has a room full of dead birds, and she doesn't know what his secret is but there's bound to be *something*. "I didn't want to have to bring it up," she adds.

And his face suddenly changes, and she wonders for a moment if she's made a mistake, if Siobhan knew something she doesn't, if she shouldn't in fact threaten a rich and powerful man while they're alone, and she thinks about yelling for Toby or vaulting over the drawers and into the living room towards the watchful eye of the house camera, but then he says, "Lauren," and, "I don't know what you're talking about," but it's clear he does, and she still doesn't know or care what the secret is, but she says, "It's okay, it's okay, I won't tell anyone, I love you, it's not a big deal, I just need you to look in the attic, just for ten seconds. Five. I promise you'll understand once you're up there."

And she feels bad, she isn't used to seeing him with strong emotions, but he'll feel better soon.

He climbs, a step and then another. His head disappearing into the dark, his torso. She sees the flickering light, and hears the buzz.

And the first thing she notices is that the tension of holding her bladder, which she had barely realised she was doing, has vanished in this new world. The easing of her whole body as she enters a life where she has not been hiding out in the bedroom.

The attic worked.

She steps forward into the doorway that just moments ago had been blocked by drawers and waits for the next husband to descend. Everything is new again; everything is back to normal and everything is different.

CHAPTER 22

The new husband likes to nestle the point of his nose at the inside corner of her closed eye, and press. The one after that likes to lick her ears, get his tongue into the crook of the curlicues. The next pretends to play music on her toes. One puts an egg cosy (in this world, she owns egg cosies) on the tip of his penis.

She lets them pass by her like leaves blowing down the road. They enter her life, she spends a day or two with them, and she sends them onwards.

At first she forces herself to do her research with each of them. She checks in on her job, her friends, her favourites, on Carter and Jason and sometimes even Rohan and Felix, to see if they're doing okay (Felix is in prison, once, which shocks her, but only for lying to people about how successful his company was, and honestly she didn't even realise that was a crime). There's always part of her that hopes she'll find Carter lonely and despondent; but he never is. He's usually with the same happy woman, hanging out in the same Denver bars.

Eventually she stops checking. The world will be changing soon enough anyway. She starts spending her sick days, replenished each time the world changes, on baking, or going for a walk, or reading books. She drops in on Elena, back from her honeymoon, on her lunchbreak, or she has coffee with Toby, who she is almost always on good terms with again. Sometimes she takes a day off and heads into town and spends money she doesn't have: tasting menus, elaborate nail art, browsing the designer bags at Selfridges and buying one and then using it to smuggle a burger into the cinema. Once she fakes an unexpected overnight work trip and goes to Alton Towers and rides the roller coasters, to see if Amos was on to something and a post-relationship amusement park might help her get over Carter, and it doesn't, particularly, but she does have a good time.

Eventually she even starts going to work after all, at least when it's at the council, to chat to Zarah and get out of the house. She has another call with the bakery guy. This time he wants to call his bakery Loaf Is All You Need, which she thinks might be copyright infringement but she's not sure. Is it at least better than the original Loaf Is What You Bake It? She thinks hard, and decides: yeah, maybe?

"We Found Loaf," Zarah suggests when they talk after the call.

"In a hopeless place? Not really on-brand with council messaging. Tainted Loaf?"

Zarah looks genuinely blank at that one.

"You know. *Ba-doomp-doomp.* You must have heard it." She pulls out her phone and plays the first thirty seconds. "Really? Nothing?"

Zarah shrugs. "Sorry, I was born this century."

"It's really famous," Lauren says. "There's a sample of it in Rihanna somewhere."

"I have no idea who that is."

"I'm eight years older than you."

"That's the spirit," Zarah says. "You're only as old as you feel."

o o

Even when she goes into work, she has a lot of spare time. There's no point in exercising: any muscles will melt away the moment she sends a husband into the attic. But she can learn, she thinks, so she studies flowers for a couple of days, thinking back to the version of herself that understood them so well at Felix's. Hydrangea, wisteria, aster, azalea. Different types of climbing roses, until she finds the one that she chose for that red wall. Then she looks up how to take better care of her little succulent, although it turns out the main thing it requires is to be left alone.

She runs out of steam on self-improvement after that, but it's good to know it's possible.

Instead she summons more husbands, and more still.

Sometimes it feels like there's a pattern, something she ought to be able to figure out. Three white Toms in a row, each one taller than the last. Five bald men with beards. Four men from the four countries to most recently win the World Cup. But the pattern always falls apart, and returns to just: men she might have liked, and who might have liked her. Every husband, she's pretty sure, is someone that she might have met, somewhere, somehow, if she'd done things a little differently. Every husband is someone she might have enjoyed spending time with, and who might have enjoyed spending time with her. Every husband is someone that she might—if things had been just a little bit different, if she'd gone to a particular party or worn a particular coat or looked in a particular direction—have married.

Which is not to say that all of them are men it was necessarily a *good idea* to marry.

There is a husband whose devotion to free speech is wearying. A husband who still goes running four times a week with his ex. A husband who claims not to be susceptible to optical illusions, who stares at the giant moon on the horizon and says that it seems like a small and ordinary moon to him, who looks at lines with angled ends and declares that they are all clearly the same length.

Some of the husbands make noises. They say words over and over. One puts his hand on her forehead as she lies in bed, spreads his fingers out and presses, a compression like all her unruly thoughts are being calmed; she misses it when he leaves, tries to explain it to the next husband but he can't get it right. One husband does forty push-ups every morning, and when she asks him how his day went, he shrugs and says, "At least I did forty push-ups." One of them balances on one leg while he brushes his teeth, she never figures out why. One saves his toenail clippings in a small jar, and jokes (she thinks it's a joke, but she never finds out for sure) that he's going to use them to make gelatine when he has enough.

Her nephew, Caleb, stays with her overnight, once; Nat has never permitted this before, and she wonders if it's because she's more respectable now, married, worth trusting with a child, or just because he's a little older. Time is, after all, still passing.

"I'm too old for fish fingers," Caleb says solemnly, confirming. Then, "I want a sausage," and he starts running from room to room and down the stairs to the front door and back up again, making zooming noises. "And ketchup!" he yells.

One husband eats two figs for breakfast every morning, whole, leaving only their stems pinched between the fingertips of each hand.

It gets colder and colder but the occasional sunlit hour allows her to believe that there are more warm days to come, and anyway, she's finding the cold-weather husbands easier to love. She likes cosy. Hot chocolates. Movies on the sofa. Men in cardigans or scarves, like big teddy bears, encumbered, adorable. In summer the husbands dressed worse, they smelled more, they were more often drunk (to be fair, so was she), they barbecued things ineptly or embarked on small-scale DIY and abandoned it halfway through. For these autumnal husbands, she feels affection more easily. She starts to keep them for three or four days, instead of one or two, and even daydreams about finding someone she would like to keep for longer. Not yet, not yet, she's still not ready. She's still getting over Carter, and making the most of the attic and its resets. But maybe soon.

She phones her mum on Tuesdays. Other than that, she accepts her calendar as it comes. An evening babysitting Magda, who pours a full carton of milk into her bag. A day trip to see her old friend Parris in Hastings, which is nice and there's a great bookshop there, although Parris spends a lot of time pointing out how much cheaper the pints and houses are. "But don't spread it around, we don't want everyone coming in and ruining it for us!" she says, unconvincing. An afternoon picking rubbish out of the Thames with a friend who is new to her; they are given an introductory pep talk which includes the warning that they should go to the doctor if they have a fever or nausea symptoms afterwards, because there's a chance it could be a disease spread by rat urine in the water. London!

A production of *Antigone* in a multi-storey car park in Peckham, with Rob and Elena and the husband; the audience is invited to chase the actors down stairwells and through mysterious doorways, and she and Rob find themselves trapped with one of the leads in a lift. The actor has a walkie-talkie, and does a valiant job of alerting production staff to the issue while remaining in character.

The husband, who booked the tickets, is annoyed to have missed out on the special individualised experience.

"I don't think it was scripted," she says. "I think the lift just got stuck," and when that doesn't cheer him up, she sends him away.

While he's up there, she heads into the bathroom to fluff her hair and swipe on some lipstick to greet the next husband. It's nice to get the new life off on the right foot. Clatter and buzz and crackle above: back on the landing, legs are emerging, and the husband climbs down and turns and, after a moment, smiles.

He's one of the cute ones. She smiles back. "Hey. Welcome to the landing." It turns out you can just say that to a husband and usually he'll accept it.

"Good to see you too," he says.

He's stocky rather than slender; looks East Asian, about her age. An accent—maybe Australian?

The house around them is tidier than usual, and brighter. A print of an old geology poster in a frame. A new yellow vase with flowers that she recognises from her couple of days of self-improvement: dahlias.

The husband is gazing around the landing as well. "Hey, seeing as I've done all that work in the attic," he says, "I would *love* a cup of tea."

"I'll bring it through to the living room," she says. Perfect. She can check her phone, look round the kitchen, scope out this life. She glances at a hall table with letters, where she finds the husband is called Bohai Strickland Zhang, and that she is Lauren Zhang Strickland. Yes, that'll work.

He's right behind her, picks up one of the letters, heads into the spare room for a minute then through to the living room.

Phone: a mix of logistical and affectionate texts to Bohai. Toby and Nat and Elena: yep, looks good, although her most recent message from Elena just reads *BARRY SPILES*, which is a bit of a puzzle. Her job is unchanged.

The kettle (new) boils. The teabags (Yorkshire branded) are out on the counter. Only almond milk in the fridge. She tries milk and no sugar.

When she brings the mugs through, Bohai is on his phone by the window, scrolling. "Tea," she says, and he looks up and smiles. He has a quality only a few of the husbands have had, of seeming to look at her with renewed attention each time instead of seeing her as familiar background. Maybe they're newlyweds.

"So," he says, leaning back into the armchair as she settles on the sofa. "What have you got planned for the week?"

"Nothing special." She pulls up her calendar: dinner with Rob and Elena, not much else. "What about you?"

"Yeah," he says. "Nothing fancy."

He takes another sip of his tea; she echoes the motion, and looks around. The windows seem brighter than usual, almost as if—oh, wait. She looks at the calendar again. For the last eight days, the calendar reads: *SHAN*.

That's why it's so clean: they had a guest. Photos on her phone show the husband and an older woman out at the park, under an umbrella. His mum? "Did Shan get back home okay?" she asks casually.

He takes another sip of tea. "Yeah, as far as I know. I mean, she'd have told us otherwise, right?"

They sink into silence again but it's not companionable; not tense either, just a little awkward. Maybe they had a big fight and they're both trying really hard, maybe something happened with his probably-mum, maybe they've got a big decision to make that they're avoiding.

"Telly?" he says, and she says "Yes" almost before he's finished speaking. Even more *Mindhunter* will do.

But the Netflix menu's "Continue Watching" is a documentary on seals, another documentary about pretending to live in the nineteenth century, and *Friends*. The husband hesitates, then clicks.

It plays: mid-season somewhere, but it's hard to be sure because it's dubbed into French.

This has come up before, husbands with whom she has evidently learned at least a little German or Arabic or Romanian; sometimes as a shared hobby, sometimes so she can say hello to his family and chat for a couple of minutes. Her French vocabulary extends to *le train, le billet, la baguette, bonjour* and how to count to twenty. This husband might not be a long-termer.

Still, their house is *so* clean; even if it's only for the sake of their visitor it would be a waste to chuck it away. She can watch twenty-two minutes of a sitcom in a language she doesn't speak. For her husband.

She browses her phone while the Friends cavort. She can't find any wedding photos, not easily—they must have been married a while—and she can't find anything in their messages to explain why things are weird either.

"Hey," the husband, Bohai, says after a few minutes. "Did you hear that?"

She listens. "Hear what?"

"I dunno, a thump? Up in the attic."

Could there be another husband? Surely not. "I didn't hear anything."

"I might check," he says. "Maybe something fell over?"

It's a shame, she thinks. She's tired. It would have been good to head to bed, have a nice sleep, see how things looked in the morning instead of dealing with another new man. Ah well. Some marriages just don't work out.

"Okay," she says. Can she be bothered putting new lipstick on to greet the next husband? She stays on the sofa and listens to this one pull the ladder down, hears him struggling for a moment to get it over the bit where you need to jerk it across at an angle.

It sounds properly jammed. "To the left," she calls out.

"Oh yeah," he says, and she hears it slide.

Huh.

"Thanks," he adds.

She's still figuring it out, she can't think fast enough. "Wait," she says.

"Yeah, just a sec," she hears him call back. She stands up, half-tangled in the blanket, lets it fall and strides through. He's only a step or two up; his head is about to disappear through the hole.

"No," she says.

"I'll just be—"

She steps forward and puts a hand up, grabs his shirt, at the limit of how high she can reach. He looks down, his face outlined by the square of the attic above him. "I'll be back in a moment," he says, annoyed.

"I don't think you should go up there," she says.

"I heard the noise again."

She knows this conversation. But she knows it from the other side.

Is she right? She can't be.

But she is. It's the ladder that gives it away; if he really lived here, he would know how to pull down the ladder. And he doesn't.

"I'll be right back," he says, and tugs the fabric of his shirt out of her hand, and takes another step up, and she's only got a moment before he's gone for ever, so she grabs again, he's two steps higher, and she says, "No, you won't. Right? You won't be back."

The husband looks down. His head is already through the hatch, the light flickering above him.

She keeps talking. "Right? You'll be off in some other attic? In a different house?"

He stops trying to shake her hand free; she keeps clutching the fabric, looking up.

"Oh," he says, and she releases him.

He takes a step down, then another, and then to the ground.

"I'm not your first wife," she says.

"No," he says, carefully.

She nods. "You're not my first husband either."

"How—how many husbands have you had?"

She thinks. "A hundred and sixty."

They're silent.

"What about you?" she asks. "How many wives?"

He nods, hand still on the ladder. "I don't—I don't know exactly. But, four years' worth. Maybe four hundred. Something like that."

"Okay," she says. She looks up into the attic again, and back at him. "If I go and make some more tea, are you going to stay to drink it?"

He's still staring at her, then he steps away from the ladder and hugs her, and she hugs back, and she's laughing and even crying and the relief, the *relief*, to not be alone in this, the astonishment of it, and she looks at his face, blurred by tears and proximity, looking back.

CHAPTER 23

They're talking fast as they settle back in the living room, sitting at the table.

"It's been *years*—"

"It started this summer—"

"All of a sudden—"

"Just climb out into a new marriage—"

They trail into silence and start again.

"I thought something was wrong with me, I kept going to hospital—"

"It's so hard to keep track—"

And again, they stop. Bohai looks around the room, and back at Lauren.

"So," Lauren says. "To be clear. You've spent the last *four years* climbing into attics, then coming down, and every time you do you've got a different wife in a different house."

He nods. "It's not always an attic. Sometimes it's a shed or a cupboard? Or a wardrobe, pantry, you get the idea. And it's—not always wives? But yeah."

"So physically, how does that work? Like, do you see it change? Does it happen as soon as you go in or when you come out? Do you get the electricity thing? I always get this crackle with the husbands, and the light comes on. But if anyone else goes up it's fine?"

"Yeah!" he says. "I get that! Like any electronics, Christmas tree lights, phones, old hard drives, they all come on. Started a little fire once, which was terrifying, ran straight back into another life and I didn't know what country I was in so I couldn't even search the news to make sure I hadn't burned the whole house down."

"Wait," she says, catching up, playing back things he's said. "They're not always wives. Girlfriends? Fiancées?"

"Nah," he says, "you know, husbands?"

"Oh! Wow, right, sorry." Should she stop prying, is she being rude? In this specific case it's probably okay.

Bohai's still talking. "So you get new husbands from the attic. Always the attic? Always husbands?"

"Yeah," she says. "Old husband goes up, new husband comes down. Wait—did *all* my husbands know what was going on? Were they faking it?"

"Nah, mine for sure don't," Bohai says. "I've tried telling them a few times. When we got on really well, or one time she was really into science fiction and I thought she might understand."

"No luck?"

He shakes his head.

"Yeah," she says, "I tried telling a couple of people and it doesn't go well."

"Can't blame 'em."

"God," she says, "I don't even know where to start. Wait, why were you going back up into the attic so fast?" Usually she exchanges the husband: it's a bit of a blow to find that the first husband with a choice was eager to exchange her.

"It felt weird. I try not to stay long if I think it's not working."

He's not wrong: it did feel weird.

"You'd know," she says. "Four years."

"Yeah, four and a half maybe," he says.

"And four hundred wives? Partners, sorry. So one a week?"

"Not really? Mostly I stay with them for maybe a day, then I move. But the longest was a couple of years."

Years! She can't really imagine it, sticking with one husband for so long and then just leaving for another world. She starts to ask for more details, but he's talking again: "Sorry, do you mind if I look around?"

"Oh," she says. "Yeah, of course."

He looks in the kitchen, and the bedroom, and the spare room. The staircase. The living room again.

He walks to the window and looks out. "This is the UK?"

"Norwood Junction. South London. You're not always in London?"

He shakes his head fast. "God no, thank fuck. Maybe one time in five. Mostly Sydney? Or Bordeaux for some reason, I guess there's something about it I like but it stresses me out because the version of me that lives there must speak French, but with my actual brain I absolutely don't."

"Wait, so you didn't understand the—"

"The telly? Nah. Did you?"

"Not a bit."

They laugh. "Yeah, sometimes I turn up and someone speaks to me in French and I go straight back into the attic. Honestly, I should just learn—I did try but every time I change worlds all my Duolingo progress resets."

"And the cities aren't random?"

"It's got to be places I might have ended up somehow, I think? Places I like? Well, sometimes I'm in Melbourne or Brighton, and they suck, but I guess love brought me there or whatever. Sometimes Singapore. Got to Perth a couple times in 2020 and stayed for a while, not usually my kind of town but it was hard to look past *Oh nobody here has Covid and everything's open, let's get brunch.* New York once, fucking amazing city, everyone there thinks it's the centre of the world and it's not, but they believe it so hard, I love it, stayed for months, but my husband was a dick and we had cockroaches in the kitchen, so. Hated San Francisco, loved LA, keep hoping I'll end up in Buenos Aires or Tokyo or something for a change but nah, not yet anyway."

"I'm always here." In her house, waiting for someone to descend from the attic.

"Makes sense. Not like you're going to wake up one morning and the attic's in Bucharest, right?"

"Yeah, I just—it'd be nice to have a change." Imagine: new things, new worlds, choosing to step through into another life whenever you want instead of tricking someone into doing it for you.

"So what happens if you go up there yourself?" Bohai asks.

"You know what," she says, "I haven't tried. It's always felt too dangerous. But it does the electricity thing if I put my head up, and it doesn't do that for anyone else except the husbands. God, maybe I should give it a go."

"Yeah, dunno," Bohai says. "It's good, obviously. Travelling without going through airport security. But with your way, you get to keep your stuff, right? Like, this is all—objects you own?" He gestures around the house.

"Some of it," she says. "A lot of it'll be yours."

"Yeah, clothes, some books; when we were in the kitchen I saw this big Dutch oven I have sometimes. But I can never rely on it. And I never know how the buses work."

She does like having Toby and Maryam downstairs, whoever's in the house with her; and she hasn't been going to her job all the time, but it's reassuring when it's there.

"That said," he continues, "a few years back I was in a cave—like, it'd never been a natural formation before, usually it's attics or sheds or big cupboards—anyway, this time it was a cave under a fucking waterfall pouring into a blue lagoon, and it was hot and we had this house on sticks, the middle of nowhere. And I'd never ever have gone there if it wasn't for the, you know." He gestures with a twiddle of his hand, *magic attic or whatever.*

"You didn't stay?"

"Nah, it was a bit much."

"Oh, come on," she says. "You couldn't adjust because your life was too idyllic and the waterfalls were too beautiful?"

"Yeah, I mean also it turned out I was having an affair with my sister-in-law which I did *not* want to have to keep up for more than a fortnight."

She leans back. "You were having an affair with your *sister-in-law*."

"I know!" he says. "I don't know what I was thinking. What the fuck, Bohai, right? It was a while back, I guess, I was young. I'm not usually having any affairs these days so I guess most of the time I've learned my lesson? And if it does look like I'm cheating I head off to a new life. It's one of my rules."

"You were going to leave here," she says. "Are you cheating on *me*?" She's mostly joking, but only mostly.

"I don't think so. I haven't had long to look into it, though. It's hard to tell sometimes, I'm really good at covering my tracks." He shrugs, apologetic.

She can't deal with the influx of new information; she keeps running back sentences in her head, trying to catch up with everything in every direction at once. "One of your rules," she says. "What are the other rules?"

"Hey," he says, "would you mind if I had something to eat? I don't know if we had dinner or not before I turned up but I'm super hungry."

"Yeah," she says. "Good call. Me too, actually." It's later than she realised, coming up on nine. They investigate the kitchen together, opening the fridge and the cupboards. Bohai lifts the lid on a big enamel pot on the oven and puts it back, pats it gently. There's half a frittata in a container in the fridge. Perhaps she's back in the habit of making them.

"Takeaway?" he says.

She checks her bank balance, and it's not too bad. No joint

account; a payment from Bohai once a month, and she sorts out bills from there. "Sure."

They go through the options. "The pizza's decent," she says, "dumplings are okay, the sushi's bad, there's an okay burger place."

He keeps scrolling. "Burritos?"

"Yeah, they'll close soon, though, so choose fast." She's been through this process with so many husbands, ordering delivery, balancing their tastes and her own.

"Can you keep stuff when the world changes?" he says, while they wait for the order to arrive. "Make notes?"

"God, if only. No. For a while I wrote a list of names whenever I started a new husband but now I just try to keep count and remember the important ones." Her formal number is a hundred and sixty, but she probably missed or double-counted a few. "What about you?"

"Oh." He lights up. "I actually—I have a little song. I add the partners as I go. I didn't start till number thirty so it's a bit vague at the start and there was a month where I was just going through them fast. But the important ones."

"A song."

"Yeah"—he's so delighted at getting to explain this—"so it's rhyming couplets but also each rhyme word from the second line in the couplet is the first word in the next couplet, to make it easier to remember. Except then sometimes I really can't make it work so I just start a new verse." He clears his throat. "Shit, I've never done this out loud to anyone before. I'm a terrible singer. Okay. Here's a bit from the middle:

Look, it's Lachlan up in Brizzy,
Me and them got plenty busy.
Busy too with Afan A,
But in a painting kitchens way.
Way too young was student Bea,

Way too grumpy Hayden Three.
Three or four then quickly passed:
Some were nameless, Bim the last.
Last with Liz I might have stayed,
Except she lived in Adelaide."

"How *long* is this song?" Lauren says.

"I don't have, like, a whole line for everyone. It's more about how much time I spent there, you know? If I think I owe them." He shrugs, a little sheepish.

She starts asking for more details, but the burritos arrive. They compare food stories while they eat, his worst takeaways, her husbands and their least-inspiring dishes.

"A fried lettuce thing," she says, that was an early husband. "A big baguette stuffed with cheese and chopped-up fake bacon and microwaved, god, it was disgusting. Oh, and so many of them have a special bolognese recipe. And it's never good." Usually when this happens the husband has an Italian ex-girlfriend from whom he learned a supposedly authentic yet surprising recipe, with one special touch: anchovies (twice), Worcestershire sauce (three times), coffee (once), buttermilk (once, particularly bad).

"Oh yeah, some of mine have that too. Like, their high-school girlfriend Maria whose sexy aunt told them to put coriander in it or something."

"Look," Lauren says, and leans forward. "You're going to stay for a few days, right? I'll make up the spare room and we can call in sick in the morning?"

"Yeah," he says, "of course. Of course. I mean, apart from anything else, I'd love to not meet another new wife tonight. You were the fourth, I had a bad run. Kids everywhere."

"You had—no, never mind. Let's get everything set up."

The bed in the spare room has been stripped, presumably after

Bohai's mum's visit, but there are more sheets in the cupboard. She can't, however, find any men's pajamas.

"I do sleep naked a lot," he says apologetically, looking in drawers. "I might not have any. Shorts?"

She finds some underpants (boxers, it turns out) and a T-shirt, passes them over.

"Weird, isn't it," he says. "Happy to lie with no clothes on next to a wife I've never met before, but as soon as we're both in on it I want to stay dressed and take the other bed."

It's true: she's had plenty of strange naked men in the house lately, but this one knows he's a strange man, and that makes all the difference.

"Night," he calls out from the spare room, through the open door and the landing and into hers, "sleep well."

"You too," she calls back. "Hey, have you had any other wives called Lauren?"

He laughs. "I don't think so. Had a Laura."

"That's acceptable," she calls back. It's like a sleepover, like camp. If she strains, she can hear him breathing as she falls asleep.

CHAPTER 24

The next morning, Bohai calls into work for her, embroidering elaborate stomach problems. She exchanges the favour by calling his co-worker at, he figures out from his phone, a training school for guide dogs.

"God," he says, "I have no fucking consistency in jobs. I don't even like dogs. Their big eyes."

"You don't like *dog eyes*?"

"Too pleading," he says.

They've gone out for breakfast at a cafe a fifteen-minute walk away, on the far side of the park. It's a Thursday morning at eleven a.m. so it isn't crowded, and it's warm for October; they find a table outside, sunlight through trees as more leaves drop. The park spreads before them: a lake, a toddler running. Summer was just starting when her first husband emerged.

There's so much Lauren wants to know: where does she start? But Bohai pulls out a piece of paper. "Anyway," he says, "I couldn't sleep last night so I made some notes."

Perfect. "Let's go."

"Okay. First of all, we age, right?" Bohai asks. "Like, it's hard for me to be sure because different lives, different lifestyles. But nowadays I almost always have these," and he leans forward and points at two furrows between his eyebrows, vertical where her own perpetual crease runs horizontally, "and, like, crinkly bits around the eyes if I'm somewhere sunny. Which is something London has going for it actually, way less UV damage, way less squinting into the sunlight because there's no fucking sunlight to squint into."

They're literally sitting in sunlight as they speak, but she stays on topic. "I do look different sometimes," she says. "But I've only been doing this three or four months."

"Yeah, tell me *everything* about how it started."

She has run through the details so often in her head, the party, the bus, Michael on the stairs. And she's said it out loud a few times as well, and it's gone badly, every time. Even now, as she explains it, she half expects Bohai to start questioning her, to explain that she must be mistaken, to laugh it off.

But: no. "Yeah," he says, "mine was just as weird, honestly. I was on this trip with friends to a holiday house in the country, back in Australia obviously. And the place was massive, so we decided to play hide-and-seek. And not to boast or anything but I'm really fucking good at hide-and-seek. So I squirmed away behind a panel in the back of a cupboard and then this buzzy static noise started so I crawled out as fast as I could and it turned out I was living by the beach with a wife called Margery."

"Huh."

"Yeah, it was a puzzle, I can tell you. I've tried renting the same big house a couple times and going back into the cupboard, just to see. But nothing happens. Then I have to head off for a new world before my husband or whoever finds out I put four and a half thousand dollars on the credit card to go and stay alone in a winery mansion."

The waitress brings their plates out and they fall silent for a minute. Bohai grabs salt and pepper and ketchup from another table.

"Next question," he says. "All husbands, right?"

"Yeah. And you get a mix," she says.

"More than half husbands. Which isn't—like, in my original life I dated more women, so it's a bit weird that it's the other way round now. But I reckon it makes sense because I'm kind of not that into marriage as a concept, you know? So I probably get carried away more with guys? With men you're like *fuck it yeah let's get married, take that, those who would deny us, I defy the looming disapproval of the law and a dozen uncles*, but with women it's more *the burden of history bids me wed you, gross*. No offence. And not that I don't do it often enough. Four hundred spouses."

"That's a lot of spouses for someone who's not into marriage as a concept," she says.

"Yeah, I think I've got to accept that I'm absolutely into marriage as a concept, but I'm also into being the sort of person who isn't into marriage as a concept, as a concept. This whole situation makes it hard to trick yourself about what you're like."

He's got a few more things on his list, but she's remembered something from the night before. "You said you have rules for marriages."

"Yeah!" he says. "When I think I might stay for a while, I do my due diligence. No cheating, no children, no visa marriages. What about you?"

"I don't really have any rules yet. Had a visa marriage once but he was great. Top-five husband. And I don't want kids but it hasn't come up much."

"Don't want them yet, or don't want them ever?"

"Not ever, I think," she says. She loves Caleb and Magda but even a couple of hours with them is exhausting. She feels like she did her fair share of caretaking when her dad was sick: Nat had been off at uni by then, so it had just been her and her mum, taking turns for a long six months before hospice care. "You too, from the sound of it?"

He wiggles a hand from side to side. "It's not that. I kind of want kids. No, you know what, I really do. But I want to actively decide I want them, you know? I don't want to go: *oh I've got three six-year-olds in this universe and I guess I love them so I've got to stay because if I climb back into the cupboard they'll vanish.* Right? When you leave a husband he's still around, he's just not your husband any more. But if you have kids, biological kids anyway, they full-on don't exist if you leave, you weren't there so they're not there either. Early on I turned up once and found out my wife was pregnant, and we didn't get on but I already felt responsible to the future kid, like: *I guess I'd better stay or it's gonna vanish.* But we were such a bad match. So in the end I left before he was born and it—I don't know—it didn't feel great. I looked the wife up after I left and she had three kids in her new life, so good on her, but obviously none of them were mine. And now if there's any sign of kids at all I leave as soon as I can, before I meet them even, before I find out whether they're stepkids or nieces or mine or whatever. Stick your head out, see Lego, pull your head back in. You miss out on the adult Lego fans as well I guess but, like, you win some, you win some, right?" And he smiles a big smile which, she thinks, he definitely believes to be charming.

"You said you'd stayed somewhere for two years?" she asks. She can't really imagine it; or rather, she can't imagine staying that long and then leaving.

He nods. "Maybe closer to a year and a half. Living in Sydney, which for me is always a good start. Married to this guy called, well, Hanwen, but he went by Jack for the Anglos. Honestly, I haven't found myself with that many Chinese partners, I guess because of the whole, like, *lo, with this marriage do I defy my imaginary critics* thing. But it was nice."

"What did you do?"

"Oh, lights and tech for a little theatre company, which obviously was all new to me. But theatres were just opening back up again and, you know, closing again and opening again, so everyone was out of practice and I got away with a lot. Then for a while I had a uni student on work experience, and that helped. I pulled a lot of *what do you think we should do, talk me through the options*, which is a godsend, highly recommended."

"That's really smart," she says.

"Right? Anyway," Bohai says, "there I was, married to Jack, who did finance stuff so I was the glamorous trophy husband, which was obviously good for my ego. We weren't monogamous, and normally that's not my thing—"

She laughs. "Mr. Hundred Spouses a Year? Mr. Slept with His Sister-in-Law?"

"Look, I'm not saying I'm always great at monogamy but I like to try. Anything else, I dunno, I get jealous. But our flat was amazing, my job was a good time once I got the hang of it, and Jack was great, I liked him a lot. We had fun. Didn't fight much. I mean, he never cleaned the kitchen but if that's the worst you can say it's a good marriage, I reckon."

"Why did you leave?"

"Ah." He puts his fork down. "It's a bit of a grim one. Jack was coming to pick me up after a show and he was in a car accident, it was pretty bad. I thought—I mean, it's not that I'm not great," and he gestures appreciatively at himself, "but probably he'd rather not be, you know, touch and go on making it. And I don't know what would have happened if he'd died and then I'd only switched worlds after, if it'd be too late. So, better reset his life for him."

"Wow. I'm really sorry."

"Yeah," he says, "anyway, I look him up sometimes and he's usually doing fine. Went to a bar he used to like till he came in once, which I thought would be just like old times but in the end I learned a few things about his tastes in casual sex that he did *not* reveal to mere husbands, I can tell you. What about you?"

"Oh," she says. "Well, I'm still new to this. There was an American guy I liked a lot, Carter, and I think he liked me. I mean, I guess they all must have liked me but he seemed really glad that we were together, you know? But he climbed back in the attic while I wasn't looking."

"Oh, wow, that sounds like a fucker," Bohai says. "Sorry," he adds to a woman walking past them with a toddler in a pushchair.

"I mean, maybe we wouldn't have worked out," Lauren says. "Obviously a week's nothing compared to two years." She can't quite imagine how she would have felt if she'd been with Carter that long, and then he'd climbed away.

"It's not a competition," Bohai says, "we can both be really sad about our husbands if you like."

They sit in silence for a minute.

"Honestly," she says, "I'd rather not."

"Yeah, me either."

"Come on," she says with renewed enthusiasm. "What's the weirdest room you've ever climbed out into?"

"Oh," he says. "There was one full of balloons. Like, up to my neck deep. There was one with eight corgis. There was one where my wife was using garden shears to cut my clothes up, that was terrifying."

"Did you figure out why?"

He shrugs. "Just climbed back in, but I dunno, probably the cheating again, right? Maybe gambling, that comes up sometimes. Like I said, seeing your life play out four hundred times is a real shortcut to all the ways you might turn out to be a dickhead. Sorry," he says again, to the same mother, pushing her child back in the opposite direction.

"Shall we head into the park?" Lauren says. The tables near them have filled up, and she doesn't want to talk about this within everyone's hearing, even apart from Bohai's exuberant swearing.

They walk towards the lake and its straggly ducks. "How do you decide when to stop?" She means: how do *I* decide.

He shrugs. "Still working on that one. You thinking about it, then? Picking one and keeping him?"

Not consciously—she's still been in easy-come easy-go mode, but it's been a long few months of fleeting husbands. There are only so many times she can spend a day skipping work and eating an overpriced lunch and buying something ill-advised and then wiping it all out.

"I don't know," she says. "I might try."

"In that case," Bohai says, "is there a newsagent's somewhere nearby? We're going to need a whole lot of Post-it notes."

CHAPTER 25

The relief of it. For the next week they stop a dozen times a day to laugh, or to say it out loud.

Nice flat you've got here, glad I climbed out of your attic.

I like this big blue pot you've brought, much better than the tartan plates the last husband had.

They figure out that they met online; no friends in common, no workplaces, different parts of town, different hobbies, lives that almost didn't touch.

"But okay, this is more fun," Lauren says. "I'm reconstructing from messages to Elena so no guarantees, but . . . it looks like you proposed at that little park near Liverpool Street, you know, where there's all those plaques to dead Victorians?"

"Oh yeah, makes sense. Love that shit. *Mother, I saved him, but I could not save myself.* Literally feeling teary now. Bet I didn't plan it or anything, it was probably, like, birds were singing and I was thinking *I cannot fucking believe I've found someone who'll come and watch me cry at heroic plaques.*"

"God," she says, "I don't think I want to know what your wedding speech was like."

They search for stories about attics and read things aloud to each other all afternoon, then write partner priorities on the Post-it notes that Bohai bought and stick them to the window.

GOOD HAIR, Bohai writes on one Post-it, then adds, OR NO HAIR. "Nothing in between."

She puts FOREARMS on one. INTERESTING SKILL. KNOWS WHAT HE WANTS. OWNS SCARF.

They look up significant exes. Bohai's Jack is single, and has just been promoted. His LinkedIn account features a recent post on the importance of insight.

"The thing we forget about insight," Lauren reads aloud, sonorous, "is that it's only possible when the subject you're addressing is just that: *in sight*."

"I know," Bohai says. "Obviously the business chat isn't something I'm actively looking for. But he didn't talk like that at home, you know? I miss him, I miss how he could always tell when I was lying, I miss his three-thousand-dollar suits." He takes another Post-it and writes, LOOKS GOOD IN FORMALWEAR. "Anyway," he adds, "I'd like to see your rich business husband do better."

She searches for Felix, who seems like he might be married to the nanny, or perhaps to someone else named Delphine. No LinkedIn, though, which makes her feel a little smug, and there's a recording of a talk he gave at a conference that's been watched thirty thousand times. She presses play, and it's incredibly boring, she gets thirty seconds in before Bohai makes her mute it, but Felix is, somehow, charismatic once the sound's off, serious face, measured gestures, lots of eye contact, the occasional business smile. They stream it to the television and watch him gesticulate silently.

"You know what," Bohai says, "I kind of get it."

Michael is married to someone else this time, not the woman who died, and his child is a tiny baby, huge-eyed, curly-haired. Jason is still running his own garden business; single, as far as she can tell. Carter isn't in Denver with his usual partner; instead, he's in Seattle with a tall blonde.

"You're prettier than her," Bohai says. "And actually he's not *that* good-looking either."

"He doesn't photograph well. It's partly the walk," she says. "The stance."

Bohai writes, WALK AND/OR STANCE IS SOMEHOW ENTIC-ING on a Post-it and holds it up.

Lauren remembers something she read a few husbands ago, after a morning spent googling *How do people decide who to marry*. Searches again, finds what she's looking for. "Hey," she says. "Have you heard of the secretary problem?"

He hasn't.

"Okay," she says. "A while back I was trying to figure out what I'd have to do if I wanted to find a husband to keep. And it turns out someone's done math about it. Like, the math that gives you the highest possible chance of finding the best partner, or hiring the best secretary."

"Those feel like really different problems."

She shrugs. "Sure, let's start with the secretary side of it, then. You're trying to find the best girl—"

Bohai raises his eyebrows. "Is this math guy from 1952?"

"—and you've got a load of interviews lined up. And each time one of the candidates comes in, at the end of the interview you decide if you want to hire her. But you have to decide right there. If you say no you can't go back to her later. And if you don't hire anyone you're stuck with whoever's last, even if she's terrible."

"I just don't think that's how job interviews work, even in 1952."

"Sure, no. But what do you do?"

"Have a set of predetermined scoring criteria so that you can work against your unconscious biases?" He gestures at the Post-it notes. "Call in references? Take them on a trial basis?"

"Mathematically," she says, "you should say no to the first thirty-seven per cent of candidates, then yes to the first person you see who's better than any of them."

When he's thinking hard, his eyes flick round, left, right, look-ing at imaginary logic. "What's thirty-seven per cent of infinity?"

Yeah, fair. "Wait, no," she says, "you're gonna die, right?"

"That's such a rude thing to say."

"How old are you?"

"None of your business."

"I'm your wife," she says.

He rolls his eyes. "Fine. I'm thirty-five."

"Then let's say you live till you're eighty-five, so fifty-five years of partners."

"Gimme till ninety-five," he says. "My family lives super old. In most lives I've still got four out of four grandparents."

Well, good for him. "That means you've got sixty-five years of spouses from when you started, so thirty-seven per cent is"—she pulls up the calculator on her phone—"twenty-four years, and you started at thirty so you should keep—shit, you should keep switching till you're fifty-four? Then you stop the first time you get someone who's the best yet."

He groans. "No. I'm not gonna do it. That'd be, what, two thousand spouses? I know what your math guy says but listen, I've been through *four hundred* already, it's not like I don't have a sense of the range of people who . . . exist. I'm not going to get any new information from making out with another sixteen hundred strangers."

"Okay," she says, "so you're looking to settle down?"

He makes a noise, *ugggh*, and sits up. "Yeah," he says, "look, things ended badly with Jack, and that was only a few months ago, and I was in that world for ages, so half the length of the relationship to get over it, right? I reckon I've got another six months or so before I need to start thinking about dating seriously. Marrying seriously."

She hadn't realised Jack was so recent. "Yeah," she says. "Okay."

"But I want to stop again," he says. "Of course I do. I want a life where I know where I'm going to be in a week. I want to . . . pre-order something. I want to buy an overambitious spice mix and then never open it and throw it out three years later way past its best-before date."

Yeah. "Me too," she says, and she hadn't been sure before but as she says it, it feels true. "I just have to find the right place to stop."

○ ○

Between the Post-its and the stories and the glory of talking openly, they neglect everything else, including their calendars, so they're surprised when, at half past seven on Sunday, Elena and Rob turn up at the door.

Lauren prepares her lie, but she doesn't need to use it: Bohai is already there, explaining while she gathers up the notes still stuck over the wall.

"I'm so sorry," he says, "my sister had to go in for emergency surgery, only appendicitis but it's still a shock, and we were waiting for news and we totally forgot you were coming. But we've just heard: she's out of surgery, she's woken up, she's doing well, they've got the appendix out. We might have to order delivery for dinner, though!"

It's perfect: a good enough excuse, but one that won't put a pall over the evening. If anything, it adds joy to the night.

In the toilet, she messages him: *Rob and Elena, Elena's the one with the hen party, they got married this summer.* But when she comes out, she finds him opening the bottle of wine Rob's brought and laughing at a joke, absolutely convincing.

"Anyway, Rob's mum," Elena says over dinner, "thinks that now we're married we have to start having kids immediately, and when we told her we were getting a dog she looked like we'd stabbed her. It's not like people can't have a dog and a baby at the same time!"

"No," Lauren agrees.

"But we do need to get a move on or else she's going to heist an egg and gestate a baby for us in the microwave, she is *obsessed.*"

Elena looks at Bohai expectantly.

"That . . . sounds sensible," he says.

"So is there any . . . news?" Elena asks.

"On . . ."

Is Bohai . . . donating sperm? Surely if that was an issue with Rob, Elena would have told her some drunk night or other. Elena continues: ". . . on the dogs?"

Oh. *Oh.* Lauren remembers Bohai's first day, the research they did into his life in London. "The guide dogs."

Bohai blinks at her.

"That you train," Lauren adds. "For your job."

"Any adorable flunk-outs?" Rob says.

Lauren can only watch Bohai, but he catches up fast. "I'm so sorry," he says, "but we've got a bumper crop this time. Sometimes I try teaching one wrong when the other trainers aren't looking, to see if I can get her to fail for you, but they're all too smart."

At the end of the night, the door closed at last behind their visitors, he flops back on to the sofa. "Oh my god," he says, "fuck," long and drawn out, "the dogs. I'd forgotten I even had a job here."

Lauren had, too. She sits on the armchair and stretches her legs on to the coffee table, and searches. "Here you *are*," she says, turning the iPad to show a photo of Bohai and three beautiful dogs. She is drunk on triumph and wine.

Bohai takes the tablet and finds another picture of him with a dog. "Definitely not my worst job. One time I did funerals. And once I did organic skincare sales."

Lauren takes the tablet back. "What's the most different the world's ever been for you?" she says. "The biggest change."

"I check the news a lot," he says, "but there's never been, like, the megafauna are back, or Australia's just won the World Cup, or the climate's settled down and we don't have to rinse out our recycling any more. Which is obviously a mixed bag because it'd be great to get to a universe that's less fucked, but it's comforting too, means we're powerless against the forces of history so we might as well watch *Mindhunter*."

"I guess. I mean not *Mindhunter* specifically."

He looks at her speculatively. "Hey, do you think we're meant to be together?"

She says "What?" like she doesn't understand, but it's not as if it hasn't occurred to her.

"As far as we know we're the only people this has happened to. If there were thousands of us, someone would've written about it, right? We'd find it *somewhere*. Instead it's just, like, there are those movies where a hard-working city girl gets hit on the head by a Christmas tree and she wakes up married to some guy with a chin, and she learns the true meaning of Christmas and then when she gets back to her original world everything is normal again but she decides to go home for the holidays after all and on the plane the guy is sitting next to her and Santa winks. You know."

"What? No."

"Yeah," he says. "Really? You haven't seen . . . ? Look, we can watch it later. God, I'm making a mess of this, sorry, but look." He sets his glass down. "We haven't really talked about what I'm doing here but I was thinking maybe it'd be nice to stay for a while longer? Not for ever, I'm not being weird, I don't really think we're meant to be together. I don't want to keep you from your husbands. But it's good to be able to talk about it, right?"

They're pretty sure they'll be able to stay in touch after he moves on, that they'll both remember, that they'll be able to email each other or get a coffee whenever Bohai's in London, but they can't be certain till they try it. And there's something special about being in this world together.

It is. "Yeah," she says. "That would be great."

"Maybe," and he sounds a little bit nervous, like he's asking too much, "maybe a month or two? It's fine if not, no problem, obviously, it's just that I'm still kinda dealing with the Jack thing and this is a great break and, you know, not to get soppy or anything but it's nice to be somewhere I don't have to constantly lie about every important thing in my life."

"I'd love that," she says. "How about you stay till the new year?"

He smiles, that admittedly quite charming smile. "Perfect," he says.

CHAPTER 26

They settle into it fast. Bohai spends a lot of time out of the house: parks, bars, nights out with friends he's never met before.

They go to a pub quiz with Toby and Maryam. Toby does flags of the world and history; Maryam takes the lead on science, and barrels through a multiple-choice language round with her mix of Farsi, German and medical Greek and Latin. There are a lot of picture rounds and Bohai, to Lauren's surprise, is great at identifying ingredients.

They're doing well, but the next round is a list of the birth names of singers and actors, under a heading: *Better Known As . . .*

They stare at the list. "Just put Marilyn Monroe for all of them," Bohai says.

"For Alphonso d'Abruzzo?" Maryam asks.

"Look, *one* of them's going to be Marilyn Monroe, do we want to get one point or zero?"

Lauren goes to the bar. It's a shame she's not more useful in the quiz but she is, at least, good at carrying four drinks at once without spilling them. But when she gets back they're on another picture round, and it's flowers.

"Oh. Wait, no. I know this. Geranium," she says. "Nasturtium, hydrangea. Don't know that one. Wisteria. Sweet pea." Two more she doesn't know after that, then: "Oh my god." Is it? It is.

"That's a rose, right? Even I know that one," says Bohai.

"That," she says, "is a Blushing Pierre de Ronsard."

They look at her.

"A climbing rose. Opens pink, fades to a creamy white."

Toby is holding the pencil.

"Maybe it'd be safer to put 'rose'?" Maryam says.

"Blushing Pierre de Ronsard," Lauren says firmly, and takes the pencil, and writes it in.

And she's right, and they even get a bonus point for it from the impressed compère, which is not quite enough to combat the fact that none of the people on the actors list was Marilyn Monroe. They land in fourth place, and win a voucher for thirty per cent off a pub meal ordered Monday to Wednesday before seven p.m. It's a good night.

Bohai fits in with her friends so neatly. He joins local groups she's never even heard of, goes to see a show at the arts centre, heads up to Walthamstow one night to join Rob for a bat walk through the wetlands.

"A *bat walk*?"

He shrugs. "Yeah, I think we look for bats. Wanna come and find out?"

"No!" She didn't even know there were any bats in London, and she doesn't care for the idea.

Lauren works from home most days, goes into the office a couple of times a week, but Bohai doesn't seem to have any daytime responsibilities. She asks whether he's still calling in sick.

"Yeah, nah," he says, "not really. I more quit my job. I mean, I guess they fired me? I haven't talked to anyone about it since I got here. I've got some savings, and I'll be off to another universe soon, right? I did answer when they called, to say, you know, *fuck you I'm done*. Then I blocked the number. I reckon it's good for employers to remember we can walk out, might teach them to treat everyone else a bit better."

"Yeah," she says. "You sure stuck it to those guide dogs."

○ ○

It's the end of October, and fireworks have been going off most nights: in the park, in gardens, a flurry of *pop-pop-pop-BANG*. They fascinate Bohai, it staggers him that it's legal to buy little exploding fires for fun. "You'd get kids burning down whole forests back home."

She gestures out of the window at the rain, the sog. "Good luck burning that."

He is only an okay housemate, careless about some chores and finicky about others, never makes the tea, but it's a joy all the same. They exchange stories. They make jokes. They spend way too much money on box tickets for a big new West End musical, at Bohai's urging: "Come on," he says, "we're in London! I wanna see the big fancy lighting effects, it used to be my job! Plus normally I never get to buy tickets for anything, or else by the time the event actually happens I'm long gone." So they do, and the lighting is certainly very impressive, but halfway through Bohai leans over and whispers in her ear: "You know, I'd forgotten that I hate musicals."

She turns. "We spent six hundred pounds on this!"

"I know!" he says. "Maybe it was a mistake!"

Oh well. *Attic!* she mouths.

Attic! he mouths back.

○ ○

The garden's a mess, but the succulent she got from Elena's hen party is putting out a new lobe, and one lunchbreak Bohai meets her at the council and they go to the fancy plant shop nearby. They've been continuing to go through money fast and, despite Bohai's encouragement, she can't bring herself to spend £180 on a tree almost as big as her, plus how would she even get it home, so she takes a medium-sized umbrella plant instead.

"Do you ever think this might be dangerous?" she asks Bohai once, scrolling through news stories.

"What, the buzzing stuff with the lights?"

"No, I mean bad husbands. Or wives, I guess."

"Oh, yeah, a bit. It's easy to get away from them if you just have to go into a wardrobe, though, right? Harder for you. Either way, at least they can't stalk you once they don't know you exist, no tangled-up finances, and you obviously don't love them so you're not trying to fight against, like, feelings."

"Yeah," she says, "I guess." She goes back to her phone, scrolls on. "No, I don't know," she adds after a moment. "I keep thinking about that thing, you know. That statistic. About how women get killed more when they're at home with a partner than when they're out walking around."

"God. Is that true?" He gets his phone.

"You don't need to google *everything*."

They criticise each other a lot, never seriously. It's the relief, she thinks: not having to pretend. And it's also just because they can; because there's no way they're going to fall out and never talk to each other again. This huge thing nobody else will ever know about or believe, shared only with each other.

"I'm gonna make a page for if someone googles 'infinite spouses' or 'magic attic,'" Bohai says. "Little note that says, 'If you're caught in an endless loop of spouses, drop me a line.'"

This seems to her like a bad idea for some reason.

"What, someone's gonna do us for bigamy?"

"Time hunters," she says. "Space cops. I dunno. No, you're right, you should do it."

He makes a Substack with one post: *Hey! I went into a cupboard once and came out in another world, and now I'm working my way through an endless cycle of husbands and wives in different versions of the universe! If this has happened to you, email me.*

"I didn't mention you," he says. "Just in case."

"Any reply?" she says after a couple of days. "To your newsletter?"

"Nah. I'll leave it up till I go, you never know."

CHAPTER 27

In December they buy a Christmas tree, a real one, guessing at ceiling heights—seven feet, eight?—and Bohai shrugs and says, "Look, I only know metric, but they wouldn't sell them if they didn't fit in houses, right?" and so they get the largest one they can and carry it back through the streets for ten minutes, stopping to change their grip and manoeuvre, almost getting stuck coming up the narrow stairs from the front door. The tree is, it turns out, definitely too tall for the flat until Bohai suggests opening the ceiling hatch and poking the tip through into the attic. Lauren puts the star on top, standing on a chair because there's no room to pull down the ladder, leaning in, tugging the tip of the tree towards her, her other hand thrust up into the attic, the light bulb above her glowing like a star itself until she lowers her arm.

It's so inconvenient: the tree fills half the landing, she has to edge around it to get into her room, the power cable to the lights has to run out from the living room (Bohai tapes it down, says he was a stage manager once, but he can't have been a good one because the tape keeps coming up). Still. It's only for a couple of weeks. She sends a picture around, and her friends pretend to admire their ingenuity, except for Nat who replies with a link to a page about how to keep down electricity costs and prevent heat escaping through the roof.

o o

They kiss, once, after a night out in town: an okay stand-up comedy show and then a late pizza, and then it turns out there's cocktails and an inexplicably 2010-themed pop night in the basement, and they're already out so why not? And when they leave at two it's so cold outside, but she's still hot from the crowded room and a hundred moving bodies, and the air is astonishing on her arms, her face, her breath billows in front of her, and they're laughing down the side street to the bus stop and she turns to tease him about the night's revelation that he knows all the words, *all* the words, to Enrique Iglesias's "Tonight (I'm Fuckin' You)," even the rap bit. And he's turning as well. And it's not exactly an accident, they both know what they're doing, but they don't turn away, and then they're kissing against a wall. She still hasn't cooled down enough to put her jacket on so she feels the rough chill of the bricks against her skin where her top rucks up at the back, and his skin in the cold air, and his mouth and hands and warm body.

They stop.

And they don't say anything. If they acknowledge what's happening they'll have to decide whether it's a good idea or not, and it really obviously isn't. So instead she leans forward, more gently this time, and he does too. But they're both tense; she can feel it. And after a few seconds she leans back.

"Yes," she says, "okay, bad idea."

"Shit," he says. "Yeah."

He hates London and she has a flat here, he wants kids and she doesn't, he's always leaving dishes soaking overnight and she kind of hates how much space his beloved blue enamel Dutch oven takes up. In some version of the world they met and didn't immediately find out every little detail and incompatibility and they got married and maybe that was good or maybe it wasn't. But in this world they know way too much, they have *Post-it notes* about each other's ideal partner, for god's sake. And they know they don't match up.

"I'm no good at staying friends with exes," he says.

"Yeah," she says. "Me neither."

And they can't risk not being friends. So they can't risk being exes. So they can't risk kissing in an alleyway.

Afterwards, Bohai starts staying out all night, every now and then. He always messages cheerfully, *Having a nice time see you in the morning*, and she mostly enjoys having the flat to herself for a change, and it's fine, it's sort of fine, though it's not uncomplicated to spend all her time joking and sharing secrets with a man she fancies enough to have married but who she can definitely not sleep with.

She could go out as well, of course. Once, in a Walthamstow pub for drinks with Rob and Elena, she drinks a bit too much, and gets talking to a stranger; perhaps she can burn off some of her energy on this man who is explaining to her with such delighted intensity that a Campari spritz is vegan and an Aperol spritz is not. Yes, she thinks, why not, but then Elena pulls her away from the conversation and says, "Lauren, what the fuck, what are you doing?" and she remembers in a flush of humiliation that she is, technically, married.

She doesn't try again. But one night, while Bohai's out doing whatever, she stands on a chair and pulls the tip of the tree out of the attic, and then shoves the whole thing sidelong, arms around the prickly branches and kicking at the base until it's budged a couple of feet and she can pull the ladder down.

It's not fair, she thinks, that she is always here waiting, that she is in Norwood Junction for ever, that the husbands come and go and she remains. It's not fair that her lives require their cooperation, that she has to cajole or trick or persuade when she wants them to leave, that she was always here in her old life and she's always here now.

What happens if she climbs all the way up?

Toby went in that one time, and nothing. She called an electrician out, once—nothing.

But the attic acknowledges her like it acknowledges the husbands, it flickers and buzzes.

She should let Bohai know, in case anything happens. He won't like it, but she sends a message—*Hey sorry trying the attic*—and turns her phone off before he can reply.

And then she climbs up. Just a normal ladder. Just a few steps. Her head through the trapdoor. It's cold, and dark despite the glow of the light bulb as she enters, and the thin fuzz in the air thickens to static, and she stops for a moment with her head in the attic but her legs still on the ladder, in the warmer air of the landing.

She steps up again, and again, and then before she stops to think too much, one last step.

The light bulb above brightens: warm yellow, then brighter, then white. A flicker behind her.

A crackle.

The buzz of white noise sharpens. It's almost a shriek. There's a smell, sweet, dusty, an edge of smoke. And the light above pops, and goes dark, and then starts to glow again.

The smell gets stronger and a smoke alarm starts below and she steps back towards the trapdoor and one foot out, another, quicker, and as she climbs the still-bright light bulb flares again and dies again, and the landing around her is the same as it's been since October, since Bohai crawled out, and she gets a tea towel and waves it below the smoke alarm until it quiets. And nothing has changed.

o o

Bohai gets home an hour later. She hears him coming up the stairs and through the landing. She doesn't get up from where she's lying on the sofa.

"Hey," he says, looking into the living room.

"Hey."

"Didn't work?"

"Nah."

He looks behind him into the landing, glances up towards the attic. She has closed the hatch. The Christmas tree is bowed by the too-low ceiling, half blocking the door to the kitchen. "Do you want me to, you know, leave early?" he says.

"No," she says, "don't, it's not that. I just wanted to know what would happen."

After a moment, he shakes his head. "Come on, let's go out."

That's his answer to everything. "It's one in the morning."

"The really bad chip shop's open till three," he says, and hands her her coat.

In the morning, they use the big bread knife to saw the top off the tree so it can stand upright without them reopening the attic, and Bohai ties the star to one of the outstretched branches.

o o

Christmas, when it comes, is good. She gets him a box of fireworks, and he gets her the big plant she couldn't bring herself to buy from the shop near work. "Plus I'm going on the first of January so there's no way you'll accidentally kill it," he says. "Not in a week."

For Christmas dinner they go to Nat's, where they eat and eat and eat, and give loud extravagant gifts to the kids, a huge box of Lego to Caleb and a toddler drum kit to Magda.

Once they've finished cleaning up they have a Zoom with their mum, who opens the box of one hundred Twixes that Lauren has sent over.

"What an odd gift," her mum says. "You know we have Twixes in Spain? They're much better here, those clever Spanish technicians put something in the chocolate to stop it melting. I'm never going to get all these eaten before summer and once it heats up they're just going to turn into a big brown puddle. But of course it's the thought that counts, darling. Thank you so much."

○ ○

At home, late evening, Bohai starts assembling two sandwiches out of leftovers. "So your mum doesn't come over for the holidays?" he asks.

"Not really," she says. "Once Dad died and I was out of secondary school she sold up and moved over to Spain. She doesn't come back if she doesn't have to. She's been at all my weddings, though."

"And your grandma left you and Nat this place, and then you both lived here through uni?"

"My university, yeah, but Nat was already working by then." It's weird that they know each other so well but there are such important parts of their lives that haven't come up.

"Oh," he says. "So she was the grown-up while you were figuring everything out for the first time. Is that why she's so . . . you know?"

Lauren laughs. "God, you'd think so, wouldn't you? But she was like that even when we were little kids. If anything, she eased off once it was just us. Actually, no, she eases off when things are going badly, and the more sorted she thinks my life is the more she tells me what to do. So it's a compliment to you that she's given us a nine-thousand-piece Tupperware set and a bunch of unsolicited advice about batch cooking, it means she thinks I've made good life decisions."

Bohai hands over her sandwich.

"What about your sister?" she says.

"She's a good kid," he says. "A lot younger, she was four or five when I moved out. So we're not super close. I think you two would get on, though. She does that thing you do sometimes of getting super polite when someone says something you think is stupid.

Which is a pretty searing critique even from you, honestly, but it's devastating when it's from your teenage sister."

Lauren doesn't think she does that, particularly. "Huh," she says.

"Yeah, exactly," Bohai says. "Just like that. Maybe it's a little-sister thing. You'll see if you meet her."

She will not, of course, get to meet Bohai's family, and that feels like a shame.

o o

On New Year's Eve, they go down to Toby and Maryam's for dinner. After they eat, they set off Bohai's fireworks in the back yard.

"Your side of the garden, though," Maryam says. "God knows what the landlord would do if he found us starting fires on his lawn."

"Yeah, no worries," Bohai says, and reads the instructions three times, and puts his swimming goggles on just in case. He pushes the sticks into the ground, then lights a taper while the rest of them stand around the corner and peer. Lauren can't see what's going on, but after bending over for a minute Bohai runs towards them. As he runs, there's a *pip-pip-pip-pip-pap* and a shower of green sparks, then a big pink plume, and a fizzing noise and silver. A column of blue-grey smoke. A jagged orange line. A shower of speckled yellow. A moment's pause, then a whistle and four or five little balls of red flame, one after another, sparks of light falling off them as they rise, then another red ball that spirals upwards before exploding at its zenith.

And finally, silence.

"Did you light them *all*?" Lauren says.

"That was amazing," Bohai says. "Amazing. Oh my god. Yeah, I lit them all, do you have any more?"

After a calming glass of wine, the four of them go to a party at

Bohai's friend Clayton's ("No idea," Bohai says, "but we're in the same WhatsApp group and apparently he has a smoke machine"). Bohai and Lauren hide in the toilet during the countdown so that nobody will think it's weird when they don't kiss at midnight, although it's obviously still pretty weird to stand in a not-very-large toilet laughing and listening to people yell "HAPPY NEW YEAR" outside.

A taxi back at half past three. "My treat," Lauren says. Spend all the money.

They sleep in and then wake up mid-afternoon, hungover, still daylit but only just. Bohai makes toast and looks around. "I feel like I should pack a suitcase or something."

She doesn't want him to go. She tries to keep it off her face, and fails.

"Yeah," he says. "But we have lives to get on with. Husbands to find. Sunlight to escape to—you know it's summer in Australia now, right? Plus I haven't mentioned this because I didn't want you to worry but I kind of ran through my savings and I've taken a whole bunch of money from loan sharks. I cannot express how much I've fucked up my financial life here, probably yours too."

"I did wonder," she says.

"Hoping for a pension plan in the next life. But okay," he says, "what if."

She doesn't even have to think about whether this is something she'd want, because she knows him well enough, now, to see how it would go if she said, *Yeah okay, stay, let's see if we can make this work, let's be strange housemates,* or even *Let's get married for real.*

"If you're going to stay," she says, which of course he isn't, "you have to stop complaining about the weather. I know it's cold but I'm not personally responsible."

"No, right, sorry, okay. Just, you know," he says.

None of those are communicative words in the traditional sense. "Yeah," she says.

"I'll visit when I'm back in London," he says. He's memorised her number; his changes a lot, but he's had the same email address since university.

It's her turn to doubt. "What if we forget? Like the husbands do. What if we don't remember each other?" She thinks again about trying to tell Elena, and Toby, and Nat, and her mum, and how lonely those first months were. She doesn't want to go back to it. But he doesn't answer, because there's nothing to say: if they forget, they forget.

○ ○

They budge the chopped-off tree out of the way again. It's easier with two.

"Hope you get someone who can deal with all your, you know, personality issues," Lauren says. "And who likes wearing suits."

"Same," Bohai says, and pulls the ladder down. "I mean, not the suits. Scarves and rolled-up shirtsleeves for you, right?"

"Well, not simultaneously. To the left," she adds when the ladder sticks.

He stares upwards. Takes a breath. Lets it out. Takes another. And all at once, faster than any husband before him, he climbs, up up up, and she expects him to stop and wave goodbye but he doesn't, and she calls after his disappearing feet, "Stay safe! Let me know when you get there!" and then he's gone.

CHAPTER 28

She looks behind her, politely, to give the world time to adjust. When she turns back the tree is gone. She hears a clatter from above. She thinks: where is he, has he gone? Then she thinks: okay, so I remember him.

And she hears her phone in the kitchen, *ding*, and she rushes through, and it's a text from an unknown number, *Lol Brighton no thanx*, and a picture of a grey view of a grey sky and a grey sea, then that disappears and a couple of minutes later there's a new message from another new number, *Okay yes sydney babyyyyy* then *no picture of the sea though, obviously we are a forty minute drive away in deep suburbia* and then a photo of a blurry moon over dark rooftops, *Look the moon's the right side up again, miss you heaps tho xxxxxxxxx xxxxxxxxx*

"Honey?" she hears from the landing. And she turns around, and there he is. Her new husband.

But not new: it's what's-his-face. That guy again. The husband, the first one. Michael.

She thinks it's Michael. There have been a lot of husbands to remember and she was either drunk or hungover or an unpleasant mix of the two for most of the time she and Michael spent together. But he was the first. She'd remember him. Right?

The first question is: is it him? "Michael," she says, experimentally.

"Yeah?"

The second question is: what the fuck?

The third question, which is kind of a subset of the second question, is: is this a loop? Does that mean she's due for Jason soon? If she cycles the husbands for long enough, will Carter eventually climb down again?

Bohai never mentioned a loop, but he's drawing on a larger pool of possible spouses: more genders, more countries, more cupboards. It might be that she's exhausted her possibilities while Bohai has a thousand left to try, the fucker.

Michael is still looking at her. "Let's go to the pub," she says.

"It's New Year's Day," he says. "Are they even open?"

Shit, so it is. "Let's go to the park."

"Aren't Toby and Maryam coming for dinner?"

Again? It's only twelve hours since she saw them in her last world. "Yeah," she says. "Tell you what, though, I'm going for a walk, clear my head. Want me to get anything while I'm out?"

"Won't the shops be closed? Are you okay?" he says.

"Yes! Yes, I'm fine, I'm just going to have a think about the . . . new year. I'll be back in an hour, that'll work with dinner plans, right?"

"Should do," he says. "Will you have time to ice the cake?"

She looks into the kitchen again, and this time notices the wire rack and large round cake. "Yeah," she says. She can always dust it with icing sugar.

Around the corner it turns out the pub's open after all. The coffee machine's off but they make her a cup of tea and she sits outside with her phone. It's very cold.

She messages Bohai, at his Sydney number: *I think I'm in a loop??* Then she checks Facebook to confirm: yes, Michael Callebaut. And she scans back and looks for pictures, and finds: oh.

WHAT? she gets from Bohai.

Wait never mind, she texts back. *I'll get back to you, it's complicated*

The photos are different.

She has seen lots of pictures of big white dresses, but you never forget your first retrospective wedding. The puff of the skirt, the flowers she didn't recognise when she first saw them but now thinks were probably peonies, Michael's brown suit.

And yet here on Facebook is a wedding from a couple of years ago, and she's wearing a close-fitting dress instead of a huge puff, it's off-white with pale-green leaves on it, and instead of a big outdoor party they're in a room with maybe fifteen other people.

Same husband different life? Is that possible, she sends, with one of the photos. *Pandemic wedding??*

Oh yeah!!! she gets back. *Had repeats a few times, I think it's when I met them some other way but we ended up together anyway?? Which husband, is it a good one?*

Michael, the first one, he was fine, she sends back, and goes to check the messages she's been sending the husband: shopping lists as always, questions about dinner, back and forth. There is not—and this is the one thing she remembers for sure—there is not a picture of a pear with googly eyes on it, even when she scrolls back and back and back again, months into the past, to the days before Elena's hen do and further still.

So. Not a loop.

She goes to text Bohai again but he's sent another message: *2 a.m. here anyway so I'm off to bed but good luck with michael 2: the return,* and then moments later *mIIchael* and then *no michaelII sorry* and then, after a two-minute gap, *twichael,* and she decides to leave it.

What does it mean that she's married Michael in two different worlds?

When she finishes her tea and heads back to the flat he has a big pot of bolognese heating up on the stove. Not another husband with a special bolognese recipe, she thinks, this is against her rules; but fine, let him add his tablespoon of balsamic vinegar or his cinnamon stick or his mince with a particular fat content. It does smell good. And the flat is looking great: tidy, nice bright paint colours, and in the kitchen the dent in the wall has been fixed again, just like the first time.

She has no idea what sort of cake she's made but she finds a chocolate ganache recipe in an open tab on her phone, some chocolate on top of the microwave, and some cream in the fridge. Sure! She'll give it a go. She opens her playlists and finds one labelled DECEMBER and puts it on while she warms the cream, and it's songs she doesn't know, girls singing with pianos, and she wonders if that means she's sad, but probably it just means it's cold and the days are short. Michael comes in to stir the bolognese and sings along to one of the choruses. He's got a nice voice.

○ ○

The ganache isn't perfect, grainier than the photo in the recipe, but she tries a spoonful and it tastes okay.

Toby and Maryam come up at seven. She knows so much about them that they don't even know themselves, she thinks. But they've always been together, in every world.

They must know a lot about her that she doesn't know as well. What her ganache is meant to taste like. What her hobbies are. What her job is, for that matter. Whether she's happy.

And maybe the different disjuncts and asymmetries are okay, maybe they balance out, because the four of them sit together in the living room, eating Michael's bolognese, talking about the new year, and it's good. Maryam recounts her hospital's best A&E New Year's Eve stories, *nobody ever found the lizard*.

The cake is pretty decent too.

○ ○

Lauren goes to work on January the third and finds, to her surprise, that she's her own boss, or rather that she's been promoted and is now the deputy head of her old department.

She's used to a gentle start to the year, but this time it's straight into calls and meetings. She remembers Bohai's advice and spends a lot of time saying "What do *you* think?" and "Do *you* have any suggestions here?" with an air that implies, she hopes, that she is being a benevolent and thoughtful leader who seeks to share power, rather than a baffled newcomer making it up as she goes along.

It's the end of the day before she gets the chance to talk to Zarah, who looks up guiltily from her phone.

"Good start to the year?" she asks, trying to stay friendly but boss-appropriate.

"Yeah," Zarah says, "getting back into it."

Lauren waits for a moment to see if there's anything else, but that seems to be it, and she can't dawdle too long; according to her calendar, she has a HIIT class at the gym around the corner. If she's looking for a world she's willing to stick with, then she needs to try living the life she finds there.

The class is horrible, and the instructor knows her and calls encouragement by name, which makes it even worse. But once she's recovered she is gratified and a little shocked by her body's capacity, the ease with which she can touch her toes, the way this version of herself has cultivated so much flexibility and strength. And the next day, when she gets home from work before Michael, she tries a handstand against the wall, like when she was a kid. Her legs go up, her arms hold—ten seconds later she lets her legs down, pushing off from the wall, left leg first and then gravity and momentum pulling the right after it until she has inverted herself again, back to standing. She stretches her arms above her head like a triumphant gymnast.

She's seen so many husbands. Not thirty-seven per cent of all the possible husbands, probably, but maybe close enough. Maybe enough to get a decent idea of what's out there. She thinks back to the lists she made with Bohai, and the things she wanted, and compares them against Michael. Vegetarian: no. Cute: yes. Genuinely notices her: yes. Feels like a good life: yes.

On the sixth of January she leans over in bed and kisses him, and grabs his hair, and he pulls her on top of him and laughs, and she rolls them both back the other way, and as the morning proceeds she discovers that in this world she owns, and uses during sex, a vibrator. She doesn't quite take to it, but there's no denying its efficiency, the pressure cooker of orgasms. Perhaps, like a pressure cooker, it takes practice to get the best out of it.

On the thirteenth of January, Bohai is in London; she calls in sick, and they meet for coffee.

What if it doesn't work, she sends, *what if we bring together two different universes and destroy everything?*

Yeah prob we won't though and if we do we won't know, he sends back.

They meet at the park where they had breakfast that first morning, and he's fifteen minutes late, which gives her plenty of time to worry; but then he sneaks up behind her and taps her on the shoulder, and she turns and squeezes him, and there they are, back in the world together.

"Wow," she says. "You look—so different."

"I know, I look like shit, all I have here are these big flannel shirts and these leggings. And god, this *haircut*. You look great; this coat looks expensive, you rich again?"

"We're doing okay," she says.

"Ooh," he says. "*Doing okay*. That's rich but embarrassed."

"How's the new life? You in town long?"

"Nah," he says, "I'm off after coffee, look at this sodden fucker of a season, plus there's black mould in our flat and I'm not an expert but I've heard that's bad. What about you?"

"I'm still with Michael," she says.

"No! The one who came back on New Year's Day?"

"Yeah."

"Wow," he says. "So that's almost two weeks, right? Is it *love*?"

"I mean, he definitely hits a lot of the assessment criteria."

"So romantic."

She laughs. "Yeah, I mean, I do really like him? And the flat looks great, he's an architect, did I say?"

"Like, at least four times."

"And," she says, "I'm still at the council but I've been promoted."

"I'll be honest, I never really understood your job."

"That's fair," she says. "It's pretty boring. But, also, if I mess up, then real people's lives get worse. Anyway, now I can ruin even more people's lives at once if I'm not careful." She's been struggling a little with the higher workload and the meeting-heavy days, and she has a funding application that she's been putting off, but it's not impossibly hard, it's not a whole different category of how to behave and what to do, and she's been feeling surprised and even proud at how well she's managing. She did wake up in the middle of the night once to worry about her team's productivity targets, but she soothed herself back to sleep by making a little to-do list and remembering that she could just change the world if things got really behind schedule.

Bohai buys them takeaway coffees, and they walk around the lake. Steam rises from their cups.

"Hey," she says, "if you end up back in London this weekend, do you want to come round to lunch? Bring your whoever, we can say we're old uni friends. Michael's a really good cook too."

"Probably won't be around," Bohai says, "the weather at home at the moment is, god, it's nicer than any weather you've experienced in your whole life, I reckon? It's hot but it's dry and everyone's still a bit Christmas lazy. And I bet I can find somewhere I'm away on holiday if I scoot through ten or twenty lives. Like: I step out of a beach hut directly on to the sand, there's the big ocean in front of me, some husband in tiny Speedos lying on a towel. Not that this frozen mud isn't also a delight."

"Yeah, okay," she says, "run on back to your spiders and sun damage."

"But," he says, "I think the weather's gonna turn and get sweaty and gross in a few days, so I could wardrobe back over then, maybe we could do something next week?"

"Can't believe you're going to abandon your sexy Speedo husband so fast," she says. "Next week would be good."

"You still gonna be with Michael?"

"I don't know." She's embarrassed to say too much in case she's wrong, in case it doesn't work out. "Maybe?"

"You *are*, aren't you?"

Her chest and her chin are tight with hope; she laughs and lets it out. "Look, he's just nice. I don't know."

She has always hated *being wrong*, the idea of doing something that turns out to be an irredeemable mistake. And with Michael she is always working out the best thing to do, and then doing it. Figuring out the ideal way to be.

"Sounds terrible," Bohai says, "but if you like it I guess you'd better lock up that attic." And he buffets her sideways with his shoulder.

She has, sort of: a few days ago she stood on a chair and put a chain and padlock around the struts of the mostly-folded-up ladder to stop it from unfolding further, and then shoved it back up and closed the hatch. If Michael pulls it down it'll only reach halfway, and of course he could still get in if he really set his mind to it and if not she'd definitely have some explaining to do. But it's something.

"That's practically a proposal," Bohai says.

"We're already married."

"I'm so happy for you."

"It's only been two weeks." She might, she thinks, be blushing. "We'll see how it goes."

o o

They spend a few hours together, then Bohai heads off for a new life. "See you next week?" he says. "I'll message you, but maybe Wednesday?"

"Yeah, perfect."

When Michael gets home he's brought orange juice, lemonade and some plain white bread. He makes her triangles of Marmite toast. "I know what you like when you're sick."

She feels a little bad, because she's had a big lunch with Bohai and she's not actually ill, but also, Michael's so nice! She's faked a lot of sickness over the last six months and she's seen who brings things home for her, who gets annoyed that the flat isn't clean even though she's *been home all day*, who takes an illness as a personal affront or instantly declares that they have the same cold but somehow more so. Worst of all are the husbands who bring jars of vitamins and special teas and check in every five minutes to see if she's okay, the husbands who won't just let her be fake-ill in peace.

But Michael sits over in the armchair and reads, and every now and then he looks up at her and smiles. Maybe the attic knew what it was doing first time round.

o o

There are a few things she doesn't like. Michael's parents are fine, but they live quite close, and his mother isn't great at calling before she pops round to drop off a bag of kumquats she saw on sale. Another objection, harder to justify: the flat is perhaps *too* stylish. Her clumsily painted succulent has been relegated to a shelf in the bathroom.

The maintenance required to keep up this elegant and energetic life is also a lot. Work is good, but harder. The flat is always tidy, and if she leaves anything on a table Michael will look at it and sigh and put it away. They get a weekly veg box which is great in theory but in practice she doesn't always want to tackle a knobbly celeriac or hyperspecific squash. Plus she's calling her own mum twice a week, and babysitting Magda and Caleb a lot—she's done it three times already and there's another evening in the calendar before the end of the month. She loves them, but they're so tiring.

"Magda's climbing," Nat warns her on her third visit. "Everything. She got a metre up the curtains yesterday, like a little mountaineer."

"Okay," Lauren says.

Nat's long-standing refusal to believe she's a capable adult was useful the first couple of times, because it meant she ran over bedtimes and what to feed the children despite Lauren's apparently regular babysitting slots, but she feels like she's got the hang of it and could now go without another run-through. But Adele, at least, trusts her, and drags Nat out of the door. "Come on," she says, "she's a grown woman, she organised a whole fundraising fair for Magda's nursery, she can microwave some mashed vegetables."

She organised a *fair*? But she hunts out photos and: yep, looks like she did.

It's good to have your life together tho, Bohai messages from another new number. *I mean, i imagine*

"It's a lot," she says to Magda, who is hitting Duplo with more Duplo. "It's good. But it's a lot. Michael and I are meant to spend all Sunday making stock and freezing it."

Magda fits the blocks together. "Yeah," Lauren says, "that's it. Keep it up. You're doing great."

CHAPTER 29

In the past she's let herself glide through her lives. But not now.
There is a time, she thinks, at the start of any relationship, when the process of falling in love softens a personality, like wax in a warm room. And so two people in love change, just a little, pushing their wax figures together, a protuberance here smoothed down but creating a dip there. It doesn't last long, the time when love can gently change who you are, and in the relationships that she's visited over the last six months, the moment has long passed. She has been presented with the shape of her new husband, and invited to either contort to fit or reject him wholesale.

But she's trying, this time, she's really trying. She feels herself warming and shifting into this better life.

Once or twice it's too much, after a night of babysitting for example, and she calls in sick and naps all day or plays games on her phone. One time she fakes a work research trip and stays in a hotel on the other side of town, and gets lunch with Bohai who's in London again, and watches YouTube videos in bed until three in the morning and forgets to have dinner, and she is not gentle and affectionate and careful and thoughtful with Michael and does not sit with him to talk through their days and share little moments (they eat at the table, every night they eat at the table, never once on the sofa with the television on).

But most of the time she does it, she lives up to the life another

version of herself has made, the life of a person whose every decision is meticulously for the best.

"Are you okay?" Michael asks her one night, three or four
weeks in.

"Yeah?" she says.

"It's just you've been skipping your book group and morning
yoga."

Ah. That's what "books" means in her calendar every second
Tuesday. She's been assuming it means *read some books*, and she's
been doing that, or at least she's been picking up a book and looking at the first page.

"Low energy," she says. "Winter. You're right, I'll get back on it."

It's good, though. This is the life she would design if she was
drunk and trying to think through the best possible version of
who she could be. Exercise every morning and some evenings too,
knowing what to do with root vegetables, spending a lot of time
with her niece and nephew, staying in better touch with her mum,
this is stuff she's sure she's written on intentional lists in the past,
and now she's doing it.

They go to an Albariño tasting night at the wine shop near Rob
and Elena's, and she worries that she's going to have to have wine
opinions, but Michael is happy to take care of that side of it, and
the rest of them get to concentrate on the drinking. It's not unbearable like she thought it might be, either; people do say "gooseberry
aroma" a few times but mostly it's the woman who owns the wine
shop being enthusiastic and excited, and people saying "Oh yeah,
I can taste that actually."

It's finished by half past nine. "Let's go out," she says as they
leave, stretching her arms into the night, wiggling her fingers to
make the street lamp shadows move.

"Where?" Elena says.

"I dunno. Pub. Karaoke. Dancing. Bus race to the twenty-four-
hour Asda at Clapham Junction."

"We can't leave Danny alone any longer," Rob says to Elena; they have a dog, here. "But I can deal with him if you two want to go on somewhere."

"There's a pub up by ours," Elena suggests once the husbands have left. But Lauren is pretty sure they're around the corner from the dessert bar where she wasted half an hour, some husband or other ago. They walk down the road; the trees have been pollarded for the start of spring, straggly tops chopped, five or six thick branches on each one stretching upwards from the trunk, crabbed hands towards the sky.

The dessert bar is busier at night. Lauren gets the rosewater ice cream again, but there's no free wafers this time. "What were we doing," she says, "this time last year?"

They pull out phones and scroll back. Elena's has pictures of herself in her living-room mirror wearing a pink faux fur coat she'd ordered in the sales. "I sent it back," she says.

Lauren's has her and Michael regrouting the bathroom.

She isn't sure what she was doing a year ago in her original world. But late January is usually a time to run out of energy and money, so nothing fun. She remembers a week of updating her CV and thinking about trying to find a new and more dynamic job and then not doing anything about it.

This is better, she thinks, and takes another spoonful of ice cream.

○ ○

She does, one afternoon, drag a chair on to the landing and stand on it to reach into the attic and unlock the padlock. She doesn't think about it too hard, doesn't quite acknowledge what she's doing. Michael hasn't noticed the lock, so he can't be trying to go into the attic anyway, so it won't make any difference if it's there or not.

Plus, she thinks as she pulls the ladder down and tests that it's still working, it's not safe to keep it locked. What if she needed to get into the attic fast for some reason? For example, a flood, or angry Labradors.

It's not like she's actively getting rid of him. She's just . . . leaving open a possibility.

And she's right: nothing happens after she takes the lock away. They go on a long, long riverside walk ending at the BFI to see a three-and-a-half-hour French film, and the walk and the film are both pretty great, even if she would perhaps not have chosen, left to her own devices, to do both on the same day.

Anyway, you can't send a husband back because he makes you *too good*. Especially not a husband who—she doesn't love him, not yet, but she likes seeing him when she gets home, she likes lying in bed with him, the sex now that she's got used to their range of equipment is excellent, if on the serious side, and she even likes it when he shows her a paragraph from some informative article he's reading. She wants to be better for him, for this life they've made.

○ ○

They're dealing with even more celeriac that Thursday—she's chopping it into large angular pieces—when someone rings the doorbell. Michael answers, and comes in with Bohai, back in London again, sodden in the rain. "Sorry," Bohai says, "sorry, I need help."

"I thought I should bring him up?" Michael says. "He was asking for you."

"Uh, thanks," she says. "Bohai. What's going on?"

This is weird. She doesn't like it. And she likes it even less when:

"It's the husband," Bohai says.

"Okay. Michael, I'll be back in a sec," and she takes Bohai down the stairs and steps out into the light drizzle and shuts the door behind her. *Don't mention the husbands in front of the husbands*, she thinks. "What is it?"

"Okay," Bohai says, "I turn up somewhere new and I'm in a walk-in wardrobe. I can hear the husband talking and I think he's talking to me or maybe we have guests, so I get out, like a normal new husband, right? But it turns out he's on a Zoom and the reason I'm in the wardrobe is because I'm listening in on his therapy session."

"Oh my god."

"I should have run right back into the wardrobe, obviously, but it took me a while to figure out what was going on—by the time he even reacted to me I was halfway across the room. Anyway, I don't know, probably he's just angry because, you know, you would be, right? Like, definitely don't listen in on people's therapy sessions, is my advice. But, you remember when we talked about bad husbands?"

"Shit," she says. "Are you okay?"

"Yeah," he says, "yeah, you know, nothing happened, it just didn't feel like a good idea to be there. He threw some stuff but not *at* me or anything."

"That's not nothing happening, that's—"

"So," he doesn't stop, "I left, and it was raining, and I don't have my phone, and I didn't really know what to do. So, uh, I went up to the main road and eventually there was a taxi and I came here."

"Yeah," she says, "yes. Okay. Of course."

"Thank fuck it happened in London, right? Imagine if I was in France or something."

"Do you want to come up?" she says. God, this is going to be hard to explain to Michael. "We could make up the spare room and get you back in tomorrow?"

"I don't know," he says. "Maybe? He was pretty angry. I don't think he's going to, like, bash in the door of the wardrobe or anything now that I'm not there, but also, I'm definitely not a hundred per cent sure that he's not? And if he does I'm not sure if I can still leave? So obviously I'd love to come up and play Scrabble with you and your guy but also, probably, I just need to get back in the wardrobe. I was thinking maybe you could distract the guy so I can run in? I grabbed a jacket on the way out and it turns out I have my keys, thank god, it could definitely be worse. I don't know, that's my best plan, sorry."

"Yeah," she says after a moment. "Of course. Let's get over there."

"Sorry, thank you, yes. Also, sorry, can you pay the taxi?"

"Give me a moment," she says, and goes back upstairs: *uni friend, he just moved to the area, having a family emergency* to Michael and *I'll call you* and kisses him and he seems bewildered and annoyed, *you never even mentioned this guy before,* but she can deal with that later. She declines a call from him in the taxi.

"I'm so sorry," Bohai says as they round a corner.

"It's fine," she says. "Do you have the guy's number? Or his name?" Maybe she can call him and pretend Bohai's hurt himself, send him to the hospital to get him out of the house.

"No," he says. "Sorry."

"It's okay," she says. "Stop apologising. We'll figure it out."

They're heading up towards Putney. It's a nice bit of town: glimpses of the river, parks, ornate fences. The house is on a little cul-de-sac, and they get the taxi to drop them at the end. The rain has slowed to an occasional spatter. The street is lined with trees and four-wheel drives. Bohai points out the house, *the one with the big vine,* then steps back from its sightline.

"Seriously," she says, "do you want to go get a drink first?"

"No," he says, "no, let's just get it over with. I was thinking maybe there was something we could do with the back garden but now that we're here the back garden is obviously totally surrounded by other people's back gardens."

"How about," she says after a moment, "I call the police and say I'm a neighbour and I've heard something going on. Then we wait here, and when they come you go over to the door at the same time? I can say I heard gunshots or something to make sure they turn up. Even if your husband hasn't calmed down, he's not going to start anything with the police literally there. You can just run in and new-world it away."

"Yeah," Bohai says after a moment. "Yeah, I guess that would work. I was sort of hoping to avoid actually, you know, seeing him. But that might be the way to go."

She remembers Kieran, who was probably fine really, and hiding in her own wardrobe, and just wanting him gone.

"God," Bohai says, "obviously it's not okay to listen in on some-one's therapy, it's not like it's an unreasonable thing to be angry about, he might be a great husband for all I know. Yeah, come on, let's go for it."

"No," she says, "okay, we can do better. You've got your keys, you said?"

"Yeah, I think so, anyway." He fishes them out: three keys on a ring. "I guess they might be for an office or something."

It's dark, and most of the houses have their curtains closed. "Okay. I'll get him out of the house. I can give you five minutes, probably? If the keys are wrong then we'll have to think of some-thing else later. I'll lead him up this road and then to the right, so if you go a block in the other direction and find somewhere to wait, you can see when we leave?"

Bohai looks at the house, the directions. "Yeah," he says, "yes, right, got it. Thanks. Sorry." He takes a moment to gather him-self. "Good, right." Then he steps away, walks a block back, turns around, gives a thumbs-up and steps behind a tree.

Her turn. A year ago she would never have done anything like this.

She walks down the street and takes a deep breath and heads up to the door and knocks. Then she steps back. No need to get too close.

The husband opens the door. Brown hair, slightly ridiculous

moustache. Wearing a knitted jumper. He doesn't look like some-one who might pull a door off a walk-in wardrobe.

"Hi," she says. "My name's Sarah, are you"—she still doesn't know his name, quick glance at the wall—"is this number thirty-one?"

"Yeah," the man says, slowly.

"Great," she says. "I was out for a walk and I came across a man who was sitting on the side of the road, he said he's sprained his ankle. He asked if I could come and let you know." She should have planned this more thoroughly. "He said his name was Bohai, and he'd left his phone at home but to ask his husband at number thirty-one if he could help."

"Oh," the man says after a moment. "Thanks. Sorry he's put you to the trouble, he's always forgetting his phone."

"Absolutely no bother. He's just a couple of blocks away," she says. "I can take you over?"

"Yeah," the guy says, "of course, just give me a minute." He glances up at the sky. "Uh, do you want to come in?"

"No," she says, "I'm fine, I like the rain."

The man disappears, then returns, shoes on; takes a jacket from the hooks on the wall.

"Just this way," she says, and gestures. Around to the right, and down another road, out of sight, counting in her head how long it might take Bohai to get in. Ten, twenty, thirty. What if the guy really has wrecked the wardrobe, and it doesn't work any more? What if the keys are wrong? She supposes she'll just say *Oh, he was here a minute ago, don't know what's happened* to the husband and then bring Bohai back to her spare room and they'll take it from there.

Seventy steps, eighty. She picks her pace up, steps in front of the man to pass some bins sitting out on the pavement.

And as she's counting she stops hearing the thud of someone following behind her and turns to look back. And there's nobody, nothing.

Her phone dings. An unknown number again. She pulls it out, hunches against the rain to keep the screen dry. *Made it. Thank you thank you thank you*

So sorry, give me ten minutes to catch my breath and I'll come back to london and explain things to your husband, let me think something up

Another message: *In prague?? Hope I'm not a spy*

And another: *You're a life saver xxxxx I'm so sorry*

Are you okay, she messages back, and then calls an Uber. Her shoes are soaked through.

And when she gets back she starts to explain things to Michael—Bohai's sent her seven different ideas for good lies and asked when he should turn up to ratify them—then she just feels too tired.

She is so damp.

"Before you explain I think I should tell you," Michael says, mouth stiff, "that I know you didn't have a work research trip."

Work research trip? What? Oh, the night she watched videos in a hotel. She imagines explaining: *I was just tired of trying to be good all the time. I really like you but have you ever considered eating crisps in bed? I'm not having an affair, I'm having a snack and a lie-in.*

"The guy tonight is a friend," she says, explaining the easier thing first. "He just moved here from Australia. His husband was angry at him and maybe violent, and he needed help getting something important from his house. I was able to help but I wasn't in any danger, and he's okay now too."

"I'm glad he's okay," Michael says, and he seems so unhappy. "But maybe I should also tell you that I looked through your phone a while back. Which I shouldn't have done, obviously. But you'd left it on the coffee table and I saw a notification come up, and it was just a number without a name, and it said something about being in town and wanting to meet up. And you'd been acting a bit off and I couldn't stop thinking about it. And a couple of days later, and again, I'm sorry, I should have just talked to you about it at the time, but I looked through your messages and that one wasn't there any more. Obviously it could have been from a spammer."

Ah, she thinks. Well, fuck.

He wants so badly for her to be able to explain everything. And she can, but the explanation would be *Yeah the message was from the guy you saw, but we were mostly meeting up to talk about how much I like you, and I didn't delete it to keep it secret, it disappeared because he climbed into a toolshed and moved to a different life.*

She doesn't think it would go down well.

"I think"—she musters up the energy for the lie—"oh, did you hear that? Is there something in the attic? We should talk about all this, but could you check?"

And Michael—perfect, self-improving, better-than-her Michael, who has made her a lemon-and-honey drink to help her warm up from the rain—Michael nods; he requires no persuading to climb into the attic.

CHAPTER 30

Another husband descends.

She feels sad. She does feel sad, doesn't she? She puts down the lemon-and-honey drink and looks away and looks back and it's gone. And when she breathes in the air of the new flat, which has lost that smell which she thinks of as *jute*, the smell of only the best decisions, the sadness swells inside her and passes up her throat and then she breathes out and releases it. And when the husband turns around and is someone new, *just some guy*, she steps forward and kisses him lightly.

She keeps him for a few days, and then moves on, and then on again. If not Michael, then who? She is in this to find her forever husband, and not to dawdle; Bohai's walk-in wardrobe experience has renewed her determination. It's time to get to work.

One husband builds model trains, the spare room filled with a winding track, and she helps out, pinching little houses together while glue dries, debating the exact positioning of a tiny cat. She enjoys it for a day, then sends him back. One husband wears T-shirts under his buttoned-up shirts, and she liked it when Carter did it but it seems weird from someone English, or maybe it just reminds her of Carter too much. She sends him back as well.

With a late-February husband she finds crocuses coming up in her garden, and she relaxes her search for a while, resting in a world where someone bothered to plant bulbs in autumn. Over the course of a week the flowers crest the dirt and start to open.

They're wonderful. But the husband himself is not to her taste; she moves on when the crocuses start to fade and she finds that nobody has planted daffodils for March.

One husband knits his own socks. One husband has a seemingly congenial coke habit which, she is shocked and a little excited to discover, she shares. She gives it a go, leaning forward and copying his movements, and she doesn't like it, but she doesn't exactly *not* like it either. A few days later, though, they go round to visit the husband's friend Padge and hang out, and after a few beers the husband asks Padge about what he's got in stock, and Padge goes to his freezer and pulls out a tub of supposed ice cream that he opens to shake out a cluster of plastic bags, and this is too much; she was willing to take drugs with the husband but she is absolutely not willing to sit with him while he buys them from a friend's empty carton of Sainsbury's Taste the Difference vanilla.

She likes the next husband, a slightly younger man called Petey, but two hours into his visit she is aghast to discover from a message she sent to Elena a couple of days ago that she, Lauren, is—somehow—pregnant. Elena's response reads *Congratulations!!(??? right?),* and then it looks like they had a long, long phone call. The process can't be far gone and she can't figure out whether she's even told Petey or whether she's keeping it a secret and deciding what to do. There's no way the pregnancy was totally accidental; her IUD should still have two years left before she needs to replace it. She wants to work out how Petey convinced her to get it removed, what's going on, what she talked about with Elena on that long call, but not as much as she wants to not be pregnant any more; she's grown used to different hair colours, the occasional new scar, but this is too much. She sends Petey back, and then cycles through another three or four husbands right away, just in case.

More husbands arrive. She sends them back. Still more husbands arrive. She stops for a while with an Alasdair, because she likes his accent, a gentle Edinburgh lilt, and when they go to his friend's wedding and he puts on his kilt she's a big fan of that too. She is genuinely hurt when she figures out that he's having an affair.

It's worse in the next world. This husband, Hōne, is from Auckland, and she has a lovely evening with him watching, thank god, not *Mindhunter* or in fact any sort of drama that they're five episodes into and that she has to pretend to understand, but instead a sketch comedy show that requires neither attention nor background knowledge. But when she heads into work the next day, she discovers that, this time, she's the unfaithful one. At first, when her colleague at the canvas-stretching store touches her on the back in passing, she assumes he is simply a creep, but then they're alone at lunchtime and he grabs her hand and kisses her and says, "I missed you so much, I can't believe I hate weekends now." No. She doesn't like the idea of herself as the sort of person who might have an affair, and it's bad enough having to figure out her relations with one man, let alone two.

"Exactly," Bohai says, during one of his London visits. "Hence my rules, as you know."

"I really hated it," she says; she was surprised by how much. It's not like she doesn't lie to the husbands plenty. "What do you think when you find out you're up to something?"

"Well. Even before all this I made a lot of bad decisions, you know? Fun decisions. But bad. So it's almost easier when it's a different version of me that did it, right, because it's *god why would he do that, the fucking idiot* instead of *why did I do that, what's wrong with me, shit.*"

He's been very apologetic about the walk-in wardrobe incident, but it's not his fault, of course; even the eavesdropping was some other Bohai. And when she thinks that she could be doing yoga every morning and understanding spring greens and joining in on Tuesday book discussion Zooms and always, always eating at the table, she's not sorry to have moved on.

"So what you're saying," he says, "is: thank you, Bohai, I'm so glad you married a terrifying shouter and then hid in his walk-in wardrobe like a creep."

"Sure," she says. "But don't do it again."

○ ○

The world remains plausible as she cycles through more men. Two times out of three, she's at the council. The lives that diverge the most are usually the ones with the longest marriages; once, in a relationship entering its seventh year, she finds she's a hairdresser. Maybe she has a surprising natural talent? But no. After speed-watching YouTube tutorials and absolutely wrecking two clients' hair, she switches.

How many are you at? Bohai sends, and she tries to count up in her head and can't; sometimes she flicks through the men so fast that they blur in her memory. *195?* she sends back, a guess.

Fast work, he responds.

How's it going there?

We're in the country which as you know is not my thing BUT, we do have a pet emu??? *Climbed out of a shed and this guy was staring me in the face.* He sends a video: a huge messy bird, as tall as a man, wide eyes, long legs, long neck, turning its head impassively.

○ ○

She decides that she's at Husband 196; or close enough, anyway. She will do better at remembering in the future.

With Husband 197 she has the flu; she sends him away in the hope that in the world with Husband 198 she is feeling better, which she is, but the whole house is painted brown, so she sends him away too. Husband 199 is a clarinettist, which she discovers when he declines to perform oral sex on the grounds that he's saving his mouth for a performance the next day. This is such a specific objection that she spends twenty minutes googling to see if it's legit before deciding that it isn't which, sure, is up to him but she still feels he could have mentioned it *before* inviting her to lick beneath his unusually pendulous balls. She sends him back with a vague sense of girl power and justice upheld.

She thinks again about the time at the start of a relationship when people soften and change, the gift of temporary mutability. Elena, who scorned reality television until she watched twelve seasons of *Survivor* in the early days of dating Rob. Amos, who hated social media when they were together but started posting daily pictures with the girlfriend after.

She doesn't always like the new versions of herself, but they help her understand the edges of who she might be.

Husband 200, then.

○ ○

The flat is tidy. She is poised for a welcoming kiss. But Husband 200 is Amos, again.

"Oh," she says, and steps back.

"Got it," he says, dropping a bag on the ground, and folding the ladder back up.

She has had one Amos before, very briefly, very early on. She supposes that both Amoses decided against breaking up with her, and moved in, and at some point deigned to marry her. This Amos has considered his options, dilly-dallied a little, thought about discarding her, and finally, perhaps ruefully, decided that he can't do better.

Fuck you, Amos, she thinks.

She should send him straight back up, but something in her wants to redress the balance. And before she allows herself to realise it's a bad idea, before she can think about how hard it's going to be to get him into the attic if he leaves the house, she smiles sweetly, and says:

"Amos, darling, I don't think we should see each other any more."

He frowns. "Yeah. I mean, that's usually the idea with a divorce."

She looks at the bag that he's brought down from the attic. She looks at him. She looks around the flat, which on reflection is maybe not *tidier* than usual so much as *emptier* than usual.

Oh, she thinks.

He is wearing a slim-fit shirt with big monstera leaves printed across a light-grey background, stubble at a careful length; she recognises this sort of get-up. He wants to look good in front of his ex-wife.

"We gave it our best," he says, with a half-smile.

"Did we?" she says. "Did we really?" In her world, he broke up with her four years ago, and they didn't even live together yet, so they've probably only been married for two or three years. She is suddenly angry; how *dare* he appear in her home only to leave, making a face like he thinks she's sad to see him go? She never thinks of him these days. She can't even remember what they used to do together other than standing in a corner and inventing new ways to feel better than everyone else. Their whole long relationship is baffling to her.

"I don't know. We tried, right?"

How gracious of him, she thinks, to *try*, to not break up with her over the phone from the queue for the Spinball Whizzer, which she now knows is not even one of the five best roller coasters at Alton Towers. "We tried way too hard," she says. "Should've given up years ago."

"Hey, steady on," that infuriating tone of diffident reason. "We can keep this civil, right?"

Fuck you, Amos, she thinks again, and then she says: "Fuck you, Amos."

"This is why it didn't work out," he says. "You weren't happy either, you just didn't want to do anything about it, so now the whole divorce is my fault."

"Get out of my house," she says.

"It's a flat," he says, picking up his bag and another one that's sitting by the kitchen door. "And yeah, it's yours, well done on having a rich dead grandmother, great work."

She has seen so many versions of the flat and this is, she thinks, almost the ugliest, a dark green in the living room with a big feathery-papered feature wall, enamel lampshades that beam the light downwards. "Cannot wait to get rid of this wallpaper."

"You fucking chose it," he says. And he picks up the bags and carries them across the landing, and walks down the stairs.

CHAPTER 31

She searches through emails and messages and photos, trying to figure out what happened.

In her original life, Amos broke up with her and quit his job and grew a beard and moved to Berlin for six months and then moved back to London, and tried desperately to stay friends with their mutual acquaintances as if he thought he could win them off her. In this version of the world it seems that instead of doing any of that, he stayed with her, moved in and bought a motorcycle.

They are not quite divorcing yet; they will give it some time, and presumably in six months or a year they will file.

She's in the house alone.

She texts Elena, *Amos came round for his last boxes*, and Elena texts back, *You okay?*, and she replies: *Absolutely.*

This is not a return to everything that used to be. The walls are terrible, the IKEA rug is a different IKEA rug, there is a small row of porcelain ducks on the windowsill.

But it's not too far.

And she is responsible to nobody.

She messages work and warns them that she's not feeling well. She is feeling *amazing*, warm and surrounded by space, no husband to decipher, no cohabitation to negotiate, no uneven split of the chores to resent or, less often, feel bad about. She looks at the wallpaper in the living room and starts taking things off the shelves, piling them in the middle of the room; then she realises that it's almost five o'clock and rushes out to the hardware store and buys a tin of the brightest white paint they have. Back at home she spins her roller over the feature wallpaper. It's textured and the paint doesn't always go into the crevices but she presses harder, big strokes, arcs of paint, as high as she can; she stands on a chair and accidentally smears a bit on the cream ceiling but never mind. She paints for an hour, then two. She texts Nat and Toby and (checking recent messages to identify other friends) someone named Taj, and asks them to come over, tonight or tomorrow or on the weekend, or the week after that, whenever they want, it doesn't matter, nobody else is going to be in the house, her schedule is clear.

The reset has wiped out her messages to Bohai and she doesn't know his number, it's always changing, so she emails him instead at his memorised address: *Divorcing!!* she says, *Won't stop the attic working, right?*

○ ○

Toby is the first to arrive; he knocks on the door and comes up to survey the living room and its streaks of white paint. Following a carpet mishap, she has laid bedsheets on the floor.

"I never liked that wall," he says. "But I thought you were meant to strip the wallpaper first?"

She tries to work the paint into the pattern's textured furrows. "There's a lot of things you're supposed to do. Do you replace your toothbrush every three months?"

"You okay?" he says, and she really is.

The mysterious Taj comes by. "Taj!" Lauren says, arms widespread, paint-streaked. Taj looks familiar, actually. Dark hair that juts out in a triangle, bright-green eye makeup, black clothes; then Lauren remembers. She met Taj at Elena's wedding! Taj was married to Amos! She hugs her and says, "Oh my god, Taj,

I'm so glad to see you," and how wondrous that they have both escaped being married to the same man, even if only one of them is aware of it. Taj has brought wine, which Lauren declines but Toby takes.

Nat comes by too, with Caleb and Magda in tow, and she only has half an hour, and she doesn't immediately launch into advice about painting and/or dating so presumably she thinks Lauren has really fucked things up. But Elena comes at eight, just as Nat's leaving, with a bag full of bread and cheese and avocados and who-knows-what. While she cuts it all up in the kitchen, Lauren enlists the others to move the rest of the living-room furniture towards the centre of the room, freeing up more walls. She doesn't have another roller, so they can't help with the painting. But it's good to see them. She has been neglecting them for too long. She's so glad to have them back.

The piled furniture and paint fumes stop them from eating in the living room, and the kitchen's too small, so they cram into the spare room, sitting on the single bed and the floor, Elena's two salads and assorted charcuterie balanced on the office chair.

While Lauren was moving things from the bookshelves in the living room, she found a wedding photo. She looks at it, close up, then at arm's length. Long white dress, black suit for Amos, Elena her maid of honour in an unbecoming peach. She changed her name this time, which would be a fucking nightmare of administration to change back if she had to follow through on it. That said, Lauren Lambert is a top-tier name; probably she only took it because it sounds so elegant. Lauren Lambert. The former Mrs. Lambert. Glamorous divorcée Lauren Lambert. There's something rather chic about being divorced, she thinks.

"Come on," Elena says, "let's not gaze at wedding photos, I reckon. We could burn it if you like? Little cleansing ritual?"

"Nah," Lauren says, "I'm good," and puts it down.

"This seems great," Taj says. "I thought you were having a breakdown."

Elena half shrugs. "I mean, not to jump to conclusions but I wouldn't say it's necessarily advisable to paint over your wallpaper, or even realistically a sign of *not having a breakdown*."

Lauren feels a little vehement, perhaps, a little excited, but it's not the sort of excitement that comes with a crash. It's the thrill of being able to do what she likes, of not having to figure out what a husband wants to do, what his expectations are, how they behave together, who sits where on the sofa, how he takes his tea and which mugs he likes, whether she should check before having her friends over, whose toothbrush is whose (a *nightmare*, every new husband). "Really great," she adds. "I'm excited. I'm excited to be on my own."

She's still excited to be on her own the next morning, when she wakes up early but due to some calling-in-sick forethought doesn't have to do anything except fall back asleep. Eventually she wakes up again and wanders from room to room, putting things in the wrong places, *deciding*.

She eats tinned peaches and a scoop of vanilla ice cream for lunch. She walks naked from room to room. She pulls the ladder down from the attic, and pokes her head up, watches the electricity flare.

She leaves the sofa and the rest of the furniture piled where they are; she'll finish painting the walls tomorrow, or next weekend. She is still excited to be alone—and the next morning, she is excited to be alone again when she wakes up to her own alarm, nobody else's, and can turn the light on right away, and rummage through drawers as loudly as she wants, and she doesn't even have to think about who is going first in the shower.

o o

Maybe she'll stay in this world for a week. Maybe for ever. She is at the council for work; goes into the office and says hello to everyone and is so delighted to see them. Wandering the area at lunchtime, she buys herself the huge £180 plant that Bohai got her for Christmas. She can barely carry it, one arm around the pot and another on the trunk, so heavy, she has to turn to get through doors without damaging its canopy. She's never going to manage it on the train at rush hour so she sits outside a Pret until it closes at eight, warming up with occasional teas, the plant on the seat opposite.

She has made notes of the care instructions imparted to her in the shop. She is happy to tend its leaves, happy with its manageable awkwardness, this big and touchy plant that needs to be taken care of, this plant that may one day be taller than she is, but which will never say *Have you seen my socks* or *Is that your third glass* or *I told you my dad was coming round* or in fact anything at all, ever. She carries it up her stairs, leaning it on every second or third step for a break, and finally nestles it into place near but not right by the window, among the piles of books and boxes that she still hasn't put back on the shelves. She doesn't name it but she does say, "There you go, buddy." Has she ever said the word "buddy" aloud before? It feels right. Hey, buddy. Need some water, buddy? Ah, come on, buddy, perk up.

She even looks up the brass plant mister she had at Felix's, but it costs eighty pounds, and her plant buddy isn't going to know the difference. She empties out a half-used bottle of beach-waves sea-salt crunchy hair spray, which is both expired and out of fashion, and fills it with water, and uses that instead. C'mon, buddy. Absorb that water. You can do it. Plump out those glossy green leaves.

Her phone dings: another unknown number, another update from Bohai on his cycle of spouses. *So many vases what the fuck* and a picture of four blue vases, then another larger blue vase, and a shelf of ten glass vases, transparent and pink and green, then an open cupboard with seven or eight glazed ceramic vases.

That night she sleeps on the sofa, surrounded by her towering piles, the curtains open so that she wakes with the sunlight. And she's still excited.

CHAPTER 32

"It takes a while to process it," Taj says while they're out for over-priced beer by the river. "I dunno, babe, this is your first divorce, I want to make sure you're doing okay."

She really is. In the years before the first husband emerged from the attic, she had felt the burden of long singleness lying upon her. Being *happy to be single* had felt obligatory, a statement of feminism or autonomy or just a way to head off coupled friends who she didn't want feeling sorry for her. The weight of that requirement had made it difficult, sometimes, to figure out how she really felt.

But now she is single *again* rather than single *still*. She reads in the bath with the door open for an hour, and thinks that she will do it all the time. (She never does, but she could.) She masturbates whenever she likes, without having to either escalate to sex or rush it through without a husband noticing. She eats dinner when she gets back from work, or at eleven, or twice, or not at all. She pops downstairs to see Toby and Maryam, or just Toby when Maryam is working, then after an hour she comes back upstairs and relishes the delights of being on her own. After so many husbands, she no longer needs to worry that she is unfit for human company; she can leave her laptop open on the other half of the bed, *yes I'm still watching, continue playing*, without wondering whether any man will ever lie there again.

She likes being friends with Taj, too. In her original life, she hadn't spent much time with single people: Elena, Maryam and

Toby, Nat, even Zarah at work, all partnered. And it's fine to have coupled-up friends, but it's different. Lauren hasn't yet figured out how she knows Taj, but it must be, somehow, through Amos, and how magnificent that he has brought them together like this, and then left them both alone.

She texts Bohai. *How's it going? I'm still single, it's amazing. The bed is so big when there's nobody else in it*

He texts back. *Yeah my wife had an affair and she's gone to stay with her sister while I figure out if I can "forgive her," should get in the cupboard and give her back the flat but it's So Nice to have a place to myself so*

She replies, *You're a terrible husband*

And him: *She's the one who had the affair*

She sends a picture of her enormous plant, which is still the only thoughtfully positioned thing in the room, furniture haphazard around it. She loves it very much.

○ ○

One Tuesday, something occurs to her: she could *date*.

She hadn't dated much, in the years between Amos and the husbands. The pandemic had put a stop to it for a while, of course. Once things had opened up again she would occasionally go out alone and wait for someone to talk to her and see how the conversation went and maybe take him home or, more often, go to his place, because you're less likely to get murdered that way, she remembers reading: nobody wants to have to deal with a body in their own flat. And then she would never see the man again, as if she could stop anything from being a *bad decision* by isolating it from the rest of her life.

Dating had started to feel impossible, the first trip to the dentist after years of neglect; who knew what flaws and expenses and cavities might be uncovered, how unfit she might be for a relationship? She'd started making a profile on one of the apps a few times, and then put it away, appalled by the process of deciding who to be and what to look for. Better to convince yourself that you're happy with what you have than to search for something else and maybe fail.

But compared to the intensity of Michael and Iain and Rohan and Jason and a dozen Davids, surely a couple of low-pressure dates should be easy?

Toby and Elena are both too coupled to be up-to-date on the apps, but Taj knows what she's doing, so Lauren heads up to the park near her flat on Saturday.

"Are you sure you're ready?" Taj asks. "A month ago you were crying on buses. Sleeping on my sofa because your flat was creepy when it was empty. Watching GIFs of baby elephants for two and a half days."

"Yeah, I'm good," Lauren says. She was living another life when that happened; she remembers none of those tears. She thinks about the claim that it takes half the length of the relationship to get over somebody. Her first relationship with Amos ended years ago, and her second lasted about twenty seconds, so she's probably good to go.

Taj sighs. "Okay. We need: close-up, distance shot, you doing something you like, you at a party so they know you have friends. And nothing where you've cropped Amos out of it. It's bad luck."

Lauren prances while Taj takes photos. "Okay, take your coat off so we can get some close-ups and it doesn't look like they're all from the same day." She stands on a ledge to get a good angle, phone raised, while Lauren stands below her on the pavement, jumping out of the way when approaching cyclists ding.

Back at Taj's flat, she puts on one of Taj's sequinned dresses, which is too big but they bulldog-clip the back, and Lauren leans casually against a wall.

"I dunno," Taj says, showing her some pictures, "my wall's too wall-y. Let's try the corridor, looks more like it might be a bar," so

Lauren stands against the dark stairwell's concrete, USB-powered disco lights plugged into Taj's laptop and perched on the steps that lead up to the next floor. "Sip! Okay, laugh. No, take the straw out. Think easy-going. Look left! Look right!"

A man in a blue shirt walks down the stairs. "Having fun, ladies?"

"We are, thank you!" Lauren says, and her eyes follow his steps: what about him? Would she date him?

The photos are ridiculous, but they go through them together and they crop and edit the colour and make an account, and she tries to write a bio. *Hello*, she writes. *I'm here because I'd like to go on some dates.*

"Sounds fake," Taj says.

I'm not fake, Lauren adds.

"Nobody reads the bio anyway," Taj says.

And they start scrolling through men. "What's your type?" Taj asks.

Lauren has listed so many criteria, written on so many Post-it notes, done so much research, married so many different men. What's her type? Well, how long does Taj have? But then, she's not looking for a husband this time. Just for a nice man to spend a bit of time with. "Someone with a hobby. Like maybe he's into crochet. Or those big tables with fake mountains and the little toy dragons that you paint and then you use them for playing games. Or . . . ice sculpture."

She likes it when the husbands have hobbies because it gives them something to do, and because it helps her to remember which is which. A dozen television husbands blend together, twenty video-games-in-the-spare-room husbands blur into one—a whittling husband stands out. But she also likes it when a man cares about a thing, when he concentrates on it, leans in, narrows his eyes or bites his lip, gives himself over to details.

Taj sighs. "I'm not saying you don't want someone who's into

Warhammer, but I promise you don't want someone who's so into Warhammer that they talk about it on their dating profile."

"I want someone who likes things," Lauren says. "I want someone who's having a nice time." It's barely a dent in her criteria list, but it feels like a good place to start.

Taj takes Lauren's phone and matches her with a tall man a mile away ("Looks like he brews his own beer," she says), and a short man somewhat closer (mentions bookbinding on his profile). Then Lauren makes her stop because tall maybe-beer-brewer has messaged her already.

"Okay, but don't get fixated on one guy," and Taj sends a message on her behalf to the bookbinder, who doesn't reply.

"Why wouldn't he reply?"

"Lots of guys match with everyone, they swipe and swipe. See what their options are and get picky from there."

Lauren has, she supposes, no right to complain about this system.

"Oh," Taj says, "and don't message for too long. Plan an in-person meet-up or don't bother."

That's fine. She doesn't want a chore, she has husbands for that; she wants an actual date, she wants to meet up in a pub and to have to check whether it's him and then laugh and get food and split the bill and wonder whether there's going to be a *spark*. "Okay," she says, and arranges for a late-afternoon drink on Thursday with the maybe-brews-his-own-beer guy.

Going on DATES, she messages Bohai.

Me too it's crazy, Bohai messages back. *Affair wife has shacked up with affair guy. But, with dating you have to explain who you are? and decide if you like each other??*

Imagine, she sends back, and wonders if she owns a hair curler in this world, and if so whether she should try to find it.

CHAPTER 33

The date, in a bar near St. Pancras so bland that she repeat-edly forgets its name even while inside it, is not at all inter-esting and she's glad they met for a drink, not dinner. In the toilet she swipes a few more men.

The next date is boring too, but on the third—with the book-binder, who got back to her after all—she feels the thing, the *spark*. The husband—no, she thinks, not the husband, the *date*—the date is slender and mysterious and flirty and when he puts his hand on her upper arm while they're saying goodbye, she's into it. The spark! There it is! She is disgruntled when he doesn't message her again, or respond to her own eventual message.

"Next," Taj tells her.

She goes on quite a lot of dates. The husbands have taught her, she thinks, not to judge. Perhaps with her expansive view of the possibilities of life, she will make all sorts of discoveries about men, and herself, and the world?

In fact the husbands have, she soon discovers, taught her to judge extremely quickly, which she has to unlearn a little. There is a thin man with a moustache who is keen to demonstrate how feminist he is, and when she arrives a couple of minutes early he is already sitting in the cafe reading Simone de Beauvoir. And sure, fine, she guesses men should read Simone de Beauvoir (she's not a hundred per cent sure, she hasn't read any herself), but not in hardback in a cafe while they're waiting for someone to flirt with, holding it up so everyone can see the cover.

Best book to be caught reading when you're early for a date? she messages Bohai when she gets home.

Uggghg books, he sends back. *Walk straight out. No readers. Gameboy advance or gtfo*

The night after, she has dinner with Maryam and Toby. "I always thought," Maryam says, "I'd be great at the apps."

"Sorry," Toby says.

"I prefer this, obviously. I just think if it had come up, I'd have been good. Can I have a go?" she adds, and takes Lauren's phone. This is something that her friends in relationships love to do, she's discovering; they want to play the game, spin through faces, imagine.

This is why Taj is better to talk to: with Taj, she doesn't feel like she's a vicarious little adventure, five minutes of make-believe.

The two of them go to a speed-dating night at an art gallery, but the speed-date activities are very intense. At one point Lauren has to spend six minutes finger-painting silently with a guy she's pretty sure she was once married to, and then for the next "date" they are instructed to sit still while their allocated men draw them. Lauren's portrait is only extremely unflattering but Taj declares hers *kinda racist, and not even for the right race,* and they slip off to the bar around the corner before they have to make plasticine models of the men in the next round.

She goes back home. She sets up another date. The process is not, she admits, as straightforward as she thought it might be. She messages a complaint to Bohai, who like her is still temporarily single, and looks up Felix, who maybe is too, and even Carter, who also, for once, seems to be between girlfriends, or at least who doesn't appear in a hundred photos with a wholesome and charming American woman living a visibly perfect life. Jason is back in

London and has twin toddlers. Michael comes up on the app, once, and she approves him—maybe this time it really is a sign—but they don't match. Fuck you, she thinks, squinting at her photos, wondering what's wrong with them; you married me twice, you don't know what you want.

"Yeah," Taj says when she complains, "it's hell, I uninstalled all the apps yesterday. I'm going to meet someone in real life. Or I'm not going to meet someone at all. Get a bunch of pets. Like the volume of a man, but in rabbits."

"No," Lauren says, "come on, dating time, a guy came up on mine who's a professor with a beard, you love professors with beards."

"I love rabbits. Let me know if you want to give it a break too," Taj says. "We can go do spinster things. Hang out and complain about the young people and get stuff done."

"What stuff? I don't have any stuff."

Taj tilts her head from side to side. "We could finish painting your living room? Put the furniture back?"

It has been, it's true, some weeks. But Lauren likes the room as it is, her friendly plant in the middle, growing new leaves, occasionally dropping an old one, the coffee table jammed up next to the sofa so that it's a fun little challenge to get into and out of. And most of all, she likes that she has no responsibility to make it normal and liveable and shareable. It's one of the things that makes her feel good about the dates not working out.

She can see how that might look bad from the outside. But it's honestly fine.

She climbs on to the honestly fine sofa and googles her exes again. After so many husbands, could Carter really have been better than the others? Or is it just that he's the only one she didn't choose to send away, and that's what makes her miss him even now? She searches the others, to see if she feels any regrets. Jason,

Rohan, Amos: no. Michael, Bohai: not really. Felix: no. Felix's mansion, which is blurred out on Google Maps but she finds an estate agent's listing from a few years back, with more normal decor: well, maybe a little bit.

○ ○

She's due a holiday, she thinks. Going to work every day, instead of mostly calling in sick and skipping out: exhausting, it turns out! Starting conversations with strange men on three different apps, and going on two bad first dates a week: time-consuming and upsetting! Taj wants her to come on a trip to Norway, which yeah, sure, sounds good, but first: what about a nice weekend in the country?

She books a cottage near Felix's house, and tells herself that it's because she knows it's a nice part of the country, definitely not because dating is terrible and she is feeling friendlier than she used to about her maybe-evil one-time husband and his millions. Three days in the country. It'll be great.

The cottage is smaller than it looks in the pictures. She unlocks the door, finds a welcome note and a bottle of indifferent prosecco.

There's nothing purposeful or special about being here, she reminds herself. But she goes for a long country walk—a good walk, a walk recommended in the local walks pamphlet that she found on the coffee table, and if it also takes her past Felix's house then that's hardly her fault—and again without thinking about it too much, she goes in the back gate. She just wants to have a look at the garden, which is different (worse). She avoids the CCTV cameras, and walks round to the courtyard outside the conservatory. Yes, Felix was a little bit evil; but only a little bit, right? And he was in prison that one time, but only once, and not for anything real where normal people suffered; just for a little light business crime.

She is exhausted and she knows that back home in her flat her

later in the year, I'd love to see a few properties while I'm around. She keeps feeling sick for the six hours that it takes him to get back to her, *of course, let me know what you're looking for.* And then she feels sick on and off for another week, and then she's on a plane, and then in an airport, and then on another plane, and then she's in Denver.

CHAPTER 34

She expects to step out of the airport and see mountains rising above her, but instead she sees: a city. A low, spread-out city, wide roads, a strange quality to the light. She has arrived on one of the sixty-five days a year without sunshine. But it feels—okay, it feels okay.

All she wants is to meet Carter once, just once, or maybe twice.

Probably there'll be nothing between them. Then she'll know that they had a good relationship that wasn't fundamentally different from any other good relationship she could have; that he is not her destiny, the purpose towards which all the other husbands point. And then she can go back and get on with her life.

Or if it feels special, she can plan around that. Maybe they'll get together immediately, sure, but that's not the only option. It could be: go home, exchange more husbands, find someone else she's divorcing, and make a slower, gentler approach. Or: switch five hundred times, a thousand, five thousand, until Carter comes back; that must be possible, right? If they're *meant to be* then there must have been more than one version of the world where they met? If she spends two hours a day exchanging husbands—and plenty of people watch at least two hours of television a day so that's not an unreasonable time commitment—if she spends two hours a day exchanging husbands, and if she exchanges on average one husband a minute, that's 120 husbands a day, 10,000 in a few months.

But first, she has to know. She has to see him. Say hello. Smile. See what it feels like when they look at each other again.

And the rest of the time she can have a nice holiday. She can look at nature, she can explore the city. Her hotel is near a train station, which she finds surprising—for some reason she'd never thought about America having trains—but comforting. A bus can go anywhere, but there're only a few ways to go wrong with a train.

She's arranged to meet Carter at his workplace on Friday; she gets to the hotel late on Wednesday afternoon and sets about getting over the jet lag. Unpacks her suitcase and hangs up her clothes, plugs in the UK-to-US power converter that she's proud she thought to bring. Showers. Blow-dries her hair, because you *never know* when you might run into an ex-husband, and heads out.

In a nearby bar she discovers the differences between the tedious London craft beer scene and the tedious Denver craft beer scene, namely (1) people in the US will try to have conversations with you even if they're not trying to pick you up, and (2) the beer contains *substantially* more alcohol, so perhaps you will let them.

She ends up speaking to a couple called Ryan and Tyler, which she is delighted by: real American names. "Ryan!" she says. "Tyler! Like in the films!" She is playing up her foreign-ness, she knows, normally she'd say "movies."

"I don't think I know anyone in a movie called Lauren," Ryan says slowly—is that a drawl? Is he *drawling*? They're not as handsome as Carter but they do have something of his expressions, his mode of being. When she thought it was love, was it just *being from Denver*?

Ryan is having a party on Saturday and she should come, they assure her, it'll be great, there'll be a bonfire and s'mores, which again feels so unlikely to her, that people actually make and say "s'mores." She should have come to Denver years ago.

"I'd love to," she says, and gives them her number. How delightful! Maybe when she and Carter meet on Friday they'll hit it off and she can bring him to the party and he'll be so impressed that she's made friends in town already and they'll have such a good time together! What a great bar. What a great city.

○ ○

In the morning, the sleep from the hangover cancels out the early waking from the jet lag, and she opens her eyes at quarter past eight.

She doesn't want to meet Carter properly until she's feeling her best, but she goes to the diner opposite his work and waits outside until a table by the window opens up, then rushes in and lays claim to it, and watches from a distance to see if he appears.

It's not stalking; it's just research.

And at 12:53, heading out for lunch she guesses, there he is. Walking along the other side of the road, looking at his phone. Wearing a suit, like when they went to Elena's wedding. Carter. Her husband.

Well, she thinks it's Carter. It's been a while, and there are a lot of guys around Denver who kind of look like him. But then he uses the knuckle of his pointer finger to press a button at the pedestrian crossing, and she recognises the gesture. It's him; it's him.

She obviously isn't going to follow him through the streets—quite apart from anything else, if he's off to look at houses, presumably he's going to drive.

So instead she decides to work through a list of the ten best things to do in Denver and furnish herself with stories about how much fun she's having.

The nearby art gallery is a huge strange building, jagged shards and looming menace. It costs money to get in, and more for her as she's not a Colorado resident, and once she's inside she wanders from room to room looking at paintings. The portraits in particular are too much: just men's faces, the dating apps all over again.

She does, however, find a shop selling the pretzel M&M's that Felix brought her, so she spends the evening in her hotel room watching American Netflix and eating three packets. And she sends Taj a picture of the mountains, and a message saying *Looking forward to comparing these to the Norwegian ones xx*, and then spends an hour anxious about not getting a reply, and then realises it's the middle of the night in the UK. Look, she thinks, everything's going fine.

In the morning she washes her hair, and dries it, and puts makeup on, then washes it off and does it again but more casual. She sorts through her clothes and puts on jeans and a shirt and a big jacket and low boots. Perhaps later, her clothes say, she will lasso a cow. She listens to "Teenage Dream" and bops gently around the room, drinking coffee, making fun of herself, but also because: who knows, who knows?

○ ○

She meets Carter in his office. Walking in, name to the receptionist, and he's there at the back of the room and he turns and— eye contact.

This is not the only time she has seen a husband while married to someone else: there was Jason at Felix's place, of course, and once her husband was a previous husband's non-identical twin brother, which made for quite a dinner party.

But Carter smiles widely when he sees her, a staggering genuine grin, and he takes three big steps across the room and puts his hand out and shakes hers, the touch of their fingers. "It's so great to meet you."

"Hi," she says. "Hey."

"Gimme a minute," Carter says, and turns back to the rumbling printer; he picks up papers and clips them together.

"So," he says as they settle into a glass-walled meeting room, "Denver! What brings you here?"

"Oh, just work."

"That's great, we'll need a load of boring paperwork about the job and your credit but I can send that over for you to fill out in your own time. Do you have a sense of the budget range you're looking in?"

"Well," she says. She's never had to deal with this sort of thing: inherited half the flat, stayed there because it was easier, doesn't know how to actively choose somewhere to live. But she's done her research. "My place in London is on the market for 500k in US dollars." She has rounded way, way up to get it into a plausible price range for buying the sort of places that Carter's selling.

"And you own it outright?"

"Yes," she lies; Amos has no claim on it, thank god, but of course, half of it is Nat's.

"And it's just you?"

"Yes," and she smiles. "But I'd love a spare room for when friends come to visit." It's important that he knows that she has friends.

"With the budget you get moving from London to Denver," and he gestures towards the window, "that shouldn't be a problem. You said you were thinking about apartments rather than houses?"

"Yeah." In this fantasy life she is not trying to cultivate plants in the hard Denver soil, she is going out to nice bars and joking with friends and maybe they all drive to a lake in the summer.

"Okay," he says, "well, we can definitely work with that. Tell me about neighbourhoods. I was in London for a year—"

"Oh, lovely," she says, in careful surprise.

"—so I can speak London boroughs. Tell me what you're interested in and I'll, y'know, translate it to Denver."

She had wondered if maybe she wouldn't be struck by him the same way here, that perhaps she had been beguiled by the quiet confidence and the sense of *being in the fresh air* that he carried with him in London. But even here, surrounded by men like him, he is her favourite.

"I'm in Norwood Junction, which is south-east, kind of near Crystal Palace? Bit further out."

"I love London suburb names. Crystal Palace!" He gestures widely. "Very *Lord of the Rings*."

She grins back. "I'd love to be more central here, though. Something like, maybe the equivalent of Bermondsey? Not in the centre-centre but with little art galleries and coffee shops and bars and stuff going on. For me that's part of the benefit of leaving London. In a smaller city I can live closer to everything." She's starting to convince herself with this: maybe she *could* move to Denver? She doesn't have a job offer but maybe she could get one?

"Okay, good guidance . . ."

"Maybe near a park." She likes nature, she thinks, she could be someone who likes nature.

"There are plenty of great options," Carter says, and he scans through some pictures, apartments, one little house. Tells her about locations: this one's near coffee shops, that one's right by a few different rooftop bars.

"Love a rooftop bar," she says. Outdoorsy! See? "Okay," as he shows her more and more apartments. "I like that one," more or less at random. "And that one," a place he's slowed down on, one that she thinks he wants her to pick.

"Good taste," he says. "How long are you in town for? Are you free Tuesday to have a look at some of the properties?"

She leaves Tuesday night; she could do it, but if looking at properties is the thing that's going to throw them together, it's cutting it tight. "You can't do anything on Monday? Or even this afternoon?"

"I don't think so," he says.

"Okay. Tuesday is great. Line 'em up. I trust your judgement."

It'll be okay. An hour or two to spend together: if romance is going to kindle, then that's enough time.

"Got anything fun planned for the weekend?" he asks as he packs up his papers and his tablet.

He's making conversation; this is the normal thing you ask someone when you meet them on a Friday afternoon. Nothing more than that. Unless it is. "Yeah," she says, "some friends are having a big bonfire party by a lake."

"Oh wow, that sounds cool."

It *is* cool, she thinks, I have friends, I made new friends in two days. She is sociable and likeable and Carter would have fun with her if they were married to each other, which they have been in the past and perhaps one day could be again. And then, like grabbing the plant mister, she doesn't let herself think it through, she just opens her mouth:

"Let me know if you'd like to come," she says.

"Oh," he says, and looks confused. But then he smiles, friendly, flattered, she thinks, and yeah, this is his job, but it seems like a real smile, and she would know: he was her husband. "I can't, I've got a friend's birthday. One of those rooftop bars, you know. But you have a great time."

"I will," she says. "I'm looking forward to it. And to seeing you on Tuesday."

"Tuesday it'll actually be my colleague Lautaro, I've got some appointments out of town. But I'll catch him up on this, and he'll be able to take you around. Have a good bonfire!" And he holds up the folder in a goodbye.

Ah, Lauren thinks. Well, fuck.

CHAPTER 35

Okay. First things first. There's no way she's spending her Saturday night hanging out by a big fire with two strangers she kind of liked in a bar while the possible love of her life, briefly single and even more briefly in the same city as her, is right there.

And there's no way she's going to spend two hours on Tuesday driving around to houses she doesn't want to buy with a man she's never even met, let alone kissed.

She messages Elena. *Mountains are fine but I don't know why they need so many of them*

She messages Bohai. *You ever been to Denver?*

She messages Toby, who is watering her plants while she's away. Well, plant—the succulent is still alive but doesn't need much attention. *How's everything going? Are the plants dead?*

They're good, he sends back, with a photo of the big one. *Hey do you want me to move your furniture back while I'm up here? It's no problem*

Of course: her living-room furniture is still, still piled in a tiny pyramid. But it's fine there, thank you very much, Toby. She throws herself back on the hotel bed, arms and legs outspread, phone face-down, and looks up at the ceiling, then over at the window.

Then she sits up, swings her legs on to the ground.

Because she still has four days left.

And she should be able to figure out where Carter will be tomorrow night. He said *one of those rooftop bars*, and how many of those can there be in one medium-sized city?

She will be there, it will be a charming coincidence, and they will hit it off, or they won't, but either way she'll know for sure.

Her mistake, not that she's made one, was to go for the outdoorsy look. Carter loved her in London, he even loved her in a bridesmaid dress, so she shouldn't try to be someone else; she should be the best possible version of herself, a charming city girl who doesn't know how horses work.

And so the next day she spends substantially more money than she has on a dress, diving hard towards the bottom of her overdraft, but it's green with a boat neck and an angular body that gathers in at the waist and narrows around her hips, and it looks amazing, exactly what you'd expect someone visiting from London to wear. She goes to a Sephora and they haul out the eyelash curlers and scan her with a device to match a lipstick to her skin tone.

Then she stops for a coffee in a park, and picks a daisy, and pulls off the petals. Always start with the answer you want, Jason said that time. *He loves me, he loves me not,* she tries, and it ends up on *he loves me not,* which isn't what she was after but she guesses uneven petals are never guaranteed. Anyway, daisies have sex by growing nectar to lure in bees that get rubbed up in pollen and then go rub it off on a different daisy somewhere else, so what do they know about love?

She sits down with a map, marks the plausible rooftop bars. There are at least seven, depending on how stringently you define "rooftop" and for that matter "bar."

The route she plans is biased towards a couple that look familiar: perhaps she has seen them in the background of Carter's many photos of his different Denver lives.

The first bar is almost empty, way too fancy. The second:

rammed, hard to find her way through, and as always she worries that she will miss Carter in the sea of men like him, but no, she's sure he's not there. The third: that's him, that's him, she thinks, but it's not. And then she turns around. And there he is.

She goes up to the bar and orders a beer. The stool is slippery, which combined with the tight skirt of her dress makes sitting difficult, and it's been getting cold fast; she wants to put her jacket on but she spent so much money on the dress so she steels herself against the temperature and brings out the book that she bought on the way, which is *Les Misérables* because it was the only vaguely impressive option in the newsagent near the park. She cannot concentrate even a little on *Les Misérables* but she can at least look at it with a thoughtful expression, and she can gaze around occasionally with the air of someone who is reflecting on something they have read in *Les Misérables* and how it illuminates the modern world.

She has learned from her first night that Americans are friendly; she is confident that she can get a conversation started. She keeps an eye on Carter's table until someone goes up for drinks: a woman with a crocheted top. She heads over.

"I love your top," she says to the woman.

"Oh, thanks," the woman replies. "My sister made it for me."

"It's so cute. Crochet, right?" The woman isn't engaging; Lauren needs to keep talking. "We don't have crochet in London," she adds.

"Oh wow, really?" The woman turns to the bartender and places her order; it's a big one but Lauren still only has a couple of minutes.

"I'm in town for a week," she tries, "so I thought I should visit one of these Denver bars that everyone's always talking about."

"They are?" the woman says. "I didn't know anyone outside Colorado ever thought about Denver."

"No, people in London say the bar scene here is great."

"That's so cool," the woman says.

"Yeah," Lauren says. "And everyone's so friendly here. In London I'd be sitting in a bar on my own but here everyone is always starting conversations."

"I guess that's true."

God, can this crochet woman not take a fucking hint? The bartender is bringing her last drink over.

"Can I help you carry those?" Lauren says, a final effort.

"Oh," the woman says. "Yeah, thanks. Do you want to join us? There's a few of us, it's a friend's birthday party."

At last. "Oh," a tone of intense surprise. "How lovely. That would be wonderful. Just for one drink."

She has finished her drink and only has water, but ordering now would mess up the plan. She can come back in five minutes once she's established herself.

So she picks up her water and two of the beers and follows the crocheted woman over towards her table, where maybe fifteen people are clustered, more people than there are seats but that's okay, her dress looks better standing anyway, and she prepares her expression of utter surprise.

And he turns, and sees her, and she lets her eyes widen, and her mouth open into astonishment. "Oh wow," she says. "Carter, right?"

And he looks at her and frowns. "Hi," he says.

She waits a moment.

"Great to see you," he adds.

He doesn't remember her.

Or rather, he doesn't *recognise* her, she thinks, and that's hardly his fault, she's dressed differently, different makeup, he was in work mode, he probably wasn't letting himself notice what people looked like in case it felt inappropriate. "Lauren. We met yesterday," she says.

"So we did," he says. "Huh!"

"So weird to see you here!" That's enough, she can ease back.

"Yeah," he says, "I thought you were going to a bonfire or something?"

"I was, I am," she says, "no, that's tomorrow."

"Do you two know each other?" the crocheted woman says. "We just met at the bar, we got talking about crochet. Did you know they don't have it in London?"

"We don't!" Lauren says. "Anyway, I met my friend for a drink here earlier," again, it's important that he knows she has friends, "but she had to run off so I stayed to read for a while," she tries to gesture with *Les Misérables* but she's left it up at the bar, "and what a coincidence." She smiles at them, plausible.

"Okay," Carter says, "well, hope you're enjoying the Denver nightlife," then turns back to the guy he was talking to.

"I'm Tia," the crochet woman, "and this is Maisie, it's her birthday, and this is Mallow."

Right. "It's so nice to meet you."

She manages to get in on another couple of conversations with Carter as the night goes on, bringing up things she knows he likes: horses, right? Tiramisu? Mostly he liked *her*. She mentions chasing after chickens once, but it doesn't go anywhere.

She warms up, at least, with the beer, and the green dress is great, and Tia is friendly and kind and asks her a lot of questions about London and her work and her hypothetical move to Denver, which Lauren is not entirely equipped to answer.

She makes one last-ditch effort at the end of the night. Tia is talking about going on somewhere else, but it looks like Carter isn't joining so Lauren declines. "It was lovely to meet you," she says loudly to Tia. "If you're ever in London, let me know—I've got a spare room if you need somewhere to stay." A spare room is presumably less impressive to people in Denver than to people in London, but it's good to seem hospitable. "Until I move, anyway," she adds hurriedly, remembering her cover story.

"That's great," Tia says. "You're okay to get back to your hotel, right?"

"I'm fine." These young cities can't intimidate her, their gridded streets can't get her lost.

"Okay. Well, you take care."

Lauren says goodbye to Carter, one hand on his arm.

"Hey," he says, "can I talk to you for a minute?"

He can! He absolutely can! Is this it? Is this the moment? They step away from the group.

"Look," Carter says, low, "I don't want to embarrass you and I'm sorry if I'm on the wrong track but it feels like maybe it's not a coincidence you were here?"

"Well," she says. Is *testing out a theory about destiny* the same thing as coincidence?

"And it's okay," he says, "I don't want you to feel bad or anything, but I think it might be a good idea if you find a different realtor."

"Oh," she says.

"Get home safe," he says, and his face is so beautiful.

She leaves without picking up *Les Misérables* or, she realises two blocks away, her jacket, but fury keeps her warm. He doesn't want her to *feel bad*? If he didn't want her to feel bad maybe he could have considered not saying anything? Also, how vain do you have to be to meet someone twice, *twice*, and immediately conclude that they're following you? And sure, she was, but not like he thought, it was just to *find out if they were destined*, which thankfully they are not, fuck him, and second, it could absolutely have been a coincidence, Denver isn't that fucking great, there aren't *that* many nice places to have a drink.

In the hotel she turns the shower as hot as it goes, and warms herself through, and washes her face and washes it again, and it's not as good as resetting the world with a magic attic, but it's as close as she can get.

Then, back on hotel Wi-Fi, notifications popping up, she deletes every email she has sent to Carter or received from him, and sorts through the evening's messages. Taj at least has forgiven her, and sent a screenshot of a guy from the dating app she's supposedly not on any more—*not for me but might work for you?*—and there's a message from Bohai saying *Lol i'm engaged*, which she can't even begin to think about, and from Amos, with a deeply gratuitous formality:

Hey, hope you're doing well. Just wanted to figure out what our plans should be about the paperwork. Big news but I'm moving to New Zealand for a bit; might make sense to do the forms and finalise it all first?

She reads it again.

The phone lights up with a follow-up message. *Maybe a coffee somewhere. Are you free this weekend?*

She puts the phone down. She doesn't have capacity for this. She will work it out in the morning. But Amos, for whom it is presumably morning already, has different ideas. The phone again: *I know this is a bit sudden.*

She throws the phone on to the uncomfortable hotel armchair by the window and it bounces off on to the ground and buzzes yet again. She picks it up. *Maybe I should have told you in person, sorry.* Ridiculous. How dare he think that she's upset because of him? He isn't in the top five things she's upset about. He can move to Pluto as far as she's concerned.

Except then she'd be stuck here, in this world where she's not destined to be with anyone, where she's lightly stalked at least two of her husbands, where she's spent all her money and then some, where she's half painted half her walls, and where Carter has politely, kindly, *perfectly* asked her to stop being a weirdo.

And her only way out is to get Amos into the attic.

Coffee sounds great, she texts back. *Sorry, noisy here, in a bar in Denver!! I'm back in a few days though, let's catch up then?* She feels her mouth twist and her arms shake but she adds another exclamation mark and hits send.

Then she plugs the phone in to charge, turns it over, and waits for sleep.

CHAPTER 36

She goes to the bar the next morning to collect her jacket, which the bartender hauls out of lost and found.

"This yours too?" he asks, holding up *Les Misérables*.

"No," she says, and sets about determinedly knocking out the rest of the top-ten-things-to-do-in-Denver list: a botanic garden, a zoo. They're rubbish.

Her plans for when she gets back aren't going great, either. She was intending to get Amos to the flat and then send him into the attic, but he's insisting on a cafe. *I just think a coffee out of the house would be better,* he messages when she pushes. *To ensure we keep it measured.*

You start a fight with a departing husband *once.* Why is he so keen to keep things measured anyway? How about accepting that things are going to be unmeasured?

This rejection feels like the others, wrapped up into one: like Carter, like swiping and messaging and *knowing* there are hundreds of men out there who would date her, even marry her, but not knowing how to get to them.

Her safety net has always been: well, if she really wanted, she could just get a new husband.

But not if Amos is in New Zealand.

She can't permit it. She is done with messaging people and awkward first dates and the supposed thrill of discovery; she's done, she will find a spouse and she will stick with him or else she will settle into her own comfortable life with her friends and she will not, she will never again, *go on a date*. Just sofas and taking things for granted for ever. She cannot *wait* to take someone for granted again.

First, she's going to need to get Amos into an accommodating mood, which isn't going to be straightforward because "accommodating" has never been his way. But she has learned a lot from her different husbands. She can do this.

○ ○

Back home, it's hard to distinguish her general post-flight malaise and jet lag from her extremely bad mood. She checks the ladder to the attic, leaves it down in readiness.

She's seeing Amos on Sunday, so she has time. First she thinks about excuses to get him back to the attic. Then she thinks about getting him drunk, but that's going to be hard in a coffee shop. Finally, she looks up drug-habit-husband's friend Padge. She remembers only approximately where he lives but he has a website advertising his marketing consultancy and his exact address is listed on a domain registry, which seems careless for a drug dealer but she supposes he's very much a hobbyist.

She dresses in grey leggings, and a big dark-blue jumper, which is woollen and she does think about fibres catching, but (1) she's never met Padge in this world so it would be weird for him to suspect her, and (2) presumably even hobbyist dealers don't go to the police to report that someone has taken all their drugs.

○ ○

Breaking into his flat is easy enough. She fakes up an electricity bill with her name and his address, so that she can pretend to live there. Then she prints it out at work on Thursday, and on

Friday she calls in sick (her boss won't be happy about it right after a holiday, but hey, she's leaving soon). She has to wait outside Padge's for five hours before she sees him leaving, which is a bit nerve-wracking. But the locksmith she calls doesn't even ask for proof that it's her place; she has brought the fake electricity bill for nothing.

And once she's inside, Padge's ice-cream containers are rammed with little bags. She shakes everything out into a Tupperware box and heads home, changing train carriages when someone comes in with a dog; she's not sure whether all dogs can smell drugs, or just the police ones.

She has until 3:30 p.m. Sunday to work out what all the little bags are and what they do.

o o

Alcohol would have been less suspicious. But she has to work with what she can get, and Amos still won't meet at the house, won't meet at a pub, *better to keep it quick*; she even has trouble getting him to come to Norwood Junction.

You're the one who wants the paperwork done, she sends in the end. *You can at least get the overground*

This sort of blame game is exactly why I want to meet in public, he sends back, but agrees. *I want us to try to be civil.*

I would love to be civil, she types, then thinks: does that seem sarcastic? *I do not mean to sound sarcastic*, she adds. *Let us engage civilly in this process.*

o o

She gets to the coffee shop five minutes early, enough time to order both of their coffees and stir the ground-up pill into his. She's tried this at home: it does work, though the coffee might look gritty at the bottom. His two sugars will help; she took a tiny, tiny sip of her trial run, and couldn't taste anything off.

"Hey," she says when he turns up. "Got you a coffee."

"Hi," he says. "Thanks. So, Denver!" he adds. "That sounds like fun!"

Given that his list of things to disapprove of has in the past included hiking, mountains and the entirety of the United States of America, perhaps, she thinks, he really is putting in an effort at this civility thing. She puts on her widest smile. "Yeah, I felt like a break, found a cheap flight, thought I'd give it a go. Everyone was friendly, the landscape is beautiful." It does, when she puts it like that, sound quite cool, the spur-of-the-moment adventure of it.

Although maybe not compared to the other side of the world. "So," she says. "New Zealand!"

"Yeah. I've always wanted to go back, ever since, you know."

"Our idyllic honeymoon?" She's looked up photos.

Now that she thinks about it, travelling around the world on a whim doesn't sound cool; it sounds like someone who is desperate to make a dramatic change but who will get to another country and find that it's still just him there, alone, no happier than he ever was. Or maybe not alone—*suddenly moving to New Zealand* does have the air of an unspoken . . . *for a woman* hanging after it.

Well, it's none of her business. And in an hour, it won't be any of his either.

"Where are you heading?" she asks.

"Wellington," he says.

"Wow!" It's so much easier to be wide-eyed and impressed when she knows she won't have to deal with him for long. She can nod and say "That sounds great" and "No wonder you want to get the paperwork sorted out, I think that's a sensible idea" and smile and let it slide off.

"And," Amos is saying, "I never loved London."

He did try moving to Berlin in her original world, but he moved back pretty damn fast. "Absolutely."

Another ten minutes on the delights of Wellington, and she can't tell whether the pill is working. "Would you like another coffee?"

"Oh, it's my turn," he says, and starts to stand.

"No, no. You slogged it over here. The least I can do is get the coffees."

The second crushed-up pill is from a different bag, in case the first batch didn't work. She stirs it furiously by the counter. "Sugar's already in," she says, as she puts the cup down.

"Thanks!" he says, delighted. Is he just happy that she's agreeing with him, or is the first coffee starting to take effect?

Another five minutes on how great it is that they're getting the paperwork done, and something is definitely happening. "Are you a bit warm in here?" she tries.

"Yeah!" he says. "I am!"

"Maybe we should get some air," she says. "Have a walk and talk through the details. We can hop into another cafe to deal with the documents."

"Yeah! That's a great idea!"

They walk up the road, Amos back on New Zealand, how good the wines are, the mountains, how London has never been right for him.

"I know," she says, "I know. You're going to be so happy."

"Not that London isn't great too," he says, generously, with an expansive gesture that takes in the worst of the local fish-and-chip shops, a puddle, a dead pigeon, a carpet shop that has been there for as long as she remembers but which she has never once seen open, and a tree that's still just bare branches even though it's almost May.

"Why don't you drink some apple juice?" She hands him a bottle from her bag, pre-prepared with vodka.

"Yes!" he says. "I love apple juice. Do you feel okay? I don't."

"Do you want to sit down? We could go to the flat? We're just around the corner."

"Ohhh, I don't know if that's a good idea."

"It is," she says. "It's a great idea. Maryam's downstairs, remember? We can ask her to check on you. And I've still got your old jacket, for hiking in New Zealand. That grey one, remember? It was expensive." Even a sober Amos surely wouldn't remember whether he had at some point in the last seven years owned a grey jacket that might be useful for his imaginary hiking future.

At the entrance to the flat, he looks up the stairs.

"Come on," she says. "You can have a nice sit-down and a big drink of water and I'll call you a cab."

He fumbles for his phone, which she has already taken the precaution of removing from his pocket. "Katy," he says, "I should let her know where I am."

Katy! There's a Katy. She holds the phone up in front of him. "Yeah," she says, "you've got a message from her. Come on." At this point she can absolutely not let him wander off unaccompanied.

"Why are you being so mean?" he says, frowning.

"You're right, I'm sorry, I'm being mean now and I was mean when we were married, and that's why it didn't work out, it was all my fault. You're going to be much happier. Katy will never be mean. But you'd better come up and get your phone and your jacket before you go home."

"I feel *terrible*," he says. "I think you should get Maryam," and then he leans over and throws up on one of the steps, and it sinks into the carpet and pools at the edge and dribbles over the next step below, and it is, of course, disgusting, but the best and most hygienic way to clear up a husband's vomit is to adjust the universe so that it was never there in the first place.

"I've messaged her," she says, "she'll be up in five minutes." Maybe the vodka was a mistake.

On the landing Amos leans against a wall. She was right to leave the ladder down in advance. She pours him a glass of water in the kitchen.

"Where's . . . where's my phone?" he says.

"I'll give it to you once you've got your big grey jacket. You need to climb up to get it and then Maryam will come and check on you."

He doesn't look good. Arguably, she shouldn't have trusted the unlabelled pills she stole from a plastic bag in an old ice-cream container belonging to an ex-husband's marketing friend named Padge.

"Come on," she says. "Up the ladder. Your jacket. Remember?"

"Okay," he says, drinking the whole cup of water, still standing upright, good. He hands it back empty, and feels his way along the wall towards the ladder. He looks up.

"Can . . . can you get it?" he asks.

"No, I twisted my ankle." And she takes his hand and places it on a rung.

"Okay," he says, and slowly sags towards the ground, then releases his hold on the rungs and lies down.

Fuck. "Okay, deep breaths, concentrate on staying awake." She can't give up. Her last couple of days have been pretty illegal, and Amos is in no state to head back out into the world. She just needs to get him up there. Is there TaskRabbit for crime support? People talk about *friends that would help you move a body* but would anyone do that for her? Honestly, she thinks, just Bohai; he's the only one who would understand the context.

"Wallpaper," Amos says; he's lying on his back on the landing, looking into the living room which is still only half-painted, and she feels more embarrassed by that than she should under the circumstances.

She calls Bohai.

The beeps of an international call before he answers. "Hey," she says.

"Oh, hi. Is this urgent? Cos—"

"Yes," she says. "It's urgent, sorry. I drugged my husband and he's kind of semi-conscious and I can't get him into the attic."

Bohai is silent for a moment.

"Okay," he says. "Right. Uh. So, I'm engaged."

"Yeah, you said."

"No," he says, "I mean, like, really engaged. I've met someone."

"You're *married*. You can't be engaged."

"No, I told you, she was having an affair, the guy left his wife and they're together now and I was just enjoying the time on my own, but then, I don't know, I met someone. For real."

"You've met five hundred people," she says, "come and help me and then fucking meet someone else—"

"Yeah," he's saying, "yeah, fair, okay, let me think. I'm on holiday, though, it's a three-hour drive to get home before I can get back in the cupboards. And then it could be another hour to find a life in London and get over to yours. Shit, Lauren, semi-conscious? He can't wait four hours, you have to call an ambulance."

"But he's right here. He's *so close*. I'll never get him in the attic if I don't do it now. And how do I explain the drugs? What if he thinks I was trying to kill him? Come on, there has to be something."

"I'm thinking," he says, "I am, I want to help."

"Okay," she says. "Then help! I really liked Michael but I still fucking helped you when you were eavesdropping on that guy—"

"I know," he said, "I *know*. But—Lauren, I like this one, I really like her. I don't want to go. Let me think."

She can't deal with this. "No problem," she says, "he's opening his eyes," though he isn't, "he's fine."

"Don't hang up—"

"I'll let you know when I'm done. Don't call an ambulance."

Phone down. He calls back; she ignores it. Maybe he really is three hours from home, but it's suspicious that he led with *I'm engaged* and not *the magic cupboard is hours from here.* Either way, she's on her own. She fills another glass of water and spatters it with her fingers on to Amos's face, then squats down and shakes him.

"Your phone is in the attic," she tries. "I heard it ringing."

"Why? What," he says.

"Kitty. She was calling you."

"Kitty?"

"Katy." She had known that, she was just being spiteful. "Katy keeps calling. It sounds important. It might be an emergency."

He tries to sit; gives up. "Can you get it? My phone."

"I can't," she says, "I twisted—" then abandons it, he's not in a state for explanations.

"Calls a lot," he says. "Always calling. She's like that. S'probably just. Bored."

"Come on, Amos," she says. "I know you can do it."

And she thinks about the moment in that other world when he traded cakes with her at Rob and Elena's wedding, his slice of not-much-icing for her slice of far-too-much, which was nice, of course it was, but wasn't it also just a little bit awful? A quiet performance of knowing her so well, a hint of old claims in front of her new husband?

She thinks as well about how much of a dick he was about *keeping things measured*, and even about getting a train to Norwood Junction. And how she really doesn't like him, and certainly doesn't love him, but still probably, furiously, reluctantly cares about him, and she can tell because the other bad husbands can't annoy her like he can. It's the tangle of shared experiences and the resentments and the jokes and the relief at it being over—they're not good feelings but they are feelings.

One last try, then.

She climbs the ladder, right into the attic, then turns on her hands and knees. Looks through the trapdoor on to Amos where he lies on the ground beneath her. "Amos," she calls. "Amos." The light glows above her, flickers, crackles, the static in the air. "Help," she says. "Please help me. I'm stuck."

Amos opens his eyes and looks up at her, blinks. She remembers when she met him, so many years ago, at some bar she didn't want to be at, and they stood in the corner being mean together.

"Please," and if he doesn't come now then that's it, it's over. And she's not faking her tears, which blur her view of him and the landing and the future. She hears the crackling sound rise, looks at the light bulb, sees it flare again and shatter and turns away quickly, shards of glass on the rough floorboards around her.

She just needs him to climb. "Please help me," she says, and gathers herself and smashes one hand hard on the broken glass, shouts, it hurts more than she thought it would, and she holds her injured hand out through the trapdoor, within his line of sight when he opens his eyes. "I'm hurt, Amos," she says, which is true, "please, I need you to climb up, something's going wrong," and the electricity is humming through the attic and she is bleeding and crying so much she can barely make out what's happening below but there's movement, a blur, as Amos finally, finally pulls himself to sitting, and then to standing, his face close below, looking up.

"Lauren?" he says.

"Yes," she says. "Please help me."

And he takes one step up the ladder, and another.

She lies back from the trapdoor to give him space, and closes her eyes, and nausea surges through her, and his head comes in, and his body, then there he is on his hands and knees in the attic, and she looks up at him. "Thank you," she says. "I'm sorry, I'm really sorry."

And she rolls back past him and out through the trapdoor, ungainly, too quick, glass embedded in one hand, dragging splinters down the ladder, and she lands heavily, squats, and she looks up and sees that one of Amos's feet is sticking out and she has to climb back up and shove it into the attic as he moves himself around. And what if this is the time it doesn't work? But she looks away and looks back with her heart pushing against itself, and—

It works.

The foot is gone.

The pain in her hand, the panic in her chest.

And she closes her eyes.

It's worked, it's worked, and her time of being single comes to an end, and her pages of searches about New Zealand and divorce and drugs disappear, she thinks, from her browser history, and Carter forgets the Englishwoman who followed him at a bar, and Amos is somewhere far away and fine, and everything is okay again.

The husband who descends barely matters; she's not going to keep him. She lies on her back on the floor on the landing. She doesn't care. She can deal with him in the morning.

The phone rings: Bohai. She answers. "It's okay," she says, and hangs up, and closes her eyes again.

CHAPTER 37

She keeps Amos's replacement for a week. They are not on good terms, and the air in the house is tense, or would be if she cared; as it is, the air around him is tense and the air around her is expansive and new. She talks to him the bare minimum, makes her own food, sleeps in the bed and some nights he joins her and some nights he's in the spare room making snippy comments and she just doesn't care.

The house is in order, nothing in awkward piles, nothing half-painted, but she misses her huge plant buddy, and on the second day she goes to the shop and buys him again with her replenished bank account. She does not go to work, or call in sick, or answer their calls when they phone her.

That weekend she decides to go away on her own, not to Denver or to Felix's village or anywhere else where she might meet a husband, but instead to the seaside, where she expects to walk along blustery sands but instead stays in her impersonal Ibis hotel room and rewatches two seasons of *Gossip Girl*.

She finally calls Bohai, her evening, his morning.

"So," she says, "you're engaged?"

"I know," he says, "embarrassing, right?" but she can hear how happy he is.

"Good for you."

"How'd you get the husband back in the attic?"

"Oh," she says. "Cried a lot and bled on him."

"Wow," he says. "Strong work."
"Didn't like it. Won't do it again."

○ ○

The next husband, call him 203, is blond and angular and the flat is almost empty, walls painted to rental magnolia; presumably they let it out and live elsewhere, and are momentarily between tenants. No. She's not going to turn landlord and give up access to an infinite supply of husbands for a guy in a polo neck. With 204, they're enormously in debt; the husband's friend is staying in their spare room to help with the bills, and that's okay, she's had plenty of housemates, but after work the husband uses his friend's motorbike to do deliveries while she does user testing for websites. She likes the guy so she sticks with it for a few days to prove to herself that she's not shallow, even when Nat pops round one night with a bunch of groceries, *We're going on holiday, we'd just be chucking these out.* She has brought no useful articles about, say, clever ways to repurpose charity-shop finds, and how fucked must things be if Nat's in no-advice mode? Lauren is relieved when she finds out that the debt is from *their stupid wedding,* which she of course doesn't even remember and which she has, she thinks, no obligation to try to pay off; she can send the husband back without feeling even a little bit bad.

205 doesn't trim his nostril hair. No.

206 is wearing a hat with a little brim even though he is sitting and watching television on his own sofa. No.

207 is angry because he has an important meeting and no clean shirts, and perhaps this is fair of him, perhaps they have negotiated an equitable division of housework and the laundry has fallen to her and she has let her side of the agreement slide, but: no thank you.

She sends back grumpy husbands, husbands she doesn't like

the look of, husbands who are not hot enough, a husband who is too hot (there must, she thinks, be a catch).

The process is, compared to the apps, an absolute joy.

She has a husband once who is big on Twitch: he plays video games and talks to teenagers about it, and makes a surprisingly good living. He has to take off his wedding ring before he streams, not because he is a particular heart-throb but because it doesn't do to remind his viewers that he is so much older than they are. He is obliged to keep up with young people's slang, which he uses in day-to-day life with an air of irony that does not in any way make it less annoying. She sends him back.

She is, she thinks, serious about this, she is in it for the husband, and there's no point pretending to herself that she might keep someone when she knows in her heart that she won't.

"I'll weed *your* garden," one husband is always saying, turning innocent phrases into double entendres. She hates it. There's no lustful intent, it's just a constant drip of a not-joke. "I'll order *your* burrito." "I'll boil *your* eggs." "I'll take *your* ice cream out of the freezer." I'll send *you* back into the attic, she thinks as she pulls the ladder down.

The next husband prods her and says "citation needed" whenever she says something he considers doubtful.

The next husband doesn't like it when she reads, will lean over and get between the book and her face, looking earnestly into her eyes. "I can be your book, all you need is me." It's a joke but it does also make it difficult to keep reading, so it's not *only* a joke. She has a fancy e-reader in this world and he will sometimes pry her hand away from it and put it on himself. "I, too, am waterproof and touch-operated," he will say. This is worse than nostril-hair husband but not as bad as "citation needed" husband.

One husband texts her updates on his bowel movements, *big one this morning fucking hell*.

One husband carries empty cups using his mouth, placing the cup over his mouth in its entirety, using suction to keep it in place, which stresses her out no end.

One husband appears and immediately makes her a coffee, which is good, but he does it while putting on an accent and making up words, "Vostre caffe con milk-io," which is bad, but if she sends him up right away the coffee will disappear. She takes it out to the garden.

Toby is weeding on his side.

"How's that going?" she calls over the fence. "Gonna put some new flowers in?"

"Nah, just getting ready for an inspection," he says. "Landlord's coming round to take photos and make sure we haven't bashed in the walls or forgotten to clean the skirting boards."

She watches for a moment, then finishes her coffee and goes upstairs and exchanges the husband. In the next life, Toby is in their living room eating biscuits, and when she looks through the kitchen window she sees the weeds have sprung back up, his chore still ahead of him.

One husband talks about his masculine energy and the natural anger of men in the modern world.

One husband likes to lie on the ground and grab at her ankles as she passes.

One husband, she discovers, likes to bully teenagers online. He will search out forums where young people are asking for advice and send messages telling them it's their fault, that they should feel bad, that they're ugly, fat, unlovable, weird, to blame for their parents' divorce or their sister's illness. To her he is a loving and diligent spouse; he makes pancakes every Saturday morning.

She can't quite take it in, has to talk it through with someone, and things are still a bit weird with Bohai after the Amos incident, so she calls Elena.

"God," Elena says when they meet in a cocktail bar and she shares the news, "is that a crime? Should you report it? Are you sure it's him, could it be a mistake?"

"I'm sure." Lauren's tone is light but she is genuinely shaken up.

"Oh, sweetheart," Elena says, "I'm so sorry. I'll get some more drinks in." Is Lauren taking advantage of her friend, who is anticipating the logistics and trauma of a real divorce? Maybe, but the cocktails will be unbought soon enough.

She sends the husband up when she gets home. In the next world she finds one of his usernames and screenshots half-a-dozen comments and sends them anonymously to his work email account, *I know this is you and I will tell everyone if you don't stop*, to who knows what effect, but either way the message is wiped out when she resets again.

One husband wakes her up in the morning by sitting astride her and spraying her in the face with the plant mister (plastic, from the gardening shop, this time). She struggles and splutters, shocked, but assumes that it must be normal, a thing they do, so she controls herself quickly and tries to cover the anger with a laugh.

"Wow," the husband says, "I should do that more often, I thought you'd hate it."

Not just a thing they do, then. She sends him back.

CHAPTER 38

It's coming into June, almost her birthday, which means the anniversary of the first husband is coming up too.

She thinks about whether she wants a party. She has a lot of friends she hasn't seen for a while, preoccupied as she has been by the husbands; and as usual some friends she hasn't seen *ever*, who she knows about only because they share a WhatsApp group or appear in each other's photos.

She's left it late to organise—a week's notice—but that's easily solved: she makes an exception to her serious-husbands-only stance and switches once, and again, and again, checking her calendar each time. By the day's eighth husband, a light-haired Irishman named Fintan (who she doesn't think she's attracted to, but you can't have everything), she finds that she has a Sunday pub lunch booked for twenty. Twenty! What a good number of friends. Happy birthday to her!

She misses Taj a lot, her constant companion when she was divorcing Amos, but you can't be friends with someone by emailing them and explaining that in a parallel world you got on really well; or even by going into the designer furniture store they work in just before coffee break and trying to strike up a special rapport, as she tries twice. She thinks it's maybe working the second time, they share jokes about a chair, perhaps if she comes in again and actually buys it she can mention *Oh, a birthday party with a few friends, you should come*, but at the end of the chat she sees Taj rolling her eyes at a colleague, an expression she recognises from when they were friends, *God, people*. She leaves, stricken with embarrassment and memories of Carter in that bar, barely managing to talk herself out of sending Fintan back straight away and wiping out her humiliation.

If she can't get Taj, at least she can get her plant buddy. She's started picking him up every time she thinks a husband shows real promise, and he's growing faster now that it's summer, more cumbersome each time she buys him. A birthday present to herself, she explains to Fintan, who seems annoyed but never mind, he won't be staying.

○ ○

On her birthday itself, the Thursday, she and the husband go out for tapas and beer at a new local restaurant. When they get home he gives her a huge unwieldy box: a fruit dehydrator, a puzzling gift that she can only assume she asked for. Sure, she can be the sort of person who dehydrates fruit. She finds a past-its-best apple in the fruit bowl and slices it up and tries to lay the slices flat but ends up eating them instead.

"What happens if we dehydrate something that's already dry?" Fintan says, and they find some dried apricots and put them in the device. It's a good birthday.

And on Sunday they walk the forty-five minutes to the pub that's not the nearby one or even the fancier one down the road but rather the far-away pub that does the nice roasts, and she has a party.

Nat and Adele are the first to arrive, with Lauren's medium-sized nephew and small niece, and both the kids are bigger than she remembered: this is what you get for ducking into another world whenever babysitting threatens. "Oh my god, her enormous *cheeks*," she says, squeezing them as she holds the plump baby, toddler maybe, and it's fine: in this world she has been putting in the work and Magda recognises her, gurgles, burps, stands tentatively on the floor and sits on her padded bum and blinks widely, does all those baby things, waves when Adele tells her to then refuses to stop waving and then the waves become big fisty thumps against the ground. Caleb runs in tiny circles and takes a karate pose and demonstrates a kick.

"Not inside," Nat says, then turns back to Magda, who is now leafing through a book. The girl isn't even two yet; one-year-olds can't read, right? And: no. Magda leans forward towards the page, closer and closer, and licks it, one big swipe of the tongue over a growling lion. Then she opens her mouth wider still and bites down, over the roaring lion's mouth, the paper pulling up and bending under her small teeth.

"Nooo," Adele says, "Magda, no, let's eat your lunch first, don't fill up on book."

Lauren resolves that she's going to be a better aunt. And a better sister! It's great to see Nat, who gives Lauren a silk scarf, all greens and blues and scattered pink-red dots, and it's true that she's printed out instructions for fourteen different stylish ways to wear it, which is perhaps not a totally necessary part of a gift, but the pattern is beautiful. Lauren feels a moment of loss at the realisation that she won't get to keep it.

Toby and Maryam next, then a guy she doesn't know called Phil, and a couple called Philip and Tess, and Phil and Philip say, "Phil five!" and slap their hands together, and then Zarah from work and her boyfriend, and, somehow, Michael, two-time-husband Michael, with his own kid, and she's delighted and baffled to see him (when she looks him up on her phone in the bathroom, she finds that they briefly dated before she met the current husband, and that they stayed friends, which is something she has never done with any ex before).

Elena and Rob turn up too, of course, and Parris, who's come up from Hastings, and Noemi. And eventually there are sixteen of them, plus the three children, sat around an awkward collection of mismatched tables, eating roasts and veggie burgers and drinking and going outside to let the kids play and coming back in, and it's—it's so nice. It's *so* nice. All these people are her friends, even the ones she's never seen before. And Elena gets up and goes to the bar and then comes back and asks for quiet, and the staff bring out a cake, all candles and sparklers, and her friends singing "Happy Birthday."

○ ○

"That was *such* a nice afternoon," she says back at home, lying on the sofa stretched out.

"It was," the husband—Fintan, she reminds herself—says.

When he leaves, she thinks, the memory of the day will be gone for everyone except her. She'll never see the Phils do a Phil five again, Caleb won't remember teaching her his newly invented kick, she won't be able to message Elena and say *That birthday cake you got me, that was great, where was that from.* She'll walk past the pub and think about the nice time she had, but whoever she's with won't remember it, even if they were with her.

June in a couple of weeks. Then she'll have been doing this for a year, a whole year that nobody else will remember and share. She thinks about the blurry picture she took with Carter at Elena's wedding, and it's not even about wanting Carter back, not any more; it's that she'd been so happy to start building a tiny shared history, and then she lost it.

"You okay?" Fintan says.

"Yeah," she says, and opens her eyes.

"Bummed out about the, you know, passage of time?"

She laughs a little, surprised. "I guess."

"That's birthdays for you. Have a twice-dried apricot, that'll perk you right up."

She takes it from him. It is hard and unpleasant, an apricot-flavoured stone. She sucks on it, holding it between her fingers.

It's a shame she doesn't fancy him. She tries to look at him with fresh eyes, imagine she's back on a date perhaps. In this world, her past self must have had chemistry with him, or they wouldn't be married; surely that's still hiding inside her somewhere? His hair is tidy, he's put on a nice shirt for her party, she likes the angularity of his nose. It's rare for her to come across a husband that stirs so little within her. She leans forward and touches him on the shoulder. No. Nothing.

Maybe, she thinks, she's worn out her ability to fancy anyone; but it's not true, she felt it for a moment at the pub, with Michael and again with one of the Phils, just that tiny spark of possibility. So: not this husband, then. But one of them. Soon she'll find someone she can stay with. Soon she'll start filling her phone with pictures that won't vanish overnight. Soon she'll be able to turn to someone and say *Hey, remember that thing we did together*, and he will, and she will too.

CHAPTER 39

She sends the husband back, and gets someone who is celebrating his own birthday.

"Did you *forget*?" he says. "Did you forget my birthday?"

She sighs. "No, calm down. It was meant to be a surprise. Go and look in the attic."

The next husband seems fine, but he heads out to the supermarket and gets back and says, "Did you know Toby and Maryam are moving?"

"What?"

"There's a big 'To Rent' sign out the front."

"Yeah," Toby says when she goes downstairs to ask him what's going on, "I told you about this, didn't I? The landlord thinks he can get an extra four hundred a month if he puts a bed in the living room."

That can't be right. "So, what, you're leaving?"

"Yeah," he says, matter-of-fact. "I mean, we're looking for something in the area, for Maryam's job."

Time is moving on without her. There's so little that's the same between one life and another: having Toby and Maryam downstairs is one of the only things that's made it home. They're her proof that two imperfect people can like each other and be happy and even stay happy.

"It's not for a couple of months," Toby says. "Good of him to give us so much notice, I guess."

She reloads the world, searches Zillow. Their flat's listed for rent here too and, yes, it's described as a three-bed with no living room. Whoever took the photos has placed two chairs in the hallway, as if to suggest that perhaps this could be its own bijou hang-out space: with a tiny kitchen *and* up to two chairs in an awkwardly shaped hall, who needs a sofa?

Another world: the same again. Another. Another.

"The new neighbours might be great too," says a temporary husband. "And you can't blame the owner—if someone's willing to pay an extra four hundred, why wouldn't you take it? If I was him I'd buy us out and build over the garden. You could definitely fit an extra couple of flats on the block."

She sends him away, and the next one, and the next. One time the TO RENT sign has vanished and she feels hope; but it turns out that the husband likes to pull down estate agent signs and leave them in dumpsters, which she appreciates in principle but it isn't going to solve her problem in practice.

It's okay, she tells herself, Toby and Maryam will end up over the road or down the hill. Maryam's a doctor, she must make decent money. They'll find somewhere. And besides, it's not for a couple of months. All Lauren needs to do is find a permanent husband by then; after that maybe their move won't be so overwhelming.

She's still theoretically assessing newcomers by her old Post-it criteria, although they're not always reliable; she's supposed to be looking for someone with an interesting hobby, for example, but once a bee-keeper turns up and she decides that bee-keeping doesn't count, because her instinct says *No, not him.* What she really needs, she thinks, is to find someone she likes enough that she sees the best in him, and then the criteria will fall into place.

The next husband she does like. They head out to see his friends the evening he arrives, and she warms to him over the course of the night and the next day and then, unexpectedly, a week. Before she knows it she's met more of his friends, they've gone to the theatre, he comes home from work stressed a couple of times and she worries about him, wants him to feel better.

His name is Adamm, with two "m"s. He is confident and outgoing in public, and at home he is a little nervous and stressed, and this is both of her types in one, the bold and the delicate, the contrast between them that only she gets to see. And she keeps him for the anniversary that he doesn't know is an anniversary, but by luck their actual wedding anniversary is two days later, and they go out for dinner, and he toasts their marriage, and in her head she toasts the attic.

She is therefore deeply affronted when he confesses that he has been suspended from his work pending a small handful of investigations into misconduct, which he explains is someone *getting the wrong end of the stick* and which will *all be cleared up soon*. She is not going to wait to find out. She sends him back, yells, "Good riddance!" after him.

"What?" the next husband says, climbing down.

○ ○

The next three husbands she sends back as soon as she sees anything wrong at all, once before he's even off the ladder: she gave Adamm three weeks, she gave him the *anniversary*, and she is outraged by his breach of her trust. Excessive moustache? No. Her own bank account is overdrawn? No.

Look, I'm glad you're happy but everyone is terrible, she messages to Bohai while someone clatters in the attic above her.

She is waiting for the dot-dot-dot of a reply when the next husband starts down the ladder, and slips.

It happens before she can register it: the foot, the leg, the husband is coming but he's coming too fast, all at once, half freefall, half a slide down the steep angle of the ladder, and he lands and he yells, loud.

She stares.

He hauls himself up: a little bit, but not far, then slips back to the ground. He's gasping, grabbing at the rungs.

Okay. Ambulance? She did a first-aid course once but that was in another world, she's probably not even qualified here. Danger, Response, Airways, Breathing—there's no danger, and he's responsive. She doesn't remember what happens if your patient isn't unconscious.

"Are you okay?" she tries.

"Fuck," he breathes, "shit, okay, maybe," and another jagged breath, and pulls himself to standing, using the ladder, one rung at a time, a grunt. He lets go tentatively. "Okay," he says. "Maybe. Yes." He takes hold of the rung again and looks at his feet and wriggles his toes.

"Okay," she says. "Good."

"Except," and he looks down, and she notices the dark stain across his trousers: he's pissed himself. That doesn't seem like a great sign.

"Maybe the shock?" she says.

"Maybe?" he says.

If she could get him back in the attic he'd be fine, but it's probably not the time to suggest climbing ladders. "I'll see if Maryam's in. Should you . . . sit down?"

"I might," the husband says, and starts lowering himself again.

Maryam is at home and comes right up, Toby with her. She squats on the ground next to the husband and tells him to take deep breaths, in and out. She asks if it's okay to touch him and takes his hand. This is what she's good at, of course. Toby looks on helplessly. "I'll make tea," he says.

"Try not to move too much," Maryam is saying, "we need to figure out if anything's broken, okay? So we know if there's anything we need to fix up. So—yep, that's right, try to stay still."

Toby emerges from the kitchen with a cup of tea in one hand and a spoon in the other. He holds the cup out. Neither Maryam nor the husband notice. "Okay, breathe in," Maryam's saying. Eventually Lauren steps around them and takes the mug. "Thanks," she says.

"Thanks," Toby says in return.

"Yeah, okay," Maryam says, "let's get an ambulance just so they can check things out." Then, raising her voice, "Could you call, please, Toby. Put it on speaker."

He holds the teaspoon haplessly; Lauren takes that too, and he pulls out his phone and calls.

"Hi," Maryam says once they get through, "for context, I'm a doctor and I'm here with my friend who's had an accident. He's an adult male who slipped and fell from an attic and there's been loss of bladder control." Lauren looks back at the dark stain on his jeans. "He's in a lot of pain, I think there's a chance of a fracture." She says some words Lauren doesn't catch, acronyms and details, communicating *this is what's wrong* but also *and I know what I'm talking about, do as I say.* "Yes, I'm keeping him still. No, the flat is on the first floor, the stairs are steep and narrow."

If someone had asked whether Maryam was a good doctor, Lauren thinks, she would have said: yeah, sure. But she hadn't imagined the efficiency, the focus, her attention narrowed in so tightly, the mustering of those around her to help.

The ambulance comes fast, maybe hurried by Maryam's knows-what-she's-doing tone, and the husband is stretchered downstairs. Lauren follows. "Are you his partner?" the ambulance guy asks Maryam (he is more handsome than the husband, Lauren thinks, but to be fair, it's hard to be handsome when you're either (a) falling or (b) lying twisted in pain at the bottom of a ladder).

"No," Maryam says, "I'm the neighbour, but—Lauren, do you want to go in the ambulance? Or do you want me to go and I'll see you at the hospital?"

"Yeah," Lauren says. "That one."

"He's doing a great job," Maryam says to her, calm, reassuring. She looks over at the husband, lying in the back of the ambulance. Yes. Good.

"Hey," Toby says as the ambulance pulls away, "I'll book an Uber."

"Yeah. I might head up for a minute and drink that cup of tea first? I think I need a moment."

The tea is lukewarm, but she sips it anyway. The ladder to the attic is pulled partway out of position, twisted in the sliders that lower and raise it.

What a mess.

"Should I make a new one?" Toby says.

"What?"

He gestures at the cup of tea.

"No," she says, "I'll just drink this one."

Toby is restless, anxious. "Sit down," he says, "you've had a shock. Maryam'll make sure they look after him." He needs soothing so he's trying to soothe her.

"Yeah." She tries to figure out how worried she is. She is certainly *shaken*, she is certainly *surprised*. Is she anxious? Is she worried about the husband?

She takes a sip of tea. She should go to the hospital. Instead, she looks into the living room. It's yellow, the ceiling as well as the walls. There's a big L-shaped sofa that barely fits in the room. An inflatable cactus almost as big as her vanished Buddy, lit up from the inside, as if this didn't already feel strange enough. She is wearing slippers, dirty from going outside. She steps out of them, still standing, and feels the shaggy rug under her feet. She should put socks on, right?

Toby is waiting anxiously.

"Could you look for a thermos, in the kitchen? Maybe in a cupboard," she says, and she hands him the tea; she has no idea if they have a thermos but it'll keep him busy for a few minutes. She finds socks in the bedroom, and a bed that, like the sofa, is too large for its space, piled high with pillows. Shoes on the shoe rack on the landing.

The husband's wallet. A phone charger. A book that's lying open in the living room. "I can only find this insulated jug," Toby says, holding it aloft.

"That'll do," she says, and starts looking for trousers. "And yeah, call a car." She finds a Tesco Bag For Life. Trousers and underwear, and a shirt, he'll want a complete change, won't he?

"It'll be here in four minutes. Are you sure you don't want me to make a new cup?" Toby says when she comes into the kitchen. He's got a funnel out, and has emptied her mug into the jug. "It's pretty cold."

"Yeah," barely listening. A toothbrush? But the eternal question: which one is his?

She should have stuck with the guy who liked to grab ankles.

CHAPTER 40

The husband was standing up and moving, so presumably the injury can't be too bad. Toby reassures her in the cab, but she doesn't really need it, which is good because honestly it's hard for a man with a wet empty mug in one hand and an insulated jug in the other to reassure.

In the hospital, they go up to the counter. "My husband was brought in," she says, "by an ambulance. He fell out of the attic."

"Of course," the woman says. "What was his name?"

Very good question. "Give me a sec." She reaches for the wallet.

"Zac Efron," Toby seems to say, beside her, which seems unlikely. But she opens the wallet, and: huh.

"Not like the actor," Toby says, confirming the bank card that she has pulled out of its place in the wallet. "Z-A-C-H E-P-H-R-O-N."

"Okay, he's just being seen," the counter lady says. "You should be able to head through soon. Take a seat."

"Tea?" Toby says as they wait, and pours it from the insulated jug into the mug. It has remained at precisely room temperature.

"Thanks. You can go if you like," she says. "I'll be fine. He'll be fine."

"I don't mind."

She has a quick google in the toilet after she finishes the cold tea, but it's difficult to search for a husband named Zach Ephron: the phone assumes she means the actor, and even when she insists that she doesn't, she bumps up against people who *do* mean the actor but are bad at spelling.

The waiting room is boring and horrifying at the same time: worried family members, a man crying gently, a teenage girl on her own with long dark hair and her head resting on her arms, which in turn are resting in her lap. Someone on the phone: "No, he's fine, he'll be fine, just some stitches."

Toby is pacing, goes round a corner and comes back with a packet of Fruit Pastilles. He opens them and sorts them by colour.

"How're you doing?" she says, and he starts making his way through the reds.

"Good. Maryam says it's under control."

Lauren is still trying to resolve her view of Maryam, constantly distracted Maryam, and get it to sit at peace with Maryam the actual doctor, who has always existed but who she has never before seen in action. She wonders if there's a version of the world where she has a job that impressive. Maybe one where she's a doctor herself? Or a scientist? Or a politician who unites the city against hunger?

Toby's on to the orange Fruit Pastilles when a nurse-or-doctor calls at the door: "Who's here with Zach Ephron?"

Toby scoops up the pastilles and shoves them in a pocket and they walk over. "We can let you in to see him now," the woman says. "We've moved him out of the emergency ward to spinal injuries."

Spinal injuries? Lauren has been imagining herself as a researcher who has discovered new and more efficient solar panels that can be made from apple peels. She is not prepared for spinal injuries.

"There's been a fracture," the woman says, "but I don't want you to panic, it's not as bad as you might think when you hear 'broken back.' He's going to have to go in for surgery, probably in the morning, and he'll be here for a week or two after that. But it's a very clean break and it's likely that he'll make a full recovery."

A week or two! Just to get out of hospital!

"He's been given some painkillers and he's sleeping," the woman says. "So we'll take you in, but it's best not to wake him."

"Okay," Lauren says. Thinks; tries not to panic. "Maybe I don't think I need to see him yet. I might go and get some sleep and come back in the morning?"

"Sure," the woman says, and smiles, reassuring. "That sounds like a good idea."

○ ○

It's almost two before she's home. The three of them get a taxi back together. Toby asks if she needs a cup of tea, but Maryam, thank god, says, "Let her sleep, you can make me a cup of tea if you want."

On the landing, the ladder is still down, out of its place and twisted. She gives it a push, but it won't fold away.

She lies in the middle of their bed, which is definitely too big for the room. Things still aren't quite back to normal with Bohai, but who else is she going to talk to? After a few minutes she messages him: it must be his midday.

Married to a Zach Ephron, she says, which is perhaps not the most pertinent thing about the husband but she would rather not think about the injuries.

OH my god, he says. *Any resemblance?*

Nnnno, she sends back. *I mean he's white and he has brown hair. He's in hospital so I don't think he's looking his best*

Whattttt, have you drugged ANOTHER husband, Loz we talked about this

He fell out of the attic, she responds.

!!!! is he ok

I don't know, she sends back, and thinks about the question some more, and doesn't fall asleep, and still doesn't fall asleep, and then does.

○ ○

Zach is extremely popular. Over the next ten days his friends come and visit him in hospital, and her friends come and visit too, his mother comes and pats his head, boxed chocolates pile up by one side of his bed, her own mother sends a giant teddy bear to the hospital (it's yellow and the heart it holds is embroidered with the message HAPPY EASTER, and her mother clarifies that it was on sale, but even so). Nat comes, holding Magda up to the bed so that she can wave her arms beseechingly and burble Zach's name. He has been moved into an individual room, after it became clear that he would be (a) constantly visited in a way that was bound to be annoying to other patients, (b) willing to share his chocolate supply with hospital staff and (c) not at risk of harming himself. A lot of serious spinal injuries are, it turns out, from suicide attempts, which Lauren tries not to think about every single time she walks past the door into the shared ward.

She is allowed to sit in on his medical briefings, and considers holding his hand in a wifely manner, but instead she takes notes.

Her work gives her a few days off, and her colleagues, who have also met and loved Zach, suggest things for her to take to him, ask about visiting hours. Zarah gives her a hat from her mum. "In case he gets cold in hospital."

"It's summer," Lauren says.

"The air-conditioning can be so intense."

Lauren doesn't get it. Zach seems perfectly nice, but this universal concern is out of all proportion.

How's your boy doing, Bohai messages. Even Bohai is worried about him, she thinks irritably, and closes the chat.

As far as she can tell, Zach has no internal life. Perhaps this is the effect of the painkillers. He blinks around the room, is delighted to see people, is pleased when she brings him things, tires easily. He responds to stimuli. He is bafflingly unconcerned about his broken back. "They say it's going to be okay!"

His family is as bright-eyed and well-meaning as he is, and as dull.

After ten days he comes home, and he's boring there too. He lies on the big sofa, and urinates into a bottle which he gives to her with an air of pathetic apology, and which she empties. He has to remain on his back as much as he can for at least a couple of weeks, so Toby helps set up an iPad above his head so that he can watch television without having to twist.

Why is he so beloved? He is a blank, a nothing, listening to podcasts and eating sandwiches that she makes for him. On days when she's working from the office she leaves the flat door unlocked so that Toby can come up to check on him and have a little chat over lunch, and she should be grateful that he's sharing the caretaking burden, but instead she is deeply irritated. Nat comes and visits again, a couple of days after Zach gets home; she brings Caleb this time, who is hushed and nervous and quieter than Lauren has ever seen him. He presents Zach with a "get well soon" card he has made, in which he has drawn several figures, each one labelled UNCLE ZACH in all caps: Zach in a hot-air balloon, Zach riding an elephant, Zach flying through the air with a red cape. And as if that wasn't enough, Nat's bursting with advice: how to support people healing from traumatic injury, foods to cook for recovery and bone strength.

For the first week Lauren wipes him down with a washcloth every night: her first experience with his naked body, sponging around the waterproof back brace, switching to another washcloth for the groin and then the butt crack, lifting the penis gently. One night it stirs, then subsides.

"Do you need, you know—?" and she gestures at it with a wanking motion.

"Nah," he says. "Haven't felt interested yet. But thanks for asking!"

He is so grateful. "Thank you so much for this," he says, almost constantly. "I love you, I can't believe how much you're doing, I can't believe I fell, I'm such an idiot."

She wishes he'd have a day of being grumpy and resentful. Instead he is pitifully appreciative of her attention, constantly urging her to go out and have fun, and, most annoying of all, besieged by guests for whom she has to make coffee and get biscuits; she has to find space for their thoughtful lasagnes in the fridge, she has to find pint glasses and jam jars for the flowers that are crowded on to every shelf.

She books a guy to come in and fix the attic ladder, and even he ends up sitting on the armchair in the living room, exchanging stories with Zach and demonstrating stretches for him to try once he's on the mend. Still, at least the ladder's working again. She pulls it down and it doesn't stick at the halfway point any more; climbs up and holds her hand above her, to check that the light still fuzzes on.

o o

Zach listens to audiobooks. He naps. He watches sitcoms, sometimes the same sitcom he's just finished. "It's soothing," he says.

Later, he starts working his way through the complete films of Zac Efron. "I never saw any of them before," he says, "but I feel like it might be time. This is amazing," and he gestures at the screen, freeze-framed in the middle of *High School Musical 2*, dancers on a baseball square. He is on extra-strength codeine, and will be for the next three months, or rather no, he won't because as soon as he's mobile enough to climb back into the attic she'll be sending him on his way.

It's not that he's a bad husband! He's cute enough now that he's not bathed in his own fluids, he's obviously got plenty of friends, his family seem to genuinely like each other. She continues to see more of Toby and Maryam than usual, even though they should be packing up their stuff, not laughing at Zach's indifferent jokes and updating him on their flat search. "We've applied for that place that's halfway to the hospital, and it's looking good," Toby tells him one afternoon. "So we should still be pretty close to you guys." She should be the one they're reassuring, she should be the one Toby is eager to stay near so he can pop up and say hello.

Elena usually refuses to come this far south but even she joins in and brings a big plate of almond biscuits. "Nightmare on the train," she says, "not carrying them, just people joking about whether they can have one, *Oh, let me take those off your hands, Oh, did you bring enough for everyone?* Fucking South London. You don't get people making conversation north of the river."

"If they wanted biscuits they should have broken their own backs," the husband says.

"Exactly! I should have told them that."

Zach is none of Lauren's types, neither gangly nor short and stocky, neither confident nor nervous, not even slightly into some arcane hobby. She spends more and more time in her bedroom, relinquishing the living room to him and his guests. For ten days she empties his piss bottles, before he's finally allowed to stand and move about delicately and he starts to empty them himself, or rather to say that he will but actually to tuck them under the sofa and apologise about them two days later when they're full and she has to empty them after all.

She goes into the office most days, and works late to have some time to herself, alone after five o'clock as the desks empty out. Or sometimes she heads up to Elena's part of town and they take terrible dance classes in old shipping containers, and she tries not to seethe when Elena asks after Zach, or hands over a book that Rob thinks he would like.

"This is your third time here this week," Elena says. "You should move. You can't live in Norwood Junction for ever just because your grandma did. The flat under us is for sale, you should have a look. Imagine being on the Victoria Line! Plus there's the Overground to Liverpool Street in fifteen minutes!"

This is the main thing people do in the suburbs, Lauren sometimes thinks: they list different ways to get into town. "Twelve minutes direct train to London Bridge," she says, the mandated Norwood Junction response.

Her trip home is pretty annoying for a journey between two places that are both supposedly so convenient for the centre of town. She thinks about Elena's suggestion. Selling the flat would be one way out of the infinite lives, at least if she could be sure that she wouldn't just drug another husband and force him to break into the old place with her.

But she's not stopping on Zach.

She's been trying to notice one true thing about each husband, to distinguish them, to accept that they are people that she has loved and who have loved her. But with Zach she keeps coming back to the bottles. Oh, and her unrelenting sense of guilt, of course. This is, she thinks, absolutely her own fault.

CHAPTER 41

One thing becomes clear as Zach slowly gets better and starts moving around the flat a little more: the injury has shocked him. He is much more upset than he's letting on.

He is scared.

And he does not want to go back into the attic.

In other circumstances she would fake a water leak, or an injury, lying at the top of the ladder and crying pitifully for help. But this husband is so friendly with Toby and Maryam: he'd call them, and they'd rush upstairs, eager to help their friend. She was their friend first! They should be helping her! Zach is also somehow friends with a maybe-a-cult family across the road and the guy three doors up who is constantly hiring skips, so even waiting for Maryam and Toby to move wouldn't help.

She has no choice but to give him time. She certainly can't pull an Amos again, firstly on principle but secondly because of all the codeine.

Bohai comes round, in London for a couple of weeks, on holiday with his not-yet-a-wife-because-technically-he's-still-married-to-someone-else. Her name is Laurel, which seems like a particular and specific blow.

"Lauren," Laurel says when they meet. "I feel like you're already my friend, baristas are always writing your name on my coffee cups." Lauren isn't quite sure if the joke is charming or obnoxious. Perhaps the ambiguity is what makes her a good match for Bohai.

"So how do you two know each other?" Zach asks, as the four of them sit in the garden under a grey sky. He has just started going outside, still always in his brace, careful and slow on the stairs, standing in the garden or walking to the end of the street and back.

"I was in London for a while," Bohai says. "I met Lauren through my partner at the time."

Laurel is very polished. She doesn't look at her phone the whole afternoon. Her hair is perfectly in place. She speaks in full, careful sentences, no *ums* or *ahs* or *nah yeahs*. She gets on well with Zach.

"Your husband seems great," Bohai says as they go up together to the kitchen to replenish the plate of biscuits and fetch more tea. "I mean, he's a bit boring, but that's your type, right?"

"Yours seems pretty good," she says, though she's not quite convinced.

"Yeah, she really is. Gonna have such a big wedding. You're coming, right? You'll do a reading? Won't be for a while, have to sort the divorce first, maybe summer at the end of next year. You'll hate it in Sydney, really huge bats."

"Look," Lauren says, tipping the biscuits off the plate and starting to arrange them again. "I like her, but is she that much better than the other six hundred partners? So much better that it's worth going through a divorce and setting up a whole life from scratch?"

He shrugs. "I dunno. I mean, maybe? One of 'em has to be the best, why not her?" He's looking in different cupboards. "So weird seeing this with a new husband, I never get to go back to my old houses."

"Come on," she says. "There has to be a reason." They spent so long on their Post-it notes. How can he just settle down on a whim with someone he isn't even married to?

He stops and looks like he's really trying to answer. "Okay," he says. "It's . . . you know. You notice something about them, and it makes you feel happy, it makes you feel lucky."

"Like what? What specific sort of something?"

"With Laurel? Uh. Right, top three. Three: really unapologetically bad taste in music. Just terrible. No idea why that does it for me but there you go. Jack had it too, I came home once and he was listening to a YouTube playlist of advertising jingles from the seventies. Maybe it's something about, you know, liking what you like? Genuinely no idea."

"Bad taste in music. Got it."

"Okay," he says. "Two: so, she does fencing, and I don't know if you've ever seen someone who's good at fencing and then they take the helmet off and they're kind of out of breath and their hair's all tousled? It's, uh, honestly, it feels inappropriate that people are allowed to do it in public."

He didn't even have *hobbies* on his Post-its.

"And one: she can tell when I'm having a bad idea. Which yeah, obviously, you don't need to say it, is almost always."

"You know what," Lauren says, "I bet you wouldn't be so keen if you'd just stepped out of a pantry into her life. It's all the logistics that make it work for you."

"Yeah, maybe. Whatever it takes, though, right?"

She shakes her head, tries to reset the conversation. "Sorry, I'm being a dick, aren't I?"

"I dunno. Little bit?"

In for a penny. Lauren hasn't been able to shake the thought that maybe Bohai wasn't on holiday when she called him about Amos, that maybe he just didn't want to leave the world he was in, to leave Laurel. "Were you really three hours from home?" she asks. "When I called you that time. It's fine if you weren't."

"Oh," he says. "When you were trying to get that guy up into the attic? Yeah, I was. We were at the beach. But I mean, fair question, I guess." He looks out the window into the garden, Laurel and Zach still chatting. "No point pretending I wasn't relieved to have the excuse. It was early days, I guess, but I liked her a lot."

They stand there for a moment, silent. Then: "I'm glad you've found someone," she says. "We should get back out, anyway. Might open some wine?"

"Uh," he says. "No. I mean it's a bit early to tell anyone but fuck it. So, I promised I wouldn't drink while she's not, and—"

"What," she says. "What. Really?"

He's beaming, embarrassed and proud at once. "I know, I mean, it wasn't on purpose but we figured, ah, go on, why not."

"Bohai! But that means you won't get sick of her and jump in a wardrobe and come round for a coffee!" She still hadn't quite believed that he would stay put.

"It's okay," he says, "she's super rich, her and her ex invented some kind of doomed VR helmet that does smells. They sold the company to Google, we came business class, I'll visit constantly."

"Wow. Wow. Have you got rid of the wardrobe?"

"It was a blanket box," he says. "Pain and a half to climb out of. Actually, I've still got it. But I'm going to break it down and chuck it out when we get back. I mean, what if I have a kid and we play hide-and-seek and she climbs in there and then she has . . . different parents? I dunno, basically I don't think you can risk having a magic blanket box when you've got a toddler. If we ever break up we'll have to do it like everyone else."

"You're not going to, though, are you? God, you're so happy it's actually revolting."

"I love you too," he says, and hugs her tight.

○ ○

Eventually she and Zach sleep in the same bed, and he puts his hand out to hold hers.

She has emptied all those bottles, made him sandwiches that he could eat while lying down, abandoned her living room for him, wiped clean his sweating body, and this is the sort of thing that one of you will do for the other sooner or later if you stay together for long enough, she thinks, but usually it's not how you *start*. She doesn't like to be tended when she is sick, she likes to be left to feel bad on her own, and that isn't Zach's way, he is trusting and wide-eyed and accepts help and attention as the right of the poorly.

He did break his back, she reminds herself, climbing out of the attic that she put him in.

He has lost a centimetre or so of height to the fall, according to the doctor. "Would you still love me," he says seriously one morning, "if I was two inches high? A tiny man. Up to your ankle."

"I would love you just as much as I do now," she says, which is not a lie, although she has long since given up the idea that nobody should ever lie about love: she has declared her affection falsely to so many husbands, one more should make no difference.

He smiles at her, grateful.

"You should head back into the attic," she says. "Get back on the horse. Otherwise you might never make it."

"Uh," he says. "I'm meant to be careful about exerting myself. But once I've recovered a bit more, for sure!"

He is working again, from home, accommodations made by his workplace, and it's like having a large capybara in her space, docile and obliging but immoveable. Sometimes she rests an object on him, like they do on capybaras in videos, a piece of food which he invariably eats, a remote control, a book, which he will leave there for a few minutes and then move to the coffee table. The coffee table itself is piled high; she clears it once a day.

"I love you so much," he says, gazing at her.

She pats him on the shoulder. "You're on super codeine. You're watching *17 Again* for the fourth time."

"I'm so glad we're married," he says.

o o

It would be convenient if she loved him. He doesn't know the fall is her fault. As far as he's concerned, she's been an exceptionally supportive wife.

But this dazed and delighted husband is not right for her.

She brings up the attic again.

"Yeah," he says, "I don't think I want to."

"No rush. I was just reading something that said it'd be good for you. Psychologically."

"Maybe next week."

Next week she lowers the ladder, still instinctively pulling to the left even though it descends smoothly now, and puts on her most matching lingerie, and calls to him as beguilingly as she can.

"Why don't we head up?" she says. "Get reacquainted."

"I dunno. In the attic?"

"It's dark up there," she says. "And mysterious."

"I'm still feeling kinda weird about it," he says, "maybe we could just watch a movie?"

God. "Fine," she says, half-naked on the landing, "no worries, whenever you're feeling better."

o o

She talks to Elena about it, to try to get some new ideas, but of course she can't explain why it's so important.

"What if he never goes up?" she says. "And there's just this lurking attic, hanging over him for ever?"

"I don't know," Elena says. "Wait till you're rich and do a loft conversion, turn it into a spare bedroom."

God, imagine, she'd never get rid of him then.

Toby and Maryam have almost finished packing for their move, and she can't bear it, the idea of the whole building empty, just her and this blank of a man. She tries pouring a bucket of water through the attic floor while the light flickers above her, then leaves the house so that Zach finds the damp patch on the ceiling and the water pooling below; but he calls a handyman, who shrugs and says he doesn't know what happened.

"Hey," Zach says, "look, I don't know how to ask this, but that water in the attic. Was that you? The guy said it looked like someone had taken a bucket up there and poured it out."

"No," she says. "What do you mean? What water?"

"The water I was telling you about? That came through the ceiling?"

"Of course it wasn't me."

"I dunno," he says, "it just feels like you really want me to go into the attic. I was thinking, maybe you should talk to someone? It must have been traumatic seeing me fall, you know? And all that work you've been doing for me, which I appreciate so much."

"I'm fine," she says. "I don't care if you go in the attic."

"Okay. If you're sure."

God. This fucking husband.

Could you fake a stuck cat? Bohai suggests. *Cute little kitten and it's up there and you need his help to get it down.* But just like the water, Zach would only call for help.

She's going to have to take firmer steps.

CHAPTER 42

The next day she calls in sick and buys a train ticket to Felix's local town. His place is an hour's walk from the station, but that's fine; she needs to clear her head.

She has a plan. She can do this.

In through his back gate, round past the swimming pool, along by the red wall, through the orchard. Part of her hopes that the code to the conservatory won't work and she'll have to find some other solution. But: *Regard the dozen men in your upstairs room, octopus.* And it clicks.

She has to move fast—it's not like last time, just two steps in and out, and she doesn't know when someone might glance at the cameras.

She goes through the conservatory, which is not arranged quite how she remembers it, and up to the games room, which has also changed. The current wife has asserted her presence more strongly than Lauren did.

She is doing a good thing. Zach's back still hurts him. He mourns his lost centimetre of height—she will return it to him.

Into Vardon's room. She looks in the walk-in wardrobe, and the desk (a box of pellets, which she grabs), then she tries the trunk at the foot of the bed. There it is: his air rifle. Nothing to carry it in that she can see; she pulls the pillowcase off one of his pillows and jams it in. It sticks out the end.

about messaging Bohai for moral support but then thinks: you know what, he might not morally support this one.

"You almost done?" she hears through the door.

"Yeah," she says.

It's time. She drops the dressing gown back over the gun, and opens the door, and smiles at Zach, who smiles back. She walks out, treating her ankle as gently as she can, carrying the bundle; he walks past her into the bathroom and shuts the door.

Once he's gone, she pulls the ladder down, then unwraps the air rifle from the dressing gown. She positions herself in the doorway of the living room. She's looking out towards the ladder, and on the other side there's the bathroom door, and beyond that the stairs. She wants to make it harder for Zach to run at her, and the door frame will help to keep her steady.

This is going to be very straightforward. During her planning over the last couple of days she has read a lot about air-rifle safety rules, and she is about to break almost all of them, but it doesn't seem like hurting Zach badly is a risk unless she's right next to him. This position gives her as much distance as possible, a couple of metres anyway, while still letting her keep the whole landing in sight. It's good. It's tactically sound.

The bathroom door opens. Zach comes out. He notices her, and takes a moment, and frowns.

"Stop there, please," she says.

"Wow, water pistols are getting really over-the-top, aren't they? Where'd you get that from?" He walks through into the kitchen, out of range.

Uh. She adjusts herself against the door frame and waits. He walks back out with a can of Coke.

"This isn't a water pistol," she says. "It's a gun. But don't panic, I'm not going to shoot you if I don't have to. I just want you to climb up into the attic and then everything's going to be okay."

"Put that down," he says, "don't mess around. It's not funny."

It feels very strange to hold a giant kind-of-fake-but-not-really gun.

Okay, down the stairs, fast as she can, and the rifle is way too obvious. Once she's outside she grabs a rake from the gardening shed and clusters it together with the rifle. Is that inconspicuous? Is that better? No, that's much, much worse; she puts it back down.

There's the gym, though, maybe there's something she can use in there. She puts the code in, goes into the first room. Yes: a badminton racket zipped up in a case. She takes the racket out and jams the air rifle most of the way in.

She takes a dressing gown and is wrapping it around the bit that isn't covered when she hears a noise.

She looks up.

The door to the pool room opens. A woman, dark hair tied back, a bikini.

Ah, Lauren thinks. It's the new her. "Laundry service," she says.

"Laundry comes on Tuesday," the woman says, very still.

Lauren turns and runs, fumbles with the door, out along the path, not looking behind because she has to move as fast as she can, but she hears nothing, and she risks a glance, and the woman isn't following her; she'll have phoned Felix, or the police, or the security company maybe; either way, the risk isn't from someone in a bikini chasing her and tackling her and wrenching the air rifle away, it's from the perimeter, it's at the exits, it's in the town. She veers away from the back gate and goes towards a wall instead, one of the ones with vines so that she can climb. She throws her bundle over and follows it up, slipping once or twice as the vines pull away from the wall, and it's fine, she can still do this. The drop at the other side is further than she'd like but she makes it, no problem, until she lands and her ankle rolls and she feels that sickening airless moment of *how bad is this* before pain rushes in. It's not great.

Okay, she thinks. First things first. The air rifle, the dressing gown. She has those.

A path curves up towards a stile and another field and then she'll be out of view of Felix's place. And she has the wall to support her. At least the field has sheep in it rather than cows, so it could be worse.

The stile will help too; on the other side she can sit and gather herself. And she makes it, and she wraps the dressing-gown cord around her ankle as a makeshift support, and goes to check train times but—

Ah. She doesn't have her phone.

Which is bad. She has dropped it, she supposes, in the gym, and the new wife will have found it, and the police must have a way of unlocking it and finding out her name.

Well. She'd better get a move on, then.

The walk to the train station is slow and excruciating. When she reaches the houses on the outskirts of the town she unties her hair and takes her jacket off in case anyone is looking out for her. At the station she sits at the end of the long row of benches, which backfires when the train comes and stops up the other end and she has to stagger as fast as she can along the platform, badminton racket/air rifle supporting her bad foot.

The journey, too, is interminable. She is on a slow train, stopping at stations she's never heard of, Little Tarpington, Pubbles. Will the Sussex police come to find her themselves, or will they phone the police in Norwood Junction? Without her own phone she can't even look up how arrests work.

She finally, finally gets to her station. It must have rained in London while she was in the country: it's wet and the pavement is slippery, and her ticket was tucked into her phone case so she can't scan to exit, has to wait till someone opens the big slow-moving access gates and rush through before they close. But she takes it easy. She's so close.

And then she's home.

She has to take the stairs slowly. "Hey, darling," she calls Zach as she nears the top.

"You're back early," he says.

"Yeah, there was a power cut, we got sent home." She s into the bathroom and props the badminton-rifle-dressing-g combo behind the door and goes into the living room fc laptop.

"I'm going to have a bath, I think," she says, looking ir spare room where Zach is working. "Do you need the toilet

"I'm good. Can always haul out one of the old bott have to."

She cannot wait to be rid of him.

Bathroom door locked, taps on. While the water runs, her ankle and watches a video where a man in his fifties how to load the particular air rifle she's acquired. She looked more like an old-fashioned wooden hunting ri would be somehow less weird, but it's full-on tactical struts and black and green. She tries raising it, loweri her finger near the trigger, then forces herself to touch as she does, not pulling but just in contact. She hadn' ning to do this right away, but she doesn't know wheth wife has found her phone, whether someone is abou doorbell to ask questions.

By the time she's gone through the video twice tl overfull even, and she knows she shouldn't dawdle a moment. Just a moment. So she strips off, anc immerses herself delicately, the water hot over her

She gives herself two minutes before she gets c back into the clothes she was wearing because she bring any others into the bathroom; they stink can't go out naked with a gun.

It's so long, so grey. She doesn't like to tou

Come *on*, Zach. "I'm not messing around. I'm sorry. I'm really sorry but everything's going to be fine in a few minutes."

"Lauren, come on, stop pointing that at me."

She is going to have to prove herself. She knew this was a risk. If a husband turned up pointing a gun at her she would climb into the attic in terror as instructed, but Zach is too placid, too easy-going, too still-on-codeine. The rifle has two pellets; she can shoot one off to the side, it'll be convincing but not dangerous, and then he'll climb up.

"Okay," she says, definitely not panicked, "calm down, stay back, okay? Watch out," and she moves the barrel away from the husband and then, once, pulls the trigger, and she doesn't know how hard she's going to have to pull but not very, it turns out, and there's a noise but it's not as loud as she'd expected and something happens fast, and what must be the pellet hits the glass on a photo hanging on the wall. The glass cracks. God, this thing might be more dangerous than she's been telling herself, maybe this is a terrible idea.

But it's way too late to back out. Zach is staring at her, horrified, as she wavers the gun back towards him. "Please climb into the attic," she says. "I promise once you've done that, I'll put this down, and we can call the police."

"Lauren, Lauren"—he has his hands extended in front of him— "this is insane, you can't—you can't point a gun at me."

She's gone too far, this is going to backfire. "It's not a real gun," she says. She should have been up-front about this from the beginning, enough of a threat to matter, not enough to make him panic.

"It's—you just shot it!"

"It's an air rifle," she says. "It's just an air rifle. But it'd still hurt a lot if it hit you and you just broke your back and I don't think it would be a good idea for you to get shot and I don't want to have to shoot you. So I need you to climb into the attic. After that I'll put it down. I promise."

Then: she hears a noise. The door at the bottom of the stairs.

Zach is looking at her, hands still out. "That'll be Toby. They're clearing out the fridge and there's some veggie sausages and some pasta sauce, he asked if we wanted them. I said to just bring them up. You should—you should put that down and we can talk about it once he's gone, yeah?"

This is infuriating, this is somehow the worst thing yet. Toby was *her* friend and here he is fucking up her plan by bringing food to her terrible husband. Can he not go a single day without checking in on Zach and doing him tiny favours? Honestly, does he have no boundaries? "Go away," she yells as he rounds the top of the stairs, and he looks in and he, too, is unable to perceive her as a plausible threat, looks at the ladder, her with a gun, Zach with his hands in front of him, and frowns like he might have stumbled into a parlour game.

She steps back into the living room to get them both in her sights.

And her foot lands on the dressing gown, balled up behind her on the floor, and her bad ankle rolls again.

And she falls.

The air rifle goes off, firing away from her as she lands on her back, sending the pellet between her feet; but not quite between them, because it has nicked her still-damp bare big toe and an arc of blood spatters backwards and forwards from it, red and wet and immediate and her *toe*. She scrambles back to sitting, then on to her knees, gun back up—they won't know she doesn't have any pellets left—but they're shouting, someone's bound to have heard, shit.

Then she looks up and Zach is paler than ever, and Toby behind him has retreated to the top of the stairs; sauce is spattered across the carpet, spilling out of a Tupperware container, frozen sausages rolling, and he's clutching the top of his leg and more blood is running between his fingers. She thinks for a moment that it's from her toe, that it's spurted magnificently right across the landing, but then Toby looks up and she sees his face and: ah. No.

"You *shot* me," he says, leaning on his other leg and against the wall behind him.

"It's not a real bullet!" she says, and tries to keep the gun level. His face, his bloodied fingers.

There is only one way out of this, and it's the same as it's always been.

"Lauren," Toby says, "you shot me, my leg, you shot me. What— Lauren, please, Lauren, put the gun down. I don't know what's going on but we can figure it out. We can have a cup of tea and a chat."

"I will. I'll put it down. As soon as Zach's been into the attic." And she steadies herself again, kneeling in the doorway, looking out at them.

Zach is crying. He will feel so much better in a minute. She is also, she thinks, crying; the snot is thick under her nose, the tears hot and then cold on her face.

"We can talk about that," Toby says. "If there's something you need from the attic I can get it, it's okay. Just, Lauren, please."

Her toe hurts so much, Toby's leg, Zach's white face and half-open mouth.

"No. Look. Zach. Please. I promise it will be okay if you climb up. I need you to climb up right now. Okay? I'm—I'm lowering the gun and I'm going to keep it down as long as I see you're climbing. Yeah?"

Zach steps forward hesitantly.

"That's it," she says. "You're doing so well. You can do this. One hand on the rung, that's right. Then the other."

She's shuffled on her knees back into the living room to give Zach space, the gun in her hands but pointing at the floor. Please work, she thinks, please work, please work.

He's climbing.

His head goes in.

Then his body.

His legs.

She can't watch; she turns away. And she registers a sudden rush of movement and it's Toby, isn't it, he's running at her, somehow, staggering, the fucking idiot, how is this the thing that he finally decides to take action over instead of standing around offering cups of tea? But it's too late, it's okay, Zach's foot disappears and all she needs is another half-second, and she swings the gun up in a wide arc as Toby rushes towards her, it's instinctive really, she just needs *a moment*, she brings it down like a club while she falls backwards again. And lands on the floor, empty-handed.

And the world has changed.

CHAPTER 43

It's okay.

It's okay. Her toe is whole again. She is lying on the carpet, legs half trapped beneath her, but her toe and her ankle are fine, the pain has stopped all at once, and she has nothing in her hands. There's no tangled dressing gown from Felix's place knotted underneath her, there's no Toby coming at her with terrified eyes, running unevenly on a leg billowing blood behind it, there's no sobbing from the attic. Just the footsteps of a normal husband doing something up there; whatever it is that normal husbands do.

It's worked.

She needs air. With the reset of the world all the chemicals have emptied out of her body, the adrenaline, the panic, but they're coming up again, she knows how this works, she's been here before; her face is clear but the tears are starting back up, and she scrambles to her hands and knees and retches, throws up, a thin yellow gruelly sick, the carpet can't get a break today, and she pushes herself to standing and rushes across the landing and down the stairs. Around the side of the house to the garden. There are a couple of plastic chairs there and she leans over on one, nausea and dizziness, and she hears someone in the garden next door and looks up.

It's Toby.

"Hey there," he says cheerily. Then after a moment, as she retches again but this time nothing comes out, "You okay?"

"God," she says. "No." She shakes her head, tries to clear it, to get air back in. She looks back up at him and stares and there's nothing in his face that speaks of his ridiculous hurtle or blood on the carpets.

How weird, she thinks, that she knows how he'd react if someone shot him, and he doesn't.

"Would you like a cup of tea?" he says. "We left packing the kettle till last," and she kneels in the wet grass by the chair and laughs and cries, and wipes the new crop of tears off her face.

"Yeah," she says. "Please get me a cup of tea."

○ ○

She is lying on her back in the grass, the empty mug in her hands, when she hears someone approach from the side of the house.

The figure draws closer, looks down at her.

A familiar face looms into view.

"Hello, Amos," she says.

"What are you doing?" he says. "You left the door wide open."

"Sorry," she says.

"And you threw up? And just came out here? You knew I had more soup reheating on the stove."

Ah, right, she thinks: Amos's pumpkin-and-lentil soup. She must have had some for lunch. That explains the thin orange-yellow on the carpet. "You're still making that, huh? You use too much cinnamon."

"And that's why you left the door wide open and the stove on?"

She doesn't have a fight in her. "I forgot," she says. "I'm sorry. Look, I'll be up in ten minutes, okay?" The sun has come out and is shining on her and the still-wet grass; she can see a pigeon perched on a branch that can't quite support its weight, and it's bobbing up and down, up and down. Her feet are bare and cold and wet, and she is maybe shivering a little, but her toes are still whole.

Amos frowns. "So you're going to leave me to clean up your vomit?"

"I'll clean it up. Give me ten minutes. Please."

He stares.

"Please," she says again.

"So I'm meant to eat my soup next to your vomit," he says.

"I guess so."

He doesn't seem to know how to engage with this.

"Please go away," she says and, after another moment, he does. She's alone again.

Only a few of the leaves above her have started to turn yellow and brown, but she can see it coming, the colours at the edges of the green, the cold in the sunlight. Summer is over, another summer, and she's spent it looking after Zach and going to pubs with Adamm and resenting her friends for liking her husband so much and, oh yeah, shooting her neighbour. The months have passed and it's getting cold again and she's married to Amos.

She needs to stop.

She reaches into her pocket for her phone, to make notes or call Bohai or Nat or Elena, but it's not there. It'll be in the house, at least, and not next to a pool in Sussex. Instead she finds a library card, a sachet of sugar and a half-filled loyalty card for an unfamiliar coffee shop.

She's had so many lives, and some of them were bad, but a lot of them were good, and maybe there isn't a single best path forward that she has to find.

The garden is a mess, but there's a bunch of unruly yellow many-petalled flowers on what is, she presumes, a weed grown out of control. She rolls on to her hands and knees and starts to consider the different blooms and then stops; she can't think about this too much or she'll never get anywhere. She takes the biggest, brightest flower, digs her fingernails in and pulls the stem off from where it joins the main plant below.

She pulls a petal off: *one more husband.*

She pulls another: *or stop right now.*

She cannot trust herself with the attic. She cannot continue with the husbands. She cannot keep seeing how things go and never making her mind up, doing things with people she cares about and then wiping it all out a few days later. Which leaves two options.

She could stop this whole thing now. Go back upstairs and break up with Amos, and probably in the end that'll be horrible rather than satisfying but she'll get through it and so will he, and she can get his stuff out of the attic for him, and fill in the forms and work out the details and go about her life. Whatever happens, she'll have to trust her future self to figure it out, without a magic attic to help.

Or she could go for one more round, one more spin of the wheel.

All the husbands are people she has chosen and been chosen by. Whoever comes next will be someone she's capable of loving. The life they live will be one that she wanted.

She will check that everything's okay with Nat and Magda and Caleb, that she's in touch with her friends, that she has a job she thinks she can do, perhaps that they do not have insurmountable debts or a feature wall covered in lightly textured feather wallpaper, and as long as the life passes those tests, then whoever the husband is, she'll meet him with as much hope and care as she can muster. No Post-it notes; just trusting her past self to have made an okay decision.

She pulls another petal.

One more husband. Stop right now. One more husband.

And then she hesitates, because she started plucking with *one more husband* and that must mean she's hoping to end there as well.

Always start with the answer you want, Jason said.

If there's an answer she's hoping for, probably she should just do that. Probably she shouldn't defer to a flower. No more tricks, no more dodging: she wants something, and she's going to have to admit it.

She stands up, dizzy, damp clothes clinging along her back, then heads around the corner of the house, tucks the half-plucked flower into her pocket. Up the stairs, hesitating where Toby's blood and pasta sauce were spilled across the carpet. She puts her shoes on, gets a bag, gets her phone—no guarantee she'll have them with her when the world changes but it can't hurt.

Amos has, in fact, cleaned up her vomit, and she feels fond for a moment—maybe he's not so bad—but he looks up from the sofa and says: "I left the book open to the recipe in the kitchen."

"What?"

"The pumpkin soup. I checked. I used exactly as much cinnamon as the recipe says."

"Okay," she says. "I guess I'm wrong about whether I like it."

She's about to leave the room, then stops. "Amos," she says. "Thank you for cleaning up. I don't like your soup but I'm glad you do. I know about the time you wanted to go to Alton Towers instead of moving in with me, and I appreciate that you didn't."

"What? How do you—"

"And I think," she says, "I don't know if this advice will do you any good or if you'll be able to remember it at all, but let's try. I think you should consider moving to New Zealand."

"We live here," he says. "You wouldn't even move to Berlin."

"Oh, love, you wouldn't have liked it, you'd have been back in London in six months, I promise. But New Zealand might work."

"Do you want to take your temperature, you don't seem—"

She doesn't stop talking. "There might be someone called Katy, I don't know much about that bit. Now, I think you're right, and I'm not well. I'm going to have a nap. I've got a blanket in the attic, do you think you could get it for me?"

And he does. A little more complaining and confusion, but he does.

And while he's up there, she runs. She can't see the new husband climb down, she can't let herself start trying to appraise him, she can't lay out his characteristics against her long mental list, because the moment she does that she'll be back on the fairground ride, two days here and two days there, and her friends forgetting everything they did together and always another husband, another back-up option waiting. So before he can start to climb down she's out the front door, down to the main road, across at the lights without waiting for them to change, and into the pub.

She sits inside in case the new husband walks past, and opens her phone. Any new husband is always the one where the messages are just *Could you get milk* or *Running five min late sorry*. She finds him quickly, and she can't help seeing his user icon, which is a photo of a pigeon, and his name, Sam. Okay. Sam it is.

She sends him a message: *Emergency babysitting for Nat, sorry, back in a few hours.*

She can already feel the temptation to change her mind: to give herself the next ten husbands to pick from, to spend just a couple of hours with Sam to make sure.

But she can't. Even the urge is proof that she doesn't have the self-control to do it responsibly. She can act right now, fuelled by her guilt and the memory of her blood and Toby's on the carpet, Zach's sobbing face, the close call. But if she doesn't shut down the attic today, she'll keep it open for ever.

She sips her beer, searches, keeps herself to the basics. Her work: the council again, and honestly, could be worse. Pension, helping people, plus everyone leaves by half past five every day. Toby and

Maryam: a group chat with photos of things they can't be bothered packing. *Do you guys want an air fryer*, a reply from the husband and his pigeon icon, *We'll take yours if you take ours*.

Bohai's number hasn't changed for months, but she doesn't
know it by heart and it isn't saved in this life's phone. He'll be
asleep anyway, and it's not like he'll be able to tell her anything
about her day-to-day existence. But even so, she sends an email to
his constant address: a link to an article she finds open in a tab
about a species of Australian crab that likes to wear sea sponges as
hats. *Don't know why I was reading this but just in case it's relevant*, she
says. *Message me when you wake up, I might have news.*

Her most recent message from Elena is the words *TWELVE
CHEESES, LAUREN. TWELVE CHEESES.* She scrolls back, and
scrolls and scrolls, more than a year's worth of scrolling, until she
finds the photo that Elena sent her of the two of them, on that
first night, and the caption she still remembers: *It must be difficult
for everyone else that we're so beautiful.* The photo is not, in fact, particularly flattering, but she copies it and sends it back: *Look at our
little faces*

A few minutes later, she gets a reply: *MAGNIFICENT* accompa-
nied by a new photo of the two of them in, as far as she can tell,
the queue for a burger truck, Lauren in some sort of sequinned
jacket, and maybe it's a picture from her own hen party or maybe
it's just from some night they've had together, but it looks like a
good time.

She has barely made a dent in her pint; she takes another sip,
and calls Nat. She's already found a photo of Caleb with Magda
on his lap, Caleb beaming and Magda glowering from under a tiny
woollen hat, so she's most of the way there.

"What's happening?" Nat says when she answers. "Is something
wrong?"

"No," she says, "I don't think so. Do you have a minute?"

"Not really, I'm at the supermarket."

"Okay, I'll just be a second. How's Adele?"

"What? Fine?"

"Okay," she says. "And just really quickly. How's my life? If I was going to change one big thing, what should it be?"

A moment's silence. "Last time I tried to talk to you about this you didn't want to hear it," Nat says.

"I do now."

"Well," Nat says. "Look. You know I think you should have gone for that promotion at work. But it's a bit late to ask for my opinion about that now, so I don't really know what to say. I guess, did you get a chance to look at that decluttering link I sent? They just email you every day and give you one little thing to do, each time it only takes five minutes but it really adds up. I think if you signed up for a few months you'd be really glad in the long run. Once you've got everything tidy it gets a lot easier to keep it that way."

"Okay," Lauren says. "I'll check that out."

"And I don't think those drinks Sam makes can actually be good for you, or at least not for your teeth, right? They're basically just vinegar and sugar. But look, as long as you're going for regular check-ups I suppose you can drink what you want."

"Thanks," Lauren says. "Is that it?"

"God, I mean, I'm just trying to find the frozen paratha and then I need to pay for all this and get it home, Lauren, it's not that I don't want to help but this is terrible timing. Can we talk tonight?"

"That's perfect," Lauren says. "Good luck with the paratha."

She sits back. Takes another sip of the beer. Whoever Sam is, she's chosen him, he's chosen her, they've ended up together, and maybe it'll be a mistake, but if she went out and found a stranger and got to know him slowly, that might be a mistake too, right? It's not like she's spent the last year demonstrating an unparalleled decision-making capacity and clear-headed ability to assess men. Who's to say that she'd be better at picking someone now than she was whenever she married this guy?

She's chosen her husband. She hasn't met him, but she's chosen him.

And if he's not right, she'll get out of it the old-fashioned way: an immense pile of onerous legal chores that wear her down over the course of many months, and a determination to keep it cordial that ultimately collapses over a missing vase that they both fixate on as a metaphor for their mutual failings.

○ ○

She heads back to the flat and hides in the back yard, right up against the window to Toby and Maryam's kitchen; out of sight, she thinks, from the upstairs flat. It must have rained again while she was in the pub, though she didn't notice; the ground is newly wet.

A noise: Toby behind her, opening his kitchen window. "Hey," he says, "are you—"

"I'm fine," she says. "I'm fine. I don't want a cup of tea." She recently shot him so she shouldn't be annoyed, but she definitely is.

"Oh," he says. "Good? The kettle's in the van so I don't think I could anyway?"

"Sorry. But yeah, I'm fine. Actually, just a sec." Hiding in the back garden is an undignified position for life decisions, but Toby was the first person she talked to about the husbands, and this is her last chance to find out more. "Are you and Maryam doing okay? I mean generally, not today specifically, I know moving sucks."

"Huh? Yeah?"

"Okay, great. No hints from her about becoming swingers?"

He frowns.

"Sorry," she says, "never mind, none of my business, as long as you're happy. One more question." Does Sam have hobbies? Does he have a beard? What's the most annoying thing he does on a day-to-day basis? What's his accent like? What's his worst T-shirt? When did she meet him? Who proposed to who? What song did they pick for their first dance?

"Me and Sam?" she says. "We're doing okay too?"

"I mean," Toby says, "looks like it to me."

Good. "Okay," she says. "Thanks. Just double-checking."

Toby looks at her. "Is . . . that it?"

"Yeah," she says. And then: "Good luck with the move. I'm gonna miss you. It's been good having you here."

"We won't be far," he says, and closes the window.

o o

Next: to get the husband out of the house. *Hey*, she sends, *really sorry but could you pop to the shops before they close and get some baking powder? I need it for a thing.*

It's a final test, in its way, because maybe he'll say he can't, or he'll pretend not to see the message, or he'll say he'll do it but not quite get round to it, and none of those would even be unreasonable things to do; but if he does any of them then she won't be able to go ahead with her plan.

She moves to the edge of the building, where she can look down the side, along the narrow gap between their building and the one next door: past the bins, out into the street. The smell of rain and the smell of slightly rotting food battle it out for dominance.

A fast reply: *np*

And about ten minutes later she hears what she's pretty sure must be the front door. She tries not to look at the husband as he leaves, but she can't help seeing a figure, in a jacket and jeans, carrying a bag in one hand. Just a glimpse. Dark hair. A blur. Her husband.

She gives him time to get down the road, then walks towards the front of the house.

She hesitates at the door. Unlocks it. Looks up.

The carpeted stairs. The landing: light green this time. Strong choice.

The kitchen: medium mess. The spare room: a fold-out sofa, a long desk. The bathroom: herself in the mirror, hair more or less the right length, the wavering line on her forehead in its usual place, a spot on her chin but she supposes that isn't permanent.

The house isn't tidy, but it's not too bad. Her huge plant is in the living room, and she has bought it so many times and nestled it into so many versions of her life that it takes her a moment to process what this means, that she must have bought it *in this life* already. What a wonder: she loves it so much and she's dragged it back from the shop so often, the same unwise purchasing decision over and over again, the same exhausting physical chore, and here it's been carried out for her already.

What a wonder, yes. But also: what terrible timing.

"Oh, Buddy," she says, and touches its unruly leaves. "I'm so sorry about this."

She doesn't have much time. She opens drawers, cupboards, picks up anything that looks important. A folder of passports, her laptop, another laptop, presumably the husband's. A box of cards and photos. She sets them on the table on the landing. Another quick look: just grab some stuff, she thinks. Who knows what matters and what doesn't? An unfamiliar mug reading COVENTRY: CAPITAL OF FUN. A concertina file in the spare room on which someone, the husband, has written BRBEAC, or, she figures out after squinting, PAPERS; she has learned something else about him, namely that his handwriting is terrible. A pillow in the shape of an owl that must have sentimental value because it sure isn't there for the aesthetics, and a couple of exceptionally ugly dishes from the drying rack as well, while she's at it. A dog-eared novel that's lying on the coffee table.

And then her little cactus, and two big supermarket bags to jam everything into. At the last minute she checks the fridge, and there's a row of glass bottles in the door, red and purple and pink, some with herbs and fruit inside them. Presumably these are the vinegar drinks Nat was talking about. Sure, why not, one of those too.

All of it on the table, ready to grab and run.

She pulls the ladder down.

And she climbs towards the attic.

The light above her starts to warm as she enters.

She climbs further and turns to sit at the edge of the trapdoor, her legs dangling out into the cooler air of the landing, like she's back in Felix's swimming pool. The attic is still dark but her eyes are adjusting and the light above is slowly brightening, and she sees the shapes around her, the shelves, the boxes, the chairs, piled curtains, tinsel, suitcases.

She pulls her legs up and leans back. She is lying down, looking at the underside of the ceiling.

The buzz of static rises, gently. In a corner she sees a tangle of fairy lights and they, too, have started to glow, brighter and dimmer and brighter again, pink and red and yellow and green and blue.

She turns her head. A heater they must have put up here for the summer, which whirrs then stops.

This is the last time she will ever be here, she thinks as she stands up. The last time anyone will ever be here. She hid up here when she was little, Nat told her scary stories here, the two of them put boxes of their grandmother's things in the corner to deal with later and then never looked at them again, her winter coat was eaten by moths here when she shoved it up in a bin bag over summer five or six years ago. She has sent so many husbands up here to supposedly carry out so many tiny invented tasks.

She opens a box, and another, just looking, just thinking.

A clock radio, which surely has been up here since her grandmother's day, blinks to life, shows 00:00 and crackles. Another box: a fan inside, spinning already, slow but speeding up, dust clouding from the blades. The heater starts again, and this time it doesn't stop.

She looks behind a shelf and sees an old computer monitor on the ground. It shows jagged pink and green, flicks off and on again: misshapen grey rectangles cascade down the screen, then it buzzes and switches to blue and yellow.

The fairy lights start to pop, one at a time, glass splitting, and the bulbs go dark but the wire itself is glowing now, the coating melting away. A box of fireworks on the shelf ignites, the clear plastic shrivelling from the heat and giving way to showers of flaring sparks.

And the smell of smoke.

She doesn't know how long everything will take to catch, but it's working. For the last time, the attic is doing whatever it is that the attic does.

CHAPTER 44

Sam finds the shelf with the baking powder, then picks up some orange juice as well, and a pack of heavily discounted salmon, and a Kit Kat. Queues for the self-check machines. Reads his phone while he waits.

There's a new bakery across the road from the supermarket, with a big sign reading, perkily, THAT'S LOAF!, which he is not at all sure about, but it's good to see something open instead of close. He should have gone in before he went to the supermarket; then he could have had a coffee and a little sit-down. But now he's got to get the salmon back to the fridge. A brownie, then. And a cinnamon swirl for Lauren.

Past the closed carpet shop. Past the bus stops. Past the dead tree.

Birds are shouting to be heard over the traffic, and a train is screeching, and he hears as well the rising and falling murmur of people outside the pub, and the beep of a truck reversing, and sirens as a fire engine pulls past him, and the shouts of the kids outside the filling station.

Past the turn at the top of the road,

and

smoke, which is unexpected; a couple of the neighbours have working chimneys but it's not cold yet

and it isn't a barbecue because the smell is wrong

and it's thick; thick grey smoke against the pale-grey sky, too much of it, and around the curve of the road there's a fire engine parked halfway down, and its lights are flashing like a disco through the haze; and he cannot, immediately, identify the smoke's source but it almost looks like it's coming from their house, so he lengthens his stride and thinks it must be a mistake, surely, he'll realise that it's fine, any moment he'll see that it's a fire in a bin, or a compost heap alight in someone's garden; but with each step it becomes clearer that the smoke is billowing from his own roof, water arcing on to it from the ground, and that his roof is burning.

The flames, just visible; orange, bright.

And smoke. So much smoke.

"What's going on?" he calls out, as if maybe it's still a misunderstanding. "What's happening?"

"Stand back, please," a firefighter is saying, "could you stand back."

The kids from across the road are lined up behind their front wall, staring, the older ones filming. Adults are standing in their doorways too, swearing, watching, coughing. The smell. Birds furious in their trees.

Lauren's not in there, right? She can't have got back in the ten minutes he was away, she must still be at Nat's looking after the kids? He pulls his phone out and calls.

The coat rack that took him three and a half hours to put together. The blanket his mum knitted for Lauren that he just got down from the attic for the colder days. The black-and-yellow plastic bag he got in that supermarket in Denmark that says NETTO NETTO NETTO. His computer, shit, Lauren's too. Their passports. Their everything. The clamour, the way the curls of smoke move but the outline, the wider shape of the billows, barely changes.

Lauren hasn't picked up.

He steps back, towards the moving van that was hidden behind the fire engine, and Toby is there, standing by a pile of boxes, staring at the building. "It's on fire," he says.

"Yeah," Sam says. He tries calling Lauren again. He is not let-ting himself feel scared when it rings out: Caleb's got the phone and he's watching videos, or Magda's got it and it's straight in the bin, or Lauren's taken them to the playground. It's definitely fine. It's fine.

Well, not *fine*, the flat is on fire. His jug shaped like a pineapple, it was so expensive, he spent two years wanting it and then decid-ing he didn't need a pineapple-shaped jug until Lauren got it for him for a wedding present, and it's pottery, right? Maybe that'll survive? Pottery is meant to get really hot?

Wait, *why* is everything on fire? Did he leave the stove on? A bat-tery charging? Is this him, did he do it?

"Do you know what happened?" he says to Toby.

"It started in the attic," Toby says. He sounds shaky.

"Shit. Fuck. I was just up there." He was only getting the blan-ket down, though. You can't start a fire by getting a blanket, can you? "Maryam's okay, right?" he says.

"Yeah," Toby says, "she's at the new place."

Sam tries calling Lauren again. She doesn't answer. He tries again. He leaves a voicemail this time, which he doesn't think he's done since maybe 2015. "Hey, where are you, can you call me as soon as you get this. Uh, the flat's on fire. Uh, let me know you're definitely not in it." He can hear in his own voice that he is not as certain of this as he'd like to be.

"Oh," Toby says. "Lauren's around."

"What? She's at Nat's." Around like what? Around like in the flat?

"No, she's over there somewhere." Toby gestures. "She was in the flat, she says the smoke alarm went off. She called the fire engine."

Sam's chest clears; then he feels it clot again but this time it's just the smoke, of course he's not breathing well. He steps back around the moving fire engine, looking for her, the terrible dense light of the air. Then he sees her, sitting on the kerb, in her sequinned jacket for some reason, legs stuck out into the road, two overflowing plastic bags beside her, and her giant plant, as tall as he is, sitting in the gutter.

"Fuck," he says as he runs over. "Lauren."

She looks up, face blank, then she focuses on him. "Hey," she says. And then, after a moment: "Sam."

"I thought you were at Nat's," he says as he kneels down in the gutter to hug her.

"I came back." She looks dazed, diffuse, half-smoke herself.

"Are you okay? Has someone checked? You were in there, did you breathe any of the smoke in?" She hates being looked after but she's just been in a fire, surely one of the fire engine guys should look her over?

"I'm fine," she says. "No, really, I'm fine. I'm just glad I was there to raise the alarm." She's looking at him; touches his cheek, then his nose, then her hand in his hair, a moment's gentle pull, and then another tiny tug on his scarf, like she's checking he's still there.

"It's going to be pretty bad, I think," she says. "I was—it looked like the attic might just burn but I think maybe it's gonna be quite a lot of the flat. Because of, you know, the nature of fire. But maybe we should move anyway, right? Walthamstow? Sydney? Berlin? I hear Bordeaux's nice."

He clambers up from his awkward squat-kneel-embrace to sit next to her on the kerb and look at the house. The pavement is gritty through his trousers, which are, he guesses, his only trousers—he's got nothing to change into, this is it, he is wearing all his clothes.

"You shouldn't have—" He looks at the things she's brought, papers, insurance, their computers, and of course, of course she shouldn't have gone running and grabbing things in a fire, but he feels simultaneously the joy of seeing that some of their things have survived, and the shock of seeing that this is it, this is everything they own.

New thoughts keep striking him, new things that this means.

"Nat's going to be unbearable," he says.

"Fuck, she is, isn't she?" Lauren says. "I hadn't even thought of that."

She leans her head on his shoulder, and he's still trying to absorb it all.

Start with the simple things. His bag of groceries. He will not be cooking the cut-price salmon today.

He pulls out the cakes instead. "Cinnamon swirl?"

"Oh," she says. "Thank you." And she takes it, and starts crying, big rolling tears, chest in and out, loud and urgent and coughing with it, and he hugs her and says, "Don't get snot on your pastry," and "It's only stuff," and "I can't believe you saved your large awkward houseplant, obviously the single most important thing we own."

"I got the passports," she says, sniffling. "And the computers. And the mug that says 'Coventry: Capital of Fun,' if that's any use to you."

"Well, then," he says.

Then she starts sniffling less, and he feels his own ability to pretend to be okay pass away from him, and the breaths through his chest start juddering, and he lies back on to the pavement and now the back of his only jacket is wet as well, and he looks at the sky and it's his turn to cry. He says, "I can't believe our fucking *house* is on fire."

He feels her lie back next to him, her hand reaching out to take his. Clamminess, his hand or hers or maybe both.

"I think it's raining again," she says. "Maybe that'll help."

She always feels raindrops first. He watches, upside down, a magpie on a gutter.

"Fuck," he says, just remembering things, the detritus of their lives. "Toothbrushes. Phone charger. Your wedding dress. The score sheet from that time I beat you at Scrabble."

She laughs. "Yeah, what a fucking mess."

The sounds of the road, the water, Toby in the background. The kids from the filling station, who have come down from the main road and are awestruck, delighted, aghast.

"That peach jam I got at the fancy market," he says. He didn't even like it much but he'd only just opened it. "Oh god, Gabby's not going to be happy."

He feels Lauren stiffen next to him. "Gabby," she says.

It had been a mistake to let the blackbird realise he could see it from the kitchen. Sometimes you just want to make a coffee and not have a bird tap irritably at the glass until you give it raisins.

"She'll be fine," he says, trying to reassure Lauren, "she'll just go back to eating worms instead, it's probably better for her," but he can't stop imagining the little blackbird trying to fly up to a burnt-out window and *tap tap tap*, and nobody there to see her. And he'd just opened a new bag of raisins. And the dish he always laid them out in, which his little brothers pooled their money to get him from the bargain homewares store when he moved out and which he never had any use for until the dickhead blackbird started coming to visit.

He closes his eyes but he can't shut out the sounds, the shouts, the water, the clatter, the crackle. He tries to feel every part of his body, his toes, his calves, his knees in a triangle before him, his back against a shirt that is beginning to get wet as the damp soaks through his jacket. Lauren next to him, and it could have been so much worse.

The smell. It's hard to accept that this is the smell of everything they own, on fire.

His hands are wet and gritty as well, he can't even wipe his face clean. "I'm so glad you're okay," he says. "I was so scared when you didn't answer your phone."

"Oh, yeah," she says, and she's still crying as well. "Sorry, I can't believe I did this but I actually left it in the flat. Who needs a phone when you have"—and she sits up for a moment, pulls something out of one of her bags—"when you have a jug shaped like a pineapple?"

"My jug!" he says as she waves it in the air, then sits up and takes it. She saved it. Of course she saved it.

"So you . . . like that jug?" she says, as he nestles it back in the bag, and she laughs again and hugs him sideways, and he finds a tea towel in the bag as well and wipes his face with it, and hands it over to her.

The flat burns before them. He lies back again so he doesn't have to see it; Lauren twists to look at him for a moment, and squeezes his knee, and lies back as well.

"Would you rather," she says next to him, "that we were married with a burning attic, or that we'd never met but you still had all your stuff?"

"What sort of a question is that?" he says.

"A hypothetical one."

"Can I just have, you know, the world where we're together and the attic isn't on fire?" The smoke above him and through the air is indistinguishable from the clouds.

She squeezes his hand. "I know it doesn't sound fair," she says, "but you actually can't."

"I guess I'll take this one, then," he says after a moment, and they lie still on the pavement.

"Okay," she says. "That's lucky. Because this is the one we've got."

ACKNOWLEDGEMENTS

Every time I get to the end of a book I read the acknowledgements and I think: *I dunno, there's no way it takes that many people to make a book though, right?*

But now I have to write some of my own, and it turns out that: oh, I was wrong, it really does.

Let's take this chronologically. Thanks first to a whole bunch of work-in-progress groups that forced me to actually get on with writing. Kaho Abe, Helen Kwok, Chad Toprak and other occasional members of that 2021 accountability group; the Game Pube WIP group; Rowan Hisayo Buchanan and her CityLit class, who were the first people to read any of the book and whose kindness about the first chapters gave me the momentum to pull the rest of it together.

Thanks as well to the Adelaide cafes in which so much of the first draft was written, especially in dot (indot? in.? baffling name, great muffins) and the Hyde Park branch of St. Louis.

Thanks to early readers, for their enthusiasm, double-checking, suggestions and plot wrangling: Katrina Bell, v buckenham and Kerry Lambeth, back when the book was twenty thousand words longer and had three endings; then Gabrielle de la Puente, Josh Hadley, Halima Hassan, Harjeet Mander, Casey Middaugh, Jinghua Qian and Sophie Sampson. Apologies to Sophie for giving her flat to Lauren, and to Josh for giving his back injury to Zach.

In the UK, my amazing agent, Veronique Baxter (who gently

explained that the very long multiple-ending draft I sent her was perhaps not the best possible version of the book), plus others at David Higham Associates, including Sara Langham, Nicky Lund, Lola Olutola, Laney Gibbons and the translation team including Alice Howe, Margaux Vialleron, Ilaria Albani and Rhian Kane. In the United States, the wonderful Gráinne Fox and Madison Hernick at UTA.

Then thanks to incredible editors Becky Hardie, Lee Boudreaux and Melanie Tutino, who spotted so many weak points and contradictions and confusions and relationships that didn't make sense and even jokes that could land a bit better, and who questioned them with incredible precision, and mixed in just the right amount of cheering enthusiasm. Then to deeply efficient and reassuring production manager Leah Boulton; and to copy editor Karen Whitlock, who knows everything, including that narwhals have a tusk and not a horn. And to many others at Chatto, Doubleday and Doubleday Canada, including Anna Redman Aylward, Asia Choudhry, Jess Deitcher, Todd Doughty, Julie Ertl, Katrina Northern, Maya Pasic and Gabriela Quattromini.

As I'm writing this, there's work still under way or about to begin from people I've never even spoken to: cover designers, translators, proofreaders and more. Thanks to all of these people, and to wonderful early blurbers.

And, y'know, friends and family. The EW Slack. The 2024 debuts Slack. My mum, who took me to every library within half an hour of our house when I was little. Terry, who listened to me read this book aloud once it was nearly done, a chapter a night, and who said I should make the stressful bits more stressful. Every friend who's swiped through faces on some app or other and showed me a few of their options and complained. Every stranger with whom I've exchanged a glance and thought, just for a moment, about a different life where they're my friend.

ABOUT THE AUTHOR

Holly Gramazio is a writer, game designer and curator from Adelaide, currently based in London. She founded the experimental games festival Now Play This and wrote the script for the award-winning indie video game *Dicey Dungeons*. She's particularly interested in rules, play, cities, gardens, games that get people acting creatively and art that gets people interacting with their surroundings in new ways. *The Husbands* is her first novel.